Bob Larson

ELM HILL BOOKS
A Division of Thomas Nelson Publishers
Since 1798

www.thomasnelson.com

To my parents Earl and Viola Larson
Their affirming love has given me the reason to believe that, God willing, I could do anything I set my mind to—including writing my first novel. They were there when I needed them, and even when I didn't. Their prayers and unwavering support always let me know my life had a purpose. The older I get, the more I love them.

✓ACKNOWLEDGEMENTS

I've never written fiction before and couldn't have done it alone. My thanks to: Margo Hamilton, who through her selfless work with victims of ritual abuse, alerted me to the mothers and children escaping the horrors of occult crime; Lori Boespflug, who lent her literary talents and intuitive insights to make the scenes and characters come alive; and Janet Thoma, who prodded me to rewrite and rewrite again, compelling me to excellence when I might have accepted adequate. Most of all, I salute those courageous women who have dared to come out of hiding and tell me their stories of abuse at the hands of secretive cults.

"Do not be overcome by evil, but overcome evil with good."
Romans 12:21

One ✓

If we listen with our hearts, the words of a small child ring with ironic clarity. Wes Bryant, talk-show host of WTTK's "Talk about Town," in Clarion, Indiana, should have known that years ago. Unfortunately, he ignored anything that threatened his comfort zone. Wes felt he had reduced his life to workable options, until the day a child's voice softly shattered his world of compromised convictions.

On Monday, October 19, 1992, Bryant sat in Studio A, as he did every weekday at five minutes to noon. The familiar surroundings hadn't changed since Wes had accepted the job five years earlier. Directly in front of him was a broadcasting console, known in radio lingo as "the board," about four feet wide and two feet deep with a complex array of switches and lights.

Looking across the top of his board, Wes could see his producer, Chuck Bailey, in Studio C. They were separated by a thick, sound proof ceiling-to-floor plate glass window.

Wes concentrated on the large white-faced wall clock. As the minute hand landed on 11:59 a.m., the second hand ticked off the increments before the start of "Talk about Town." Wes and Bailey eyed each other, adrenaline flowing as the moment arrived when Wes would be heard by the largest radio audience in Columbus County. The clock hands converged at twelve; Chuck Bailey jabbed his left index finger toward Wes; and Bryant's right index finger punched a brightly lit button on the board, triggering "Talk about Town's" opening jingle and announcement.

"And now, the host of "talk about Town,' your friend and mine, Wes-s-s-s Bryant," intoned the prerecorded "intro" that began his three-hour show.

Over the door leading to WTTK's Studio A, a bright red ON THE AIR sign gleamed. Wes Bryant's microphone was on.

"Hello, Columbus County! This is your host, Wes Bryant. Today's show is brought to you by the Crowell Implement Company on West Third Avenue. Call Crowell for all your farming and garden implement needs! From the biggest tractor to the smallest motorized lawn weeder, they've got you covered. Look in the Yellow Pages under Farming Equipment or call 555-1654. If it's weeds you're after or corn you need planted, call Crowell."

West winked at Bailey, as if to say, "The show's on the road," and leaned over the huge control board in front of him, with its sliding volume controls, lighted buttons, switches, and digital readouts of sound levels. An impresario of the air waves, Bryant knew the location of every ON/OFF switch or volume control-no small feat.

The board rested on the closed end of a large U-shaped broadcasting module. The extended arms of the U served as counter tops that held additional equipment. To Wes's left was an open area where he laid information pertaining to the show. To his right, a computer video screen displayed information about caller's names, ages, sex, and their comments or questions. The screen was wired to a computer in the producer's room, Studio C, directly in front of Wes. Chuck Bailey's job was to make all the show's elements sound right—the topic, guest selection, and pacing of callers. Bailey screened incoming calls, typed relevant details into the computer, and sent short messages to Wes in Studio A on a special note line on the computer readout. Studio B, to Wes's left, was a small newsroom from which headlines were aired at the top of each hour. Wes was ready to depress the start button on channel one, which would trigger the musical tag line for the Crowell Implement commercial.

At the precise moment his live commercial endorsement ended, Wes pushed a button that beckoned a prerecorded jingle: "when you need a farming tractor, go call Crowell. When you need a weed extractor, go call Crowell. If you're planting seed for growing, Crowell equipment helps the sowing. When you harvest, you'll be crowing, 'I called Crowell!'"

It wasn't literate poetry, and it wasn't pretty. Even an expensively produced, uptown singing commercial couldn't make it palatable, but it did sell tractors, and that kept Wes on the air. To Wes, that's what mattered.

Chuck Bailey signaled Wes to open the phone lines to callers.

"The number you dial to give Columbus County your opinion is 555-8773. That's 555-8773. Go to your phone now, and call me. Whether it's a comment of complaint, this is the time to express it. Don't keep your views to yourself!"

As Wes talked, he simultaneously glanced down the station commercial log sheet in front of him. Like a pilot's checklist, the station log was his flight plan. He read: "12:05, play Green Thumb spot."

Only one of the four phone lines at Wes's right was flashing, so he needed to stall and give the audience a chance to start calling.

"In a moment, we'll take calls from across Columbus County. But first, this message."

Wes activated the ON button for board channel two, which started the playback deck containing the Green Thumb commercial. "Don't know what bulbs to plant in the fall? Can't decide what to do now to prepare your garden for next Spring? Well, don't wait until April . . ." Green Thumb didn't have the same financial clout as Crowell Implement, so they settled for a simple announcement. No fancy singing or clever rhymes, just the basic facts about their business. Wes had heard the commercial so often he didn't watch the clock on his board. He knew exactly when it would end.

A small station like WTTK had to have good broadcasting equipment. Radio was a highly competitive industry, and audiences were fickle, even in rural Indiana. "Talk about Town" got good ratings, so Warren Crews, the station owner, bought the best for Wes. Everything was state of the art. Tape cartridge playback machines sat within easy reach next to the computer on Wes's right. Cartridges containing continuous loop tape fit snugly in the slots of these machines. When activated, they automatically cued the start of whatever sound was wanted, in this case the Green Thumb pre-recorded commercial. After going through the play cycle, the cartridges cued up again to where they had started, so the sequence could be repeated.

During the commercial breaks, Wes seemed amazingly relaxed, almost disinterested, as if his mind was floating away. He jotted down notes about possible topics to provoke his audience if calls came in slowly. He loved to start a good argument, but he could turn on the charm quickly when needed.

At the precise moment the announcer on the commercial said, "Call now," ending Green Thumb's sales pitch, Studio A's ON THE AIR sign flashed again, and Wes came alive. He resumed his banter. "That number to call and '*Talk* about Town' is 555-8773. Our first caller is on line two. Welcome, this is Wes Bryant."

"Can I talk to Mr. Wes?" asked a small, frail voice.

"This is Wes Bryant. You sound very young. How old are you?"

"I'm nine."

"What's your name?"

"Jennifer."

"Do you have a last name, Jennifer?"

"Yes, . . . but I can't tell you."

Wes didn't like to start things off this way. He wanted a controversial caller right up front, someone to rant about the upcoming school board referendum or complain about the ineptitude of City Hall. Wes decided to get rid of Jennifer fast.

"Why did you call me, Jennifer? I bet you don't want to talk about the potholes on West Seventh Avenue."

For a moment, silence. Then Jennifer's thin voice could be heard sniffling.

"Are you crying? Is something wrong? Jennifer, can you hear me?"

"I'm afraid of them! I've gotta talk to somebody." Jennifer spoke slowly, carefully choosing each word. "I heard your voice on the radio and called the number. You sound like a nice man, Mr. Wes. You're not mad at me, are you?"

"No, I'm not mad. What do you mean, you're afraid of 'them'? Who's 'them'?"

"I can't tell you. They hurt me bad. They'd hurt me worse if I told. Just be my friend?"

"Sure, I'm your friend. But who hurt you?"

As Wes waited for Jennifer's reply, he looked at Bailey. Wes's expression, a mixture of consternation and irritation, said, *Why did you dump a kid on me to start off the show?*

On the computer screen, Bailey cued Wes to wrap up the conversation and move on to the next caller, a farmer wanting to know the long-range weather forecast for the fall planting season.

Abruptly, Jennifer's voice punctured the silent communication between Wes and Chuck: "I gotta go now! A car's coming! I like you, Mr. Wes. Good-bye."

"Jennifer? Jennifer? Are you there? Hello, Jennifer?"

Probably some cantankerous kid who got one too many lickings and wanted me to say her parents were wrong, he thought. Wes took a deep breath and quickly checked his log: "Promote tomorrow's show before taking five-minute newsbreak."

"In a moment, we'll look at what's going on around the world, First, I want to remind you about tomorrow's show. We'll hear from County Clerk Ed Morgan about the recent reassessment of property values in Columbus County. I know that's got some of you upset, so don't miss it. And now, a short break so you can catch up on today's headlines."

Wes threw the switch marked NETWORK SATELLITE FEED. Instantly, a nine-foot-wide satellite dish in WTTK's backyard pulled down the signal from a satellite circling 22,500 miles overhead. With less than a second's delay from its point of origin, a New York newscaster's voice was telling Columbus County about events in Central America and the Middle East.

Wes headed for Studio C to confront his producer in person. He was upset. Part of Bailey's job was to make sure every show started on a high note. A nine-year-old kid complaining about parental discipline was hardly a winner, even on a bland Midwestern talk show like this one.

"What're you trying to do, ruin me?" Wes yelled at Bailey. "Why'd you give me that kid, Jennifer?"

"I feel just as bad as you do," Bailey answered lamely. "You know I usually screen callers thoroughly before giving them to you, but I thought she'd be cute. I expected her to say something nice about you, and you could move on from there. Sorry it didn't turn out that way."

"Just make sure it doesn't happen again today—or ever," Wes

snapped angrily. "You've got two more hours to get me some good callers! Controversy! Conflict! People mad at me, people mad at the government. I don't care if they're on the political left or right, just make sure they stir up some excitement. And for Pete's sake don't let Old Lady Spencer on again! She just gripes about the price of vegetables at DeGroff's Market. Everyone's tired of her, especially me."

Wes Bryant wasn't the seemingly composed man admired by many in his hometown of Clarion, the Columbus County seat. At forty-three, the landscape of his existence was littered with shattered relationships and unfulfilled dreams. The hairline of his light brown hair receded slightly. His self-indulgent lifestyle resulted in a poorly balanced diet and twenty pounds of extra weight, and his stout, six foot frame no longer resembled the once-virile body that had dazzled football coaches and made cheerleaders sigh, His coat pocket flaps always seemed to be half in, half out, and the crotch of his pants was permanently creased from lack of pressing.

"Calm down, Wes," Chuck retorted. "Get in there. I'll do my job here. You keep up the energy in there."

Once the newscast ended, Wes returned, solicitous, cajoling listeners, provoking people to pick up their phones. What happened off the air had little to do with his professional personality, the only one the radio audience ever got to know.

"Talk about Town" couldn't end soon enough for Wes and Bailey that day. Jennifer's confusing call started things off badly, and the rest of the show limped along on the same theme. Callers continually asked Wes what he knew about Jennifer and what he intended to do. Wes repeatedly explained that he had no idea who she was and had no way to contact her. He was irritated that callers in the second and third hours of the show, who had heard about Jennifer secondhand, distorted his conversation with her. By the end of the day, Wes had to reassure some listeners that, to his knowledge, Jennifer wasn't being violently beaten.

Two fifty-nine, Eastern Daylight Saving Time. Wes had one minute to wrap things up.

"Don't forget, tomorrow Ed Morgan from the county clerk's office will be my special in-studio guest. Thanks for listening today. The opinions expressed by me, my callers, and guests are not necessarily those of WTTK or its owner. Remember, what you can't tell the president, can't tell the mayor, and can't tell the boss, you can tell Wes Bryant! They may not listen, but I will. Good-bye, Columbus County."

Wes pointed to an announcer in Studio B. WTTK's afternoon stock and feed market report was next. The announcer saw Wes's signal, turned on his microphone, and the ON THE AIR light for Studio B lit up, signaling the end of another episode of "Talk about Town."

Wes disgustedly grabbed the papers on the table in front of his microphone: voter bond issues, city street repair reports, Chicago futures market prices—the exciting stuff of Smalltown, U.S.A. talk radio, America's last neighborhood fence and perhaps the last bastion of democracy in the CNN/Big-Three network dominated broadcasting industry.

After Wes pushed down the top on his briefcase and snapped shut the clamps, he turned to Chuck Bailey, who had joined him in Studio A. "What about that business of someone hurting that little girl? Suppose she's in real trouble? You know, Chuck, we read about abuse all the time. A kid gets battered, and nobody pays any attention until it's too late."

Before Bailey could respond, Wes answered himself. "But what am I supposed to do? I don't even know who she is or where she called from. It's not my problem. I don't know what to do about that kind of situation, anyway. That's for the police to handle."

"Suppose she calls again? What do you want me to do?"

"Guess we'll have to play that one by ear." Wes picked up his briefcase and walked to the door as he reminded Bailey, "Make sure that Morgan guy shows up. I'd like to talk to him about the property tax on Polly's house. I still make the payments as part of the divorce settlement. Can you believe it? It's gone up fifty dollars a month since we split five years ago."

Wes left the studio and turned down WTTK's only hallway. His office was directly opposite Studio A, allowing him quick access to do the show. Doors on each side led to the offices of advertising personnel and various management people. Photographs of the rich and famous who had once graced WTTK with their presence adorned the wall on one side of the hallway. Photos of authors on book tours mingled with pictures of local and state politicians. One presidential candidate from ten years ago had stopped in Clarion to pick up votes and had been photographed shaking hands with Warren Crews.

"Great show, Wes!" someone called, as he trudged down WTTK's cramped corridor.

"Who was that kid?" someone else yelled.

Wes disinterestedly waved his hand, shrugged off their questions, and headed out the door to the parking lot. He wondered who she was too, and why her frightened voice bothered him so much.

At this stage of his life, Wes Bryant wasn't inspired to get out of bed, since morning brought the dreaded dawn of another insipid day. Alone, divorced from his high-school sweetheart, and lonely for Misha, his nineteen-year-old-daughter, he plodded from one day to the next.

The seven-thirty alarm deafened Wes. He didn't want to wake up to a clock radio. He detested the clever digital devices delivering melodic strains on cue and a snooze bar for five minutes more escape, even though radio was all he had in life. Instead, he had a quaint alarm clock, reigning with terror over sweet sleep. Sometimes the alarm malfunctioned, leaving Wes to rely on his inner self to signal a new day.

Wes detested his first glance in the mirror. Polly had called his eyes gentle, until she saw the anger of love gone bad flaring through them. Once, he had been the most important person in his daughter Misha's life, until the divorce pulled them apart. Little Jennifer, the nine-year-old caller to "Talk about Town," thought he sounded like a nice man. But what if she could see his eyes? Nothing nice about them. Tired, saggy, listless.

Robin Leach would never send a camera crew to film the décor of the small apartment where Wes lived. The bedroom was a disaster area. If it was ready to be washed, it lay in a pile in a corner. If it was ready to be worn, it hung in the closet or lay on the dresser top. Clothes were piled helter-skelter so Wes could search through them randomly before rushing out the door. A faded plaid flannel blanket lay across the bed.

The wall on one side of the short entrance hallway was bare. The other sported a collage of football photos from his glory days before an injury sidelined his life. The living room and kitchen looked as if they had been furnished with K-Mart blue light specials, laminated this and plastic that. A floral-patterned couch that had seen plenty of use graced that longest wall, and in the center of the room in front of a TV was a beat-up, brown recliner, his favorite place to watch weekend football or lean back for a nap.

Thirty minutes later, Wes walked out the door. The mug of morning coffee next to him in the car helped awaken a brain bombarded by too many disappointments in life. One advantage of living in a small, middle-American town was never being far from anywhere; within five minutes, he arrived at the station.

Wes pulled into the parking lot of WTTK, a red brick building like many others on Main Street, a relic of the forties, untouched by time, because if was too valuable to replace and too run-down to refurbish.

Hand-painted red letters on a front picture window, "WTTK-Columbus County's Voice of the People," were the only indication it was a radio station. Just inside the front door, a small foyer contained ugly green vinyl chairs. On the wall, various certificates of merit and recognition from local civic organizations expressed appreciation for WTTK's role in community affairs. As Wes stepped inside, he was greeted by Brenda, the stout receptionist with a narrow sense of humor that complemented her poor taste in clothing.

"Good morning, Wes. Got time for a great joke?" she asked. Wes winced and waved her off as he rushed toward his office.

"Hi, big guy," said Ted Winkler, the traffic control manager, who was responsible for making sure the show and commercials aired on time and were properly logged for the Federal Communications Commission. Ted tucked his ever-present clipboard under his arm and headed into Studio C just as Chuck Bailey was coming out the door.

"You look like death warmed over," said Chuck. "What's the problem? No sleep last night?"

"I always look this bad," Wes responded nonchalantly.

"Yeah. But today your worst looks worse."

"Had a lot on my mind last night."

"Polly and Misha again?"

"Naw, haven't seen either of them in weeks."

He hadn't. Polly didn't want him around. Even after five years, she found it too painful to be reminded of what could have been. Misha was another matter. She had always been happy to see her dad. Yet he was uncomfortable around her, so they seldom saw each other. Daddy's little girl had matured into Daddy's little stranger.

Every time Wes thought about Misha, a sense of failure overwhelmed him. It was more than the miscarried marriage. Wes felt as though he was responsible for Misha's maladjusted life. When he admitted this to her, Misha always replied, "Daddy, I've got my own problems. It's not your fault I'm so screwed up." Wes didn't believe it.

Wes looked at Bailey. "Chuck, I've been thinking about that Jennifer kid all night. What *should* we do if she calls again today?"

"It's up to you, Wes. If she's really in danger, I can't tell her to call back later—and I don't think she'd give me a number, anyway. If you want, I can tell her she's not on the topic today. After all, you've got that county clerk lined up."

It was a way out. If Jennifer were a spoiled brat, he could deal with that. But if she *was* being hurt, the risk was too great to ignore. The truth was, Wes did care. Probably too much for his own good, he surmised.

"It the kid calls again," Wes instructed Bailey, "go with it. Try to find out where she is before you put her on the air. Meanwhile, I'll check my *Columbus County Courier* files for any hot items we can use on upcoming shows."

Wes spent the rest of the morning sequestered in his office, poring over newspaper clippings about local issues. It was a tedious exercise, but unavoidable if he wanted to stay on top of provincial scuttlebutt. After an hour of scanning dozens of insipid reports on the high drama in Columbus County, Wes kicked his feet up on top of his desk, leaned back in his chair, and let his chin drop to his chest. Wes wasn't sure how long he dozed, but Chuck Bailey's abrupt intrusion nearly jolted him off his chair and sent a batch of jagged-edged newsprint flying.

"Three minutes to show time," Bailey called, as he opened the door slightly and leaned into Wes's office.

Wes groggily shook his head. Ted Winkler handed him the daily commercial log, ad he walked toward Studio A. Wes was unsure about most things in life outside that room. Inside the studio, seated in the big, high-backed easy chair in front of the microphone, he was transformed into a self-assured voice of the people.

Studio A wasn't lavish or massive. It was about fifteen feet long and ten feet wide, sufficient to broadcast a local talk show. Three microphones were needed—one for Wes, the two others for his occasional guests. Not many people in Clarion were willing to go against Wes Bryant on the air. He wasn't the smartest guy around, but he could outtalk almost anyone. Wes leaned back to savor the recognition that escaped him beyond WTTK's walls. Ed Morgan, Columbus County clerk, sat opposite him.

"Is the position of the microphone OK?" Wes asked.

Morgan, a nondescript, passive man, nodded affirmatively, ill at ease with the thought of confronting thousands of people on radio and a little defensive about trying to justify their higher tax bills. Ed wiped the beading sweat from his brow. After all, he was facing Wes

Bryant, a hero to the average man on the streets of Clarion who was fed up with life's deal of the deck and anxious to tell anyone who would listen what to do about it.

The ON THE AIR light flashed above Studio A's door. Wes was being handed the ball, and he was ready to run with it.

"Hello, Columbus County! This is Wes Bryant."

The next minute he continued the standard monologue. A few complimentary words about a sponsor. Reflections on the weather. A comment or two about some local political issues. The opening of the show was so routing Wes could utter it with complete detachment.

Suddenly, Chuck Bailey began motioning frantically for Wes's attention. Wes looked at the computer screen on his right and read, "Jennifer! Line 3! Yes or no?"

Wes froze. He was ready to cash in the county clerk's credentials. Local politicians were a dime a dozen. He made a living blistering their hides on his show. Ed Morgan wouldn't make it through the first round with him, and besides, Wes had his own tax bill he wanted to fight about.

Yet part of Wes wanted some mileage out of showcasing the possibly pathetic story of an abused youngster. He could get on his soapbox, rant and rave about out "insensitive society," call in the social services people, and be a hero. Another part of him cared, really cared. This was a Wes that not even Wes knew, the inner man who couldn't ignore the voice of a fear-stricken little girl.

"Before we go to my guest, Mr. Ed Morgan, I'm going to talk to a young lady who called yesterday at the start of the show. Her name is Jennifer.

"Hi, Jennifer!"

No response.

"Jennifer, are you there?"

"Oh, are you ready to talk to me, Mr. Wes?"

"Yes, Jennifer. Yesterday, you said someone was hurting you. If you want help, you have to tell me a lot more."

"I don't want help! You can't help! The Dark Raven said so. Nobody can help me."

The fear in the child's voice transfixed Wes. His muscles tensed, and he began tapping the pencil in his hand against the desk. "Jennifer, if someone is hurting you, I want to know. Where are your mommy and daddy?"

"My daddy is dead. The nasty people said he was killed in a car crash. I don't know where Mommy is. She was hurt in a car crash. I haven't seen her in a long time. Not since I saw her sleeping in the hospital. The doctor said she would sleep for a very long time."

We could see Ed Morgan growing increasingly nervous. He had feared Wes would flay him alive. Now, he was being ignored, upstaged by the disembodied voice of this child. Wes suspected Morgan's mind was on important work at the county clerk's office. Requisitions to approve. Purchase orders to pay. Instead of attending to these critical tasks, he had to drive all the way across town, at least a six-minute trip, to sit silently, while Bryant talked with an emotionally disturbed child.

"Well, who are you talking about . . . the nasty people? And who is the Dark Raven?"

Full Moon "They're coming! I have to go! I don't want them to hurt me! If I'm good, they won't hurt me so bad when the moon is big."

Click! The sound of the phone going dead was an emotional sledgehammer. Wes looked at Bailey with raised eyebrows and an expression that asked, "What should I do?"

"Go to a commercial!" read Bailey's computer message.

"My guest today is Columbus County Clerk, Ed Morgan. Our topic is the increasing property tax rate in the county. You can talk to Ed or me by dialing 555-8773. More in a moment, after this message from your friends at Hartfield Fertilizer."

Wes pushed a button, and familiar words echoed through the studio: "Do you want to increase crop yields by 30 percent or more? Well, Hartfield Fertilizer has a way to . . ."

Wes reached to his control board and turned down the studio speaker volume. "I'm coming out to talk to you, Chuck," We said over the intercom. "Get Winkler in here to run the board and play a couple of extra commercials to kill some time."

Ignoring the county clerk, Wes hurried to Studio C. "I can't deal with this, man!" he blurted.

"Take it easy," Bailey counseled. "Maybe it's a hoax, especially since the kid referred to a dark raven. Sounds like an overactive imagination, if you ask me."

"Well, I *didn't* ask you." Then Wes began to calm down. "Sorry, Chuck. I didn't mean to be rude, but that girl Jennifer really shook me up."

"Look, you can't do anything about it now. We'll talk about it after the show. Maybe we should call the police, get a tracer on the line if she calls gain. Just get back in there, and do the best you can with Morgan. In a couple of hours, we can get back to this. Go on! Finish the show!"

"I'm not going to sit around and wait for her next call, Chuck, I'm going to find out who she is and where she's calling from. If she's a brat, I want her out of my hair. If she's in danger, I'll do something about it!"

For once, Wes decided not to back down from adversity. In the past, when only his ego had been at stake, he had backed off. This time, a little girl's life was on the line.

Or was it?

Two

Early Tuesday evening, more than four hours after "Talk about Town" had ended, Wes relaxed in his beat-up brown recliner, stale coffee and dirty laundry within arm's reach. His dark brown eyes seldom flashed with excitement unless he cornered an unprepared guest on the show. Off-mike, he gazed blankly, a man observing life rather than living it.

Like that now, he disinterestedly flipped through pages of an old *Sports Illustrated* magazine lauding football greats of the previous season. The TV, tuned to ESPN, droned on in the background, as glib commentators discussed who was most likely to win this year's Heisman Trophy. A lone corner lamp bathed the room in such shallow light Wes might have dozed off if it were not for what preoccupied his mind.

Jennifer's second call refused to leave his thoughts. Abruptly, he decided to phone Larry Bender, assistant editor of the local newspaper, the *Columbus County Courier*. Wes knew he was the last person Larry expected to hear from. They were hardly buddies, which was partially due to different lifestyles. Contrary to Wes's scruffy appearance, Larry dressed meticulously and conducted himself as befitted Columbus County's social elite. Wes read Larry's weekly editorial column and often quoted from it. When he picked up the phone to dial Larry's home number, he realized Larry would instantly suspect a purpose beyond casual conversation.

"Larry, this is Wes. Wes Bryant. How're you doing?"

"Wes! Haven't heard from you in a while. How's the talk show going? I hear good things about it."

Wes wasn't sure if Bender meant that or if he was using flattery to put him off-guard. "Ah, it's OK. Same old grind. Cover local events one day, politics the next. Spend an hour here and there on farming news. Whatever the local controversy might be, as if there's any real controversy in Clarion."

"You don't sound too excited."

"C'mon, Larry. What's exciting about prodding city hall to change the timing of a stoplight so traffic won't block an intersection to the only fast food restaurant in town? Give me a break!"

"Let's face it, Wes, life at the *Courier* isn't exactly the fast lane. So, what do I owe this call to? A favor or a loan?"

It was a cheap shot, but on target. Wes didn't like to admit that he had forged few friendships. When he did venture beyond his comfort zone, he either needed something or was broke.

"I'll pretend you didn't say that, Larry. Truth is I do need a big favor. Could I check through some old *Courier* clippings and files? I'm curious about a car accident that happened in the last year of so."

"Why don't you ask the police?"

"Because I don't want them involved until I know more," Wes explained.

"Want to tell me what this is about?" Larry asked.

Wes knew Larry suspected something was up that might interest

Courier readers. "Not yet. But I'll fill you in when I know more. It could be a wild goose chase," Wes said to dull Bender's curiosity. "No sense wasting your time if there's nothing to it."

"Wes, you can check any files you want, under one condition. If you hit on a hot story, I want first rights to it, OK?"

"Yeah, sure. But I've got my own condition. If what I'm looking for involves anything that would invade a child's privacy, it's off-limits to you or anyone else. Fair deal?"

A child's privacy? That piqued Larry's interest. Since when did Bryant have a soft spot for kids? If he was interested in the welfare of a child, he must have an angle to exploit for his talk show.

Bender's silence made Wes wonder if he would agree. But Wes figured, in the end, Bender would comply so his readers wouldn't be cut off from the story.

"All right, fair deal. Want to come by the office in the morning?"

"No. I want to do it tonight."

Tonight? Now, Larry was really curious. "All right, Wes. If it's that important, meet me in front of the *Courier* in fifteen minutes."

Wes threw on a jacket, pulled his marginally reliable Toyota out of his driveway, and headed downtown. Driving to the *Courier*, Wes was on automatic pilot. Clarion was one of those towns that was too big to blink and miss, but with a three-minute catnap, you could ignore it completely. Most people never knew it was there.

They took the Interstate 360 bypass and whipped by.

Visitors noticed the feedlot smell that floated over the central city when the wind was right. Locals were long since accustomed to it. Every Saturday, thousands of hogs and cattle passed through Clarion on their way to Chicago meat-packing plants and death. Some said the town itself had died long ago when the trains quit coming and the interstate was built. Since then, Clarion had become a freeway exit with an Exxon truck stop and café serving the best cinnamon rolls between Indianapolis and Lafayette.

Halfway to the *Courier*, Wes was stopped at one of the few traffic lights on Third Street. As he waited, he glanced to his left at the familiar neighborhood fast food shop, Mac's Drive Inn. Wes had worked there while meandering through college. Flipping all-meat patties seemed so long ago. He remembered the aroma of fries, snapping like popcorn in fresh cooking oil, and the incessant hubbub of hungry customers pressing forward in line, bellying up to the burger bar. That job had been the promise of better things to come.

Wes hadn't intended to stay in Clarion. The local community college was supposed to have been a pit stop on his way to the big time. He planned to make his mark playing football, then he would marry a rich man's daughter and move on to bigger and better things. However, a knee injury during his freshman year ended those sports aspirations.

Better things had never come. Just different ones. A stint at DeGroff's grocery store, checking the lettuce. A few months at Reliable Ralph's Used Car Lot, selling slicked-up, fourth-hand jalopies. A job fitting shoes at J.C. Penney's. Nobody back then knew Wes was a talker, except when he had to save himself from one of the many messes he fell into: fist fights, arguments over girls, shaky deals. Only after Polly left did Wes accept the thankless assignment of trying to improve WTTK's poor ratings by launching the county's first talk show.

Lots of live-by-satellite stuff came in over the networks. But Clarion needed its own, something that concentrated less on current events and more on Friday night's football game. Enter Wes. Nothing else to do. Nowhere in particular to go, and no one to account to. Certainly, Warren Crews thought it was risky. But if Wes failed, so what? He didn't matter much to anyone, and his demise wouldn't be greatly mourned.

A couple of months later, Crews concluded his hunch had been right. "Talk about Town" was a hit. People didn't mind that it was Wes. They just wanted to talk to someone. Anyone. And Wes, with his lightning-fast quips and devil-may-care attitude, fit the bill. As long as he bashed the big guys, he was Clarion's titan of talk. From noon to 3:00 p.m. each day, Wes assumed the persona of the man he had always wanted to be, a leader who formed opinions rather than regurgitating jaded ideas, a man people came to for answers.

He didn't understand why something at the core of his soul was forcing him to find out if Jennifer's plea was bogus or authentic. A force pressed him forward, but he quickly ignored the thought of divine intervention. He had abandoned God years ago in a doctor's office after being told, "You'll walk again, but, with a knee like that, your days of playing football are over."

Wes's daydreams en route to the *Courier* were interrupted by the motorist behind him. He looked into his rearview mirror and saw an impatient man gesturing in disgust, pointing at the stoplight, and honking.

Gunning the engine and moving down Third Avenue, he turned left onto Clarion's main drag. Larry Bender stood in front of the *Courier*, motioning to him. Wes pulled to the curb, parked, and got out of his car. It had been months since he had seen Bender. He hadn't changed: three-piece pin-striped suit, slight build, horn-rimmed glasses, pale complexion from spending too many days and nights poring over page proofs, and small thin hands that belonged to an academician. Twelve years before, Larry had come from upstate Indiana to hire on as a string reporter. Clarionites hadn't been sure he'd fit in, but he eventually gained their confidence by writing a series on price-fixing by local seed and fertilizer dealers. Soon, he was promoted to assistant editor.

Wes and Larry had gotten to know each other at Clarion Middle School functions, PTA, school plays, and the seasonal celebrations in which their daughters participated. Beyond that, they didn't socialize, but Wes hadn't forgotten the editorial five years ago when his talk show first aired. When everyone else had adopted a let's-see attitude toward his doing big city stuff on radio, Larry had encouraged his readers to listen.

With our mini-shopping centers and pre-designed housing developments, Clarionites no longer stand on street corners to visit. We hardly know our new neighbors. Perhaps "Talk about Town" will restore some of the camaraderie we once enjoyed. If we don't talk to each other about what really bothers us, it won't be Wes Bryant's fault. Tune him in! Better yet, call him.

Wes shook Bender's hand and said, "Thanks for coming down tonight. This may take a couple of hours. Got something to keep you busy?"

"Are you kidding?" Larry answered. "Tomorrow's edition includes a special supplement on fall harvesting, and it's nowhere near ready. I'll show you where our archive copies are kept, and you can look until you find what you want. I'll be in the layout room, checking copy content."

Wes had never been inside a newspaper building. He thought it strange that, after more than thirty years of reading the *Columbus County Courier*, he had no idea how words actually got on paper. As they walked past the reception desk into the newsroom, Wes was struck by the messiness, even worse than his bachelor apartment.

Stacks of paper were piled randomly on the dozen or so tightly cramped desks-heaps of clippings from previous editions, computer printouts, photos, rolls of wire service paper with jagged edges, and press releases from agencies, corporations, and public interest groups. Amidst the clutter and overflowing ashtrays, half-empty coffee cups reeked of stale brew, which contrasted with the friendly smell of sharpened pencils. Pens and paper clips lay scattered on desks. Scrawled notes were taped to the edges, sides, and tops of computer monitors perched on each desk.

"No offense, Larry," Wes commented, "but this place is a mess! Who cleans it up?"

"It is clean. We're sticklers about neatness," Larry said, grinning mischievously.

"You mean, it always looks like this?"

"Hey, the people who work here are journalists, not brain surgeons. Every newsroom I've ever seen looks like this. Must be a disease that strikes newspaper reporters," Larry laughed. He led Wes through the layout room where strips of typeset stories awaited their places in tomorrow's edition, past the photo lab where front-page pictures were developed, and into the classified department where a bank of phones waited for calls about cars for sale and apartments to rent. Larry pointed to a narrow room filled with steel warehouse-style shelves. Each shelf was piled high with past editions of the *Courier*.

"Everything from the last twelve months is in that section over there," Larry explained. "Going backward from that, just look on the shelves next to the wall. In reverse chronology, go from left to right. We've got two years' worth in here. If it's not here, you'll have to look at microfilm. You can spread the newspapers out on the small table in the rear. Just put them back after you've finished."

"Thanks," Wes replied. "I'll yell if I need anything."

Wes hadn't anticipated this chaos. He thought a newspaper morgue would be more organized, like the library, that Larry would

call up a computer file labeled "Automobile Accidents" and refer
him to every car wreck in the last seven years.

Where should I start? Wes wondered. Last winter? *Lots of accidents
happen when roads are slippery.* He started looking at Thanksgiving
time, when the first snow usually struck Clarion.

As Wes flipped through the newspaper pages, a few memorable
events caught his eye. The story about the nursing home fire just
after Thanksgiving. And the misappropriation scandal in the
County Building and Works Department that broke just before
Christmas. He had almost forgotten about the fallen minister of
Clarion Community Church, who got caught in January skimming
funds from the missionary account. National televangelists had
nothing on Columbus County, though Clarion's corruption was on
a decidedly smaller scale.

February . . . March . . . early April. Wes was ready to give up. It
was nearly eleven o'clock, and he had probably pressed Larry's gra-
ciousness far enough. He got up from the newspaper-strewn table and
walked through the narrow corridors between row after row of
Columbus County Couriers. Exasperated, he leaned his head against a
steel reinforcing cross bar and rubbed the back of his tense, aching neck.

What am I doing here? He wondered. *If Jennifer really is in trouble,
let me find what I need to help her!*

That interlude gave Wes the stamina to look through one more
stack of newspapers.

The first two weeks of April lay in front of him. As Wes lethargically reached for the first day's reading, he remembered a freakish spring storm that had hit Columbus County Easter weekend. Maybe that was it. Frantically, he flipped newspapers right and left, descending through the stack.

There is was! How could he have forgotten the bold headline? CHICAGO FAMILY OF THREE INVOLVED IN FATAL SPRING STORM ACCIDENT.

Wes skimmed the article, like a child tearing through wrapping paper on Christmas morning, anxious to grasp the gift inside:

One member of a Chicago family of three was killed and the others seriously injured when their car skidded into a guard railing near the Clarion exit on Interstate 360. There were no eyewitnesses to the accident, but Sheriff Arnold Hancock arriving at the scene said it appeared that a patch of ice caused the driver, 36-year-old Dr. Gregory Simpson, to lose control and crash. Simpson was pronounced dead upon arrival at Clarion Municipal Hospital. His wife, Annette, 34, daughter of the late Rev. and Mrs. Earl Kirkwood, was reported in critical but stable condition. Nine-year-old Jennifer Simpson survived with minor cuts and bruises.

Wes stared at the blank wall in from of him. Jennifer wasn't a hoax. What was *really* going on in Columbus County, while the general populace worried about hog prices and soil conditions?

Wes hurriedly restacked the April issues on the shelf and rushed to Larry's layout room.

"Larry, I found what I was looking for. Thanks a lot," he said.

"So, now do I get in on this?"

"Not yet. I need to check some more stuff. But at least I know I'm on the right track. You've been a big help. Sorry I kept you so long."

"No problem. I got a lot of tomorrow's work done, so I'll sleep later in the morning. Give me a minute to turn out the lights. Want a cup of coffee before going home?'

"Not tonight. I'll take a rain check. I need some time to think before I hit the sack."

Wes stepped out the front door of the *Columbus County Courier*, feeling that he had hit pay dirt. One article about an insignificant car wreck on a busy interstate had convinced him the kid was sincere.

A cool October wind scattered crisp, colorful maple leaves around his feet. He pulled his suit coat collar around his neck. Tomorrow, he'd check out Clarion Municipal Hospital. If Annette Simpson was still there, she might be in trouble.

The nearly full moon cast his shadow far down the sidewall, as if he were being followed by something dark and faceless that imitated his every move.

Things get a little crazy this time of year, he thought.

Halloween was less than two weeks away.

√Three

Clarion Municipal Hospital, a forty-five-year-old brick structure built after World War II for returning veterans, was no high-tech center of modern medicine. CMH, as it was known to locals, could handle bodily injuries, minor surgery, and pregnancies. Most incisions were for Caesareans, and most stitches for general abrasions. People didn't stay there for long-term medical care. No piped-in cable TV or private rooms with bath. Just the basics to fix people quickly and get them home. Major medical treatment was referred to Indianapolis, fifty-five miles down the road, where internal organs could be analyzed and diagnoses made with the latest medical technology.

Wednesday morning, the day after his visit to the *Courier,* Wes Bryant was skeptical about finding Annette Simpson at CMH. Six months had passed since the accident, and lingering health problems needing prolonged supervision would have been handled elsewhere. Still, he had to check CMH. Perhaps he could learn where she had been transferred.

As Wes walked into the lobby, Clarion's finest—and only—infirmary seemed downright boring. Nurses didn't scurry through the halls, looking harried and frazzled. Nor did somber, handsome doctors hurry around with charts clutched to their chests to diagnose still another patient. The typical hospital antiseptic odor was masked by a musty scent of old woodwork and the outdated fabric of well-seasoned curtains on elongated windows.

"May I help you?" asked the sternly efficient receptionist.

"Yes. I'm looking for someone who was a patient here. She was admitted after a car accident last April. Name is Annette Simpson. Can you check your records and tell me when she was released?"

"Ill do my best. Please take a seat in the waiting area."

Wes remained standing, while the reluctant receptionist pulled out a cardboard box and thumbed through tattered five-by-seven index cards. Wes stalked to a pop machine, stuffed some change into the slot, and pushed the diet soda button, his answer to health. He sat down and thumbed through a three-year-old copy of *National Geographic*, scanning, he poignant photographs. They reminded him of Jennifer, a face he'd never seen, and he tossed the magazine aside. The receptionist interrupted his thoughts.

"Sir, I have the information you wanted."

Wes hurried to the desk.

"An Annette Simpson was admitted here Friday, April 10, but I show no record of her dismissal. It appears she's still a patient here."

Wes smiled, inwardly elated and hopeful of getting some answers to Jennifer's strange story. "Can you give me her room number?"

"Are you a member of the family?"

"Well, yes. Second cousin," he mumbled.

"You'll have to come back after 6:30 p.m., during visiting hours. And you'll need her physician's permission to see her."

"What's his name?"

"Sorry, I can't give out that information. Don't you know?"

"The family never mentioned him by name. Look, I have to see her! It's very important."

"I can't help you. Hospitals have rules, you know."

The receptionist looked down at some papers, tacitly dismissing Wes.

"Yeah, I noticed," Wes replied, condescendingly. He considered asking for the head nurse, then vetoed the idea. Clarion Municipal Hospital had no intensive care ward for the critically ill. Why such formality to see a patient who'd been there six months? And why was Annette Simpson's doctor's identity such a big deal?

Slowly, Wes made his way down the front steps of CMH. Chunks of concrete had crumbled off the front edges of each step, making his downward navigation somewhat precarious. He reached out to steady himself with the handrail. Wes wondered if such structural neglect indicated similar disregard for the patients.

What now? Wes couldn't give up that easily. Should he disguise himself and sneak in? It was almost 11:30 a.m. He barely had enough time to get to WTTK and do the show. CMH would have to wait.

Little more than three hours later, another episode of "Talk about Town" was history. Wes's mind was miles away, thinking about Clarion Municipal Hospital and Annette Simpson. He took off his headphones and laid them next to the microphone. Next, he signed off the program log, carefully checking to be certain every announcement and commercial had been aired. Leaning back in his chair, Wes released his tension with a sigh. He went through a post-production procedure, turning off all buttons on the control board as he rubbed the tense muscles in the back of his neck with his other hand. NO matter how many times Wes did "Talk about Town," the stress of live radio took an exhaustive toll. "To other people, it looked like fun. To him, it was a job, a tough job.

"Great show today, Wes," Chuck Bailey said. "You really did a number on that arrogant guy from the Agriculture Department. Imagine trying to convince us Washington cares about farm foreclosures! If some radio exec from Chicago had driven through town and heard you today, we might have had a tough time keeping you in Clarion!"

"Thanks. Some days, I appreciate your compliments more than you know. Can you wrap up everything for tomorrow's show without me? I have to leave right away on personal business."

"Sure, By the way, that Jennifer kid didn't call back today. My guess is, you scared her off. She couldn't think of any more tall tales to tell you. Just as well. I hate seeing you get sidetracked with that stuff. Hurts the focus of the show."

"Yeah. You're probably right. But if she does call again, try to keep her on the line long enough for me to take a commercial break and talk with her off the air."

"Sure thing. Listen, Wes. I hate to bring it up, but you did cut it close today. Had a few of us worried. Try not to fly in at the last minute before the show, OK?"

"Sorry about that. See you tomorrow, with time to spare."

Wes stepped from the studio into the path of Ted Winkler, the traffic control manager.

"Wes, I need to see you for a moment," Ted said. "You've got to do some commercial voice-overs for tomorrow's show. It'll just take a few minutes."

"Sorry, Ted. Can't do it today."

"But Warren told me to make sure you did them today!"

"Well, just tell him I had pressing family problems and couldn't stay."

"Misha in trouble again?"

"No, I've just got to go."

"Just five minutes of your time?"

"I said no!"

"OK, OK!"

Wes ran his hand through his hair and took a conciliatory step toward Winkler. "I'm sorry, Ted. I've got a lot on my mind. I'll do it before the show tomorrow. Promise." Winkler slapped him on the shoulder and scurried off, apparently pacified.

Wes usually left by the front door, but, afraid of running into other staff members, he hurried down the hallway past the restrooms and out the back entrance to the alley. Wes walked with his head down, carefully avoiding spilled garbage from the Mid-Town Café next door. The sound of his footsteps reverberated against the brick walls, forcing him to deliberately watch each step. He was limping today, a sign of too much stress, not enough rest. That old sports injury always flared up when he least wanted to be reminded of it. His whole life would have been different if it hadn't been for that warm, late summer afternoon at Clarion Community College football practice.

If only he hadn't tried to make that quick cut around the right end of the line. He had run that play hundreds of times, but on that occasion he was determined not to turn the action to the outside. Fool everybody, and break it for a big play. It was only a scrimmage, not a real game, but his reputation was on the line, and making the team depended on proving himself in preseason.

No one touched him. The sod under his right foot just gave way a little when he planted the cleats. Down he went, writhing in pain. The smell of freshly mown grass usually stirred his adrenaline, but he lay facedown in the turf that day. One careless step had destroyed all he had hoped to be. Remembering made his belly knot up with the hot resentment that always lay there.

That knee injury cost him a football scholarship and an easy academic road. The professors didn't treat him like a Saturday afternoon superstar. He was just another dues-paying student, who was expected to make the grade or fail. And he failed a lot. The college athletes he had hoped to befriend ignored him, too busy being heroes themselves to care about a one-time high school football star.

For a long time, no one wanted to be near Wes. His humor was sarcastic; his conversation, cynical. But Polly Anderson, his high-school sweetheart, seemed to understand. She was the only bright spot in his life, a pretty girl who let him rant for hours about life's inequities. Wes accepted her kindness as love; her compassion, his due. They married his freshman year.

At times, Wes secretly wished there had been no "Talk about Town." Perhaps he might have become desperate and patched things up with Polly and God. But now, he felt permanently estranged from both. Polly was gone for good. God? He was still hanging around somewhere, the elite deity who regarded failures with bored, impersonal pity. God didn't care about ex-heroes; he was a fan of champions, sitting in heaven's grandstand and cheering winners on to victory. Before he'd been hurt, Wes had thanked God every day for giving him a strong body and natural athletic skills. But after the injury, he hated God. It was grossly unfair that one second's misstep should rob him of everything. If God was that callous, there was no place for him in the scheme of Wes's life.

Wes rounded the corner, turned left, and walked to WTTK's parking lot. He had to get into that hospital. He started his car, drove out of the WTTK parking lot, and headed for Clarion Municipal Hospital. WTTK had a back alley entrance, so might Clarion Municipal Hospital. He'd seen people accidentally wandering the halls of WTTK, thinking they were in another building after coming through the back door. Why couldn't he "mistakenly" wander through the back door of the hospital?

Wes drove around the hospital, looking for a parking place. He spotted a side street, pulled into it, and parked. A few seconds later,

Wes was walking down the alley behind CMH. To his relief, no one appeared to investigate when he accidentally kicked an empty beer can, and it clattered down the alley.

The back entrance to Clarion Municipal Hospital, a black steel door with a sign declaring DELIVERIES, loomed on his left. Wes put his hand on the knob and turned it, even though he expected it to be locked. The door swung open noiselessly. Wes faced a long, cold corridor. He took calm, deliberate steps forward. Closed doors every ten feet or so lined the hall. Were these patients' rooms?

There were no names on the doors, only handwritten numbers on plain construction paper that someone had posted with thumb tacks. Wes approached a corner. Should he go forward or turn right? Right, he decided. Ten steps later, he reached an information center. Patients' charts hung from large nails hammered in the wall. No one was around. Wes started reading clipboards, one by one.

"May I help you?"

Wes whirled around to see a girl, barely eighteen, confronting him. He wasn't a quick thinker, except in front of WTTK's microphone, so he hesitated as he sought a rational explanation.

"Yes," he answered. "I'm from Millican's Pharmacy, down the street. Mr. Millican asked me to check if patients at CMH are treated with generic drugs more than brand names, so we can correct our inventory accordingly."

Millican's Pharmacy was an advertiser on the show. Wes had been sick of their commercials about generic drug prices, but he vowed never again to resent doing their spots.

"Why didn't they tell us you were coming?"

"Actually, it was a last-minute decision. Mr. Millican wanted me to check personally on my way home. There was no one at the reception desk, so I just came down here."

"All right. If you need any help reading what's written, check with me. You know how doctors scribble."

Wes managed a respectable chuckle. "Yeah, I sure do. Started out in pre-med myself and still can't write my own name clearly."

The nurse's aide smiled and walked down the corridor.

Trickles of sweat formed in Wes's armpits and ran down the sides of his chest, despite the cool draft in the hospital. He wiped his forehead on his shirt sleeves and picked up the clipboards again. Four patients' reports later, his eyes fixed on the words: "Annette Simpson, Room 16. No admittance without permission of Dr. Michael Blackwell."

Blackwell? Wes Bryant thought he knew the town's doctors, but he had never heard of Blackwell. Room sixteen was back down the hallway toward the exit door. He had walked right by Jennifer's mother and hadn't known it. Wes hung the chart back on the nail, then resolutely headed toward door sixteen. He pushed it open, stepped inside, and pulled the door shut. Then he stood silently, heart pounding, surveying the shabby room.

A small bed and a folding chair in a corner crowded the room. Chunks of plaster had fallen from the walls, which were unadorned except for an emergency sign depicting the building's layout and accessible exits. No windows or phones. Even the standard plastic drinking containers and tissue box were missing. Next to the bed, an intravenous tube slowly dripped the contents of a suspended bottle of liquid into the arm of a sleeping figure.

Wes cautiously approached the bed. A woman lay there. He looked down at her pallid face. Dark circles blotched the skin under her eyes. Her body, covered by a stained sheet, was almost childlike in size. Wes's heart pounded so hard his ears hurt, but he had committed himself to this exercise and had to see it through. He leaned toward the intravenous bottle to read its label; water, glucose, and Thorazine.

Suddenly, the woman's eyes opened. They were glazed and she had trouble focusing. Her lids opened and shut, opened and shut. Slowly, she brought her gaze to focus on his face.

Speaking in hushed tones, Wes drew close to the woman and asked, "Are you Annette Simpson?"

She stared at him, tried to lift her head, and failed. Moments of silence passed, adding to Wes's confusion. Finally, she spoke in a husky whisper. "Annette . . . yes. Who are you?

Hearing the woman speak those words thrilled him. Quietly, fearful of scaring her, Wes answered, "Never mind. I can't stay. Do you know why . . . you . . . are . . . here?"

Annette Simpson looked puzzled. Unkempt strands of dull auburn hair lay on her forehead, partially covering her eyes. Laboring over each syllable, she said, "The car wreck . . ."

"That was *six months ago*. Why are you still here?"

The furrows on Annette Simpson's brow deepened. She didn't seem to understand.

"I know about the car wreck," Wes prompted. "Were you hurt badly? Is that why you're still here?"

"No . . . not badly. Dr. Blackwell says I have to stay . . . a few more days. What do you mean . . . six months?"

"That's how long it's been since the wreck. Six months."

Annette moved her head from side to side. "No," she said. "I just got here . . . a few days ago."

Had she been in a coma? Was she suffering from amnesia? Wes dared stay only a few more minutes, so he chose his words carefully. "Where is Jennifer?"

"My daughter?" The muddled, apathetic look in her eyes cleared.

"Yes."

"She's down the hall." Annette Simpson tried to raise herself on one arm, but fell back against the pillow.

Wes didn't want to upset her further. He'd learned enough to know that Blackwell had misled his patient. Now, he had to find out why.

"I have to go."

"Will you come again?" The woman's dark eyes pleaded with him. "You're the only one I've seen . . . since the accident . . . besides Dr. Blackwell."

"What about the nurses?"

"Oh, no . . . Dr. Blackwell says I'm . . . too sick. He's the only one who treats me. He looks after Jennifer too."

Annette's brittle voice cracked. Wes noticed her parched lips were covered with scabs that had bled recently. She motioned for Wes to come closer.

"Has Greg . . . Had his operation?" she asked.

Operation? Gregory Simpson was dead. What had Blackwell told her, and why?

Wes evaded her question. "You just rest. I'll come back soon, OK?"

"All right." Tell Greg's parents . . . sorry we didn't make it . . . for Easter."

Parents? Everything Annette Simpson said raised more questions. Had the accident damaged her mind?

It was out of character, but Wes bent over the bed, softly brushed aside the errant stands of hair crisscrossing her brow, and kissed the woman's forehead. She caught her breath, then her lips parted as the words thank you trailed off. Slowly, her eyes closed, and her head fell to one side. Wes adjusted the lumpy pillow and pulled the sheet around her. He had to get out, now.

Wes stepped back into the empty corridor. Moments later, he was out the back door. Jennifer's story was true! There was a real Jennifer, with a real mother in a real hospital.

But Blackwell? Gregory Simpson's parents? Jennifer's plea for help? He could stop now and presume the best or he could pursue his strange fascination with Jennifer's call.

The rising moon was nearly full and ringed in bright red. Wes couldn't remember whether it meant good or bad weather, but it couldn't change Jennifer's situation. Her fear of a "big moon" would be growing by the hour.

Four

Wes slept poorly that night. He awoke several times to unanswered question: Who was Dr. Blackwell? Why had he lied to Annette Simpson about her husband and daughter? What was Thorazine, the stuff in the IV bottle?

Wes was impatient for Thursday morning so he could call Mike Millican, the proprietor of the pharmacy. Perhaps Millican had heard of Thorazine. As the dark hours crept toward morning's light, Wes wondered where to go for help. Who could he trust?

Wes glanced at his watch: 7:05. He heaved himself out of bed, feeling tired and cranky. He walked barefoot to the kitchen, started coffee, and showered. Afterward, he read the paper and finally called Millican's Pharmacy at 9:00 a.m. when they opened. Mike Millican answered the phone.

"Mike, this is Wes Bryant. You've done some advertising on my talk show."

"Sure, Wes. I listen to you all the time. Have you on in my store. But I can't buy any more ads right now, not until business picks up a little."

"That's not why I called. A friend of mine is real sick, and his doctor wants to give him a drug called Thorazine. Ever heard of it, Mike?"

"Yes, but I don't know much about it. I'll check the *Physician's Desk Reference*. It lists all the new drugs on the market. Wait just a minute. I'll have to go into the other room to find it."

Wes could hear Mike lay down the phone and clunk through the room, only to return a moment later.

Millican mumbled as he traced through the drugs beginning with *th*. Wes wondered how any doctor or pharmacist could keep track of all the exotic names that sounded so much alike.

As Wes waited for Millican, he glanced at his watch several times. Wes's life revolved around twelve noon when "Talk about Town" began.

"Found it!" Millican was back on the phone. "But I don't think your friend wants to take any. Thorazine is a powerful drug that's used to treat mentally impaired people. If not administered properly, it can cause severe spatial disorientation. The patient loses all sense of time—who he is, what's going on. Real dangerous stuff. Used by psychiatrists to control psychotic behavior in wards for the criminally violent."

It all made sense now. Annette Simpson had been held hostage by the drug Thorazine and the mysterious Dr. Blackwell.

Wes thanked Millican for the information and headed to work. The rest of that morning, and all during "Talk about Town," he wondered why Blackwell would give such a potent drug to Annette Simpson. As he prepared to end the show and was playing the last commercial break, Chuck Bailey rushed into the studio.

"It's her, that Jennifer kid! She's on the phone again!"

Wes had hoped she'd call again. Something about this particular child reached him more than the hundreds of callers he'd listened to before.

As the last commercial faded into the jingle signaling "Talk about Town's" return to the air, Wes instructed Bailey to keep Jennifer on the line.

"As soon as the show's over, transfer the call to my office. I'll talk to her in private."

"I'll do my best," Bailey assured him.

The final minutes of the show inched by. Hog price reports, weather forecasts, field harvesting conditions. The fabric of rural Indiana life seemed frivolous compared to the fear Wes had heard in this child's voice.

Seconds after Wes uttered his farewell to the radio audience, he rushed to his office and settled into his oversized, well-worn desk chair. Unlike the well-equipped studios, WTTK didn't provide expensive offices. Flashy images conceded to functionalism, and furnishings had been there longer than current workers could remember. Wes's chair squeaked as he tilted backward.

Line three lit up. The phone beeped, indicating a call transfer. Wes paused before pushing the button to take Jennifer's call.

Should I say anything about her mother? He wondered. *Should I keep quiet about visiting the hospital?*

Wes often asked probing, even embarrassing question on "Talk about Town." Why was he so nervous now? He picked up the phone.

"Jennifer? This is Wes Bryant."

"Hi, Mr. Wes," Jennifer said, her voice fragile and frightened. "I had to talk to you today." There was a tense silence before she continued.

"I'm scared of what's gonna happen."

"What are you talking about, Jennifer?"

"I don't know. It's an important night. It's the night of my color nation."

Color nation? Wes wondered. "What's a color nation?" he asked.

"I'm gonna be queen of something," Jennifer answered.

Wes felt panicky. He couldn't understand her. He didn't want to lose her again. His thoughts whirled . . . and then, he had it.

"You mean coronation!" He exclaimed.

"Yes, color nation," Jennifer repeated.

The breakthrough added more to Wes's confusion. A nine-year-old wouldn't be involved in such a ceremony. She must have misunderstood or distorted something she had overheard.

"When is the coronation?" Wes asked.

"At midnight."

"Where?"

"Where they always take me. The Mounds of Elders. It's dark outside. They cover my eyes when they take me there."

Wes tipped forward in his chair and leaned across his desk, gripping the phone handset. His neck muscles tensed as he wondered how to pull more information from the girl.

"Can you describe the Mounds of Elders?"

Jennifer spoke hesitantly, softly. "The dirt is high when we walk around. It's hard to remember. I always drink juice before we go, and I forget stuff." Silence. Then she blurted, "I don't *want* to remember!

It hurts."

"Have you told anyone else about this?"

"Just you, Mr. Wes. You're the only friend I've got. The nasty people won't let me talk to anyone. They say the Dark Raven wouldn't like it. I have to go! They might catch me."

"Can you write down a phone number, Jennifer?" Wes asked hurriedly. "It's my house. You can call me any time, even at night."

"I'll get a pencil," Jennifer responded.

Long moments passed. Then to Wes's dismay, he heard adult voices in the background. He stuffed an index finger into his right ear, closed his eyes, and listened intently to the barely audible sounds. Heavy footsteps approached.

The phone went dead.

Wes groaned and slumped forward on his elbows. He clenched his fist around the receiver, wishing it could magically reconnect him with Jennifer's voice.

What were Mounds of Elders, and where were they? Wes decided to see if he could find the answer in the Columbus County Library, Clarion's monument to books.

The library was the kind philanthropists built at the turn of the century in Smalltown, America-red brick, unimaginative architecture. Only its prominent location in town signified the community's former regard for knowledge. Wes hadn't entered its weathered wooden doors for years. As a kid, He'd spent many Saturday afternoons immersed in children's books, long before the adventure of reading was diluted by cartoon characters prancing across a flat screen.

Stepping inside the library, he noticed that the groove-and-tongue slatboard floors still creaked as he walked toward the librarian behind the old gray metal desk. The lofty ceiling supported whispering fans that occasionally shrieked like a night owl diving upon prey in a quiet wood. The musty smell of old wood mingled with the peppery scent of yellowed paper in even older books, some peering at him through frosted panes of glass.

"May I help you?" the bespectacled librarian, the *gendarme* of Columbus County's sacred volumes of literature, demanded. She tilted her head down to stare over her bifocals.

"Could you tell me where I'd find some books on local history?" Wes asked.

"We don't have many like that, at least not serious works of history. The Columbus County Historical Society puts out two pamphlets, which might be useful. Can you be more specific about what you're looking for?"

"I'm not really sure." Wes preferred not tot mention the Mounds of Elders, which might stir the librarian's curiosity. He smiled at her and looked down at the floor, hoping to appear noncommittal.

"Why not talk to Katherine Caldwell? She knows more about what's gone on here than anybody in Clarion, maybe in Columbus County. She's collected all kinds of books and relics. Who knows what will happen to all that stuff when she dies? We hope she wills it to the library. I'd give it a corner where we could keep it for peo-

ple like you." The austere woman pointed to a floor-to-ceiling book-
case in a far corner of the reading room. Then she volunteered, "I've
got her number, if you'd like it. Her address too. She lives in that old
Victorian house on First Avenue, the one with the Gothic gables."

The librarian scribbled on a piece of paper and handed it to Wes,
her hands shaking slightly. "If I were you, I'd call Katherine. She can
save you a lot of time, if you're looking for something specific."

"Thanks," Wes said, slipping the paper into his shirt pocket. *I might
as well ask her while I'm here, after all. No use beating around the bush,
he thought.*

"Have you ever heard about something called the Mounds of Elders?"

The librarian's staid expression shifted, and her head twitched
unnaturally. She faltered only a moment before replying, "I don't
believe I ever have. Why do you ask?"

"No special reason."

Wes knew the librarian was making a subtle effort to mask her
surprise. He'd bet she knew something about the Mounds of Elders.
He'd wager even more that she certainly wasn't going to tell him
what it was.

"Thanks again," Wes said and abruptly turned away from her
inquisitive gaze.

As he made his way down the steep library steps Wes still wondered
what the librarian knew about the Mounds of Elders. He headed down
First Avenue, searching for Katherine Caldwell's address. He found it
quickly, an odd house that children had believed was inhabited by a

witch. The frame slanted a little where the foundation had settled over the decades. A wrought-iron fence with evenly spaced, spear-pointed vertical rods surrounded the property. The gate creaked as it opened, and the porch steps seemed to sag under his weight.

Wes knocked on the heavy door, half-expecting the fragile building to collapse. Beveled glass rattled in the door's windowpane.

Silence.

Wes knocked again. Heavy lace curtains covered the door window, so he couldn't see inside. He stepped back a pace to offer a better view of himself. Slowly, the door opened. A thin, elderly woman in a dark blue silk dress that had been fashioned in another era stood before him. Rims of white ruffles encircled her neck and wrists. Her thick white hair was twisted to the top of her head and pinned there. Wispy bangs fell over her brow. A carved wooden cane hung over her left arm. She looked surprised, though not alarmed, by his presence.

"May I help you?" she asked.

"My name is Wes Bryant. The librarian gave me your name and address. I'm trying to find out some things about the history of Clarion, and she said you're the expert. Could I ask you a couple of questions?"

The tall, frail-looking woman glanced down momentarily, as if pondering the merits of this stranger's request. Then a smile flickered across her colorless lips, and she said, "Come in. I wasn't expecting anyone, so please excuse the unkempt appearance of my home. You're welcome to ask a few questions."

The interior of Katherine Caldwell's home looked as if it had been preserved at the turn to the century and then maintained there after as a landmark. A dark, wooden, curving staircase dominated the center of the entryway. To the left, a small parlor displayed a deep burgundy velvet loveseat and several ornate chairs with petit point seats. An old-fashioned pump organ squatted in a corner, the kind city people pay big bucks for in antique stores. Katherine motioned to Wes's right, inviting him to join her in the living room.

Delicate white lace doilies adorned two lamp stands at each side of an old leather couch. A marble-trimmed fireplace dominated one wall. At each end of the room stood large, leaded glass-front cabinets, one filled with china and the other with leather-bound books. A scent of lemon mingled with the dusty smell of the faded blue draperies that hung motionless, framing several tall windows. French doors at the back of the room opened on an overgrown garden shaded by giant oaks. Remnants of a broken marble birdbath lay half-hidden in tall dry grass, and a dilapidated toolshed sank into leafy shadows at the far end of the yard. The elderly woman led Wes to the leather couch and seated herself opposite him in a high wing-backed chair.

"May I offer you something to drink?" Katherine Caldwell asked.

"Thank you very much, but I have only a couple of questions," Wes responded. "I understand you qualify as the local historian."

The elegant woman was unmoved by the attempted flattery. "It's my longevity, not my expertise, that gives me perspective on Columbus County's past. What would you like to know?"

Wes settled into a corner of the couch and crossed his legs as the soft old leather whispered under his thighs. :Do you know a place called the Mounds of Elders?"

Katherine Caldwell leaned forward, supporting herself with the cane. Her frail voice lowered. "That's a strange question. People ask me all sorts of things—about former politicians, where certain family members are buried, even rumors about lost treasures. But no one ever asks about the Mounds of the Elders. Most people aren't interested in that kind of history. How did you learn about them?"

Wes noted Katherine Caldwell's distinct emphasis on "Mounds of *the* Elders" and hesitated, struggling to fit his response into a believable framework. "A person at the radio station where I work mentioned them. It sounded like local folklore, so I thought it might be interesting to look into."

His simple answer apparently sufficed. The woman folded her hands in her lap and recrossed her feet, one ankle over the other. "What do you want to know?"

"I'd appreciate any information. Where and what are they, for example."

Katherine Caldwell stared at him for what seemed minutes, then eased back into the chair. She straightened the ruffles at her neck and gazed toward the French doors. She spoke softly, turning her face back to the room.

"It was the year 1806. The local tribe of Miami Indians was suffering through a severe winter. The food they'd stored was running low, and the whole tribe worried about what to do. The chief and older warriors wanted to stay, but the younger braves were determined to pack up everything and move farther west in search of food. It was just a friendly disagreement at first, the kind that happens frequently between generations. But as more and more Indians died that harsh winter, the division intensified.

"Eventually, the young warriors rose up against the elders of the tribe and killed them. Such a thing was unheard of among the Miamis, respect for older members of the tribe was so great. The tribe moved westward but didn't make it very far. A week-long blizzard in February of 1807 wiped out the entire tribe somewhere in southern Illinois.

"Other clans of the Miami tribe heard about what had happened. The following summer, they met at the spot where the massacre had occurred. A legend soon was born that the elders came out of their graves at night to avenge their deaths. A medicine man claimed the only way to scare away the angry spirits was to erect large earthen mounds, shaped like animal predators. Indian w/ arrows Mystery House

"Since the Indians feared bears and wolves most, they erected a series of earthen mounds, about two feet high and six feet long, shaped like these predators crouched for an attack. The mounds were laid out in a pattern of straight lines with occasional angles that formed three large triangles. The Miamis worked all summer clearing the land and hauling in dirt. Strangely, a dozen Indians Three Triangles died from mysterious diseases and accidents. Their bodies were then buried in the mounds.

"When they were done, a medicine man performed a ceremony and placed a curse on the mounds, promising death to anyone who disturbed them. It worked. No one has ever cleared or farmed that land. The spirits of the animals represented by the mounds supposedly guard the area to make sure the elders' spirits never return to haunt any other clan of the Miami Indians."

Leaning on the cane, Katherine rose from her chair, slowly brought herself erect, and walked to the fireplace. She stood for a moment, staring into the blackened, empty grill. Then she turned to face Wes, thrusting back her shoulders with surprising vigor. Unsmiling, she said, "I don't know why you're asking about the Mounds of the Elders, but my advice is, Stay away! The trees surrounding them could have been cleared and the land farmed, but nobody ever tried. If you want my opinion, they were smart."

She took several steps toward Wes and looked sternly at him. "Anyone who walks among the mounds risks arousing the spirits of the elders, who seek revenge on any living man. If you don't believe in spirits, then at least believe in the curse!"

Wes met her eye and decided to go for it. "Where are the mounds?" he quietly asked.

"I don't think you heard what I said, young man. Stay away! The mounds mean nothing but trouble."

Suddenly, her tall frame slumped, and she retreated within herself. Sighing deeply, she said, "Oh, I suppose you'll keep nosing around, and someone will tell you. If you must know, they're about five miles southwest of town on old Route 193. Farmland and tall cottonwood trees encircle the mounds like sentries guarding against intruders."

Wes arose. "You've been very helpful. Don't worry. I'll remember your advice, and I promise not to bother you again. Thank you for your time."

Walking toward the door with him, Katherine repeated in a tired voice, "The mounds are best forgotten. Stay away from the spirits of the elders, young man."

Wes glanced into her faded, weary eyes and didn't respond. Katherine Caldwell clearly believed in lingering curses and bad-mannered Indian ghosts. They were part of her era, not his. He would drive out old Highway 193. If there really were mounds shaped like wolves and bears, he'd find them. That would be easy. But a raven? A dark raven? What would he look for, and where would he find it?

Five

Driving those five miles down old Route 193 late Thursday afternoon took a strangely long time. Cracked asphalt and eroded shoulders dispelled any idea that it was well-traveled thoroughfare. As a kid, Wes had roamed this country and investigated the dilapidated homesteads that had been hacked out of wild land. Once he had come upon an old caved-in sod house, a relic that epitomized the simplicity of nineteenth-century living. On another such safari, he had stumbled upon—and almost fallen into—an exposed cellar that yielded a few bullsnakes and dozens of magazines from the '20s and '30s. Wes had spent that afternoon thumbing through yellowed pages of Montgomery Ward and Sears catalogs, fascinated with the merchandise of his grandparents' era.

What would this safari reveal? Wes both anticipated and dreaded the answer.

The flat, monotonous landscape floated mirage-like in the afternoon autumn haze as Wes drove slowly between harvested fields. Every detail now assumed a new significance, as though he were looking at it through a magnifying glass. High, thin clouds made several passes at the sun, depleting its warmth just enough that Wes wished for a heavier jacket. He rolled up the car window, watched the odometer, and scanned the countryside for signs of the Mounds of the Elders.

Wes passed cornfield after cornfield of skeletal dried stalks standing in disheveled ranks. White frame farmhouses flanked by towering barns and silver silos butted against the blurry horizon. Looking like afterthoughts, small cement porches protruded from the two-storied houses. Detached garages sheltered family sedans and ailing tractors. Poplar and cottonwood trees clumped near farm buildings that fanned out toward fenced fields, dotted with herds of Hereford cattle. The stocky animals lumbered down to drink from scattered ponds that glinted pale yellow in the clouded sun.

One or two mongrel dogs guarded most farms, crouching by the roadside and barking furiously at approaching cars. Two such animals flung themselves at the wheels of Wes's car and galloped furiously behind him for several yards. Then they trotted back to their grassy lookout, panting vigorously after failing to vanquish the metal monster.

The odometer read 4.5 miles. Wes slowed down and scrutinized his surroundings, as the odometer turned to 4.7 miles . . . 4.8 . . .

How will I find this place? I hardly know what to look for, Wes mused.

On his right he spotted a narrow rutted road, branching off between two cornfields. A half mile away was a stand of trees. He turned into the dirt road and angled the wheels between two deep grooves, worn by heavy farm vehicles, hoping to avoid high-centering the car.

The car bucked and rattled along the furrowed road. Certainly no casual passerby would venture down such a precarious trail after dusk.

Approaching the trees, he saw a small turnout where he could abandon the two-track trail. He carefully maneuvered the front wheels across the ruts, pulled off the road, and parked behind some tall, thick bushes to avoid being seen if someone drove down the road. He presumed he was alone out here, but he couldn't be sure.

The old lady's story about spirits and whatnot had made him paranoid. He was here to look around. If mounds shaped like animals were hidden beyond that cluster of trees, he wanted to see them.

He got out of the car and locked it—he rarely bothered in town—wondering what inner fear had subconsciously motivated him to do so. He walked about fifty yards to the trees, made his way through another forty feet of dense woods, and strode into a circular clearing that fit Katherine Caldwell's description. He stepped forward cautiously, acutely aware of the uneven, rocky terrain. A few feet ahead, he noticed tall grasses that partially concealed several elevated sections of earth. Were they the mounds? He wished he had been wearing boots, but he couldn't do anything about that now.

Warily, Wes started stomping down the vegetation around an elevation in the southeast corner of the clearing. Dry weeds crackled and snapped under his feet. As he tramped, the earth revealed a peculiar configuration approximately six feet long, three feet wide, and eighteen inches high, just as Katherine Caldwell had described. As Wes looked more intently at the clearing, he could see the grass had grown to varying heights, as if the ground underneath were raised in certain areas. It required little imagination to make out the triangular patterns Caldwell depicted. But he saw no specific shape.

There wouldn't be any defined wolf or bear shapes, not after nearly two hundred years. The shapes would have eroded long ago, Wes reasoned.

He continued tramping around the clearing until his pant legs bristled with burrs and bits of leaves, and foxtails became imbedded in the threads of his clothing. "Indian curses, right!" he muttered sarcastically, glancing at the pale setting sun, wishing again he had worn a warmer jacket. The physical exercise didn't quite compensate for the chill that had enveloped him upon entering the clearing.

Suddenly, something rustled behind him. Hot fear shot through his belly. Wes spun in a crouch, ready to run or defend himself. He looked up to see an angry red squirrel, running up a tree, chattering and scolding him for intruding. Sweat had popped out on his skin and mixed uncomfortably with the chill. He felt like an idiot, and told himself as much. If he expected to make any pertinent discoveries out here, he'd better start acting less fearful. He went back to work.

Each time he found an elevation, he stomped down the growth until a mound formed. Within the hour, he had identified five elevated areas, seemingly manmade. He speculated about what he'd find if he could drive a shovel or an axe into one of the rounded dirt heaps. Would he uncover arrowheads and flint stones, like those he had dreamed of finding as a youth while hiking through plowed Indiana fields? Would the shovel blade slice through buried bones? And what about the infamous medicine man's curse?

Wes didn't believe in the hocus-pocus of spells, potions, and hexes. A rational man didn't give serious consideration to spooks and spirits, but he admitted, he was uncomfortable out here . . .

whirling around like a crazy karate fighter at a harmless squirrel, his heart beating like a runaway engine. Something about the place gave him the willies, no doubt about that. God forbid anyone should see him stomping around in weeds on top of some very ticked-off Indian ghosts! They'd lock him up.

No matter how he reasoned with himself, he remained uneasy. The trees cut off his view of everything beyond the circular area. He was only five miles from town and maybe a half mile from the highway, but he felt isolated. If any place could get caught up in a curse, this would be it. Katherine Caldwell's warning tolled like funeral bells, "Stay away, young man."

Wes shivered. Glancing around, he peered at the sky, uneasy that little daylight remained. He walked to one side of an area of flattened vegetation, hugged his arms around his body, and gazed at the trampled landscape before him. Wes couldn't deny the obvious regularity of the earth elevations. These had to be the mounds. More pieces of the puzzle dropped into place. He was sure he had found the ceremonial site, but what was he supposed to do now?

Nothing, Wes decided. He needed time to form a plan of action. Pensively, he walked away from the clearing. *What strange ceremony would take placed at midnight tonight on these burial grounds?* Wes shivered at the unformed thought. When he reached the trees, he looked back at the exposed mounds. For an instant, he imagined a moonlit sky and the figure of a very small, frightened child reaching her arms out to him.

Wes hunched over in the chill autumn air. He drew his shirt collar around his neck and headed back to his car, grateful it was still sitting there, concealed by the bushes. He slid behind the steering wheel and sank back on the seat, tired to the center of his being. Six hours remained until midnight, the appointed hour of Jennifer's coronation. He knew intuitively that his uneventful life had reached a turning point. He could head back between the ruts of the precarious dirt road and try to convince himself this place wasn't connected to Katherine Caldwell's strange story. In time, he might even convince himself that Jennifer's odd conversations were the product of a child's overactive imagination.

Should he sit there, shivering, waiting for a child's nightmare to unfold? Even if it did, what could he do about it? This was none of his business. He didn't even know Jennifer.

Wes turned the key in the ignition of his car. The motor sprang to life, ready to take him away from an encounter for which he felt completely unprepared. He reached for the gear shift and put the car in drive. Yet Wes couldn't take his foot off the brake. Sure, he could drive back to Clarion, but how would he live with himself? Too many questions remained unanswered. He decided to stay and wait for midnight, no matter what the bewitching hour might bring.

Wes took the car out of gear, turned off the motor, and sagged back against the seat. Then he made sure the doors were locked, tilted his head back, and closed his eyes.

I've got a long wait, so I might as well catch a catnap. He concluded. *If some group is going to meet at the mounds, I'll need all my energy.*

Minutes ticked away into hours. The sun set in red-orange glory, leaving him in darkness. Wes's mind drifted in and out of a dream-sleepstate. He didn't want to expose himself by turning on the car's interior light to check the time, so he switched the key to the accessory position and read his wrist watch dial under the pale light of his car radio.

Nine p.m. I've been sitting here three hours. Three more hours to go. Wes didn't want to think further about it so he drifted back to sleep.

A fluttering, guttural whirring nudged Wes out of his sleep. Had he left the motor running? Groggily, he reached for the car key. It was in the OFF position. He cracked open his car window, and the sound swelled into a steadily increasing rhythm. A full harvest moon had ballooned upon the horizon to bathe the night in a brilliant glow. Trees and fence posts cast dark shadows. Tilting his watch toward the digital light, Wes read 11:30 p.m. "The whumping sound whipped the heavy night air, then abruptly rushed in overhead, beating percussively at Wes's eardrums.

An invisible force rocked the car. Piles of leaves and chunks of cornstalk swirled as though caught up in an early fall snowstorm. Wes grabbed the steering wheel with both hands, as though preparing for an earthquake.

In a panic, he rolled down the window and poked out his head.

It's a helicopter! Right above the trees where the mounds are!

The immense power of the helicopter's propeller created a mini-hurricane that swayed the giant cottonwoods and sucked up leaves and branches and everything else not firmly attached to the ground. Larger than any helicopter an area farm photographer or the traffic reporter for an Indianapolis TV station would use, the aircraft was painted in shades of military camouflage. Wes had almost made out the emblem on its side when the helicopter turned to a different angle, lowered, and vanished into the circle of cottonwoods.

Suppose the people in the helicopter discovered his car? Wes feared having no way of escape and being stuck in the middle of nowhere with heaven only knew what kind of loonies! He had always wondered how men who were scared to death in the dentist's chair kept cool on the battlefield. Now, he knew. Adrenaline. Doing replaced thinking.

Wes cautiously got out of the car and inched forward, trying to stay concealed in the brush. He could see frost forming on the tips of the branches and a faint wisp of smoke blowing through his nostrils. Staying low to the ground, Wes crept from three to tree, pausing intermittently to scout ahead. Grit flew through the air into his eyes. He squinted and turned his head against the gusts from the still-hovering craft. Finally, he found a stump several feet in diameter and crouched behind it, raising himself up slightly to peer at the scene spread before him in the moonlight.

The helicopter had settled to the ground, and Wes saw several figures scurrying around in the swirling debris of broken tree limbs, half-decayed leaves, and dry grass stalks. A dozen more people disembarked from the helicopter and began unloading large crates. As

Camouflaged Helicopter

the whirling blades slowly came to a halt, four men dressed in battle fatigues and carrying rifles burst from the dusty haze and dashed to positions at the four corners of the clearing.

The dust settled. Leaves and debris floated to the ground in the ensuing calm. The deafening sound of the helicopter blades gave way to silence. Wes became conscious of his heartbeat and heavy breathing. He remained on the ground behind the stump, his face close to the decaying bark, a guard only inches away. *I can't move!* Wes thought in his cramped position. *If I even take a deep breath, this guy is going to find me. There is no way I can get a better view now.*

None of the apparently all-male participants spoke. Two of the men removed robes from the crates and distributed them to everyone except the guards. The black cloaks, which were nearly invisible in the darkness, were distinguished by the glistening of interlocking triangles on the front. Wes watched as several men picked up a wire mesh cage that had been placed in the center of the clearing and moved it onto one of the mounds.

The full moon illuminated the small cage, and as Wes craned his head around the stump, he could see the naked figure of a small child inside. Straining to see better, Wes perceived that the child wasn't alone in the cage. An animal was also held captive. The child hunched on the floor of the small cage, unable to rise. Something moved, undulating in dozens of wavy lines. *Snakes were crawling in the bottom of the cage! Is that Jennifer?* Wes wondered. His skin felt clammy.

A twig snapped by his ear, and Wes tried to control his surprise. The guard had moved to get a better view of the ceremony; his musky aroma and the odor of sweat from both him and Wes caused Wes's stomach to churn. *As if this night weren't bad enough already,* Wes thought, *Now I have to deal with a bad blind date!* He tried to get his mind off the impending vomit that his stomach was trying to deliver, and strained his eyes in the direction of the strange ceremony.

The group began lining up in front of a tall figure who seemed to be their leader. They drew candles from their robes and lit them. Then holding the flickering candles, they marched solemnly behind the leader, crossing back and forth in the clearing, as though enacting a familiar ritual. They walked in triangular patterns around the individual mounds, back and forth, with the deliberation of a mock funeral procession.

Wes wondered if they were invoking some kind of power from the mounds or conducting the ceremony to honor whatever was buried there. Then the procession formed a triangle around the cage. The silence was broken by chanting from the leader. One end of the triangle opened so Wes could see into the center. The top of the cage had been lifted, and the small girl stood motionless on the ground, seemingly unaware of the biting cold, despite her nakedness.

A member of the group stepped forward with a large, writhing snake and draped it around her neck. The animal from the cage was at her side. Was it a dog? Wes couldn't tell, until the animal turned, and he saw the small horns of a goat.

Wes felt helpless. He wanted to rescue the innocent child, but he knew he could do nothing to stop the proceedings. Armed guards scrutinized the area continually.

"Hail, our queen!" a deep-throated voice intoned.

"Hail!" the others responded.

"Hail!" voiced the guard near to Wes.

Like The Invocation of the Owl.

"Dark Raven, descend upon us with your power. We call you forth from the night, from the netherworld of the dead. Honor us with your presence. We present to you our queen!"

Wes's body ached, but it was too dangerous to move. The guard might hear the underbrush crack if he changed his position. Cold sweat trickled down his cheeks, tickling his skin. He dared not wipe it away. The slightest move might reveal his presence, and who knew what these crazy people might do?

One by one, each of the participants bowed before the shrouded leader, who stepped forward and placed a crown on the child's head. In unison, the men untied the ropes around their waists and parted their robes. The leader stepped behind the child and shouted at her. She didn't respond. He shouted again and struck her with a whip. Silently, she staggered under the blow. Was she drugged or is a trance? Another blow from the whip. The child stepped forward. Wes saw her white face in the moonlight, as he had imagined her hours ago on the mounds. But now she didn't raise her arms toward him in supplication. She obediently knelt in front of the partici-pants. Wes turned away in revulsion.

The retching spasm Wes had feared finally gripped his insides, spewing vomit into his mouth. He dared not spit it out. Steeling himself against the putrid smell that burned his nostrils, he swallowed hard. Wes looked up again and watched the child proceed from one participant to the next, performing fellatio in the name of an ancient Indian curse.

They're worse than animals! How could they make a child do this?

Two of the robed men then placed the young victim on top of the wire cage. The leader picked up the small goat, held it over his head, chanted, and handed it to the men. One took its front legs, the other its back legs. They extended it over the child's head and began chanting. Wes saw the leader take a long, slender knife from under his robe. He held the blade skyward, pointing in the four primary directions, while invoking eerie words.

Deliberately, the leader put the knife blade to the goat's neck, and slit it with a sudden stroke. The slaughtered animal's body jerked spasmodically as blood poured from the dying goat over the girl's head. Wes was astounded that one small animal could contain so much blood. The crimson tide saturated the child's body, while she sat motionless, eyes staring blankly.

Why doesn't she run? Scream? Why doesn't she do something . . . anything? Wes wondered. *She must be so heavily drugged she can't fight back.*

The men who held the goat wrapped its body in a cloth and placed it in a crate. The robed figures lined up again and passed before the child, kneeling in front of her, dabbing their fingers in the blood on her body, and blowing out their candles. Each then drew his hand to his face. Wes could see them touching their foreheads with the blood.

Finally, a cage containing a large bird wearing an ornate hood was taken from a box. The black bird was removed from the cage and placed upon the girl's shoulders. Wes knew its sharp talons must be digging into her tender flesh. The leader plucked a feather, dipped it in the crimson blood still coursing down the child's naked body, and placed the feather in her left hand. Then he took her right hand and led her around the mounds in the same pattern that had started the ceremony. Each participant silently followed.

Wes remembered trampling down the grass hours earlier, the burrs on his pants, the rocks that had cut his shoes. The child was walking barefoot across these stones and sharp blades of grass. Within minutes, the procession ended. In split-second timing, Wes heard the whump-whump of the helicopter motor starting. While the guards watched, the participants removed their robes and placed them in crates. Everything was loaded on the lumbering craft, whose horizontal blades swept in slow motion. The men climbed aboard, and the child was handed up to them. Finally, the guard who had been beside Wes and his three comrades jogged backward toward the ship and disappeared into the swirling dust. The evacuation was completed in a few minutes, and the camouflaged aircraft lifted into the sky and sped off into the darkness.

Wes breathed deeply. He slowly straightened his cramped, bent knees and stretched his aching legs. His joints and muscles hurt, and the tenseness in his neck had given him a ferocious headache. He took quick, short breaths like a marathon runner gasping for air at the end of his course. Then, overcome by the ordeal, he fell in the scattered leaves, clenched his fists, and beat the ground in anger and frustration. He stared into the brilliance of the moon, wishing he could erase from memory the events he had seen.

Will anyone believe this? Who can I tell? What can I do? Wes agonized.

He had never thought much about evil. There were good guys and bad guys, cops and robbers, saints and sinners, but this was like stepping back to an ancient realm of mythology. He rose to one elbow and looked back at the clearing. Did he dare walk in there now? What malevolent powers of nearly two hundred years ago now sulked silently among the Mounds of the Elders?

Wes decided it was pointless to investigate further. So much had happened to him in just four days, his emotions were on overload. Shakily, he rose to his feet, brushed leaves from his clothing, and haltingly walked back toward his car. The simplicity of his past had been inalterably changed. If little Jennifer had actually been crowned into an ancient and evil royal family, Wes knew that he, too, had been inaugurated into a stark realization of hell on earth.

Six

Wes knew he had witnessed a crime, the intentional abuse of a minor. He had to go to the police, but how could he explain what he had seen? He doubted they would believe him. The next morning, he called Chuck Bailey and did something he had never done before.

"I can't come in today," Wes told Bailey.

"What's wrong?" Bailey questioned. "Can you talk about it?"

"No," Wes shot back tersely. "I just can't make it today."

"Who's going to do the show?"

"I don't know. One of the jocks. Maybe you, Chuck."

"Is it that kid, Jennifer? Is that why you're upset?"

"You've been my friend for years," Wes answered. "You know I don't always pay my bills on time or keep my apartment looking real neat, but I've never let you down on doing the show. Today, I just can't do it. Tell Warren anything. Say I'm sick, bedridden, at death's door. Get me off the hook today, and I'll be in bright and early Monday morning."

"Sure, Wes. Whatever you say."

Wes couldn't postpone the next unpleasant step. He had to go to the Columbus County Sheriff's office. He had been there before to pay traffic tickets and follow up stories for the show, but, like most people, he didn't want to be involved in a personal confrontation with the police, especially if his credibility were going to be in question.

Police are cut-and-dried people, Wes thought. *How will they react? Enough people in this town think I'm off-base for some of the things I say on my show. What will they think of a story about ancient Indian burial grounds and spooky spirits under a full moon?*

The sheriff's office was a cement-block building on the corner of East Fourth Avenue and Main Street. The police spent most of their assigned hours at the west end of town, where approaching motorists often failed to notice the thirty-five-mile-per-hour speed limit. Wes pulled into a visitor's slot and made his way into the building. He approached a uniformed officer at the front desk. "Can you tell me where to report a crime?" he asked.

"What kind of crime?"

"I'd rather not say," Wes answered.

The officer looked at him, bored and disinterested. "Is it a serious crime?" he asked.

Columbus county crimes mostly involved running stop signs and jaywalking. How could he get through to this guy? "Yes, it's a *serious* crime. I'd like to talk to the sheriff."

"I suppose you could talk to him, if he's not busy. I'll check. Have a seat."

Wes glanced around the room as he waited for the officer to return. Obviously, the county's finest didn't operate on a big budget. The walls hadn't been painted in years, and almost every tile on the linoleum floor was cracked or chipped. Pictures of former sheriffs hung on the walls along one hallway, and on the wall behind him were two black and white photos of Arnold Hancock, one as sheriff of Columbus County for more than three decades, the other as battalion commander of the Clarion-based National Guard Reserve unit.

"I understand you want to talk with me. Didn't get your name."

Wes looked up to see Arnold Hancock, an overweight fleshy man, partly bald, tall and erect. Patches of puffy skin lay under his small, beady eyes. His hands were on his hips, his right arm resting on the handle of his holstered gun.

"Yes. I'd like about fifteen minutes of your time, Sheriff. I have to speak to you privately."

"Let's go to my office," he said, as he motioned toward a side hallway.

Bulletin boards lined the long corridor, filled with random announcements about wanted fugitives and various police directive. They passed an office where a bored dispatcher slouched in his seat, doing crossword puzzles. In another room, several uniformed officers sat around desks, laughing and joking.

Arnold Hancock's office was small. The sheriff sat down in an old wooden swivel chair, tilted it backward, and swung his heavy boots on top of the desk. He put his arms behind his head, tilted it to one side, and asked, "You've seen a crime committed?"

"Yes, sir," Wes responded.

"Before we go to the trouble of filling out a report, you'd best give me a few details."

Wes realized he hadn't introduced himself. "My name is Wes Bryant. I work for station WTTK.

"You're the guy who does that talk show the first part of the afternoon, right?"

"I'm the guy."

"I've heard of you. What kind of crime did you see? Not much happens here in Columbus County. You must have seen something pretty serious to take the trouble to come down here."

Wes didn't know where to start. Somehow, he had to explain the ceremony at the Mounds of the Elders. Should he mention Annette Simpson? How much should he tell about Jennifer? On the radio, Wes said whatever came to mind. If he said something dumb, he could always make it right the next day. Talking to the sheriff was different. He had to choose his words carefully, or he'd be taken for a fool.

Wes sat upright, looked squarely at Sheriff Hancock, and asked "Ever heard of a place called the Mounds of the Elders?"

Sheriff Hancock's eyes narrowed. "No. Can't say I have."

"It's out on old Route 193, about five miles from town. I was there last night. I saw something I think was a crime. That's why I'm here."

Hancock reached up to scratch his thin, gray hair. "Go on," he said. "I'm listening."

"There's a grove of trees with a small clearing in the middle. A helicopter landed there last night, and a bunch of people got off with snakes and guns. They performed some kind of religious ceremony. Killed a goat."

Sheriff Hancock lifted his feet off the desk, flung them around in front of him, and leaned forward in his chair. He gazed intently at Wes, resting his left elbow on the desk top. "That's pretty hard to believe, Mr. Bryant. Don't take me for a country jerk. I've been around a little, and I don't like to waste my time. Understand?

"Yes, I do. But I'm telling you what I saw. A helicopter *did* land out there last night, and a dozen or so men put on some robes. They had this little kid in a cage. They made her do terrible things . . ."

The sheriff crossed his arms over his chest and leaned back in his old swivel chair. He stared at Wes for several moments, grimacing. "If you've got a drinking problem, I'm not the guy to talk to. Or if you're doing drugs, you know Columbus County. I'd bust you in a minute if I found an ounce of marijuana on you."

Wes had feared this kind of reception, but he forced himself to act calmly. He stood and placed his hands palms-down on Hancock's desk. "I don't to drugs, and I wasn't drunk. I saw that helicopter. They did kill that goat, and they held it over that little girl and let the blood pour all over her!"

Whack! Sheriff Hancock's fist thundered as he hit the desk. "That's it!" he said. "I won't listen to this! I've been sheriff of this county for thirty-one years. Nobody has ever insulted my intelligence like you have today!" His chest heaved in barely contained indignation. "I don't know what your game is, and I'm not interested. You're a known wise guy, not exactly a reliable citizen, from what I hear.

"But let's just suppose you did see something. Maybe it was some kind of ritual? So what? It's a free country. You can worship that door knob over there for all I care," Sheriff Hancock said, gesturing toward his office entryway. "We've got a Constitution in this country, you know. Acting like a fool in the woods at midnight isn't my idea of religion, but if it's somebody else's, there's nothing I can do about it. Whether they got there in a helicopter or in a Mercedes means nothing to me. Evidence, Mr. Bryant. Evidence is what it's all about. I can't send a deputy out on a wild-goose chase without some evidence. You got any?"

Wes felt enraged. He sat back down in the chair. "I'm just a talk show host, Sheriff, not Perry Mason. I told you, these guys had guns. What could I do? Ask them for a bullet to bring back to you?"

Sheriff Hancock lifted his elbows off the desk and tilted back again in his chair. His body language conveyed both irritation and self-assurance. His dark blue eyes stared almost viciously. "Don't smart off to me! If someone was out there with guns, of course you couldn't do anything. What about after they left? Didn't you check the place to see if they left anything behind?"

"I got out of there fast. I'm no hero. I was scared stiff."

Sheriff Hancock slowly rose from his chair and walked over to a filing cabinet. He thumbed through some files and pulled out a stack of papers. Returning to his chair, he threw the documents on top of his desk. "I've heard about this kind of thing before. This is an FBI report from the National Center for the Analysis of Violent Crime in Quantico, Virginia. It deals with the kind of stuff you claim you saw, and the FBI says that police officers should avoid wasting time on so-called ritual crime."

Before Wes could say anything, the sheriff grabbed the document and began flipping through it. "Listen to this on page six: 'Far more crime has been committed by zealots in the name of God than has ever been committed in the name of Satan. The actual involvement of the occult in a criminal case usually turns out to be secondary, insignificant, or nonexistent.'"

Sheriff Hancock looked at Wes, as if to ask, *had enough or do you want to hear more?*

Wes dropped his eyes. He didn't want to hear more of Hancock's efforts to debunk what had been the most horrific experience of his life, but the sheriff wasn't finished. He read on: "'The law enforcement perspective on occult crime requires avoiding the paranoia that has crept into this issue. Unless hard evidence is obtained and corroborated, police officers should avoid being frightened into believing that Satanists are performing criminal ceremonies requiring investigation. An unjustified crusade against such activity could result in wasted resources, unwanted damage to reputations, and disruption of civil liberties.'"

Wes fidgeted in his chair, then reached to zip his jacket. He had long since gotten Sheriff Hancock's point and saw no reason to hang around.

"I'm a public servant, paid to uphold the Constitution and enforce the penal code, not the Ten Commandments," Sheriff Hancock added.

Wes rose to his feet and headed for the door.

"One more thing, Bryant. What were you doing out there in the first place, if you were there? How did you find out about this place . . . what did you call it?"

"The Mounds of the Elders," Wes responded, glancing back over his shoulder.

"Yeah. The Mounds of the Elders. Who told you about it?"

Wes turned around, one hand on the door knob. He was going to take a parting shot, whether Sheriff Hancock liked it or not. "What difference does it make how I knew about the Mounds of the Elders if what I've told you didn't happen: Why worry about a place that might not exist or a naked kid who was sexually abused and bathed in animal blood?"

Sheriff Hancock straightened his six-foot-three frame and stared back at Wes with equal intensity. "Helicopters, ceremonies under a midnight moon, and even a blood ritual involving an abused child. This is Columbus County, Indiana, not some backward, voodoo-infested Louisiana bayou. Even if it were, I couldn't arrest someone for practicing black magic, unless you could prove a crime was committed."

Hancock stepped around the corner of his desk and sat down on its edge. "Tell you what I will do, though. If you can supply any logical, solid evidence, I'll check it out. But unless you can come back with some cold, hard facts, my advice is don't go wandering after things that go bump in the night."

Wes nodded his head in assent and walked out the door, angry and discouraged. He left the police station, opened the door of his car, and slipped behind the wheel. Again, he was tempted to forget the whole thing. He'd done his civic duty, but he could still taste his own vomit, and if he closed his eyes he could see the image of a frightened child huddled among slithering snakes. He had to do two things. Find someone who would believe him, and get Annette Simpson out of that hospital so he could tell her what was happening to her daughter.

Wes didn't have many friends. Most were beer-drinking, poker-playing buddies, not the kind to buck public opinion. As Wes started the car and pulled out of the police station parking lot, names of people he knew in Columbus County flashed before him: business friends, casual acquaintances, men and women. There was no one. He turned down Main Street, saw the familiar sign saying, "Clarion Municipal Hospital. Turn right."

Then it struck him. Clarion Municipal Hospital wasn't just where Annette Simpson was being held against her will, sedated by a potentially dangerous drug. It was also where twenty-odd years ago the kindest man he'd ever known walked into his life—the Reverend James Christoble Carmichael.

S e v e n

Carmichael . . . the Reverend James Carmichael. Why hadn't Wes thought of him before? When he had been hospitalized for his injured knee more than twenty years ago, the Reverend Carmichael dropped in on Wes, who was watching a Saturday afternoon football game on television in the patient lounge. Carmichael stuck his head in the door and asked, "Mind if I watch with you a few minutes?"

The Reverend Carmichael knew his football, all right, but he also knew a lot about living. He was black, and, in a mostly white town like Clarion, the two races didn't mix much. Carmichael was the first black person Wes had ever known. They talked about God a lot that dark, bitter day in the hospital. The reverend listened with compassion, as Wes vented his anger at God for the drastic disruption the injury had made in his life.

"Remember," Carmichael had told him, "God is big enough to handle your hurt. Go ahead, lay it all on him! That's what he's there for. Give him your pain, your bitterness, your disappointments. If you don't tell God about your anger, he can't do you any good."

After his release from the hospital, Wes hadn't seen the reverend again, but he knew he should have called Carmichael years ago to thank him for coming into his life at that particularly depressing time. Wes spotted a gas station with a phone booth and pulled up to it. Wes grabbed the phone book. C-Car-Carmichael. Reverend James

Carmichael, #10 Applegate Lane. Wes dialed the number. No answer. After returning to his apartment, he tried again throughout the day, and still no answer. Finally, that evening, he reached a woman who identified herself as the Reverend Carmichael's wife, Hanna. "James will be gone until Sunday's services," she told Wes. "He's performing a wedding out of town." Wes decided to visit Carmichael's church that Sunday and ask the reverend what he should do about Jennifer and the Mounds of the Elders.

Sunday morning, Wes woke up with the sun, read the paper, and drank coffee until 9:00 a.m. He dressed with special care, brushed his unruly hair into submission, and trimmed his fingernails.

Faith Apostolic Tabernacle, located on the outskirts of Clarion, was different from any church he knew. The building itself was white clapboard, and the parking area was muddy from late fall rains. Inside, the ceiling of the small church stretched upward into a high V, braced by aged wooden beams. Where the roof met the wall, long steel bracing rods went from one side to the other to stabilize the structure. The windows consisted of plain frosted glass. In front, alter rails stretched along each side, and boxes of tissue were placed strategically every few feet. Everything was clean, free of dust, tidy. Light filtered down upon people who sat quietly, squeezed into the pews, shoulder to shoulder, waiting for the service to start. Wes was the only white person in church that morning, but the congregation seemed to pay little attention to him. Maybe they were just too polite. Whatever the reason, he felt at ease.

A large woman sitting next to Wes smiled. "Sister Wilma's my name," the woman whispered to Wes. "That's Reverend Carmichael sitting behind the pulpit. Wait 'til you hear him preach! He's anointed by the Lord."

"Let's all stand and sing, brothers and sisters," said a gravelly voiced song leader. On cue, the organist began. He didn't just play the old Hammond. He pumped it into action. All around Wes, people started swaying. They clapped hands rhythmically. No one used song books. The people didn't need printed notes, telling them what to do when the Spirit moved.

"Glory, glory, Hallelujah, when I lay my burdens down!" They sang from their hearts and, from what Wes knew about black poverty in the county, these people had plenty of burdens to lay down. Wes had serious concerns too—Jennifer and Annette Simpson, for instance, as well as his daughter, Misha. Yet, for the moment, within the walls of the Faith Apostolic Tabernacle, he felt free from the inner turmoil that had dogged him since Jennifer's frightened voice had interrupted his life.

The congregation was the choir. To Wes's left, women sang the soprano parts. On his right, men's voices blended the rich bass, forming a single vocal instrument. The very young bounced up and down in rhythm with the swelling voices. Spry old ladies in elaborate hats beamed at the little ones, acknowledging in their hearts the safety of this small sanctuary.

The singing ended, and the organist played a bluesy interlude. The congregation quieted and walked around the tiny church, hugging each other. People came over to Wes and shook his hand. This was hands-on Christianity. Touching, embracing, loving. Wes had never felt anything like it. He vowed right there that, if he and God ever resumed talking to each other, he wanted to speak this language.

"And now, brothers and sisters, our beloved pastor, the Reverend (organ chord) . . . James (organ fanfare) . . . Christoble (organ chord) . . . Carmichael (organ finale)!"

The congregation clapped and shouted, "Praise the Lord!" loud enough to raise the spiritually dead in some of the white churches downtown. As if responding to a silent signal, the people took their places again in the pews.

Reverend Carmichael smiled that big smile Wes remembered so well. His eyes glowed with a love that Wes hadn't often observed upon the faces of frocked ecclesiastics. An old man in his seventies, he had a youthful energy that many men half his age lacked. His full head of thick hair was tinged with white, and a few deep laughter lines marked his strong, square-jawed face. When he smiled, his teeth gleamed almost luminously, contrasting sharply with the dark hue of his skin.

"Today, my text is taken from Matthew 21:42: 'The stone which the builders rejected / Has become the chief cornerstone.'"

Carmichael's voice boomed, "That stone is the rock of ages, Jesus Christ! He knows about rejection. He knows about suffering. He knows about heartache."

From the pews, glad voices rang out: "Amen! Hallelujah! Preach it!"

"Brothers and sisters, our people know how it feels to be rejected and despised. We know what it means to be downtrodden and left out."

"Yes, Lord!" an usher shouted.

"That's right!" Sister Wilma, the woman next to Wes, echoed.

"Jesus knows too!" Reverend Carmichael assured his congregation. "When Jesus walked the earth, he couldn't save many rich people. He couldn't heal many high and mighty people. But the poor heard him because he came to set the captives free! We know about being captives, don't we?"

Strangely, Carmichael looked at Wes. *Why?* Wes wondered. He wasn't black. He'd never been a slave. No one owned *his* soul.

As if answering the questions in Wes's mind, the Reverend Carmichael continued: "Brothers and sisters, you don't have to be black to be captive. You can be captive to your own fears. You can be a slave to your own greed. You can be in bondage to your selfish desires, wanting what you want more than what God wants for you. Jesus won't change the color of your skin, but he will change the condition of your heart . . . if you ask him!"

"Amen! Hallelujah! Thank you, Jesus!" the crowd shouted.

As if their response was too feeble, Reverend Carmichael implored, "I said, you got to ASK him!"

"A-MEN!" the congregation roared.

"Now, if you want to ask him, just get out of those seats and come down to the alter! Lay down you burdens! Don't be a slave any longer! Give you life to the Lord! He'll take care of you! Don't let that old devil pride keep you down! Humble yourself before Jesus! Let the *Lord* lift you up!"

The organist interrupted the sermon with the stirring chords of improvised, soul-felt music. These people were gloriously happy to be alive. When the small room became still again, the Reverend Carmichael pounded the pulpit and his voice thundered as if it would rattle the windows of the tiny church.

"This old building you know as Faith Apostolic Tabernacle will fall down someday; yes, it will! But the tabernacle of the Lord will stand forever! If your faith rests on this building or this preacher, you got trouble! Keep your eyes on the Lord, brothers and sisters!"

Now, Wes saw the purpose for the boxes of tissue. All around him, people wept. Some left their seats and marched to the front of the church. They didn't go to lay down black burdens: they cast down human despair, sickness of the soul, and frail beliefs.

Wes wanted to go to the front with them. He wanted to get rid of his anger toward God for the injury that had ruined his future, the hurt of his disintegrated marriage, the pain of not knowing who he really was, and the feeling that his only value was expressed from noon to 3:00 p.m. each day during "Talk about Town."

He almost stood to join then, when a lump formed in this throat. Wes bowed his head and tried to recapture the strange serenity he had felt too briefly moments before. He wasn't sure about the actual existence of the devil, but if Satan were real, his nickname was Pride.

People didn't leave the Faith Apostolic Tabernacle after the benediction. A half hour later, they still stood around, laughing and talking. There were new babies to hold, tales to tell, hands to shake, and prayers to pray. Making his way through the exuberant crowd of people, the Reverend Carmichael approached Wes, holding out his hand and smiling broadly.

"Welcome to our little church," he said.

"Thanks," Wes responded. "You're something else behind that pulpit."

"Oh, not really," Carmichael said modestly. "I just put out the words the Lord gives to me. First time here?"

"First time."

"Hm-m-m. You look a little familiar to me. Have we met before?"

"Oh, about twenty years ago. I hurt my leg playing football and was laid up for several weeks in Clarion Municipal Hospital. We watched a football game on TV together."

"I remember!" Reverend Carmichael exclaimed, tossing his head back in laughter. "You sure changed a lot. Me, I've hardly aged at all, have I?"

"No, doesn't look like it, Reverend Carmichael."

"Now, watch out! You know where liars go," he said, laughing again. "And cut out that reverend stuff. Folks just call me James."

"OK, James."

"Sorry, I can't remember your name. Twenty-some years is a long time at my age."

"Wes Bryant."

"Are you the same Wes Bryant who does that talk show?"

"That's me."

"Well, bless my soul! My parishioners just love your show. They've never forgotten that series of broadcasts you did on the Ku Klux Klan. Still lots of Klan members around these parts. Some of my people have had threats from them."

"Sorry to hear that."

"What brings you to our church this Sunday morning?"

"Well, Rev . . . I mean, James, you preached about it this morning, about laying our burdens down. I've got a burden I can't lay down on anyone."

"Then lay it down on Jesus."

"I'd like to do that, but right now I need the help of a human friend, and you're the only one I feel I can trust."

"Why me?" Carmichael asked with surprise. "You hardly know me."

"That's true, but I've never forgotten how much I trusted you with my feelings. I need someone I can trust completely."

"Well then, let's sit down in this pew, and you tell me about it."

Wes started form the beginning. Jennifer's calls, the effort to locate her mother, and his fear for the safety of both Jennifer and Annette Simpson.

"You'll think this next stuff is crazy, but please . . . please, James, just listen."

Carmichael settled back in the pew and signaled for Wes to continue.

The reverend's expression changed, as Wes recounted the horror and torment that happened at the Mounds of the Elders. Like the gaze of an injured animal, his eyes saddened as Wes explicitly described Jennifer's ordeal in the snake-covered cage, and he began to weep, his tears forming small rivulets on his dark, weathered cheeks.

"As God is my witness, I saw these things happen. And if this kid I saw at the ceremony is Jennifer, her mother is lying in Clarion Municipal Hospital, drugged out of her mind, and some so-called doctor is keeping her that way. Believe me, James, I didn't go looking for this mess. But I know that little girl who called is the same child I saw so horribly abused the other night."

The reverend shook his head slowly back and forth. He covered his eyes with one hand, bowed his head, sat silently a moment. When he looked back at Wes, Carmichael's face was twisted with pain. "I believe you, Wes. It sounds like the work of the devil to me. What have you done about it?"

"I did what I thought was the right thing. I went to the sheriff. He all but threw me out of his office."

Carmichael nodded his head again, then sat back against the wooden pew and remained silent so long Wes thought he might have gone to sleep. Finally, the reverend spoke, his voice indescribably weary, as though decades of weight rested upon his soul. "I won't throw you out of the house of the Lord. You didn't come to this little tabernacle by chance. Give me some time to think about what you've told me. It's too much to handle all at once. Let me sleep on it . . .

and pray about it. Just give me some time to think."

The two men rose from the pew, one of them with a heavier burden, the other with a lighter one. They shook hands, and Wes walked slowly out of the little church. As he drove down the dirt road, he realized he had spent too much of his life bearing burdens alone.

Eight Fight

After the ceremony at the Mounds of the Elders on Thursday night and Carmichael's Sunday sermon, Wes felt trapped between heaven and hell. At the Mounds, he had witnessed human depravity at a level lower than he could have imagined. Conversely, the Faith Apostolic Tabernacle service revealed a bit of heaven on earth that was also beyond his experience. He felt suspended between good and evil. Yet straddling fences no longer seemed to be an option for him.

Neutrality was a useful, often advisable posture on "Talk about Town," since it afforded him the chance to play one side against the other. He could flip-flop and champion whatever position provoked the greatest interest from his listeners. But what worked for radio ratings wasn't feasible in this situation. A nine-year-old child had been brutalized, her mother was imprisoned, and he had witnessed the clandestine desecration of an innocent human soul.

Wes rolled out of bed that Monday morning, October 26, planted his feet flat on the floor, and held his head in his hands. He felt deeply compelled to take action, perhaps illegal action. Annette Simpson had to be freed. No one had ever accused him of living an exemplary life—he sometimes stayed out too late and had occasionally fudged on his income tax—but he'd never done anything really bad, nothing like kidnapping.

Though the thought of executing his ideas unsettled him, Wes didn't question his basic plan. He would sneak through the back door of Clarion Municipal Hospital and, somehow, take Annette Simpson out of there. As he swigged a last cup of coffee before leaving for WTTK, he looked in the hallway mirror. Aside from shaving and combing his hair, he didn't look at himself much, but just now he was comfortable with his reflection.

The morning and early afternoon passed quickly. Wes tried to act nonchalant. To those around him, it was a normal day, but to Wes, it was a day he'd make critical decisions that could affect the rest of his life. Before he knew it, "Talk about Town" was over.

"Great job, Wes!" Chuck Bailey said, jotting down some notes for the next day's show.

"Who's my guest tomorrow?"

"Bud Short. He's a new candidate for city council. Says he wants to do something about that feedlot smell on the west end of town. Don't know how he's going to accomplish it without offending farmers, but we'll see what he says."

"Just get me some facts to pin him down. Cow manure isn't the most stimulating subject in the world. In fact, it stinks!" Wes chuckled.

Chuck laughed. "I'll have some stuff on your desk by the time you get in tomorrow morning. Want to come over tonight for a beer, watch some television? There's a prize fight on one of the cable channels."

"No, thanks, I had a pretty hectic weekend. Think I'll get to bed early. Talk to you in the morning."

Wes walked out the front door of WTTK, wondering what his life would be like by morning. If his plan for the next few hours didn't come off, he could land in jail.

Wes pulled his car out of WTTK's parking lot and drove to Clarion Municipal Hospital; he parked in the same spot he'd used on the previous visit to CMH. He walked down the same alley to the same delivery entrance. Once inside, he headed for room sixteen. No one was in sight, so he gently nudged the door and stepped inside. The door swung shut noiselessly. The sheets had been tossed aside. The bed was empty! The stand holding the IV bottle of Thorazine was gone.

Oh, no! Wes panicked. *Blackwell moved her, or maybe somebody from the Dark Raven got her.* As he stood there, his veins throbbing with adrenaline, something banged at the doorway. Before him stood a frail woman in a disheveled hospital robe. Lank strands of hair hung in her face. With one arm, she steadied herself against the door jamb. The other clung to a tall metal pole with casters on a tripod base, from which an intravenous bottle dangled. Wes recognized Annette Simpson.

Annette stared blankly at Wes. A faint glimmer of recognition began to register. "You came here before," she stated flatly. Her voice sounded hollow, though stronger than on his previous encounter with her. He decided the only way he could reach her was through blunt honesty.

"Yes. I want to help you. I think you're in danger."

Her face remained expressionless. It was obviously difficult for her to concentrate. Her eyes closed, and Wes wondered if she was going to sleep. But they opened again, and she sighed heavily.

She spoke in a barely audible tone. "I've been up and walking today. I can't find Jennifer. She's not here. Do you know where she is?"

"Not exactly. I've seen her. That's all."

"Are you a minister?"

"No. Just a friend."

He heard muffled noises far down the hallway. A car horn blasted nearby. Wes hated the smell of hospitals, and this one was no exception, but he had to give Annette Simpson time to process what he presented to her. The distortions of a drugged mind were strange enough, let alone his mysterious appearances in her room.

Finally, she spoke again. "I'm not supposed to leave this room. But I noticed that the IV stand had rollers . . . I wanted to walk . . . down the hall. No one saw me." Her pupils were dilated, her breathing shallow.

Time was short. Wes had to press on. "Listen carefully," he said. "Dr. Blackwell lied to you. Your husband is dead. He was killed in the accident. Blackwell is drugging you so you don't know what's going on. Jennifer needs help! You've got to let me take you out of here!"

Wes could see Annette trying to focus on his face, his words. She asked for water, and he found a glassful on a nightstand. He held it for her while she sipped the stale liquid. She stared wide-eyed at him, then said, "I'm awfully weak. Today, I walked. First time since the accident. Very tired." Annette sighed heavily and closed her eyes again. "Please help me."

"Are you injured? Can you leave the hospital?"

"I'm not hurt . . . just tired. I can't think straight. Who are you? . . . Did you say?"

"Never mind. You must trust me. I'll help you find Jennifer. Will you cooperate?"

Annette's brow furrowed. "I'll do anything to help my daughter."

"Listen, then. I'm going to take that tube out of your arm, pick you up, and carry you out of her. But you must cooperate."

"Yes. I want to. But . . . the nurses? What if they see us?"

"We'll have to risk that. My car's just outside. I can get you out of here real fast. How often is your room checked?"

"No one comes in here except Dr. Blackwell, a couple of times a day."

Wes knew nothing about the legal implications of what he was doing. Was it kidnapping if he had Annette's consent? Or would it just be a violation of the hospital code or some civil law? Could he be sued for endangering someone's life or for intervening between a patient and a medial doctor? All his questions were swept away by the sudden, stark memory of a small, naked child huddled in a cage swarming with snakes.

Wes took Annette's arm in his hands, gently pulled back the adhesive tape, eased the needle from her flesh, and quickly placed the tape back over the puncture wound. He let the IV drop, slowly dripping its poisonous contents onto the floor. He took his hands away and stared into her dulled eyes. Quietly, patiently, he urged, "When I lean over the bed, I want you to reach up and put your arms around my neck."

"I don't think I can."

"Just do your best. I'll help. I'm going to put my arms under you, then lift you up."

"Wait! Is my purse here?" Annette interrupted.

Wes quickly looked around the room, then saw a crumpled leather bag he had missed before. He picked it up and glanced inside. "It's empty," he said, tossing it back on the floor.

"Let me look," Annette insisted.

Wes gave her the bag, and she fumbled inside. For a moment, Wes's conclusion about the purse's contents matched the despairing look on Annette's face. Then Wes saw a slight smile cross her lips as she removed her clenched fist from inside the bag, a lint-covered gold chain dangling from her frail fingers. Annette unfolded her hand, and Wes saw the chain was connected to a small gold cross.

"It was a gift from my father when I was confirmed," she said. "I've never been without it since."

Wes draped the chain around her slender neck and tightened the clasp. The cross sparkled in contrast to Annette's pale skin.

"Here we go," Wes said, as he leaned down and steadied her arms around his neck.

Annette's thin body seemed light in his arms. She laid her head on his shoulder and leaned against his chest. Wes placed his foot against the door and shoved it open. He looked out and carefully scanned the area. He saw no one. His heart thumped, and sweat soaked his back. Wes stepped into the hallway and cautiously made for the exit.

As he reached the delivery door, he bent his knees, cradling Annette Simpson close to his body, extended his hand, and turned the handle. He nudged the door open and stepped into the alley.

Although Wes's mind was racing, his body seemed to work in slow motion. He walked toward the car, balancing his burden carefully, his legs laboring as though wading through knee-high wet snow. It took an eternity to open the car door and maneuver Annette Simpson into the back seat. *Was anyone watching? Were alarms being set off?* he wondered.

Wes slammed the back door and ran to the driver's side. He threw himself behind the wheel and jammed the key into the ignition. Just as the motor turned over, a sleek sports car rounded the corner and turned up the alley.

Wes put his foot on the gas pedal and fought the impulse to race away. He saw a tall man in a dark suit get out of the sports car. As the man turned to lock the door, Wes saw his thin face and black beard. The man walked to the delivery door, paused, and stared at the open door. He reached out and swung it back and forth a couple of times, then shook his head and walked inside.

Wes forced himself to pull away at a normal speed. He turned the corner onto Archer Street, feeling better with the hospital out of sight. It occurred to him that he hadn't planned his next move. Where would he take Annette Simpson? Wes glanced back over his shoulder. She lay on the seat, her head on an old jacket of his. She wore only the tattered hospital bathrobe. Wes turned on the car heater full blast.

Annette needed total rest and proper food. That meant someone had to look after her. Again, he had only one choice . . . the Reverend James Carmichael. He wanted to stop and call first, but he knew he couldn't take that chance. Just thinking about what was happening at the hospital right then made his heart beat erratically. Wes headed down the old dirt road toward Faith Apostolic Tabernacle. He glanced intermittently into the rearview mirror where he could see Annette Simpson. She lay perfectly still, and Wes gained a strange sense of comfort in seeing her there.

Wes coasted into the church yard and surveyed the surroundings. He spotted what he assumed was the Carmichael home, a small brick house about fifty yards away. A large wooden porch spread across the front of the house. It contained a few worn lawn chairs and an old-fashioned wooden swing, suspended by heavy chains from the porch ceiling. Wes remembered a similar swing from his childhood and felt a sudden, overwhelming need to let its relaxing sway block out the fear and anxieties of the last hour.

He parked far enough away from the house so no one inside could see Annette Simpson in the car, then climbed the solid front steps to the porch, walked to the door, and knocked. A tall, stately black woman, holding a shiny metal pot in one hand, a dish towel in the other, answered. A colorful print dress draped loosely on her large frame. She continued wiping the pot in her hand as she looked at Wes, sizing him up.

"Is this Reverend Carmichael's home?" Wes asked.

"Yes. I'm his wife, Hannah. Can I help you?"

"I'm Wes Bryant. I really need to talk to the reverend."

Hannah Carmichael grinned broadly. She turned and put down the pot and dish towel, and threw open her arms. The next thing Wes knew, he was engulfed in a bear hug like those he'd seen after Reverend Carmichael's sermon.

"James told me so much about you! I'm sorry I didn't get to meet you yesterday morning. Come in! James is raking leaves in the back-yard. I'll get him."

"I'll just wait here."

"All right. I'll only be a minute."

Wes didn't want to leave Annette Simpson unguarded.

His anxieties compelled him to return to the car and look in on her. She hadn't moved. He stayed there, leaning his back against the side of the car, his arms folded. James Carmichael would either think he had performed a heroic act that warranted assistance or that he had behaved like a criminal.

"Howdy, Wes!" Carmichael called from the porch. He walked down the wooden steps. "Been thinking about you all day. Awful lot of things to consider," he said, walking toward Wes with an outstretched hand. "Haven't made up my mind what to do about it."

Wes grasped the strong dark hand in his own, grateful for the solidity of this man who had given him so much already. "Well, I'm afraid there's not much to think about anymore. I didn't wait for you. I sort of took things into my own hands," Wes said, drawing

Carmichael's attention to the back seat of his car.

The Reverend Carmichael leaned over, cupped his hands around his eyes, and peered into the car window. His mouth dropped. He turned quickly to look at Wes in puzzlement, swung back toward the car to look in the window again, then stood in silence. Slowly, he stepped backward and said, his voice low and harsh, "Who is that? Is she dead or alive?"

"Oh, she's alive, all right. It's Annette Simpson. I carried her out of a hospital room. She wants to find her daughter."

"You kidnapped her! Good heavens, man! I'm a preacher! I can't mess with this! I spent my whole life telling people to respect the law. You can't just sneak into a hospital and hijack people!"

Wes shoved his hands into his pants pockets and took a step forward, advancing toward the car in symbolic defense of the woman inside. His voice sounded rough as he answered, "I saw a little girl, naked and brutalized in the woods not far from here. And some character who calls himself a doctor was pumping her mother—the woman in my car—full of poison, messing up her mind with drugs. What if they decide to kill the girl or this woman? I told you about going to the police. You know that didn't do any good. Help me, man! Help me!"

Carmichael's shoulders slumped. He paced back and forth, shaking his head, muttering under his breath as if arguing with himself. Every few steps, he kicked some dirt and raised his right hand in a gesture of perplexity.

Wes heard a screen door slam. Hannah had obviously heard the two men yelling at each other.

"What's going on, honey?" she called to her husband.

Carmichael whirled around, his dark eyes snapping. He was clearly angry. He barked, "You know that woman Wes talked to me about, the one whose daughter he says was in some kind of evil ceremony, the woman in the hospital? Well, Wes kidnapped her! She's right there in his car!" the reverend pointed at Wes's battered vehicle as though it contained contraband goods.

The Reverend Carmichael turned toward Wes, staring silently. Wes felt he had just one chance to say the right thing and gain their support. "I'm not a theologian or a lawyer," Wes said, a note of desperation in his voice. "I'm just a talk show host. I'm not sure what's right and wrong anymore in this crazy world. I only know I couldn't sleep at night for thinking about that poor kid in the woods. I had to do something, even if it meant breaking the law. What does God want me to do? Pray? Dump the whole weird mess on some spiritual waiting list until all the answers come down from heaven?" Wes was angry, too, and tired. He felt as if he had been running uphill for hours. "I don't know much about that book you preach from, but I heard it says something about treating others the way you want them to treat you. Well, that's what I did. And I can't look after this woman. I know I should have asked you first, and I apologize for that. But if you don't help me, nobody will!"

An awkward silence followed, until Hannah's husky voice broke through, commanding, "James, get that woman out of the car. Carry her inside, and put her in the guest bedroom. While you two argue about what's right and wrong, she's lying there freezing. Go on! Get moving!"

James Carmichael and Wes Bryant looked at each other, suddenly aware that they had been quarreling about principles while Annette Simpson lay helpless.

Without a word, James opened the car door wide, then turned to Wes and nodded. Carefully, they eased her off the seat. Wes took her in his arms and carried her into the house.

Hannah led them to a small bedroom in back of the house. The room was brightly decorated and smelled sweetly of lavender. A handcarved wooden cross hung on the wall, and Wes wondered if the reverend had done the woodwork. An old well-read Bible with tattered pages lay on the nightstand. The Carmichaels obviously had used the Word of God more than once to help a lost or troubled soul. Hannah had richly embroidered the cloth covering the nightstand with brightly colored lilies of the valley and small delicate angels. As he surveyed the room, a strange blend of peace and self-pity overcame Wes, and he wasn't comfortable with either.

Hannah turned down the spread to fresh white sheets, plumped a couple of pillows, and waited for Wes to put Annette into bed. "Watch her while I warm up some broth. Tuck those covers around her," Hannah said. "Try to make her comfortable."

While Hannah was in the kitchen, Reverend Carmichael and Wes maintained an uneasy silence, glancing at the inert figure in the bed. Wes was aware that he had imposed upon James Carmichael, but he didn't know what to say. Carmichael knew he was compromising his principles as a minister for this man he barely knew. Finally, he broke the silence. "How long do we look after her?"

Wes glanced at him, relieved.

"A couple of days, at least. When the drugs wears off, I'll ask her where Jennifer could be. The thing that worries me most is getting that kid to safety."

Carmichael reached out and put an arm on Wes's shoulder. His voice softened as he said, "You've had a tough day. Why don't you turn in early? Hannah and I will look after her tonight. You can curl up on the living room couch, in case we need you. I'll get a pillow and some blankets."

Wes nodded. James was right. If anything went wrong, he should be there. He could pass by his apartment in the morning and get ready for work.

Wes spent a restless night, and it wasn't just because of the cramped couch. His overactive mind retraced again and again the events of recent days, circular reasoning that left him stranded on the inescapable fact that he had stumbled across a frightfully dangerous group that operated beyond the law.

The first rays of the morning sun filtered through a window in the Carmichael kitchen and jolted Wes out of a fitful sleep. He couldn't remember where he was and why he was lying fully clothed on a couch. Then the enormity of his circumstances descended with all its ponderous weight.

Wes gingerly pushed back the blanket and got up. He stretched his stiff limbs and approached the door to Annette's room. He pushed it open and saw James soundly sleeping in a lounge chair, head tilted back, gently snoring. Hannah sat in a chair by Annette Simpson's bedside, next to three women, Sister Wilma, whom he remembered from the church, and two others Wes also faintly recalled seeing that Sunday morning. The four were crocheting and sewing quilt squares, each one handcrafted with small stitches and perfect detail.

Hannah smiled at Wes as he peered in, and the other ladies nodded to acknowledge his entrance. "She slept most of the night without a sound because she was in the Lord's hands, Mr. Bryant," Hannah said softly. "After you went to sleep, I phoned and asked my friends to join me. We prayed all night that she'd be kept safely in the arms of Jesus. It's the devil that's after her, you know. It's him we're fighting."

Hannah gestured toward the Bible on the nightstand. "That book tells us that the love of God is a lot more powerful than the wicked one who stalks our souls," Hannah added resolutely.

Wilma and the other kept crocheting as they murmured affirming amens under their breaths. Wes couldn't think of a better place for Annette to be and wondered if God had brought James Carmichael's name to his mind.

As if on cue, Annette Simpson stirred and opened her eyes. She lay silently, then turned her head toward Hannah, raised herself on her elbows, and asked, "Who are you?"

Without waiting for an answer, she slowly moved her head and saw Wes. Recognition lit her face, followed by a frown. "You carried me out of the hospital . . . I remember . . . going out the back door."

She glanced around the room, studying its contents. "Is this your house?"

James had awakened and sat silently, watching the thin, pale woman.

Wes answered her. "These are friends of mine, the Reverend James Carmichael, pastor of the Faith Apostolic Tabernacle, and his wife, Hannah."

"You're welcome in our home, child," Hannah said. "And you're in all of our prayers," she added, motioning to Sister Wilma and the other ladies who were quilting.

"Amen!" the three ladies affirmed in unison.

Annette Simpson relaxed, resting on her back. Her eyes were surprisingly clear. "Who are you? Did I know you from somewhere?"

"Not before I saw you in the hospital. It's a complicated story. Not that I mind talking to you about it, but let's take it a little slowly. I want you to know that I . . . we'll help you, whatever you need. Please trust us."

"I trust God," Annette answered somewhat defensively, as she looked at Wes in frank curiosity, then glanced toward the others at her side. Sorrow and compassion were etched across the tired lines of Hannah's and James's faces. The other women sat silently, waiting to offer consolation.

Annette's hands flew to her face in alarm. "Jennifer! Where's my little girl?"

Annette's troubled mind had finally emerged from her drugged state far enough to understand her child was missing. She choked back tears, as she searched Wes's face for an answer to calm her fears. "I have to find her. I have to know she's alive!" Annette exclaimed.

Hannah leaned toward the bed and took Annette's hand. "Child, you have to trust Mr. Bryant. He brought you here to safety, and God brought him into your life to find your beautiful girl. I know in my heart the Lord will show him the way to find that young'un of yours.

Hannah embraced Annette, pulling her close to her matronly bosom. As Annette cried in anguish, Hannah continued to comfort her. "Jesus has a plan. We don't always understand it, but we have to believe it. I know you have Jesus in you heart, and he's been holding your hand to guide you down life's path. Right now, that path seems to have veered off in some strange direction. But, honey, Jesus knows what he's doin'. He's gonna be bringin' your little one home soon.

"Right now, he's using us to look out for you, and it's something we gladly do. Like I always tell James, we may not be rich with the world's things, but we're rich in God's love. And when it's time to enter those pearly gates, that's all that matters. So, don't you go forgetting the Jesus who's been with you and your little girl all these years and let that old devil knock you down."

James Carmichael reached over and took Annette's hand in his. Wes noticed that, despite his calluses, the touch of the warm flesh of this man of God calmed Annette.

"Child, you listen to what my Hannah said," the reverend assured Annette. "She's been the Lord's biggest cheerleader for years." Annette smiled through her tears, as he went on. "I sometimes think she ought to be the one wearing this preacher's collar instead of me." He motioned to his ecclesiastical trademark, which peeked out from the overlapping flesh of his neck.

Hannah took James's hand in her hand as both of them reached out to touch Annette's shoulder. Then Hannah began to softly pray that God world look down on all of them and defeat the evil that had taken hold of the Simpson family. When they finished, Wes walked over to the bed and patted Annette's thin arm. "It will all work out. I'll do everything I can to find Jennifer," he said.

He walked toward the bedroom door. "Don't get up," he said to the Carmichaels. "I'll see myself out. Thanks for all the help. I've never asked so much from anybody in my life, and I'm grateful to you."

James and Hannah said farewell to Wes as he walked out of the room. This simple house was the only safe haven Annette Simpson had at the moment. Wes's eyes were bloodshot, and great dark circles lay beneath them. He was bone-tired, jittery from lack of sleep. His head had begun to ache. "Talk about Town" and the staff of WTTK seemed incidental, unwelcome intrusions upon the mission that had been thrust upon him.

Misha! His daughter's name struck him. What if Misha had been caged and whipped, forced into bestial acts? The mental image was unbearable, and an enormous wave of pain bludgeoned him. For the first time since he had faced the truth of his shattered leg twenty-four years before, Wes wept. Foreign words swelled into his heart like soft echoes from a forgotten time: *Help me! Someone, please help me find Jennifer.*

Nine

Tuesday and Wednesday of that week, Wes Bryant shuttled between his apartment to change clothes and the radio station to do his show, hurrying to the Carmichaels' house immediately after he went off the air. He maintained a vigil over Annette Simpson, alternately sleeping on the couch and sitting by her bedside. While recognizing Annette's need to sleep and give her body and mind the chance to recover, he felt a pressing constriction of time. Each passing hour was a threat to Jennifer's welfare, and he needed to talk to Annette. Wes knew she believed that God had a plan for her and Jennifer, but he was not sure he shared that belief.

Hannah Carmichael fed Annette rich broths and thick vegetable soups, patiently urging her to take nourishment. A bond of trust grew between the two women. Hannah talked about the church and the quilts for the needy that she, Sister Wilma, and the other ladies were making. She also spoke to Annette about the faith she would need to pull her through her pain.

"God is there, child." Wes overheard Hannah tell her.

"He's there for those who have set aside their vanity and pride and have given their lives to him for the sake of others. You have to believe that Jennifer will be home soon and that Wes is being guided by the hand of God to bring her back. The power of God is pure and unstoppable. So hold tight to your love and trust in Jesus, and you'll find the hope you need."

Annette listened, and Wes could see she was keenly aware of Hannah's sensitivity to her bizarre situation. She understood on both an intuitive and a spiritual level that she had crashed into a conflict that would exact an enormous price from her. Yet she knew few specifics of the past six months and the incredible rescue from the drugged limbo of the hospital, which had destroyed the boundaries of her once-normal life. Truth and fact had been distorted beyond recognition. Hannah and James felt her fear, extended their love, and with God's help created an oasis of safety for Annette Simpson.

On Thursday, the third day of her covert residence at the Carmichael's, Annette sat up in bed and asked, "Where's the man who brought me here?"

Hannah explained that Wes Bryant was at the radio station and would be by later that afternoon. Annette was sleeping when he pulled into the driveway just after four o'clock.

"She asked to see you," Hannah said, meeting Wes at the door. "She's coming around, not so groggy today. She seems to be think-ing clearly."

That was good news. Wes had worried a great deal about Annette's condition and the possibility of physical or emotional relapse. It had been dangerous enough to sequester her without medical attention, and Wes was uneasy about the emotional impact of what he had to tell her. The shock would be brutal, if not lethal, to her recovery.

Wes pushed open the door to Annette Simpson's room and walked to her bed. He pulled up Hannah's chair and quietly sat down, gazing at the small woman. After the few days of care by the Carmichaels, Annette Simpson's appearance had dramatically changed.

Hannah Carmichael had brushed Annette's shoulder-length auburn hair to a copper shimmer. Annette had shed the anemic hospital pallor, and color had returned to her skin. She was an attractive woman with delicate, small features. Her blistered lips were healing, and her gaunt cheekbones had partially fleshed out. Wes reached out to push back a few strands of hair from her forehead. She opened her dark brown eyes, scrutinized him a moment, then smiled. *Well,* Wes thought happily, *that's an improvement!* He returned her smile and withdrew his hand.

"Thank you for everything you've done," Annette said in a low voice. "I'm grateful. I know almost nothing about you, or why you took me from the hospital. How did you find me?'

James came into the room and stood just inside the door. Annette sat up higher in the bed as Wes adjusted her pillows. "I feel so much love in this house. I feel safe and cared for, even though I know something's wrong. I dreamed you told me Gregory was dead."

"That was no dream, Annette. I told you that the day I took you from the hospital."

Annette put her hand out, and Wes clasped it in his. "You also told me Jennifer was in trouble. You have to tell me what you know. She's my *daughter.*"

A great hollow of dread formed in Wes's stomach. How could he tell this fragile woman of the brutal indignities her daughter had endured? How could any mother tolerate descriptions of the scenes he had witnessed that black night? Where was the toughness he'd depended upon for so many years on the show?

Wes looked into Annette's questioning eyes. It was his responsibility to reveal the terrible facts; no embellishment or deletion would make it easier to tell—or listen to.

Wes leaned closer to Annette. Her face boasted a pale shadow of rose across its cheeks, and her eyes were wide in anticipation. Her hands lay loosely on top of the spread. "Please, go ahead," she said quietly.

Wes ran a hand over his unruly hair, drew in a deep breath, and began talking. "It started with a phone call from Jennifer on my radio talk show 'Talk about Town.'

Too often Wes's verbal style as a talk show host spoiled over into conversation with others—a verbose, fast-paced, sometimes overbearing delivery that could intimidate and seem rude. What he had to say now was too important to risk that kind of misunderstanding. Choosing his words with painstaking deliberation, Wes explained the events leading to Annette Simpson's dramatic escape from Dr. Blackwell's control.

All the while Wes watched Annette carefully, studying her reactions. She seemed disassociated from her surroundings, totally immersed in his words. Her hands had tightened their grip upon each other, but he saw no other outward signs of distress. She seemed remarkably composed. Wes looked away from her direct gaze, dreading the sound of his own voice.

Again, she insisted he continue, "I realize this is painful for you. But I have to know the details. Please trust me, like you urged me to trust you when I was in the hospital."

Wes couldn't circumvent her logic, nor could he avoid his task. He spoke of the ceremony that night at the Mount of the Elders, and the intense expression in Annette Simpson's eyes turned from shock to inexpressible pain. The tiny lines on her young face seemed to deepen as if her mother's heart were aging before his eyes. He tried to imagine how he'd feel upon hearing about systematic, degrading abuse of his own daughter, Misha.

Wes cleared his throat and plunged onward. "The only reason I'm involved is because Jennifer called my show and said she needed a friend. She was pretty sacred. Annette, I want to rescue your daughter from the evil that has claimed her. But I need your help."

For a moment, Annette turned her head aside, looking to the opposite wall. She put her hand to her mouth and rubbed her lips in frustration. Slowly, she turned to look at Wes. Then that beautiful, soft smile Wes had seen before curled across her face.

"You're a very brave man." She touched his arm in a reassuring gesture. "But wouldn't it be best for me to go to the police? Surely, they would help."

"It's no use. I already tried. I didn't give any names, just told them what I'm telling you. Sheriff Hancock—he's been sheriff forever—he half accused me of doing drugs." Wes looked at Annette carefully. Her eyes clouded with tears, but she seemed composed enough for him to ask her the question he's been so anxious to pose. "Do *you* know where Jennifer is?"

"No. Maybe with my husband's parents. As you know, Dr. Blackwell told me she was in the hospital too."

Blackwell. Wes felt the heat of rising anger. Was Blackwell one of the hooded men at the Mounds of the Elders that night?

Wes rose from the chair in which he had been sitting, excused himself to Annette, and went to find James. Twenty minutes later, Wes returned to Annette's room with the reverend, who said, "I think I can help you. There's a lawyer who attends my church, a bright young man just out of law school. I practically raised him like a son. He'd probably know some places and people to check, things we don't know about. Suppose I call him? I wouldn't tell him the whole story, just that we have to find a missing child."

"Yes, that's fine with me," Annette assented. "What do you think? She asked, looking at Wes.

"Let's see what he says," Wes agreed. "There's nothing to lose."

Annette smiled and lay back on the pillows. She looked tired, but not debilitated. Wes's admiration of her had increased tenfold in the past hour. Polly could have used some of her toughness and good sense.

He took Annette's hand, squeezed it reassuringly, and then impulsively leaned over and kissed her forehead. Smiling, Annette closed her eyes and pulled the bed covers to her chin. She turned toward the window, through which the late afternoon sun sank swiftly toward dusk.

Before Wes left the Carmichael home, James told him more about Manley Harris, whose agile mind and persuasive speaking abilities had earned the respect of his university colleagues. Yet his color had prohibited his landing a position with a prestigious firm in the city. He had returned to his home town, Clarion, and established a small practice dealing with personal injury claims, divorce cases, and bankruptcy proceedings, mostly cases experienced attorneys wouldn't handle without big retainers. Bluntly stated, Manly worked cheap and maintained a steady flow of business. He wasn't earning a fortune, but he attracted enough clients to provide what he needed most—courtroom experience.

"I'll call him in the morning," Carmichael said, as he walked Wes to his car. "I'm sure he'll look for any court documents for us."

Wes and Reverend Carmichael shook hands and said good-bye. On the way back to the apartment, Wes tossed around in his mind a thought that hade been nagging him. What if Dr. Blackwell were holding Jennifer hostage as he did her mother?

All that Thursday night, Wes thought about ways to trace Blackwell. By the time the first rays of the morning sun slanted through the curtains of his bedroom window, he had devised a plan.

After his morning ritual of coffee and powdered sugar donuts, he called Clarion Municipal Hospital. When the operator answered, Wes said, "This is Millican's Pharmacy. We've got a delivery for Dr. Blackwell. Can you tell me when he'll be in?"

"Dr. Blackwell doesn't keep regular hours here."

Wes persisted, "Could you at least call Dr. Blackwell and tell him the delivery is on its way? I'll have it here about four o'clock this afternoon."

"Sure, but I can't guarantee he'll show up. Like I said, he didn't say when he'd be back."

Wes felt amateurish and ineffectual, but if the receptionist could reach Blackwell, he might be compelled to check out the package. If Blackwell did show, he'd follow him. If he didn't, nothing was lost.

When "Talk about Town" ended that afternoon, the Reverend Carmichael, who had arrived earlier during the show, was waiting just outside the studio door, looking satisfied. "Manley Harris found some interesting information this morning. Seems the father's parents, Harold and Eunice Simpson, have sole custody of Jennifer. A Dr. Blackburn, Black . . ."

"Blackwell," Wes offered.

"Yes, Blackwell. He certified Annette as mentally and physically unfit. Manley also said papers were drawn up to commit her too. They just weren't filed yet with the courts in Chicago."

"I knew it!" Wes gritted his teeth. "But the Simpsons are supposed to be in Indianapolis. At least, that's what the newspaper said. Jennifer called locally." He looked at Carmichael. "My friend, I think there's more here than we imagined. When you get home, tell Annette what Harris found out. I won't come by until later. I've got something to do first."

Wes and James headed straight for their cars. Wes drove to

Clarion Municipal Hospital and parked where he had a full view of the front entrance and the back alley, then he settled down to wait. He remembered the sports car and the poor view he'd had of the man with the dark beard. Somehow, without concrete evidence or logic, Wes felt certain this was his man.

Four o'clock. No Blackwell. No sports car. Wes rotated his stiff shoulders and rubbed his neck to relieve tension. This was his best shot; he had no alternative plan. Four-thirty. Still no Blackwell. Wes's eyes burned from his intent staring at the alley and entryway. Five-thirty. Nothing had broken his monotonous vigil.

I'll give it fifteen more minutes, Wes muttered to himself. *No point sitting here all night.*

Moments later, the sports care swung into the alley. It had to be Blackwell! Wes tapped his fingers on the steering wheel. The car stopped abruptly, and the man with the dark beard got out, slamming the door. He stalked into the back entryway, looking neither left nor right.

As Wes waited, he thought of the next scenario he would have to play out—trailing the automobile. In the movies, the hero stalked the villain through heavy traffic, sneaking behind buses, kicking in the afterburners to head the killer off at a conveniently empty intersection. But he didn't see how he could follow anyone inconspicuously in Clarion. He could hardly hide behind Lambert's Country Milk truck or the post office jeep that puttered along the town's wide streets. And if Blackwell spotted him, he could dust his Toyota in seconds.

The hospital back entrance door swung open. The man he thought was Blackwell strode to the car, obviously annoyed he had been summoned to the hospital under false pretenses. He swiftly backed out of the alley, screeching his tires as he drove away.

Wes started his motor and headed in the same direction, hoping the man ahead was too preoccupied to notice him. When Blackwell turned off Main Street, Wes slowed down to remain at least two blocks behind the sports car. For several minutes, Wes failed to realize that they were speeding along old Route 193.

If following discreetly in town was problematic, Wes felt a hundred times more exposed on this lonely country road. The Indiana flatlands provided no declines or curves for concealment. One glance in his rearview mirror, and the driver might see Wes's car. Wes was forced to stay much farther back. He calculated his car's speed precisely so Blackwell remained in sight as a dot on the horizon.

Suddenly, the dot disappeared, as though the car had turned onto another road. Wes increased his speed, the risk of being spotted now secondary to losing his quarry. Scrutinizing both sides of the road, Wes searched for a place where the car could have turned.

There it was! The sports car was parked in a driveway in front of a white frame farmhouse about a hundred yards off the road.

To avoid attracting attention, Wes drove at a steady speed past the driveway. About a mile beyond, Wes saw the grove of tall cottonwoods where the Mounds of the Elders were located. He gripped the steering wheel tightly as he remembered his panic when the helicopter had zoomed in, the fear that had pounded in his veins at the sight of the armed guards, his revulsion at the blood dripping from the freshly slaughtered goat.

Wes pushed his thoughts away from the mental images associated with those cottonwoods. He drove on several miles, then turned and headed back. What next? He couldn't stop at the farmhouse. Even if Jennifer were in that house, it would be foolish to force his way in alone.

As Wes approached the driveway, he slowed down and surveyed his surroundings. This could be his only chance to study the location. He strained to memorize important details: a vegetable garden behind the house, an old clothesline, like people used before washers and dryers became staples of American life, a detached garage with double doors, a small, neatly trimmed front lawn, a harvested corn field in back, two plowed fields on either side. No farm machinery in sight. Maybe the land was leased out.

As Wes drove away, he mentally recorded everything he had seen. Once he approached the outskirts of Clarion, he headed toward his apartment, anxious to stretch out in his own comfortable bed. He badly needed the rest. The muscles in his right forearm twitched with the sensation of a light, feathery movement up and down his arm. This old nervous reaction, which had always bothered him when he was stressed, added to his tiredness.

Wes parked his car in the driveway of his apartment, got out, and stretched his tense muscles as he strode up the walk. Something was stuck to the front door. As he drew closer, his eyes widened in disbelief. A sheet of paper with dark writing was nailed to the door. Wes yanked the knife from the wooden door and took the paper in his hands as cold sweat broke out under his shirt. The blurred writing declared, "Back off or the girl dies! This is written in her blood."

Suddenly, Wes heard tires screeching and the sharp crack of a rife shot. A window in his apartment shattered as Wes threw himself to the ground and rolled. A car sped by and careened around a corner. He lay in the grass, panting, drenched in sweat, shaking uncontrollably.

Slowly, his body quieted. Wes rose and staggered toward his front door. Questions hurled themselves at him: *Did they miss me intentionally? Would they really kill me? Will they try again? Who are THEY?*

Then an appalling thought slammed through his terror: *If I don't quit, I could be responsible for Jennifer's death!*

Wes sagged forward, as if kicked in the back of the knees. He slumped down on the front step, still clutching the note. Shards of splintered glass glinted in the pale light.

This wasn't like "Talk about Town." He'd been a tough guy many times behind that microphone. He could turn the bravado on and off whenever he wanted to pin a guest to a wall or sympathize with a troubled soul. But now, *he* was trapped in a deadly corner. Jennifer's life hung by a thread. His own life was in jeopardy, perhaps Hannah's and James's too. And what about Annette's safety?

Wes couldn't go to the police for protection. Sheriff Hancock would accuse him of creating a bizarre scene with bloody notes and broken windows to gain attention. But blood *had* been taken from a child's body to write a death threat. A bullet *had* been at his home . . . or at him.

The image of the desolate child at the Mounds of the Elders flashed before him again. He saw her pale arms stretched toward him.

√ Ten

The next day, Saturday, October 31, Wes didn't tell Hannah or James, let alone Annette Simpson, about the bloodstained note. He told his landlord and a neighbor that some kids had thrown a rock through his window, probably in retaliation for a show he'd done the week before condemning teenage drug abuse. That seemed to satisfy their curiosity.

Wes spend most of that Saturday at the Carmichael house, talking with Annette as she rummaged through some clothing that Hannah, Sister Wilma, and the other ladies had collected for her and Jennifer. The weather was unusually warm for late October, the kind of Indian summer day folks in Indiana relished before the onslaught of winter's harshness. All day long, Wes marked time in his mind, waiting for the evening hours to arrive, a time he had personally appointed to intervene on Jennifer's behalf.

That night, after bidding farewell to Annette and the Carmichaels, Wes headed down Route 193 in the direction of the lone house that Blackwell had led him to.

About a quarter mile before the house, Wes spotted a turnoff into a cornfield. He pulled to the side of the road, turned the car around toward town, and shut off the motor. He sat in the darkness, looking toward the unimposing house, Jennifer Simpson's alleged prison. He had to find out if she was there.

Wes recalled that, as a kid, he had helped his Uncle William on a nearby farm. Irrigation was used extensively in Clarion County, and typically, water was siphoned from ditches that ran perpendicular to each field of long rows of corn. Alongside such ditches, narrow dirt roads allowed pickup trucks to patrol and supervise the flow of water. It occurred to Wes that the field between him and the house must have such a utility road, which would be hidden by the tall stalks of corn on either side. If he could find it, he could approach the house without being seen, probably even get safely within half-a-football–field's length of it. Then he would have to summon the courage to investigate further.

Whoever these people were, they were deadly serious. If any of them were in that house and saw him, Wes knew that, out here in the country, they could shoot him without worrying about anyone hearing the gunfire.

Wes found the irrigation ditch road exactly where he expected it to be. He pulled onto it and got out of the car, leaving the keys in the ignition. He eased the door shut noiselessly and carefully picked his way through the waist-high underbrush and weeds.

A slice of waning moon hovered well above the horizon behind high, thin clouds. Wes could see well enough to judge each footstep. His movements were stealthy and deliberate, totally unlike the small boy's happy meandering behind Uncle William to check irrigation tubes.

Wes counted cornrows to offset his anxiety about what might happen at the house . . . 127 . . . 128 . . . 129. Row upon row.

Straight, narrow stands, grown from modern agriculture's best hybrid seed. The wealth of Columbus County.

Wes reached the edge of the cornfield and crouched behind a clump of bushes a hundred yards or so from the house. A yard light illuminated the back door. Were there guard dogs? Electric fences? Farmers used such easily erected wire barriers to confine herds of feeding cattle in harvested cornfields. They were impossible to see at night and delivered a healthy jolt.

Two cars were parked behind the house, the sports car and another with words painted on its side. Wes squinted to focus better. The words catapulted through space toward him—COLUMBUS COUNTY SHERIFF.

Wes stepped from behind the bushes and stalked toward the house. He was conscious of crunching dirt clods beneath his feet. His eyes darted swiftly over the white farmhouse, alert for a curtain being pulled back, a light going on. A couple of windows were lighted from within. He had to get close enough to look inside.

Suddenly, Wes froze, unable to believe what he saw in the evening light. On the back steps under the light was a small figure . . . a child!

Could it possibly be Jennifer? Adrenaline rushing through him, Wes slowly walked toward the silent figure. Time seemed suspended. Thirty yards, twenty yards from the steps. The rustling wind in the dried corn stalks muffled the sound of his approach.

What should I say? What if she gets scared and screams? Wes wondered. He walked to about ten yards from the rear entrance. The he hunkered down, trying to appear less threatening, and spoke softly, almost whispering, "Jennifer?"

The child had been stroking a black cat in her lap. At the sound of Wes's voice, she turned toward him, her head moving slowly. The cat screeched, leaped form her lap, and dashed into the dark.

The blonde-haired girl stared at Wes, not moving. She wore a blue windbreaker over a blue and white checked shirt and navy pants.

Wes's thoughts raced wildly. Here she was, the fear-ridden voice that had called "Talk about Town," the naked figure in the snake-infested cage. She seemed paralyzed now, unable to move.

"Jennifer, it's me. Mr. Wes. The man on the radio." With excessive caution, Wes rose to stand quietly, arms at his sides. Then he drew closer to the steps and knelt to her eye level. The child's eyes were wide, pupils dilated in the dark, her skin pale as milk. "Remember me, Jennifer?" Wes Bryant from the radio talk show. I've come to take you to your mother."

The child stared at him with her large blue eyes. Wes slowly held out his hand, palm up, and waited. Again, with gentle urging, he spoke. "Your mom wants to see you, Jennifer. She's in a nice house with nice people. Come with me."

He extended his hand farther toward her. The child somberly put out her hand. Her flesh touched his, and her fingers curled into the security of his bigger palm. In a single smooth movement, she jumped into Wes's arms, a low moan in her throat that almost broke his heart. She clutched him with desperate intensity and buried her face in his jacket.

At that moment, Wes's mind flashed back over the many times as a young father he had stretched out his hand to Misha, felt her tiny, supple fingers cradled in his. Wes wondered if things might have turned out differently had he offered his hand more often to his own daughter.

"Good girl!" he whispered to Jennifer. "You're brave! Hold on, now! We're on our way." Somewhere within the house, a door slammed. Wes's heart thudded hard against his rib cage as the child cringed in his arms. He had to get out of there!

Wes wrapped his jacket around the child, clutched her tightly to his chest, and stood up. He walked steadily toward the cornfield, struggling to stay calm. Then as he drew closer to the field, he began running into the vegetation. Plunging deeper into the field, he pumped his legs faster toward the car. Hot needles of pain from the old leg injury shout through his leg, but he kept running.

Wes reached the car, yanked open the door, and put the girl on the front seat. Then he ran to the driver's side and flung himself behind the wheel. Hitting the ignition key, he stomped hard on the pedal. The car shot down the narrow road, spewing dust and scattering gravel, finally fishtailing onto Route 193.

Wes studied the rearview mirror intently, blood pounding. He was almost overcome with the need to laugh. He'd snatched a full-grown woman out of her hospital bed, and now he had stolen a little girl out of nowhere.

He'd heard the food wasn't too good in the state penitentiary. That thought reminded him of Arnold Hancock. He wasn't out of the woods yet, not by a long shot.

When he saw the town lights, Wes slowed down and turned on his headlights. He jumped when Jennifer's voice broke through the darkness. "Take me to Mommy. Mr. Wes. Please?"

"You bet, honey! That's where we're going right now. Just hang on a little longer."

"How did you know the nasty people let me go outside to pet Blackie before I go to bed? It's the only time I go out of my room. Blackie lives outside."

Wes smiled at her, but he had no answer. Was it a fortunate twist of fate or the answer to the Carmichaels' prayers for help that he found her just at that moment? He wasn't sure.

Jennifer inched across the seat and leaned her head against him. He put his arm around her, driving with one hand. He remembered driving many miles with Misha like this. During the months that followed the split with Polly, his bitterness had deepened until Wes swore never to become emotionally available to another human being. It felt good to be needed again.

Wes parked in front of the Carmichaels', then turned to Jennifer and almost shouted, "Your mom is staying here. Boy, is she going to be happy to see you! Are you ready to go inside?" Jennifer nodded her head. Wes got out and took the child's hand. Together, they hurried to the front door. Wes knocked. Hannah pulled back the curtains of the front window and quickly let him in.

Annette Simpson and Jennifer saw each other at the same instant.

Jennifer ran to her mother, screaming, "Mommy!"

Annette dropped to her knees and opened her arms to Jennifer. "My baby! Oh, my baby!" Annette moaned, swaying back and forth, rocking her daughter.

Jennifer whimpered, "They hurt me . . . Oh, Mommy, they hurt me so bad." Anguished sobs poured from the little girl.

"It's OK, darling, it's all right! Nobody can hurt you now."

James Carmichael stepped into the living room and put his arms around his wife.

"Thank you, sweet Jesus. Oh, thank you, Lord," Hannah said, as she wiped away tears spilling down her cheeks. "You've brought the tiny lamb back to the fold."

Hannah and James were weeping, and Wes found that his face was also wet. He wiped at his eyes with the flat of his hand, reached into his pocket for a handkerchief, and blew his nose.

Annette got to her feet and led Jennifer to the sofa. She held her child, unable to speak.

"I've got to go to the church and prepare for tomorrow's sermon," James whispered to Hannah. "I may be a little late, so don't wait up for me. Why don't you get some milk and cookies for Jennifer. You know how much little girls like cookies."

Hannah followed James into the kitchen. "Oh, James, that child has got to be so scared and hurt inside. When you get to the church, please say a prayer for all the pain she's carrying in her little heart. And thank God for bringing her back to her mama."

James hugged his wife and nodded. Turning to walk out the back door to the church, he said, "We've got a lot to be thankful for tonight, Hannah. We've seen miracle of the Lord right under our own roof."

Wes stood in the kitchen doorway, unable to think. Hannah led him to a chair and pushed him into it. He put his head back and tried to relax while Hannah fussed in her cupboards. She arranged cookies on a plate, poured two glasses of milk, and handed them to him on a serving tray. He returned to the room where Annette still held her daughter in her arms. She stroked her daughter's matted long blonde hair and crooned endearments to her. Wes was surprised to see his hands tremble as he held the tray out to them.

"Would you like to hear some music, Jennifer?" Hannah asked.

The fine-featured child smiled and nodded. Hannah went to the old upright piano in the corner of the living room, took a hymn book from the piano seat, and sat down. Her weathered, agile fingers caressed the keyboard as the chords of hymns Wes remembered from childhood filled the peaceful living room.

"Rock of ages, cleft for me, let me hide myself in thee," Hannah's rich alto voice accompanied the music. As she sang about God's protective presence, Wes realized his once-meaningless life had taken on a positive direction.

The headlights of an automobile flashed through the front window as a car turned around in front of the church. Wes rose quietly, went to the window, and glanced outside. In the faint moonlight, he saw the car driving away.

Who would be out here at this time of night? He wondered. Perhaps someone to see the Reverend Carmichael. Funny they hadn't come to the house first.

Jennifer lay across her mother's lap, almost asleep. "Let the water and the blood, from thy wounded side which flowed," Hannah sang as she played the closing chords of "Rock of Ages." Wes motioned for her to follow him to the kitchen.

"I need to talk to James for a few minutes," Wes said to Hannah. "I hate to interrupt him, but I really need his advice about what to do next." Uncharacteristically, he reached out and hugged Hannah.

In the darkness, Wes carefully made his way the fifty yards or so to the church, guided by the glow of the lights streaming from the window for the Carmichael house. He walked to a back door of the church, which led to the Reverend Carmichael's office, and knocked several times, but no one answered.

He must be talking on the phone or maybe he's in another part of the building. Wes walked around the small white clapboard church to the front door, which was ajar. He entered the tiny foyer leading to the sanctuary and noticed a light in the pulpit area. Where was James? Who had left the lights on? Something was wrong. Carmichael wasn't in the church as he said he would be.

Wes walked down the center aisle between the empty pews. As he came closer to the altar railing, Wes adjusted his eyes to the light, straining to see an object on top of the pulpit. A reddish-brown substance streamed down the weathered wooden sides. Wes jumped over the alter rail, ran the last few feet to the sanctuary, and felt a sledgehammer blow to his belly. He sank to his knees, groaning, "Oh, God . . . dear God."

A black cat that looked like Jennifer's Blackie was impaled on the pulpit. The animal had been spread-eagled on it back and its paws nailed to the wood. Its throat had been slit and its belly sliced to expose its innards.

Wes grabbed the sides of the pulpit, unconsciously putting his hands in the still-warm blood. He retched and struggled to breathe. The blood splotched his skin and mingled with his tears. The quiet sanctuary had been raped by evil.

Hands smeared with cat blood, Wes arose. The he saw a note tacked to the pulpit beside the cat's head. Written in blood like the note pinned to his own door yesterday, it read:

The holy for the innocent!

A fair exchange.

E l e v e n

Wes Bryant stood motionless in front of Apostolic Faith Tabernacle's desecrated pulpit, like an austere cleric ready to deliver a sober sermon. His eyes darted about the sanctuary in panic until his gaze fell on a faintly illuminated stained-glass window. It soft glow depicted an angel. Heaven and hell stood side by side on this Halloween night.

He had to dispose of the cat's remains as soon as possible. *I remember seeing a shovel in James's backyard,* Wes thought. *Have to move quickly so Hannah doesn't see this. I need a bag or something to put the body in.*

A jumble of thoughts continued to shoot through his mind, like bullets racing toward a distant target. *There must be some rooms behind the choir loft. Has to be a garbage basket in there. I'll put the cat in that. Need something to pull those nails.*

Wes jumped from the platform, went through a side door, and ran down a hallway. He looked in several rooms before finding a metal garbage basket. Further search led him to the janitor's closet. There, he found a pair of pliers and hurried back to the defiled pulpit.

He worked quickly, removed the nails and lifted the cat's carcass into the basket. Using paper towels from the bathroom, he wiped away the blood from the pulpit and his hands. After he finished, only four small nail holes and barely detectable stains in the dark wood marked the sacrilege.

Wes carried the metal basket out the side door and walked deliberately to the Carmichael backyard. A shovel leaned against a tree. About fifty feet behind the house, Wes found some loose soil and started digging. In less than ten minutes, the bloody carcass was buried beneath the brown Indiana soil.

What will I tell Hannah? Could say James was called out on an emergency. She'd know that isn't true. Hannah's too smart. Wes determined to tell her the truth, minus the cat sacrifice. He stepped into the Carmichael kitchen and called for Hannah.

"What took you so long?" she asked.

Wes stood silently, unsure what to say.

In a matter of seconds, Hannah Carmichael sensed something was dreadfully wrong. "Sit down, Wes," Hannah said, motioning to a chair. "You look pale, like you've seen a ghost. Where's James?

"Gone!" he said, burying his head in his hands.

"Gone!" Hannah gasped. "Gone where? What's happened? Where's James?" Hannah's voice rose with each question as her eyes quickly filled with tears.

Wes went to the sink for a glass of water. He gulped deeply, drinking the entire glassful in one swig, then he walked over to Hannah and put his arms on her shoulders to steady her. "The people who had Jennifer have taken James."

"How do you know? Maybe James went into town for a while. Perhaps one of his parishioners called . . . ." Hannah thought of every plausible excuse. Then she gave in to her fear and sat down at the table. She leaned her head back against the high-backed chair and covered her lips.

Wes sat down beside her. He reached in his shirt pocked, unfolded the bloodstained note he had found on the pulpit, and laid it on the kitchen table. Hannah studied it for a moment and muffled a shriek of horror. She rocked back and forth, her arms wrapped around her body. "We've got to call the police."

"Can't do that. Some of them are involved, including Sheriff Hancock. Don't tell anyone! It's too dangerous. Put Annette and Jennifer to bed while I think about what to do. Do you have a gun around her?"

"Just an old shotgun that James used to hunt pheasant. But please don't load it! James is a man of peace. He wouldn't want us returning violence with violence."

"Look, Hannah," Wes shouted, in a voice he belatedly realized was too harsh, "these people are killers! They'll stop at nothing. I'm not a man of God, like your husband. I'm scared, and I'm not going to sleep here tonight without a gun at my side."

Wes stood to his feet and paced several times across the kitchen. He shook his head in disbelief, as if conversing with an unidentified entity about what he had seen in the church. Then Wes said, "Maybe James escaped. He could be hiding somewhere outside. I'm going to look around and see if there's any trace of him."

Though Wes knew that his search was pointless, he opened the kitchen door and stepped quietly into the night. What moon there was had slipped under a cloud, and darkness surrounded the Carmichael house. Wes felt his way, one hand touching the side of the house to keep his bearings. He rounded the front corner of the house and paused, trying to focus his eyes on the dark surroundings. Snap! A twig cracked behind him, and a heavy weight struck the back of his head. He struggled to steady himself, then his knees buckled, and he slumped into a deep voice.

———————

Wes was jolted to consciousness by the sharp pain of something cutting into his wrists. He shook his head to free it of grogginess. He had no idea where he was and no sense of how much time had elapsed since he had stepped out of the Carmichael kitchen. As he slowly regained his senses, he realized that he was sitting on a floor, knees bent, his arms tied behind his back. He tried to move and soon discovered that the limits of his confines resembled a closet. When he wiggled his arms in the darkness, the cords binding his wrists gnawed into his flesh. His head throbbed with pain.

Suddenly, the door to his prison flew open. Two strong hands grabbed him under the arms and lifted him to his feet. Wes labored to maintain his balanced, feeling as if every muscle in his body had atrophied. Several strategically placed candles provided the only light in the large room outside the closet. The walls were painted pitch black. The darkness, coupled with Wes's blurred vision from the blow to his head, made it difficult to see anything very clearly. A dozen or so people wearing long, hooded robes mingled silently. Wes strained to make out their faces.

They're wearing masks, he thought. *Animal faces, wolves and bears.*

One by one, the masked creatures passed in front of him, staring into his face. Wes presumed they were trying to frighten him, but they need not have bothered. His entire being pulsated with enough terror to last a lifetime. He jerked his body left and right to see how firmly his captors held him. At his slightest movement, the strong hands holding his arms tightened, pinching his biceps at precise pressure points to induce pain.

No one spoke. Suddenly, a door at the far end of the room opened. Wes heard a loud thud as someone dressed in a white hospital smock was thrown to the floor. A black hood covered the victim's head. The body thrashed about violently.

An imposing figure stepped through the doorway, and everyone in the room turned, grunting animal sounds in acknowledgment of his presence. From underneath his robe, he took a large hypodermic syringe and knelt by the struggling figure on the floor. He nodded to others to help restrain his prey. Then he shoved a needle into the victim's arm, and the body went limp.

As Wes watched, the body was dragged to the center of the room and laid on its back, arms and legs spread-eagled. The leader took several lengths of rope from a table and handed them to the participants. A heavy-set, robed figure pounded some large metal stakes into the wooden floor with a hammer. The ropes were tied about the ankles and wrists of the victim and secured to the stakes. The leader then administered another injection to the victim. In moments, the inert body jerked back to life.

One of the figures, who held a bowl of white powder, knelt near the body. He took small quantities of the powder in his hands and let it sift to the floor in carefully proscribed amounts to form an intricate triangular design. Wes assumed it was some kind of ritual incantation.

When the artist was finished, the leader walked to a table and picked up a six-inch-long smoking pipe. He took a long puff, slowly exhaling the smoke. Each member of the group puffed in succession, passing the pipe until everyone had participated. Then the leader took a goblet and scalpel from the table and approached the bounded victim. Lifting the corner of the hood, he made a quick motion with the scalpel and quickly placed the goblet near a vein in the victim's neck.

Wes muttered to himself in shock: *Blood's collecting in that glass!*

The leader took a long black feather in one hand, the goblet in the other, and walked to each person in the room. He dipped the feather in the blood and made the mark of a triangle on the forehead of their mask.

Once again, Wes surged forward against his bonds. This time, he felt cold metal at his temple, as one of his captors held what felt like the barrel of a handgun to his head. Whoever these people were, Wes knew they would kill him if he interfered.

Wes felt a sharp pain shoot up his spine, as a jab in his back made him lurch forward. His captors pulled him toward the dying body on the floor. Wes looked down at the hooded victim, wondering why he was held captive to this evil. Then the member who had secured the body stepped in front of Wes and pulled back his mask. Sheriff Arnold Hancock stood there.

"Welcome to the Order of the Dark Raven. We're not afraid for you to know who we are. Nobody would believe you if you were crazy enough to tell what you've seen tonight."

One by one, each participant, except for the leader, removed his mask. The faces were stil barely distinguishable in the dim candle light. Wes glanced around the room to see who he might recognize. Several were women. One female face seemed to stand out. *It's the librarian!* Wes said to himself. *No wonder she acted so suspiciously.*

Wes had no trouble spotting Dr. Blackwell. His swarthy complexion and dark beard looked all the more sinister close up. Others looked like people he had seen throughout his growing up years in Columbus County, but before he could venture a guess as to their identities, Hancock spoke.

"Interested in knowing how much influence we have in these parts?" Hancock sneered. "I'll tell you some of who's here. That's Judge Thornton Lassiter over there. Helps us when we need a favorable decision from the *justice* system. To your left is William Christie. He's the U.S. Congressman from our district. I thing you've already recognized Dr. Michael Blackwell. And, oh yes, on your right is the Reverend Marvin Randall, pastor of Clarion Community Church. There are a lot more on the team I'm not telling you about. Got most of the positions covered, haven't we, Bryant? Like I said, who'd believe a has-been football player and loudmouthed talk show host if he spoke out against us?" Hancock arrogantly concluded.

"This will catch up with you someday," Wes retorted.

"Look around you again, Bryant. And don't forget who I am. In Columbus County, the Order of the Dark Raven is justice."

Hancock let out a laugh that echoed off the hard walls and floors, then he turned toward the victim, kicking the body sharply in the side with his boot. Hancock walked nearer to Wes and looked him coldly in the eye. "Like to say good-bye to a 'saint' before he has a little "accident'?"

Hancock nodded to one of the others, who knelt by the body and ripped off the hood. Wes stared into the terrified face of Reverend James Carmichael. A rag had been stuffed in his mouth. His eyes were glazed in terror.

"What are you going to do with him?" Wes demanded.

Hancock replied with a fist aimed at Wes's midsection. Wes doubled over in pain, gasping for air.

"I'll do the talking here, Mr. Talk about Town. This county isn't going to miss one less nigger. As for you, be grateful you're a local radio 'star.' Otherwise, we'd have killed you days ago. Explaining your demise might be a little too risky for us, unless you push us too hard. As for the girl and her mother, we know where they are, but we're a little reluctant to confiscate them, as long as you're in a position to cause trouble."

Hancock grabbed a fistful of Wes's hair and sharply jerked his head upward. He pulled Wes's face close to his, while the men on either side of Wes tightened their grips on his arms.

"You've got the girl, now we've got a suitable sacrifice. Like the note said, for now, that's 'a fair exchange.' If you'll butt out, we'll leave it that way."

"You filthy pig!" Wes blurted.

Hancock jammed his knee into Wes's groin. Wes collapsed in a flash of hot white pain beside James Carmichael.

"Listen carefully, Bryant. The reverend is done for, but you can save your own skin if you'll forget what you know about us and the Mounds of the Elders."

Wes staggered to his feet. The pain in his back and groin convinced him this was not time for heroics. He breathed heavily. He had to control his anger.

"By the way, I'd like to introduce you to two other people," Sheriff Hancock sneered. Hancock motioned to Wes's captors, who shoved him toward two people standing near Reverend Carmichael's feet. Wes looked into the faces of a man and woman whom he guessed to be in their late fifties. Their hair was tinged with gray, and Wes shuddered at the thought of these middle-class American people embracing such brutality.

"Let me guess," Wes ventured. "Harold and Eunice Simpson?"

"That's right," Hancock answered. "You've met everyone you need to know, for now."

Hancock motioned toward Carmichael on the floor.

"Normally, we only punish those who actively interfere with our plans," he said, "but in the reverend's case, we'll make an exception. He's not a faithless failure like you, Bryant. He believes . . . in God . . . and knows the power of the Dark Raven. Now that you've told him about us, we can't risk his praying to his God. Besides, the Dark Raven will be pleased with such a holy offering.

Wes's captors pulled him to the far end of the room. A half-dozen of the still-hooded figures began chanting monotonously. The rhythm of their words reminded Wes of the Indian chants he had heard at Columbus County fairground pow-wows he'd attended as a kid, but he words weren't entirely Indian. They mingled with consonants and harsh guttural infections.

Slowly, the Order surrounded the Reverend Carmichael, chanting louder and louder. Their circle grew smaller, until one of them jerked the rag from Carmichael's mouth.

"Wes, don't worry about me!" Carmichael gasped. "They can kill my body, but my soul belongs to God . . ."

As Carmichael spoke, the room erupted with mocking laughter, but it couldn't drown out the reverend's voice. He shouted in biblical cadence, "Oh God, deliver me from the workers of iniquity, save me from bloody men . . ."

Before he could finish, Hancock lunged at Carmichael with a knife. The group parted, and Wes could see Blackwell kneeling over the reverend's body. He ripped open Carmichael's chest with the bloody knife. Then he thrust his hand into the gaping wound, grasped Carmichael's pulsating heart, and, with precise surgical motions, severed its arties and veins. Holding the bloody prize in he palm of his hand, Blackwell grinned at Bryant and thrust Carmichael's heart toward him. Then he methodically cut small pieces of the heart, handing each member of the Order a portion. Like an unholy communion, each one put their piece of the "saint's" body in their mouths and chewed.

"The power of the Dark Rave is strengthened when we consume the heart of the innocent and holy," Blackwell explained arrogantly.

"You animals!" Wes screamed.

"You're right," Hancock responded. "We are animals. Descendants of the wolves and bears who guard the Mounds of the Elders."

The physical pain in Wes's head seemed nothing compared to the emotional torment that overwhelmed him now. A cloud of abject terror rose within him as Blackwell approached him with another syringe.

"Got a headache? Poor boy. Here's a little something to help you sleep if off."

Wes felt the needle go sharply into his arm and watched Blackwell slowly depress the plunger. Then like drawing the curtains to darken a room, Wes felt his eyes close and a rush of warm, drugged blood surge through his body.

The next thing Wes Bryant heard was Hannah Carmichael saying, "Wes, wake up! Can you hear me, Wes?"

Wes came to his senses and looked around. He was lying on the ground next to the front steps of the Carmichael house.

"I waited for you to come back in the house. Then I finally came outside and found you lying here. What happened?"

He couldn't tell Hannah what he'd seen until his mind cleared. He wondered himself if it was a horrible nightmare. Then the pain in his groin reminded him all too well how real the past hours had been. Slowly, Wes stood to his feet and staggered into the house. Annette and Jennifer had gone to bed. He threw himself on the couch.

As Wes collapsed, a car drove up. Hannah rushed to the window to see who has there, hoping it was her husband. Wes could see the reflection of blue and red lights shining through the window and reflecting on the wall opposite him.

"It's a police car," Hannah said, hurriedly going out the front door.

Wes wanted to go wither, but his aching body and clouded mind immobilized him. He wasn't sure how much time passed as he faded in and out of consciousness. Hannah returned and fell to her knees beside the couch. "It was a highway patrolman," she moaned. "Oh, Lord . . . James is dead! A Hit-and-run! They found his body down the road."

Hannah laid her head on Wes's chest and began weeping as he wrapped his arms around her. *I can't tell her what really happened,* he thought. *I've got to get someone to look after her . . . get Annette and Jennifer out of here, for their safety as well as Hannah's.*

Wes looked up to see Annette standing at her bedroom door.

"What's going on?" she asked.

"There's been a terrible tragedy," Wes answered, speaking loudly enough to be heard over Hannah's anguished weeping. "It's James. He's dead. Please sit with Hannah while I make a call."

"Oh, dear Jesus!" Hannah cried. "Not my James!"

Annette rushed to Hannah and smoothed her hand over her shoulders.

"He was praying, doing the Lord's work. I knew he could be called home any time, but, God, why now? Why so violently? He was a man of peace!"

Annette listened, as her own tears fell. She had known James Carmichael so briefly, but the faithful preacher, his wife, and members of the congregation had made an immeasurable impact on her life.

Wes walked quickly to the kitchen and thumbed through a well-used telephone directory, looking for Manley Harris's name. He was the only person Wes knew to call for help.

Wes dialed the number. As he impatiently listened to the phone ring, he heard a muffled conversation in the living room. In her grief, Hannah rambled almost incoherently about what a good man her husband had been, his love, his devotion to his parishioners.

"Hello," a groggy voice answered.

"Manley Harris?" Wes asked.

"Yes. Who in blazes are you, calling at this ungodly hour?"

"I'm Wes Bryant. The guy who does the talk show on WTTK. I'm a friend of James and Hannah Carmichael. Something terrible has happened. Reverend Carmichael is dead, and Hannah needs you. Can you come immediately?"

He heard Harris groan. Wes waited, his heart heavy as lead, remembering the loving relationship the minister and the young attorney had shared. Finally, Harris responded. "How did he die?"

"There's no time to explain," Wes answered. "Just hurry, please!"

Wes hung up the phone and returned to the living room. Hannah looked at him with a drained, perplexed expression, a thousand questions reflected in her bewildered gaze. Wes sat next to her and spoke to Annette. "Wake Jennifer and get her dressed. Collect whatever clothing the church ladies gave you. We're leaving immediately."

Wes spoke so calmly and resolutely that Annette didn't question his stern directive. She headed for the bedroom. Wes turned to Hannah. "We've got to get them away from here. Their survival depends on it. I've spoken with Manley Harris. He's on his way here to stay with you. Your husband's death wasn't an accident. You have to know that. And the people who killed him will stop at nothing to harm Annette and Jennifer. As soon as Manley gets her, I'll try to get Annette and Jennifer out of this crazy town. There's not time to explain everything now. Just trust me."

Hannah patted Wes's hand and wiped tears from her swollen eyes. "Do what you must. Manley's my boy. He'll take good care of me, and the Lord will see me through. James always reminded me that we should never fear man. He can harm the body, but he can't touch the soul."

He words drove deep into Wes's heart as he remembered the horror of the reverend crying out the same words before the knife plunged into his body.

Justice! Was there any? Was the faith of Hannah and James a true anchor in tough times, or only a comfortable explanation for the inexplicable pain of life? Wes was determined to find the answer to that. Without it, nothing made sense.

"I'm so tired," Hannah said. "I'll just lay down and rest here on the couch 'til Manley comes."

Wes nodded and plumped up a couch cushion, then placed it under her head. Soon, Harris's car pulled up, and Wes stepped out on the porch to meet him. As they shook hands, Harris asked, "What happened? How did the reverend die?"

"I can't explain the whole thing now," Wes answered. "I can tell you this, though. James was murdered by the same people involved in that child custody case he asked you about. When Hannah feels better, ask her to tell you about Annette Simpson and her daughter, Jennifer. I've got to get the two of them out of here, *tonight*. Can you look after Hannah?"

"I'll stay with her until morning, then Sister Wilma and some people from the church can take over," Harris responded.

"Good," Wes said. "We'll talk more later. I don't know when, but I'll get back to you. Don't mention our conversation to anyone!"

Wes and Manley stepped in the house. "I'm sorry to rush you," Wes said to Annette, "but we've got to get out of here. Do you have your stuff together? We need to be on the road in five minutes!"

"Go, child," Hannah implored. "Go with God, and know that my James's prayers for you have been answered. You'll be safe in the arms of Jesus. More now than ever, the Lord will be watching over you and Jennifer."

Annette looked lovingly at the stout black woman. From the expression on Hannah's face, she could see that, without having children of her own, Hannah evoked in Annette the same maternal assurance her own mother had, years ago.

"God bless you," Annette whispered. Then she added more confidently, "We'll be back, Hannah. We will be back."

Hannah motioned Annette and Jennifer toward the door. Jennifer staggered slightly, half-asleep. Wes took her by the hand and led her to the car, where she laid down in the back seat. Annette sat in front next to Wes.

As Wes shook hands with Harris, Hannah walked to the passenger's side of the car, reached through the open window, and warmly embraced Annette. "Goodbye. God be with you," Hannah said, her voice steady.

Wes started the car, pulled out of the yard, and headed down Applegate Lane. He had no idea where the three of them were going. He only knew they had to escape the evil of Columbus County and hope that, wherever they ended up, justice would be there.

Dream – In a red square box.
Crying band them over + over
then bells ring.

Twelve

Wes's thoughts were a whirlwind: the kidnapping of Jennifer, the dead cat in the sanctuary, his abduction at the hand of the Order, and the murder of James Carmichael. The convergence of these traumas had reached sensory overload. His aching body and tormented emotions combined to induce a state of shock.

Two things kept Wes sane: his responsibility for Annette and Jennifer Simpson and his fear for his own life, in spite of the Order's assurances that his "star" status spared him from their murderous intent. Wes also felt responsible for Hannah Carmichael. The Reverend Carmichael's death was a direct result of his rescue of Jennifer.

It I hadn't gone to James with my store . . . if I hadn't brought Annette Simpson to his house. If . . . If . . .

"What do you know about Reverend Carmichael's death?"

Annette's question jolted Wes back to reality. He hesitated to speak about the night's events.

"I don't want to tell you everything I know right now. Trust me. It involves the people who had Jennifer, and they'll stop at nothing to complete their mission of evil."

"So, what about us? Are they still looking for Jennifer and me? Will Hannah be all right?"

"I think we're all safe for now. Hannah doesn't figure in their plans. James wasn't in their original scheme either, but since he was a man of God, I thing destroying him appeased them, like the surprise in a Cracker Jack box."

Wes continued across town through secondary streets to the freeway on-ramp to Interstate 360. Two right turns, a left, and they were headed toward Chicago. Annette watched the interstate signs flashing by as traces of mist collected on the window.

Wes momentarily turned on the car's interior light to look at his watch and saw through bleary eyes that it was 2:00 a.m.

About fifty miles down the road, Wes started looking for a motel with a vacancy sign. He passed a Motel 6 and a Days Inn before spotting the blinking neon light of the Travel Weary Lodge.

"I'll get us a room," he informed Annette. "I need some rest. It's not safe for me to drive."

Wes pulled into the motel driveway, parked, and walked to the door. The vacancy sign was on, but no night clerk was on duty. Wes pounded on the front door several times. Finally, an elderly man in a bright orange and red bathrobe appeared and let Wes in. "Hi, there! How many people?"

"Three. We need two beds."

"Three adults?"

"Two adults, one child."

"That'll be $37.50, in advance. Cash, if you've got it."

Wes hesitated. He didn't know how long his money would have to last them. Looking in his wallet, he found the remains of his last paycheck, some crumpled fifty-dollar bills. The motel clerk sensed his hesitancy.

"I'll have to charge you 10 percent extra to use a credit card. I'll need an imprint before you can get a room key."

Wes handed over a credit card.

"Mighty late to be out on the road," said the inquisitive clerk. "You and the missus plan to drive all night?"

"Yeah. But we got tired and had to stop."

"That's smart. There's free breakfast in the lobby. We start serving at seven o'clock. Juice, rolls, coffee. Nothing fancy, but it gets the day started."

Wes took the key, got back in his old Toyota, and drove down a long row of doors to their room at the back of the motel. "I only got one room," he said to Annette. "You can sleep with Jennifer. It may be awkward, but we'll have to make the best of it. I won't leave you two alone tonight."

"That's OK. We'll make do. You can have the bathroom first."

The arrangement felt strange to Wes. This woman wasn't his wife, not even his girlfriend. What would Jennifer think? Well, tonight it didn't matter. Wes carried Jennifer from the car and gently put her down on a double bed. Her tiny body twitched, as if she were having a nightmare or was in some kind of internal pain. Within ten minutes, everyone was in bed.

Tired as he was, Wes couldn't sleep. He lay in the second bed, stared at the ceiling, and watched the blinking neon sign outside reflect through the small slits of Venetian blinds. Where would they go tomorrow? What about "Talk about Town"? Dozens of questions raced through his mind, warding off the slumber his aching body craved.

The blast of a car horn outside the motel room abruptly awakened Wes at 6:50 a.m. after a couple of hours' sleep. He walked to a window and opened the blinds. An angry husband at the wheel of an automobile gestured for his wife to get in the car. They exchanged heated words, then drove off.

Sunday, November 1. Decision day, Wes thought. *I'm the surrogate husband and father of Annette and Jennifer. I can't just dump them somewhere and hope for miracles.*

Quietly, Wes opened the door and stepped outside into the crisp autumn air. He spotted a dilapidated lawn chair a few feet away and sat down. The early morning sun warmed him. Wes tilted back his head, soaking in the sunshine, thinking about what to do next. Half an hour later, Annette joined him. Wes gave her his chair and sat down on the edge of the curb where his car was parked.

"We really don't have much choice," he said. "We have to find a place where no one knows us. It's not safe for us back in Columbus County."

Annette glanced at him inquisitively. "Those people, Wes, do you think they might have abused Jennifer?"

Wes looked at Annette, unsure of what information she was seeking.

"Well, I told you about the ceremony that night. I don't know if there was more after they left or not. Why are you asking?"

"Jennifer was crying in her sleep last night. When I held her and rubbed her shoulders, she jerked and there were spots of blood on her slip."

Wes's eyes filled with concern as Annette described her horror of the night before.

"I pulled off her slip and found strange marks and wounds. There were open sores—almost like something had ripped her—along her shoulders and small punctures along her neck and thighs."

The raven! Wes thought. *They placed that foul bird on Jennifer when they crowned her.*

Wes winced as the memory of Jennifer's soft skin being torn came to him. Even in the darkness, Wes had been able to see the bird against the moon, as it screeched in triumph. He tried to shake the scene from his mind and return to Annette. Then he remembered the snakes. Bile rose in his throat, and he fought to regain his composure. Slowly, his attention came back to Annette, and he heard her speaking to him.

" . . . any idea at all, Wes?"

"Idea?" Wes answered, still distracted.

"Could it have been injections? Was she drugged?"

"I think she was drugged, Annette, but that isn't what the marks are from."

"What then?"

"There was a raven, Annette, the symbol of the Order. It was placed on her shoulders that night at the mounds."

Annette's eyes misted with tears.

Wes continued. "There were also snakes in the cage with her. I assume that's where the punctures came from."

Shaking her head and wiping her tears, Annette took a deep breath. "Wes, could the snakes have poisoned her?"

"I don't know. Why?"

"She said her stomach hurt last night. She told me it burned like fire inside and she couldn't sleep."

Wes added this development to his growing list of questions. At that moment, he decided that he had to tell Annette about last night and what he had been forced to witness.

"Annette, they sacrificed Reverend Carmichael last night. I saw it. The most bloody, horrible thing you can imagine. Evil so unspeakable, no one would believe me if I told them."

Annette's hand shot to her mouth, and she gasped in shock, eyes wide. Her head sank to her chest as she whispered, "Is Jennifer safe?"

"I don't know. We can't go back to Clarion until the Order's exposed, I'm sure of that."

"But what about your radio show?"

Wes motioned toward the motel office. "There's a pay phone down there. I'll call my producer. You get Jennifer ready, and we'll hit the road. I'll get coffee and donuts for you."

Wes walked to the office and dialed Chuck Bailey.

Might as well tell him some of the story, he thought. *Chuck will thing I'm crazy, but nothing I tell him will make sense.*

"Chuck, it's Wes. I can't make it in tomorrow."

"Are you sick?"

"Sort of. Fact is, I don't know when I'll do the show again."

"What's that mean? Are you quitting?"

"Maybe. I'm not sure. I can't come near Clarion right now."

"What have you done? Got some debts you can't pay off? Did you get into a fight with someone?"

"No. It involves that girl, Jennifer. She really is the victim of a dangerous cult, involving the most powerful people in Columbus County."

"Wes, are you drinking again? Come on, big guy! Level with me."

"Chuck, I'm completely sober. Don't believe me if you don't want to, but try to buy me some time with Warren. Tell him a friend is dying and I can't leave him. That's half-true."

"I can't guarantee the boss won't fire you," Chuck warned. "I'll try to stall a couple of days. After that, I don't know. Try to get back on the job, fast."

Wes hung up the phone and started to leave the booth when he remembered Larry Bender. Bender had given him the first information about Jennifer from the *Columbus County Courier* files. He had promised to let Larry know if there was a story. This was a story all right, but if his best friend Chuck Bailey didn't believe it, would a skeptical newspaper man? Wes figured he had nothing to lose, so he got Bender's number from information and called.

"Larry, it's Wes Bryant."

You caught me as I was leaving. I've been thinking about you a lot. Wondered what happened after that strange night you looked through those old issues of the *Courier*. What's up?"

"You wanted to know if I stumbled onto something. Well, I have. Forget your reporter's skepticism. You'll have a tough time believing what I'm about to tell you."

Wes didn't tell Larry everything, only that he had uncovered a murderous cult of powerful people in Columbus County. Wes mentioned no names.

"Can I trust you, Larry? Really trust you?"

"Sure, Wes."

"Larry, I mean *really* trust you! Do you swear?"

"OK! OK."

"I'm going to put some names on a piece of paper and mail it to you in an envelope marked confidential. Don't open it! But if I'm found dead any time soon, the names of the people responsible for killing me are inside."

"Wes, is this a joke? I swear, if this is some cheap publicity stunt . . ."

"Larry, I'm not kidding, and I'm not drunk. If you want proof, check with the coroner's office this morning. You'll find out that the Reverend James Carmichael—you know, that black preacher on the edge of town—was found dead last night. They're going to tell you it was a hit-and-run. Don't believe it. Ask to see the body. If they don't let you, there's a good reason. Check it out."

"OK, Wes. Mail me the envelope. But you can't leave me hanging like this forever. If I don't hear from you in thirty days, I'm going to open that envelope."

"Thirty days. You got it. I'll be in touch before then. Thanks, Larry."

Wes hung up the phone, wandered into the motel entry area, and found a tray of assorted pastries laid out with juice and coffee. He wasn't sure which donuts Annette and Jennifer would like, so he picked chocolate-glazed and multicolored sprinkles. He almost chose one with pink icing but decided to leave it in the company of a fly who eyed him from its center.

Juggling the donuts, juice, and coffee, Wes walked outside and returned to their room. He tapped on the door with his foot, trying not to disrupt his balancing act.

"It's me, Annette," Wes called out.

Jennifer opened the door and immediately grabbed Wes's leg, nearly causing a donut disaster.

"Donuts!" Jennifer cried. "I *love* donuts, Mr. Wes."

"Well, you'd better let me come in or you'll have them spilled all over the place," Wes laughed, as he walked into the room and set their breakfast on the nightstand.

Jennifer reached for the multicolored donut and began eating the frosting. "Mr. Wes," she said, "thank you for taking me away from the nasty people."

Wes put down the tray and hugged her tightly. "Don't worry about them, Jennifer. You're safe now with your mother and me."

Two hours later, they approached the outskirts of Chicago. It was a strange homecoming for Annette and Jennifer. Distant skyscrapers beckoned mother and child back to the time before an icy road and a freak April snowstorm stranded them far from home. Shopping sprees in the Loop, dips in Lake Michigan on warm summer afternoons, and the wide-eyed wonder of Marshall Field's Christmas windows were vague memories now.

"What happened to Tickles?" Jennifer blurted, unexpectedly.

Annette explained to Wes that Tickles was a calico kitten Jennifer's best friend had given her as a birthday present. The cat earned its name because of a game the two to them had worked out. Jennifer laid on the floor wiggling her toes and rocking her feet back and forth. Tickles pretended he was a ferocious jungle beast, and Jennifer's toes were prey to stalk, and she giggled as his hair tickled her feet. Wes was puzzled, not sure what had brought the memory back to Jennifer.

The night before, it had seemed sensible to head toward Chicago. He hadn't thought about what returning to Annette's former hometown might mean to her. Would Annette be satisfied to stay anywhere but home, now that her expensive North Shore residence, filled with furniture from the Chicago Mart and designer clothes, was only forty-five minutes away? Getting lost in the big city of Chicago could work only if they stayed away from Annette's house.

Before Wes could express his concerns, Annette spoke. "If we're going into hiding, we should stay on this side of town. Do you have any idea what to do next?"

Wes shrugged his shoulders. "We can't keep paying for motel rooms. I don't have that much money. We have to find an apartment, get you settled in, and figure out what to do from there."

Even though the real criminals were Sheriff Hancock, Dr. Blackwell, and their cohorts, Wes felt like a fugitive. For an undetermined time, he, Annette, and Jennifer would have to live in a new world based on lies. Everything about then—their names, their personal histories, their families—everything would be lies.

Wes pulled over to a parking place near a newspaper stand. "I'll get a copy of the *Tribune*," he said to Annette. "Let's see what kind of apartments we can get on this side of town."

For the next hour, Annette and Wes sat in the car, reviewing classified ads. They dismissed most of the apartments because of cost or location, and it was clear that Wes's money wouldn't go far in Chicago.

"This might be it." Annette said excitedly. "One bedroom. 535 square feet. Gas oven. Mini-fridge. Third floor. No elevator. $225.00 per month. No security deposit. 2519 Calhoun Street. Landlord on premises."

We cocked his head cynically. "Doesn't sound like much to me," he said.

"Beggars can't be choosers," Annette quipped. "It's the only thing I've seen on this side of town. Can't hurt to check it out."

OK, you know Chicago. Show me where to go."

Wes followed Annette's directions, and fifteen minutes later they pulled up in front of a narrow three-story building covered with off-white aluminum siding. On one side was a neighborhood dairy mart, the kind frequently found in old Chicago ethnic neighborhoods, offering sundries, dairy products, newspapers, magazines, candies, and a supply of basic groceries. A laundry squatted on the other side. Tattered paper signs were taped to the window: "Quarters available in the dairy mart two doors down," "Detergent for sale," "No food or smoking allowed inside." The rest of the window was plastered with poster promoting the Police Athletic League, a local high school play, and miscellaneous announcements about garage sales, people needing jobs, and civic functions.

The small apartment building was about thirty feet wide, and three apartments were stacked on top of each other. Directly across the street, a bar welcomed patrons with a huge flashing neon sign that said, "Happy Landing." It looked like a seafaring tavern where sailors spent off-duty hours.

"Wait in the car," Wes said. "I'll see if anyone is home."

Wes knocked several times before the only door to the building opened, and a robust woman in her sixties greeted him. Her graying hair was pulled back tightly into a ponytail and was held in place by a single rubber-band. She wore a plain, blue and white print, cotton dress and an apron with tiny, bright yellow flowers.

"Sorry I didn't come right away," the woman said, wiping her hands on a dish towel. "I was in the kitchen doing my breakfast dishes. Thought I'd better get to them before lunch time. Name is Hattie MacKenzie. What can I do for you?"

"I read your ad about an apartment for rent."

"Two flights up. I live on the main level, and a gentleman who works at a local machine shop is just above me. This apartment just for you?"

Wes hesitated. He hadn't thought things through. For a slit second, he saw himself behind the microphone of "Talk about Town," answering a caller with the quick wit that made his show a success. "No, my wife and daughter too."

Hattie looked at him inquisitively. "It's a small place. Maybe you didn't read the ad closely. I need to rent it, but are you sure it's big enough?"

"It'll do if we like it," Wes said. "We can't afford much."

"Moving to Chicago permanently?" Hattie asked.

Wes stuttered. "Ah, yeah. We're moving here from downstate Indiana."

Hattie flipped the dish towel over her shoulder. "Let me show you the apartment." She took off her apron, folded it neatly, and placed it on the back of a chair behind her. She put the dish towel next to it and took a nylon jacket from a hall closet.

"You've got to walk up an outside flight of stairs on the side of the building. Sorry there's no inside entrance. That's the way they built these buildings."

Hattie motioned for Wes to step outside. He followed her around the corner of the building and down a narrow passageway between her home and the laundry. A wooden stairway toward the rear of the building led to the second and third floors.

"Have to be careful in the winter. Make sure you get all the snow off or it gets real slippery. My back bothers me too much to clean the steps. You have to do that . . . thought you ought to know."

Hattie walked up the steps slowly, placing each foot firmly on the wooden planks and grasping the handrail to steady herself. She was spry for her age, but it was obvious her joint didn't move the way they once had. At the top of the stairs, she unlocked a door.

Wes stepped inside. He hadn't expected much and wasn't disappointed. The door opened into a small kitchen, which led to a tiny room that could serve as a living room. A bathroom and single bedroom were located down a short hallway.

"It's furnished, you know," Hattie said, pointing to a dilapidated couch and a small wooden table and chairs that Wes surmised the Goodwill would reject. "You're welcome to use the pots and pans in the cupboard. The bedroom is at the front, facing the street. Don't know why they built it that way. Seems smarter to put the bedroom at the back where it's quiet."

Wes wasn't sure if the three of them could live in such cramped quarters. He looked again at the cracked and peeling leather couch. That's where he'd probably sleep, and it didn't look at all comfortable. He imagined the alternative—lying on a blanket spread on the hard linoleum floor.

"Pay your own utilities," Hattie said. "There's a meter under the stairs below. The utility company checks it each month. Not too expensive. You can heat a small space like this for around forty-five dollars a month, even in the winter. Electricity will run you another twenty-five to thirty dollars, unless you got one of those microwaves or run the TV a lot. Do you have a TV?"

Wes shook his head. "No."

"Where'd you say you came from?"

"Clar . . . Clarisville," Wes answered. "Clairsville, Indiana."

"Never heard of it. Used to live outside Indianapolis. Thought I knew every town in Indiana."

"What's it near?"

Wes swallowed and faked a cough, stalling for time. Inventing information spontaneously was difficult. How many more questions like these would the three of them face in the weeks ahead? *We'll have to role-play our assumed identities and be ready for anything,* he thought.

"It's just down the road from Grafton. That's where we did most of our shopping. Hardly anything left in Clairsville, except a small café, and implement supply company, and a filling station."

"M-m-m. Well, if you're interested in the apartment, I need a month's rent in advance. Want to think it over?"

What's to think over? Wes mused. *No sense spending another thirty or forty dollars on a motel room tonight.* "I'll take it," Wes answered.

"If you pay by check, I can't let you move in right now. Have to wait until the check clears."

"No. I've got cash."

"That's good. What'd you say your name was?"

"Wes," he answered.

"Last name?"

"Uh, Milton. Wesley Milton." *My old high school science teacher, Milton, Tony Milton. Haven't thought of him in years. Strange he should come to mind,* Wes thought.

"Come on downstairs. We'll fill out the papers so you can get your things moved in."

There wasn't much to fill out. A form indicating a former address and a credit reference, both of which Wes quickly devised, and a pledge to pay in advance each month.

"Probably should have a damage deposit," Hattie said. "Guess I'm too trusting. In my time, folks took responsibility for what they did."

"I'll make sure we don't hurt anything," Wes offered. Hattie thanked him, and he walked out to the car. Jennifer was asleep in the back seat, and Annette was dozing, huddled in a cloth coat Hannah Carmichael had given her. The vague aroma of Hannah's sachet lingered.

Wes awakened Annette and said, "We've got a place to stay. I've given the landlord one month's rent, so for the next thirty days, this is home. Tomorrow, we'll pick up some groceries and clothes."

Annette roused Jennifer, and they climbed the rickety outside stairs of 2519 Calhoun Street to apartment number three.

"Mommy," Jennifer said. Her face grimaced. "It hurts me when I climb up the stairs."

Jennifer looked around at Annette and then at Wes. She lowered her voice to a barely audible sound. "My tummy and my . . . private parts."

Annette turned to Wes and unspoken rage gleamed in her eyes. She paused to regain her composure, then responded softly, "Maybe your legs just went to sleep in the car. Take it slower."

Jennifer bit her lip and continued up the stairs, as Wes and Annette silently shared the pain of Jennifer's abuse.

Once inside, Annette and Jennifer surveyed the place; Wes waited in the kitchen. Mrs. MacKenzie knocked on the door, her arms loaded with blankets and sheets.

"Thought you might need these. Saw you walk in without anything. I can't let you keep them, but if you need them for a night or two, it's OK."

"Thanks, Mrs. MacKenzie," Wes said. She probably wondered about their coming to Chicago with just the clothes on their backs, but she said good-bye cheerfully enough.

"I'm tired, Mommy," Jennifer said. "Can I go to bed?"

"Sure. Give me a few minutes to make it up."

"I'll help," Jennifer offered.

In minutes, the bed was prepared and Jennifer was tucked inside the sheets.

"I think it's safe to leave you two here," Wes said. "I'll run next door to the dairy mart and pick up some coffee, juice, and cereal for morning."

When Wes returned, Annette was curled up on the couch, almost asleep. He put water on the stove to heat, and measured instant coffee into cups. The two of them talked for several hours about what had brought them to Chicago and what to do next. As dusk approached, Wes heard a voice coming from the bedroom where Jennifer was sleeping. He asked Annette, "Does Jennifer talk in her sleep?"

Annette instinctively reached for the gold cross around her neck. "No." she whispered. "She never has. Why?"

"Thought I heard her."

Wes motioned Annette to follow him, and they tiptoed down the hallway toward the bedroom door. The closer they got, the more distinct the voice became. Wes turned the knob and pushed the bedroom door open. Jennifer sat naked in the middle of the bed, her back to the door, staring at the window where the Happy Landing sign flashed on and off. She rocked gently back and forth, muttering, "My soul belongs to Dark Raven, my soul belongs to Dark Raven." Jennifer's rhythmic motions synchronized with the timed flashes of the triangular-shaped Happy Landing sign, which Wes concluded must have triggered a conditioned response.

"Jennifer," Annette cried, rushing to the bed and throwing her arms around her daughter.

Jennifer's glazed eyes looked through Annette. "Who are you?" she asked. "I am Dark Raven's queen. Don't touch me! Dark Raven doesn't like it. I belong to him."

Annette drew back in horror. Jennifer's voice had changed, and the expression on her face was unlike any Annette had ever seen. It was as if another personality had taken over.

"Who is he?" Jennifer demanded, pointing at Wes. "He's bad! Go away!"

Then to their utter amazement, Jennifer lay back on the bed in a sexually receptive position.

"Come, Black Raven," she crooned. "I am yours."

Voice changed.

Thirteen

Wes and Annette stood helpless before the strange scene. Then abruptly, Jennifer snapped out of the trance. She seemed baffled and exclaimed in a normal voice, "Mommy, I'm cold! Where are my clothes?"

As if a switch had been thrown deep in Jennifer's psyche, the persona of the queen vanished. Jennifer's curled up into a fetal position, tucking her knees into her chest. She glanced sideways at Wes, embarrassed by her nakedness. Annette grabbed the blanket and threw it over Jennifer. Wes, too, was flustered by the child's unnatural actions.

Annette stroked Jennifer's brow to comfort her and said "It's all right. You had a bad dream. Go to sleep. Mommy will come to bed in a little while."

Annette went to the window. "Dear God," Annette cried. "Please help me, and please help Jennifer . . ." As she silently faced the window, the lights from the Happy Landing sign cast her shadow against the opposite wall. She pulled the curtains, dimming the intrusion of the flashing sign.

Annette then turned to find Jennifer already fast asleep. She leaned down and kissed her daughter's soft, moist cheek that moments before had been flushed. "Sweet dreams, my baby. Mommy loves you, and God is watching over you."

Annette motioned for Wes to follow her and stepped softly from the room, closing the door behind her.

"I wish I knew what that was all about," Annette said. "It scares me."

"Me too."

"Wes, I think it's obvious now—Jennifer was physically abused, wasn't she?"

Unable to erase the sexual image of Jennifer moments before, Wes shook his head despairingly. "I think you're right, but I have no idea what happened in there. Some kind of psychological reaction. It's like Jennifer became someone else."

"Do you think I should take her to a doctor?"

"Maybe. But first, we've got to find you and Jennifer new identities."

"What's that mean?"

"I've already told Hattie my name is Wesley Milton. Now, you've got to become someone else. A new name. A new past. A new future. You've seen those TV programs about the government witness protection program where someone testifies in a trial, and the government gives him a new identity."

"I don't watch that much TV. How does it work?"

"Start from scratch. Program you and Jennifer into being new people. I've been thinking about it, and the only place I know to start is the graveyard."

"The graveyard! What do dead people have to do with it?"

"If we walk through a graveyard and find tombstones of people about your age and Jennifer's, we could trace who they were and build your identities around them. Maybe we could even get some legal documents to verify your identity."

Annette sighed deeply. "It's too much for me tonight. Let's talk in the morning before Jennifer gets up."

Wes reached out to comfort Annette. As he put his big arms around her small body, she curled into his chest and hugged him hard in return.

"How will you keep warm on the couch?" Annette asked.

"I'll use our coats. That'll get me by tonight. Tomorrow, I can buy some blankets. Don't worry! Go back in there with Jennifer."

"Good morning. How about some cereal?" Wes said to Annette the next morning, as he heard her footsteps on the bare wooden hall floor. "I didn't know what you and Jennifer liked, so I got one of those variety packs. A little of everything, some healthy stuff and some sugarcoated junk. Take your pick."

As Annette prepared her cereal, Wes continued. "I left earlier and talked with Hattie, told her I had an aunt buried somewhere in South Chicago and asked where the nearest cemetery was. There's one about five miles from here, Pleasant Hills Cemetery. It's not my idea of how to spend an exciting day, but we're going tombstone snooping!"

"Are you suggesting we romp around cemetery headstones and pick a name, hoping we get a good one? But Wes, my religious upbringing makes me uneasy about showing disrespect for the dead. I don't think I can handle that." Annette put her head in her hands and began to cry softly.

Wes gently touched her shoulder, but kept silent. He knew she needed to release her feelings.

"I'm sorry," Annette said, sniffing and wiping tears from her eyes. "This isn't going to be easy. I was the daughter of a minister as well as the wife of a successful doctor. Now, my future identity lies in the former life of someone buried in a graveyard." She pushed her chair back from the table and stood.

"I know this graveyard thing sounds morbid, but we have to trust each other. We must do that for Jennifer. Remember, she trusted me first."

"I'll get Jennifer up," Annette responded. "If you have some Rice Krispies, please pour her a bowl. She used to like them."

Wes and Annette ate hurriedly while Jennifer only picked at her cereal, again complaining of a stomachache. Then they drove to Pleasant Hills Cemetery. In Columbus County, cemeteries were located on the edge of town with room to expand and allow for adequate landscaping. But the unpretentious Pleasant Hills Cemetery was separated form the small bungalow homes only by an intricate wrought iron fence, a reminder of the Victorian ear. Its arching gate displayed a painted wooden sign. The rundown atmosphere made Wes wonder how he would feel about burying his loved ones there.

After parking their car inside the gate, Wes, Annette, and Jennifer began looking for tombstones that weren't too weathered. The sky was dark and cloudy, typical of the endless overcast days awaiting Chicago's stark winters. Many of the small headstones bore simple messages. A few were embellished with longer epitaphs, recalling memorable deeds of the deceased. Most were small granite stone lying flat on the ground, unpretentious to an outsider, but a loving reminder to family members. Several brass vases filled with plastic flowers squatted here and there, colorful, if artificial, interruptions on the dreary landscaping.

"Here's one," Annette said, pointing to a rectangular gray slab. "Heidi Hansen. Born the same year as Jennifer. Died last year from pneumonia. Will this work, Wes?"

"We can try it. Let's jot down the information, then find one for you."

That was more difficult. They walked along row upon row of tombstones, looking for one close to Annette's birth date.

"Here's one, Mommy!" Jennifer yelled. She had run ahead, frustrated at their slower pace. Wes and Annette doubted Jennifer's enthusiasm until they saw the stone: "Helen Logan. 1955-1991. Loved by all who knew her."

"So, it's Heidi and Helen," said Annette, stoically. "Has a nice, alliterative ring. I guess we need to find out who these people were and how to act like them."

Wes knew the hard part had just begun. His experience with Larry Bender and the *Courier* had taught him about newspaper morgues. Getting access to big city newspaper archives wouldn't be easy.

They walked briskly back toward the entrance of the cemetery, anxious to leave the dead behind.

"Why don't we see if people in the neighborhood can tell us about Heidi Hansen and Helen Logan?" Wes suggested. "Both must have lived in this area." Wes paused and pointed in the direction they had just come from. "Did you notice that shopping area a couple of blocks back, where we turned off Fitzsimmons Street? Suppose we go in a few stores? I'll ask for Helen Logan. You check out Heidi Hansen."

They left the cemetery and drove to the shopping area. When they arrived, Annette asked, "What do I say about Heidi Hansen?"

Wes pondered her question, then answered, "Say you're Heidi's aunt. You're in Chicago on business. Her mother was you ex-hus-band's sister, and you didn't know them well, but you think they lived here, and you'd like to see how they're doing. If anyone gets too inquisitive, cut the conversation short and leave. If they take the bait, see how much they'll tell you. Then go to another store. Keep asking clerks, customer, anybody you meet, until you can piece some things together."

Wes pulled the car into diagonal parking space, in front of an antiquated parking meter still showing forty minutes of unexpired time. As he got out of the car, Wes put two dimes into it to make sure it was working. With a satisfying click, the needle registered another forty minutes. Annette got out of the car, and Jennifer shut the door behind them.

"Wes, what are you going to do?"

Wes walked a few more steps, searching his thoughts, then he responded, "I'll say Helen Logan was a friend of my wife. They haven't been in touch for years, but the last address we had was in this area. I'm in the vicinity on business—might as well use your line—and want to contact Helen as a surprise for my wife. How does that sound?"

"I don't know if anyone will believe any of this," Annette answered, "but we have to try."

"Mommy, what do I do?" Jennifer asked plaintively, feeling left out.

"Stay as quiet as possible. Do you understand what we're doing?"

"Well, sort of. You're afraid the nasty people will find me, and you're hiding. You want me to be someone else, right?"

"You got it!" Wes responded. "It's easy to decide who you are according to those tombstones. It'll be harder when you have to *be* those people—I mean, really be Helen and Heidi twenty-four hours a day, no matter what. I'll take the left side of the street, you take the right. Let's meet at the end of the block on your side. Jennifer, hold your mother's hand. Don't get lost!"

"I won't, Mr. Wes."

Wes tucked his hands in his pockets and darted across the street to beat the light. He was uneasy about letting Annette and Jennifer out of his sight, even though the Order probably couldn't have traced them this quickly.

His first stop was Harry's Hardware store. It wasn't like the hardware stores found in suburban shopping malls, with wide aisles, carefully organized bins and shelves. This was a real hardware store, the kind Wes had known as a kid, where you went to find nuts and bolts, hammers and pliers, pocket knives, and dish strainers. Narrow aisles led through a maze of practical items.

"Can I help you, young man?" an old gentleman in faded blue overalls asked. "If we don't have it, you probably don't need it!" he added, chuckling.

Harry's Hardware was a one-man show. If Wes had wanted three-eights-inch bolt, two-and-a-quarter inches long to fit a clutchhead screwdriver, he knew Harry could find it fast. Wes hoped information about Helen Logan would be as easy to come by.

"Actually, I didn't come in here to buy anything. I need some information about a person I'm looking for, and I hope you can help."

Well, I'll do what I can. I was raised in this neighborhood and know just about everybody and everything that goes on here. What can I do for you?"

Wes reached into a gin of bolts and took some in his hands, studying them, taking time to collect his thoughts. "I'm in the vicinity on business. An old friend of my wife lived around here. She hasn't seen her in years, and I thought it would be a nice surprise if I found her. Helen Logan. Ever hear of her?"

The man dropped his eyes and jammed his hands in his overall pockets. "Yeah, I knew her, all right. She was a right nice lady. Never hurt any one. Don't know why it happened."

"What do you mean, *was?*" Wes asked, feigning surprise.

"She was killed last year, just a couple of blocks from here. Raped too. The police never found the guy." Harry lifted his eyes and looked squarely at Wes. "It was evil, downright evil. Helen Logan never did nothing but good. She didn't complain when her husband, Dwight, left her. She went out and got a job at the South Chicago Diner. What makes people do evil things? I mean, really evil things. Just no sense to it." Harry the hardware man shook his head and kicked one boot against the other. "There's no real justice in the world these days."

He added, "If you want to know more about Helen, go to the South Chicago Diner. Ask for Evelyn. She used to wait tables with Helen. Turn west as you leave the store, and you'll walk right into the diner a couple of blocks up."

"Thanks," Wes said. "I'll do that." He put the bolts back in the bin. Then he asked, "You wouldn't happen to have a three-eights-inch bolt and two inches long that would fit a clutchhead screwdriver?"

Harry took off his hat and scratched his head. "Can't say I do. I got an inch-and-a-half, but not two inches."

Wes grinned. "Thanks! Just thought I'd ask."

As Wes stepped outside, he glanced down the other side of the street. Annette and Jennifer were leaving a clothing store. They walked up the street, then turned into a flower shop. They were safe. Wes headed toward the South Chicago Diner. *I was there for Jennifer. Why was no one there to rescue Helen Logan the night she was brutalized?* he wondered.

But maybe someone was there, Wes thought, someone who chose

not to become involved. After all, he could have ignored Jennifer's calls. He didn't have to go to the library and Katherine Caldwell's house. No one forced him to make that lonely trek into the Indiana farm fields to those grass-covered mounds. Wes couldn't answer the hardware man, but he could partly answer himself: Justice is silent when those with the power to act against evil do nothing.

Wes was so lost in thought, he almost walked by the South Chicago Diner. Its name had been hand-painted on the widow, which was framed by red and white checkerboard curtains. Wes stepped inside, triggering a tinkling bell that announced his arrival. He sat at a table and studied the menu: hamburgers, reubens, French fries, home-baked pie.

A waitress in her late twenties approached and asked, "You want to look a few more minutes, or have you decided?"

"Just a cup of coffee, please. I want to talk to a waitress named Evelyn. Is she here?"

"If you mean Evelyn Ronson, she's in the back, giving an order to the chef. I'll tell her you're here. Black or white coffee?"

"Black."

In a few moments, the waitress returned with coffee and said Evelyn would be out soon. Wes sipped slowly, thinking about what he'd say. He'd have to be very careful if she asked personal questions about his fictitious wife's relationship with the late Helen Logan.

"Can I help you? Renee said you wanted to talk with me."

Wes looked up into the face of a young woman whose bleached

blond hair was pulled back inside a hair net. "Evelyn? I'd like very much to talk to you. It will take a couple of minutes, though. Have you got time? If you're with a customer, I can wait."

"I'll ask Renee to look after things. Be right back."

Evelyn Ronson spoke briefly with the other waitress, then joined Wes at the table. He set the stage with the same story he'd given Harry the hardware man. Then Wes said, "I thought maybe you could give me a little information for my wife, like, what Helen did the last few years, anything old friends might hold onto."

"We didn't spend a whole lot of time together outside the restaurant, but when things were slow, we'd sit around and talk. I got to know Helen pretty well. I still don't understand why it happened. Why kill her for a few lousy bucks? She didn't look rich or anything. If they were going to mug someone, you'd think they'd hit some high rollers in downtown Chicago. How long since your wife saw her?"

Wes reached for his coffee cup and took a long drink. "I don't really know. My wife mentioned her only a few times. I think they lost touch about ten years ago."

Evelyn lowered her head slightly. "Helen came to Chicago looking for a new life, like a lot of kids in the Midwest do. Somewhere along the line, she met this guy named Dwight Goodwin. I saw a picture of him once. Not bad looking. Blond hair, looked young for his age. Dwight was a salesman. I don't know what he sold, but she said he was on the road a lot. I guess that's what tore the marriage apart. He never even came to her funeral. I was there, but just a handful of people showed up. Her parents and a brother, David, who lives in Des Moines."

"What sort of a person was Helen Logan?"

"Kind! That's the best thing I can say about her. She always helped out when I was busy. Even gave me the tips and wouldn't take a dime for herself. I figured some day she'd get enough money to leave, maybe go back to college and finish her education. She always wanted to be a vet. Loved animals. She kept a dog named Cicero, a cat named Plato. Strange names for animals, don't you think?"

Wes gestured in vague agreement. "did she have any hobbies" What did she do for fun?"

"Mister, when you're a single woman making it on your own and living off tips, there's not much you can do for fun! Go to a few movies, bowl now and then. Women like Helen and me don't belong to the country club crowd, y'know!"

"Did she ever talk about her family?"

"No, just that they were poor farmers out in Iowa, some little town. I think it was Altonville. Not sure about that." Evelyn's voice was beginning to sound irritated and impatient, as if she were beginning to get suspicious about Wes's questions.

Wes put a couple of dollars on the table. "Thanks for your time, Evelyn, also for the coffee."

Wes rose and started to leave. "Mr. Milton," Evelyn said, "why would someone like Helen get killed for nothing? I blame myself, y'know. I should have walked home with her that night. Maybe they

wouldn't have jumped the two of us. Have you ever heard of anything so cruel and pointless?"

Wes shrugged his shoulders and thought of Jennifer.

"A lot of strange things go on in our world," he answered vaguely.

Wes stepped into the street, grateful he was allowed to uncover
so much information about Helen Logan so quickly. He saw Annette
and Jennifer step out of a corner candy shop and stand by the stoplight, waiting for him. He crossed the street and caught up with
them. "Well, Mrs. Logan. How are you this afternoon, and how are
Cicero and Plato?"

"You'll find out soon enough. First, tell me about Heidi Hansen."

Wes, Annette, and Jennifer headed toward their car. During the
short drive back to their apartment, Annette explained what she'd
discovered about Heidi Hansen.

"Heidi's parents were a young couple named Frederick and
Estelle. Frederick drove a delivery truck for a local manufacturing
company. Estelle did housecleaning for well-to-do families somewhere in the suburbs. They lived a couple of blocks from here, but,
after Heidi died of pneumonia, they went back to Mississippi where
Estelle's parents live. It shouldn't be too hard to track down information about Heidi. She was born nearby at St. Joseph's Hospital."

"I think we've got enough to go on," Wes said. "Now, we have to
decide what to do next."

They returned to the apartment, and Annette asked Jennifer to
play in the bedroom so she and Wes could talk privately about the

day's events. Annette and Wes sat in the kitchen to plan their strategy. Before they did, Wes addressed an envelope to Larry Bender at the *Columbus County Courier* and wrote CONFIDENTIAL in large letters across the front.

"What are you doing?" Annette asked.

"Larry Bender, the assistant editor of the *Courier,* helped me find you. He let me go through some old newspapers that led to where you were. I called him yesterday morning from that motel, told him a little bit about the situation. I didn't mention any names, but said I'd mail him the full story about who's involved in the Order of the Dark Raven. If he doesn't hear from me in thirty days, he'll open the envelope. Just a precaution, in case something happens to us."

Annette nodded. "Let me have a piece of paper from that pad. I'm going to write down everything we've learned about Helen Logan and Heidi Hansen. If Jennifer and I have to become these two people, we've got to study what we know about them."

Just then, they heard the sound of shattering glass and a scream from the bedroom. Wes and Annette froze, staring at each other in horror. Each knew what the other was thinking: *Has the Order found us?*

Fourteen

Wes threw open the bedroom door and was met by a blast of cold air. Broken glass lay everywhere. An errant baseball rolled across the floor, bouncing against pieces of the broken window's sharp edges before coming to rest against a large section of pane. Wes carefully stepped across the room and looked out the window. On the street below two frightened boys tilted their heads back and stared up at him. One wore a baseball glove, the other nervously swung the offending bat back and forth, as if it were a pendulum pacing off the time until the inevitable scolding.

"Hey! What're you guys doing?" Wes yelled as if the broken window were insufficient testimony. The startled boys bolted, ran around the nearest corner, and disappeared.

Jennifer had draped herself in a blanket and was standing across from the window in the corner. *At least it wasn't an attack by the Order,* Wes thought, weak with relief. Annette stood in the doorway, gawking at the destruction. Realizing their only concern was avoiding the broken glass, Annette ran to Jennifer and pulled her into her arms. Jennifer reacted violently, pounding her fists against Annette's head and breast, screaming, "I hate you! I hate you!"

Startled, Annette froze, her arms wrapped tightly around the little girl. Jennifer clenched her hands into fists. With her long blonde hair flying wildly, she jerked her head back and forth in frustration. "Why didn't you stop them? You let them hurt me! You're not my mother! I hate you!"

Annette and Wes looked at each other in confusion. As suddenly as her fury had erupted, Jennifer's knees buckled. She leaned backward and slowly slid down, her body limp. Her head rested against her bent knees as torrents of sobs wracked her. "It's all my fault," she cried in anguish. "I was a bad girl! The Black Raven said so. That's why you didn't stop them from poking me."

Jennifer's body shook feverishly. Befuddled, Wes realized he had to stop the cold November wind. He ripped the sheet from Jennifer's bed and stretched it across the window. He secured it by stuffing the edges into the crevices of the window frame, not the best solution, but a stop gap.

Someone knocked at the door. "That's probably Hattie MacKenzie, wanting to know what happened," Wes said, as he turned and walked into the small living room.

It was Hattie indeed. "Did they break another window?" she exclaimed as Wes opened the door. "I've told those crazy kids a hundred times, 'Play ball on the play-ground!' But, no, they play in the street. Not the first time this has happened. Broke my front picture window once. I was napping and nearly had a heart attack. Kids don't care these days. And parents don't care either.

It's a disgrace, I tell you, a disgrace. I suppose there's glass every-where. Anyone hurt?"

Wes shook his head.

Hattie went on, "I know a handyman a few blocks away who installs glass. Can probably get him out here in an hour or so. What about your wife and little girl? Are they OK?"

"They're fine. We put a blanket over the window to shut out the cold. Don't worry."

"Told those kids a hundred times, 'Don't play baseball in the streets' . . . but would they listen? It's the parents' fault, simply irresponsible. Ought to punish them for letting their kids run loose . . ." Hattie continued her monologue, muttering disgustedly, as she slowly descended the steps.

"I got Jennifer calmed down and she's resting," Annette said, as Wes met her in the hallway. "Let's leave the glass alone for now. The sheet covering the window works pretty well. I don't want to disturb Jennifer anymore. That was a bad shock for her."

Wes nodded in agreement. "I'll make you a cup of coffee," he said, putting his arm around Annette to console her.

Annette slumped into a kitchen chair, her head resting on her arms, which were folded on the table. Wes put his hand over hers. He felt helpless.

"Did you hear what Jennifer said?" Annette asked, lifting her head and staring intently at Wes. "She wanted to know why I let them hurt her. She thinks I was there! How could she?" Annette doubled up her fist and pounded the table in frustration. "I always tried to protect her when Gregory was around. She should remember that!"

Annette grew pensive for a moment. Wes sensed she was recalling some unpleasant memories. He leaned forward, touched her arm, and asked gently, "What is it? Did Gregory ever abuse Jennifer?"

Annette stared at her hands, her forehead furrowed in contemplation. "If you'd asked me that question a year ago, I would have been shocked. But, in the past few days I've been looking back, and a lot of things make sense." Her mouth tightened into a frown, and she sighed deeply. "How could I have been so blind?"

Annette sat silently, eyes closed. Finally she spoke, haltingly, each word an attempt to expunge her self-assumed guilt and shame. "Gregory was very aggressive sexually while we were dating, and he was like that until I got pregnant. I wouldn't say he was kinky, exactly, but he liked some unusual variations. You know, different ways of . . . doing it." The words came hard for her.

Wes understood her apprehension. "Hey, you don't have to tell me your private life," he reminded her.

"It's OK. You might as well know," Annette assured him. "Before Jennifer was born, Gregory had a strange obsession with my getting pregnant. It was more than a newly married husband wanting a child. I *had* to have a baby, and it *had* to be a girl. Gregory was firm about that. A lot of couples have sexual problems when a wife gets pregnant. But Gregory lost all sexual interest in me. When I told him I was going to have a baby, he never touched me again. All he talked about was the baby. I was like a baby factory, a breeding machine.

"I was afraid to have an ultrasound because, if it had been a boy,

Gregory might have asked me to get an abortion. He insisted on picking the names, and he only considered girls' names. Jennifer was the name of an aunt way back in his father's family. Gregory was so sure I would have a girl that, by the fifth month of my pregnancy, he told me the baby's name was Jennifer.

"When Jennifer was born, Gregory was obsessive about raising her. He monitored what she ate, the toys she played with, even the people he allowed to touch her. An uncle of mine visited once, and Gregory wouldn't let him near Jennifer. I thought he was just a very jealous father, but it was more like he owned her. Jennifer was a product of my body, but my pregnancy was incidental to Gregory. In fact, after she was born, he ignored me, though he was very affectionate with Jennifer," Annette said, her voice trailing off as if she had hit a raw nerve deep in her psyche.

Wes looked at Annette, puzzled. For a moment, she stared blankly at him. Then she went on. "Once, when Jennifer was only a few months old, I found him in the nursery, licking her body and touching her . . . I yelled at him to stop. He got very angry, and I thought he was going to hit me. That's another thing. He was two different people. One minute, the doting father and model citizen, the next a raving maniac. I never knew what would set him off, but once he got riled, I kept my distance."

"Did he ever hit you?"

"No. He was too smart for that. He had subtler ways of intimidation. Once, he left on a business trip and took the keys to the car and house so I couldn't leave. I nearly ran out of food. When he returned, he acted like nothing had happened, just wanted to know if I had obeyed his instructions about taking care of Jennifer."

Wes and Annette heard the sound of a door closing and turned to see Jennifer walking toward them, rubbing her eyes.

Wes quickly changed the subject. "Hello, Jennifer. Been sleeping?"

Jennifer nodded. "Mommy, it's so cold in my room. A sheet's over the window, there's broken glass all over the floor, and my tummy hurts."

Annette put her arms out to the little girl in the cotton slip. "Sit down. Mommy will make you a cup of hot chocolate. How's that?"

Jennifer smiled. Annette got up to boil water, and Wes carried on the conversation. "We need to go over the details about Heidi and Helen, so you two can assume your new personalities tomorrow. Then we'll make up a job history for you, Annette. Suppose we say you worked at a McDonalds's in Altonville? We can concoct where you worked in Chicago before waitressing at the South Chicago Diner. Know of a place around the North Shore that we could add to the resume?"

"There was a delicatessen a few blocks from our house. Hirschbaum's Deli, a kosher place. How's that sound?"

"OK. So, it's slicing corned beef and serving bagels at Hirschbaum's Deli. That'll work."

Annette set the hot chocolate in front of Jennifer, who slurped it loudly. "Jennifer," Annette interrupted. "Remember your manners! Sip slowly, or wait until it cools down."

For an instant, Jennifer stiffened like any child being disciplined. Then her expression relaxed. "I will, Mommy, but it's hot," she protested.

A knock at the door interrupted their conversation. It was the handyman Hattie MacKenzie had sent to repair the broken window. "Let's leave while he's fixing things," Wes suggested. "It'll do us good to get out of here for a while. Besides, I have to call Larry Bender before he goes home at five and tell him the envelope I promised is on its way."

Wes let in the handyman and mumbled that they would be back soon. Then he picked up their three coats and followed Annette and Jennifer out the door. As they descended the steps from their apartment, Jennifer put her hand in her mother's. "Mommy, you know I love you, don't you?'

"Of course, darling," Annette answered.

"I mean, *really* love you," Jennifer insisted, squeezing her hand.

Once they reached the pavement and stood in the narrow alley, Annette knelt in front of Jennifer, placing both hands on her shoulders, and asked, "Why do you ask that question?"

"I don't know," Jennifer said. "Funny things are inside my head." She looked at the ground, kicking a piece of broken asphalt. "Part of me doesn't like you very much because you let them hurt me."

"Jennifer, I would never let anyone harm you! Never!"

"Yes, you did!" Jennifer shouted. "You stood there while they put those things in me! I asked you to stop them, and you didn't."

"What things?" Annette asked.

"You *know*! Those long sticks. They put them right here," Jennifer insisted, pointing to her buttocks and groin.

Annette swallowed hard. "Honey, I don't know who you saw, but it wasn't me."

"Yes, it was!" Jennifer persisted. "You were standing outside the circle of fire around me. I couldn't see your face, but you had on that red dress you wear to parties. My head felt funny, but I heard your voice. You didn't stop them. It hurt bad with those things inside me!"

Jennifer burst into tears. Wes knelt beside Annette, putting his arm around her shoulders as she hugged Jennifer tightly. Both sobbed uncontrollably. Though it was painful for mother and daughter, Wes *no* partly understood Jennifer's earlier outburst against her mother. *The Order had someone imitate Annette, wear one of her dresses,* he thought. *What a clever way to destroy her confidence and make Jennifer hate her mother.*

A harsh burst of wind blew in their faces, reminding them that they were huddled together in a cold South Chicago alley. Wes motioned for them to follow him on down the narrow passage toward the street. They walked down the block to a pay phone booth. Jennifer and Annette waited while Wes dialed the number of the *Columbus County Courier*.

"May I speak with Larry Bender?" Wes asked the switchboard operator. She didn't answer. "Hello," Wes said. "Is anyone there? I want to talk with Larry Bender."

"May I ask the nature of the call?"

"Larry is a friend of mine. Please, this is a long distance call. If he's not in, tell me when I can call back."

"Just a moment, sir. I'll let you talk to Mr. Darrell Skinner, our senior editor."

Wes waited impatiently. He pulled back the accordion glass door and told Annette he was on hold. He fidgeted with the coin return slot, nervously flopping it back and forth. He thumbed through the battered Yellow Pages that dangled from a slim chain on the metal shelf under the phone.

"Hello, this is Darrel Skinner. May I help you?"

"I want to talk to Larry Bender. He's a friend of mine."

"Who's calling?"

"What's the difference, mister?" Wes answered angrily.

"I'm afraid it's not possible to speak with Mr. Bender."

"Well, when *can* I talk to him?"

There was a long pause on the other end of the line.

"You haven't heard?"

"Heard what?" Wes exclaimed, frustrated.

"Larry's dead. Killed in a car accident. He was following up a story on the death of a local minister, the Reverend James Carmichael. He left the coroner's office—not sure why he went there—and was on his way to Carmichael's house when he apparently lost control of his car and rolled down an embankment.

"You know where Eighth Avenue turns into a dirt road on the south side of town, where it goes down along the river? The road's about twenty feet above the water at that point, and Larry missed the curve. Sheriff Hancock found the car this morning. He just left my office a couple of hours ago. Sorry to tell you this so abruptly. What'd you say your name was?"

Wes lowered the receiver and let it dangle, suspended by its metal cord. In the distance, he heard Darrell Skinner calling, "Hello, hello! Can you hear me?"

He opened the door and walked out of the phone booth, his eyes filled with tears. Annette and Jennifer had been looking in the window of a nearby drugstore and walked toward Wes when they heard the phone booth door creak open. Annette saw Wes's dazed look and avoided asking questions.

"Where will it all end?" Wes asked, staring beyond Annette. He took Jennifer's hand in his right hand and Annette's hand in his left and headed back to their apartment. By now, the repairman would have finished patching the broken window of apartment number three, but Wes knew it would be along time—if ever—before the lives of Annette and Jennifer could be put back together.

Early Tuesday morning, Annette and Jennifer set out to buy a jacket and a nightgown for Jennifer and some essential household items. Wes waited anxiously in apartment number three, flipping the dial to check out what talk radio offered Chicagoans. He seldom had time to hear competitors, and it fascinated him that the same tactics he used in Columbus County to keep listeners calling worked in the Windy City too. Afterward, he scanned some dog-eared paperback novels a former tenant had left in the closet to keep himself form watching the clock and wondering where Annette and Jennifer were.

At noon, Wes heard voices outside and then a knock at the door. He threw his arms around Annette and Jennifer like a relative who hadn't seen his loved ones in months. "Boy, am I glad to see you guys! You have no idea how worried I've been. Sit down.

What did you get?"

Annette and Jennifer took off their coats and joined Wes at the kitchen table. They opened their bags and spread out a variety of foods, cooking utensils, towels, and paper needs. Wes checked out several of the items and said, "My day wasn't exactly dull. Aside from listening to the radio and reading, I called from the phone booth on the street to talk with some people in Altonville, Iowa, and boy, do I know a lot about you, Helen Logan!"

Wes held up a stock of yellow legal pad sheets. "Here are my notes. I called the Altonville Chamber of Commerce and told them I was thinking about moving there, needed to know about schools and so on. Then I called the schools to get information about Helen. I passed myself off as an uncle, said I was writing a family history for a reunion. Everyone was helpful!"

Wes laid out the facts. "Helen Logan was born at a hospital in Altonville—eight pounds, ten ounces. A nurse checked the records and told me her tonsils and appendix had been taken out. She attended Jefferson Elementary and Patuska County District Junior/Senior High School. At sixteen, she had a bicycling accident and broke her arm. It caused complications, and she had to have therapy the rest of her teen years."

"Hope I can make out your scribbling and remember all of this."

"You can't go by my notes. We'll have to role play until you get it down pat."

"When do we check up on Jennifer—I mean Heidi—to find out more about her?" Annette asked, reaching over to pad Jennifer's arm. She noticed that Jennifer was rubbing her stomach. "Is something wrong, honey?"

"My tummy hurts."

"Does it hurt like before?"

"Yes. But it hurts worse today."

"Why didn't you say something sooner?"

"I didn't want to worry you."

"Jennifer, if you feel sick, tell Mommy. We're right near a hospital. We could ask a doctor to look at you and also check on getting a copy of Heidi's birth certificate for identification."

"No!" Jennifer panicked. "I don't wanna see a doctor! They hurt people! The nasty people have doctors. They fixed people when Dark Raven hurt them! Please, please don't make me see a doctor!"

Annette knelt by Jennifer and put her arms around her. "Real doctors don't hurt people on purpose, honey. They help people and make them better."

Jennifer wouldn't budge. She stood her ground, and her body stiffened. "I don't wanna see a doctor! They hurt people! One of those men who poked me was doctor, and he hurt me bad!"

Another puzzle piece slipped into place. Not only had the Order of the Dark Raven sent someone to imitate Jennifer's mother to break that bond of trust, they also had medical pretenders, or genuine doctors like Blackwell, who performed despicable deeds.

Annette refused to encourage Jennifer's fear, regardless of its painful origin. "Jennifer," she said, touching her daughter's arm. "Mommy says you need a doctor."

Jennifer's defiance softened, then she abruptly threw her arms around Annette's neck. "OK, Mommy. I'll do it for you."

Half an hour later, Wes, Annette, and Jennifer stood in front of the largest hospital in South Chicago. A tall statue of the Catholic patron, St. Joseph, loomed above the entrance.

They stepped through the hospital's front door and walked up to a receptionist. "May I help you?" the woman at the counter asked.

"We'd like to see a doctor," Annette answered.

"Do you have an appointment?"

"No," Annette said. "But my daughter isn't feeling well, and I'm very worried about her."

The receptionist shuffled some papers on her desk and picked up the intercom. She made two calls, then replied, "Dr. Olinger can see you in an hour. Go back out the front door and around to the emergency entrance at the rear. Ask for him by name."

"Thanks," Wes said. "I'd also like to see about getting a copy of a birth certificate while we wait."

"That would be at our records division, down the hall to the right."

"Records division? Down the hall to the right?"

The receptionist nodded.

Wes thanked the woman, and the three of them started down the hall. Halfway down, Annette and Wes stopped and looked at each other. They hadn't discussed what to do next, and the situation was confusing. They were afraid of blowing the covers they'd pieced together. Annette grasped Wes's arm, pulled him toward her, and whispered, "What will we say when we get in there?"

Wes replied in a low voice, "Tell them that Heidi's mother, Estelle Hansen, lost Heidi's birth certificate when they were packing to leave for Mississippi. The elementary school in Mississippi requested proof of Heidi's age for enrollment. You're a friend, and Estelle called to see if you could pick up another copy."

When they got to the records room, Annette followed Wes's advice. The secretary was young and seemed distracted, so Annette hoped the girl's preoccupation would prevent her from asking too many questions.

"I don't know if it's OK to give out that information, except to a family member," the girl protested.

"But Estelle has no way of getting here from Mississippi. They have very little money. Can't you please do something?"

"All right," the girl said. "Let me check the files."

She soon returned with a record of Heidi Hansen's birth. "You'll need a certified copy if you want to use it for anything official. I can't get that now, but I can mail it. What is the Hansen address in Mississippi?"

Annette responded hesitantly, I don't know their new address. They didn't tell me. Could I pick it up in a few days so I can forward it to them?"

The young records keeper looked up for a moment, as if questioning what she was doing. Then she started writing on a piece of paper. "Well, it is a little irregular, but I'll make an exception."

When they finished in the records room, Wes, Annette, and Jennifer headed back out the front door to the emergency room. Like trauma centers at most big city hospitals, St. Joseph's emergency room bustled with activity. Every molded plastic chair in the cramped waiting room was filled. Many people seemed dazed from the pain of their wounds.

Occasional groans and muffled cries of pain issued from behind a wall of white curtains. This was no arena for minor afflictions. Gunshot and knife wounds and assorted physical trauma brought people here. Some were victims of crimes. Others had been involved in mundane chores when an errant saw, the careless swing of a hammer, or the screeching tires of a speeding automobile had interrupted their lives.

Doctors and nurses strode in and out of the waiting room, calling patients' names. They didn't lack compassion, but long hours of endless drama and human suffering had numbed them. Wes filled out the necessary forms, remembering the information he had garnered that day regarding Heidi Hansen. He hoped no one would access computer records that could reveal her real location beneath the grassy slopes of Pleasant Hill Cemetery.

"Heidi Hansen," a nurse called out, as she walked into the waiting room. "Dr. Olinger will see you now."

Jennifer didn't respond. Annette touched her leg and whispered, "Heidi, they're calling you!"

"Yes, ma'ma," Wes said, jumping to his feet to compensate for Jennifer's lack of response. "Where should we go?"

"Follow me down the hall. I'll put you in a room where you can wait for Dr. Olinger. He should be coming out of surgery any minute. Right now, we'll take you daughter's temperature."

"It's just a tummyache," Jennifer protested.

"There, there, young lady," the nurse said smiling, the first display of human warmth Wes had seen in the waiting room. "We have to follow a routine with every patient. You might have just a tummyache, but in this emergency ward nobody sees a doctor without the routine. Come on," the nurse said, taking Jennifer's hand. "Ben—Dr. Olinger—is a nice man. You'll like him."

The nurse directed them down a hallway to an austere examination room with light mauve, plastered walls. Jennifer sat on the one chair in the room, while Wes stood to one side. Annette leaned against an examination table covered with fresh white paper.

"I feel lots better, Mommy," Jennifer said. "I really don't need a doctor."

Annette tilted her head and frowned, wordlessly letting Jennifer know enough talk had been bantered about. Wes wasn't sure how thin the barren walls were, but every sound they made reverberated around the room. He put his index finger to his lips to hush Jennifer and Annette, the said quietly, "Let's not talk. It's best to stay real quiet while we wait for the doctor."

They waited a long time. Dr. Ben Olinger's surgery involved a motorcycle rider who had collided, helmetless, with a freight truck on the interstate, resulting in severe head lacerations, the nurse explained a half hour later."

"He's washing up now and should be here in a few minutes."

A short while later, a gray-haired man in a starched white coat entered the room. "Hi. I'm Dr. Ben. Who's Heidi?"

Annette quickly pointed to her daughter, taking no chance that Jennifer would forget her assumed identity.

"I want you to sit on this examination table, young lady. Come on! Hop right up here."

Jennifer grabbed both sides of the chair and hung on tightly. She turned her head aside, refusing to look at Dr. Olinger.

"What's this, Heidi? You don't want me to examine you" I've got three grandchildren of my own, and I raised two little girls. This is only going to take a few minutes. The nurse told me you have a tummyache. Maybe you had too many hot dogs, and you just need some ice cream," he said, smiling.

Jennifer peered at him suspiciously from wide eyes, then slowly stood up. Dr. Olinger took the opportunity to lift Jennifer onto the examining table. "How long's it been since Heidi's seen a doctor?" he asked, looking at Annette.

"It's been a while," Annette answered, buying time. "I don't know. Maybe a year or more."

"Well, then, I want to be more thorough. I'll only be five, ten minutes. I wonder if you two could step out of the room a moment?" he said to Wes and Annette. "Even though it's just a tummyache, I'd like to do a complete examination, including blood tests."

"We'll be right outside the door," Wes said.

Ten minutes passed, then fifteen, Wes and Annette glanced at each other with increasing apprehension.

Suddenly, a shriek pierced the plaster walls, jolting Annette to attention. She recognized Jennifer's voice.

"I'm going in there, Wes!"

Wes discreetly followed Annette into the examination room. Inside, Jennifer wildly flailed her arms and legs, screaming, "Don't touch me! Don't poke me! It hurts!"

Dr. Olinger was standing back from Jennifer, looking shocked and puzzled.

"Heidi, please calm down! I'm going to speak to your mother outside," He motioned Annette toward the door. Knowing Dr. Olinger wasn't going to touch her again, at least for the moment, Jennifer stopped screaming. Trembling, she drew her legs up until her knees met her chest.

Outside, Dr. Olinger beckoned for Wes and Annette to step down the hallway where Jennifer couldn't hear.

"You'll have to help me with Heidi. If there's pain or discomfort in her pelvic region, I should perform an internal examination. It's not uncommon for young girls to be sensitive about a gynecological examination, especially at her age, but Heidi's violent reaction is unusual. If you wish, I'll go no further. It's up to you. But it would be in the best interest of your daughter to proceed.

"If that's the way you feel, Dr. Olinger, I'll do what I can," Annette answered. "I've never seen Heidi like this, so I'm not sure what will happen."

Annette and Dr. Olinger returned to the examination room. Wes stayed outside, wondering what would happen next. He listened carefully and could hear the sounds of scuffling and muffled cries from Jennifer. Then everything grew quiet. Wes waited as the minutes multiplied. He paced the corridor until, finally, the door opened, and Annette walked out. Her face was ashen. Dr. Olinger followed her.

"I'm sorry," the doctor said. "I'll let you and your husband talk about it. After you decide what course of action to follow, I'll meet you in my office, Room 6-A, at the end of the hallway."

Annette watched Dr. Olinger walk away. She seemed immobilized. Wes expected her to turn around and walk toward him. She didn't. The echo of Dr. Olinger's footsteps grew faint as he proceeded down the long hallway. Finally, Wes stepped behind Annette and gently placed his hands on her arms. Annette stiffened, then slowly turned, her cross held tightly in her right fist. She looked at Wes with tear-filled eyes, and collapsed against his chest, sobbing. Holding her tightly, Wes let her cry out her pain and fear.

Eventually, Annette stifled her sobbing and blew her nose on Wes's handkerchief. "Wes," Annette said, looking up at him, "Jennifer's g-g-got . . ." Annette broke down again, her chest heaving. From deep within, she drew the strength to tell Wes, "Jennifer has gonorrhea."

If he hadn't been comforting Annette, Wes's own knees might have buckled. He held Annette while they both tried to assimilate what the illness might mean to a nine-year-old child's physical and emotional health. Then he led her to a chair in the hallway and gently pushed her into it. He knelt by the side of the chair, speaking the only words he knew at that moment: "I'm sorry."

Through her tears, Annette went on. "That's not all. Dr. Olinger says Jennifer has been vaginally mutilated. He first noticed bruising on her breasts and the scars of small holes on various parts of her body. The holes were in twos, side by side. Wes, they *were* snakebites."

Wes buried his face in his hands. If he'd had a gun at that moment, he'd have killed Dr. Blackwell, Sheriff Hancock, and all their kind. He wanted to scream, but Annette needed his support, not his anger.

"Dr. Olinger says the mutilation in the vaginal area is so bad Jennifer may need surgery. She also has anal damage, but he's not sure yet what to do about that. He doesn't want to complete the examination unless she's under an anesthetic. He did put a few stitched in her shoulder wounds. They were deeper than I thought."

A muffled groan rose from deep within Annette's throat. "This is all a bad dream, isn't it?" She cried. "No one could be so evil! No one could do that, could they?"

Again, that hazy vision of a caged child and shadowy figures performing despicable acts returned to Wes's mind. But sexual torture?

"Wes," Annette said through her tears, "the doctor wants to admit Jennifer to the hospital as soon as possible and begin tests. I'm afraid to leave her alone. What if Dr. Olinger is like that Dr. Blackwell? What if the nurses are part of this Order you talk about? Suppose this is a plot to torment Jennifer further? Wes, I can't think!"

Wes felt Annette's paranoia. He knew he had to help her make a wise choice, but he had never had to make decisions that profoundly affected other people's lives. It was one thing to give off-the-cuff comments about politics or religion during a talk show, but nobody took that seriously. Now, his decisions would affect the child's mind the rest of her life—and his own, as well.

Sixteen

"I'm Michelle Milthorpe," said a nurse whose silver-streaked dark blonde hair was pulled back and covered at the ends by a nurse's cap and veil, which Wes assumed was the appropriate dress for a nurse in a Catholic hospital. "Dr. Olinger asked me to keep an eye on your daughter while you talk with him," she added, smiling kindly.

Wes and Annette hadn't noticed the nurse walk up. Her crepe-soled shoes had cushioned the sound of her arrival, but they probably wouldn't have noticed anyway. Both were too befuddled about what to do next.

Nurse Milthorpe's soft blue eyes instantly set them at ease. She was a handsome woman in her early fifties, with strong features and a smile that projected confidence and strength. She waited politely for a response.

"Thank you," Annette said. "We'll speak with Dr. Olinger in a moment."

"Take your time," Nurse Milthorpe said. "I have some books I'm sure will interest your daughter. We'll have a nice visit. I'll take her to a more comfortable waiting room just around the corner. What's her name?"

"Jen . . . *Heidi*," Annette said, correcting herself.

"Come on," Wes said. "We can't put off talking to Dr. Olinger forever." As he turned to walk to Dr. Olinger's office, it occurred to Wes that he should have been more apprehensive about Nurse Milthorpe, but something about her allayed his fears.

Annette walked slowly down the hallway, leaning against Wes and looking as if she would fall down if he miscued one step sideways. Wes knocked on the door marked 6-A, and Dr. Olinger let them in.

Like everything else at St. Joseph's Hospital, his office was sparsely furnished. A single plaque hung on the wall behind the doctor, signaling his graduation form Loyola University, School of Medicine. A crucifix adorned the wall across from his desk. He sat behind a battered steel-framed desk in a faded tan leather chair frayed at the top where it met his back. Dr. Olinger rested his elbows on the chrome arms and folded his hands together with his braced index fingers pointed upward. He nervously moved them back and forth. As he tilted his head down, his lips almost touched his gesticulating fingers. Annette and Wes waited for him to speak.

"I know this isn't going to be easy. I wish I could blunt the seriousness of the situation, but I can't. Please understand, too, that several laws govern how I approach this predicament."

Wes narrowed his eyes and looked intently at Dr. Olinger. "What do you mean?"

"Medical ethics—and the law—mandate that any time a sexually transmitted infection is found in a pre-pubertal child, it must be considered evidence of sexual abuse until proven otherwise. Nonsexual transmission of sexually transmitted pathogens is extremely rare in children. Our hospital also has policies requiring a psychological examination of the victim, in addition to whatever medical treatment is needed."

Dr. Olinger tilted back in his chair, unfolded his hands, and gestured with his open palms toward them to ease the tension. "I have our lab run a fast analysis on the smear I took from Heidi's vagina, and it confirms what I suspected—the presence of gonorrhea. But generally, if there's one sexually transmitted disease, others coexist. We must do a full battery of tests—laboratory studies, urinalysis, wet mounts of cervical discharge, and cultures of the rectum. Once we identify all the existing STDs—sexually-transmitted diseases— we'll attempt to identify the carrier. I'm also concerned about the obvious physical abuse because to the bruises I saw and the shoulder wounds I stitched."

The emotional impact of Dr. Olinger's words fell like hammer blows. Wes and Annette sat dejectedly, as if the doctor were a judge pronouncing a horrible penalty.

Dr. Olinger had averted his head, feeling equally uncomfortable. He peered from underneath his eyebrows and set his gaze on Wes. "The most pointed question I have to ask is for you, the child's father. You can lie to me, but you'll endanger Heidi's life if you do." Dr. Olinger took a deep breath, rested his elbows again on the arms of the chair, and refolded his hands, his index fingers nervously twitching again. "Have you sexually abused your child?"

Wes had acted behind the microphone many times: false bravado in the face of an antagonistic caller; gut-wrenching empathy when hearing a tale of human woe; outrage at an injustice; feigned shock upon hearing something he was not expected to know. Now, he not only had to pretend he was Heidi's father, he also had to seem indignant about the accusation against him. Wes straightened in his chair, threw back his shoulders, and gripped the armrest. With a tinge of shock and a full measure of disgust, he stared at Dr. Olinger and said, "I understand why you have to ask that question. The answer is *no*."

Without hesitation, Dr. Olinger replied, "Do you have any idea who might have molested Heidi?"

Wes fought to keep his face expressionless, though his gut was churning. *Of course, I know—well, not exactly, maybe not which specific member of the Order infected Jennifer,* Wes thought. "I have no idea," Wes said, shaking his head.

"Neither do I," Annette added, through silent tears.

"The tests and surgery are expensive," Dr. Olinger pointed out. "Do you have insurance?"

"No," Wes responded.

"We do have a public assistance credit program you can apply for. The nurse can tell you all about it, if you like."

"Thank you," Annette said. "I'm sure it will be helpful." She paused for a moment, then looked straight into the doctor's eyes. "What does all of this mean? How serious is a sexual disease in a child Heidi's age?"

"It depends on the response of her immune system, which determines how quickly she will respond to treatment," Dr. Olinger answered. "I can give you more details later. You're both too shocked now to understand a lot of technical information."

Dr. Olinger arose and stepped around the side of his desk, looking at Wes empathetically. Then he moved to the door and opened it for them. "I hope you decide quickly about further treatment. If Heidi suddenly complains of extreme pain in the cervical region, please bring her to the emergency room immediately and ask for me. I'm sorry I can't stay with you longer. If you'll excuse me . . ."

Wes and Annette thanked the doctor for his help and stepped into the hallway. "Well, this settles one thing. I have to go back to Clarion," Wes said.

Annette looked stunned. She hadn't anticipated Wes's leaving, certainly not at this time.

"I know there's no worse time for me to leave, but if Jennifer needs intensive medical treatment, I've got to make some money. Going back to 'Talk about Town' is the quickest way to do it—if the boss will let me have my job back."

"It's not safe back there! I won't let you do it," Annette protested. "Jennifer needs you. I need you!" she said, eyes brimming with tears.

Wes hadn't heard those words in years, especially from a woman. A lump came to his throat as he realized Annette meant what she said. Annette needed him emotionally. "Talk about Town" brought fame and notoriety, but with a price. At times, Wes felt like a prostitute. He felt used—used to sell advertising, used to dispense opinions, used to say what others wouldn't or couldn't.

Going back to Clarion would be a double whammy. It meant leaving Annette and Jennifer alone to live their assumed identities and survive by their wits. It also meant risking his own life, even thought the Order seemed reluctant to do him in. It also raised serious questions about the triumph of good over evil. The Reverend James Carmichael and Larry Bender were dead because of their association with him. Though he found it hard to accept, it appeared that evil was winning.

Still, Jennifer had been rescued, and Annette no longer lay drugged and incoherent in that hospital. If Wes was going to question the evil around him, wasn't he obligated to acknowledge credit for the goodness he had experienced? Who was he to pass judgment on what God did or did not do? Wes concluded his philosophical debate by turning his attention back to the current problem. He was nearly broke and had no money to cover Jennifer's medical costs. Returning to Clarion wasn't an option; it was a necessity. He had to get in the car and drive south, back to hell.

Still reeling from the shock of hearing about Jennifer's condition, Wes and Annette walked in silence to the room where earlier they had seen Nurse Milthorpe take Jennifer. As they eased the door open, they saw Jennifer and the nurse seated on an old sofa with numerous colored pictures lying between them.

"Have you been drawing some pictures for Mommy?" Annette asked.

"Yes, Nurse Mil . . . Milthor . . . Oh, I can't say it right."

"Mil-thorpe," the nurse said slowly.

"Mil-thorpe," Jennifer mimicked. "She gave me some paper and crayons and asked be to draw whatever I liked. This one's for you, Mommy," she said, handing Annette what appeared to be clouds floating over patches of green with creatures resembling cows and horses.

"Thank you. It's beautiful. I'll treasure it forever," Annette said, folding the picture and placing it in her purse. She turned to the nurse. "It's very thoughtful of you to spend such special time with Heidi."

Nurse Milthorpe blushed and accepted the compliment. "It's your daughter who's special, and she needs some very special care."

"What's this?" Wes inquired, motioning to another stack of pictures Jennifer had drawn.

"Nothing," Jennifer replied. "Just some drawings of things I think about a lot. Nurse Mil . . . Milthorpe asked me to draw whatever was in my head."

Wes picked up the sketches and held them where Annette could see, as he thumbed through them. They depicted strange scenes of stick figures arranged in triangular patterns. Other scenes portrayed what appeared to be red blood and tears mixed with mountains and trees he recognized as the Mounds of the Elders. He fingered the curled edges of the paper and noticed that Jennifer had drawn so hard and furiously in certain places that the paper was torn and deeply etched in color. His eyes unexpectedly misted over, and he quickly wiped away the tears.

Taking a deep breath, Wes turned to Annette. "Tell Heidi about the 'visits' we're arranging for her and Nurse Milthorpe."

Annette nodded and looked at her daughter. "Dr. Olinger wants to start helping your tummyache as soon as we can."

Jennifer hesitated, then glanced out of the corner of her eye at Nurse Milthorpe. "Will I be with her all the time?"

Annette looked at Nurse Milthorpe. "Will that be possible?"

"By all means. I work exclusively for Dr. Ben."

Until that moment, Wes hadn't realized what a somber child Jennifer was. *I've never seen her smile, not the way she's smiling now,* he thought. *Those drawings have released something inside her.*

"Can we do more drawings together?" Jennifer asked Nurse Milthorpe.

"Of course, Heidi." The nurse got to her feet and leaned over to brush back the hair from Jennifer's forehead "I'm glad I made a friend," she said. "Remember, Heidi, friends always care and love you. They never make you hurt."

Wes reached down and took Jennifer's hand in his and smiled at Nurse Milthorpe. "Thank you again. You've obviously made a big impact on Heidi. We'll look forward to seeing you again."

The nurse smiled back at Wes and walked to the door, watching as the unlikely trio faded down the corridor. As the three of them left the hospital, Wes picked up the evening edition of the paper at a newsstand and thumbed through it.

Suddenly, spreading the newspaper wide to the lifestyles section, he yelled, "Annette! Look at that headline! DARCY LINMORE, THREATENED WITH COURT ACTION FOR ASSISTING UNDER-GROUND MOTHERS."

While Jennifer looked in a nearby store window filled with electronic games, Wes and Annette read the article with wonder and disbelief.

> A 37-year-old Chicago area woman, Darcy Linmore, threatened with legal action by the District Attorney's office, continues her efforts to shelter women who are fugitives from custodial cases involving child abuse.
>
> Mrs. Linmore's quest took a step backward last week when a district court judge ruled she would have to stand trial for assisting a Wheaton, Illinois, woman escape with her child. Four months ago, the Wheaton woman had claimed her ex-husband was sexually abusing their daughter. Authorities now believe Darcy Linmore is hiding the mother and daughter.
>
> Ten years ago, Mrs. Linmore divorced her husband and testified in court that her daughter was a victim of incest. The judge insisted there was insufficient evidence to prevent Mrs. Linmore's ex-husband from seeing the child. Mrs. Linmore took the child into hiding for two years. During that time, her ex-husband was arrested in another state for child molestation.
>
> "If the courts had listened to me in the first place, other innocent children would not have been abused," Mrs. Linmore says.
>
> Darcy Linmore admitted leading weekly support groups at a clandestine location. Women interested in further information should call 555-1200.

"Are you thinking what I'm thinking?" Wes asked exuberantly. Annette nodded her head. "There's a pay phone at the next corner. Let's go!"

Wes quickened his pace, and Annette grabbed Jennifer's hand as they followed him.

"Wes, do you really think they might be able to help us? This isn't a custody or a divorce situation."

"The article said they shelter women and children in dire circumstances, didn't it?" Wes answered. "I think you and Jennifer qualify! Even if they can't help, we have to give it a try. Maybe they can point us in the right direction."

Annette tugged at Jennifer to hurry along. As the pay phone came into sight, they were out of breath from their haste and the anticipation of contacting Darcy Linmore.

When Wes got to the phone booth, he hurriedly dialed the number in the newspaper. A woman's soft voice answered.

"Mrs. Linmore?"

"Who's calling?"

"I read the article in today's newspaper about the work of Darcy Linmore. How do we talk to her? We need to know more."

"Who's 'we'? Who are you?"

"A friend of a woman whose child has been abused. Please meet with us! We've got to talk with you."

"Our support group meets tonight. But I have no idea who you are," said the voice on the phone. "You can attend under certain circumstances. Tell me where you are, and someone will meet you there. You'll have to be blindfolded on your way to the meeting site. Who's coming with you?"

"My friend, the woman I mentioned." Wes paused, realizing they couldn't leave Jennifer alone. "Can we bring her daughter too? We have nowhere to leave her."

"Normally, we discourage bringing children to our meetings, but I suppose someone could look after her. You name the place. A four-door, silver-colored Honda will pick you up at 6:30."

"How about the corner of Calhoun and Ogden in South Chicago? I'll wear a tan overcoat. There will be three of us. The little girl is nine."

"We'll be there. Remember, 6:30. A four-door, silver Honda."

"Got it," Wes said, hanging up the receiver. He stepped from the phone booth, looked at Annette, and heaved a sigh of relief. "I have no idea what we're in for, but now I know we're not alone."

Seventeen

Everyone in South Chicago knew the corner of Calhoun and Ogden. Three years ago, an ambulance on an emergency run had collided with a station wagon and killed a family of four. The intersection had been excellent for retail store outlets, but people were sensitive, even superstitious, about the tragedy. The liquor store, dry cleaners, automotive supply shop, and dress shop that had operated profitably here were vacant and boarded up. Wes felt spooky about being there with Annette and Jennifer.

Hosting "Talk about Town" had taught Wes to be wary of newspaper reporters. What people read in the papers and what they heard on radio and television often didn't resemble reality. *What if Darcy Linmore isn't who she says she is and our lives are endangered?* Wes wondered. Still, he had to believe that the *Tribune* reporter who had interviewed Darcy Linmore had done his homework.

Wes grew edgy as 6:30 arrived and no silver, four-door Honda appeared. By 6:40, Wes concluded Mrs. Linmore had decided she wanted no part of his problem. He had almost decided to go back to the apartment when a silver, four-door Honda with tinted windows turned the corner of Ogden and pulled to the curb. Wes leaned over and squinted, trying to identify the occupants. The back door flew open, and a voice shouted, "Get in! Quickly!" Wes held the door and motioned to Jennifer and Annette to enter, then followed them. They crammed themselves into the back seat. In the darkness, Wes couldn't see the faces of the driver and his passenger.

"Put these on," the female passenger said. Over her shoulder, she handed Wes three pairs of eyeshades, the kind sold in drug stores for insomniacs. Wes held them a moment, questioning again the sanity of following this bizarre plan. The woman said sharply. "Put them on if you're coming with us. If not, get out of the car."

Wes gave two of the eyeshades to Annette, indicating for her to put one on Jennifer. Jennifer sat calmly while Annette slipped the covering over her eyes, then donned the second on herself. After they were securely blindfolded, the Honda drove off.

No one spoke for a while, finally, the woman in front said, "I'm sorry we have to treat you this way, but you could be a police officer or, worse, someone sent to infiltrate our group. The safety of many mothers and their children is at stake. We can't take chances."

Minutes passed in silence. The car turned every few blocks, probably, Wes surmised, to elude anyone who might try to follow them.

"Is your case a custodial one?" the gruff-voiced driver asked.

"Not like a divorce decree, if that's what you mean," Wes answered as he vaguely explained their situation in terse statements, still suspicious of their escorts. Silence followed for ten or fifteen minutes, then the car stopped.

"You'll have to leave the blindfolds on until you're inside. We'll lead you by the hands and give you an idea of where you're stepping. Don't worry, we'll make sure you don't fall. I'll take the little girl's hand on my left and her mother on my right," the female passenger said. "You'll be led by the driver," she added, touching Wes on the arm.

The three blindfolded passengers waited until they could hear the back doors opening. Hands reached in for them. After they walked forty or fifty feet, a screen door opened, then the main door, and moments later they were inside. They were led down a short corridor and through a doorway, then seated on a couch. "The light will seem too bright when the blindfolds come off, so you might want to cover your eyes," the female passenger said.

One by one, the blindfolds were removed.

Wes rubbed his eyes and squinted, adjusting to the brightness. They were in a small, unpretentious room with a couch, two easy chairs, a coffee table, and an old portable black-and-white television sitting on a stand in the corner. Next to the wall opposite them was a sewing machine with a chair in front of it. An ironing board held a stack of clothes. The opposite wall sported an oil painting of mountain peaks, the kind of mass-produced art found at starving artists' fairs.

"I'm Darcy Linmore," said the woman standing in front of them. "Welcome to our support group, 'Believe the Victims.' Before we join the others, I want to get more information about you. A friend of mine will take care of your little girl while we talk."

Darcy Linmore pushed open the door and soon returned with her friend, Michelle Milthorpe. Jennifer squealed delightedly and ran to her outstretched arms. Unaware of the extraordinary circumstances of this reunion. Darcy exclaimed, "I can see you two will get along famously!"

At first, Annette and Wes looked at each other in shock, too stunned to speak. Then Annette said, "I must admit it's a little mind-boggling seeing you again today, but a pleasant surprise."

Nurse Milthorpe smiled, then took Jennifer by the hand and led her out of the room. Darcy turned to Wes and Annette. "We'll help if we can, but we need to know some facts. If you don't feel comfortable telling me something, that's OK. But the more you share, the more we can help."

Mrs. Linmore's relaxed smile put "Annette and Wes at ease. Wes admitted who he was and how he had come to know Jennifer and Annette, whom he referred to by their assumed names. He skirted details about he Order but told Darcy Linmore enough to let her know that Jennifer had been physically and sexually abused. The longer he spoke, the more Darcy Linmore's eyes flashed with anger. She had heard similar stories, Wes knew, but familiarity with abuse hadn't dulled her empathy.

When Wes finished, Darcy knelt directly opposite them and took Annette's hand in hers. Tears formed in her eyes and trickled down her cheeks. "You're not alone," she said, reaching into the pocket of her full skirt for a tissue. "Let's go meet the others."

She put an arm around Annette, directing her and Wes down a short hallway to a larger room, where three women sat on metal folding chairs arranged in a U-shape. A man stood behind the woman in the center chair.

Darcy led Wes and Annette to overstuffed chairs that faced the three women seated on the opposite side of the room. Annette sank into the center easy chair, while Darcy sat on her left. Wes eased himself into an old green plaid chair to Annette's right so that they formed a loose circle with the people across from them.

Darcy said, "Let me introduce you to the people here. They're all using pseudonyms because they feel safer not giving their real names. That's Marie on the left," she said, pointing to a petite brunette in her late twenties.

"Next to her is Isabel." A woman who seemed to be in her early forties, with coal-black hair and dark, piercing eyes, smiled at them.

"Behind Isabel is her boyfriend, Angelo." Angelo, a man whose rough hands and strong build indicated he was a laborer, nodded his head and smiled at Wes.

"On the right is Roberta. If you don't mind, Roberta, we'd like to hear from you first," Darcy said.

A slim, plain woman with reddish-blond hair, Roberta cleared her throat, put her hands on her knees, and straightened her back. She wore no makeup, which accented her tired, worn look. She started to speak, but her lips quivered and she seemed to be afraid of losing control. She reached into her long hair and twisted a strand around her index finger. Finally, she spoke.

"It's hard to know where to begin. The last five years have been such a nightmare that it's hard to make sense out of my life. I suppose the best place to start is the night I walked into my six-year-old daughter's bedroom and saw all her dolls and toys arranged in a circle. She sat in the center. I'd never seen her do thats. She said it was so they'd all be safe."

Roberta clutched her throat, as if choking off pain that rose from deep inside. Isabel reached over and squeezed her hand. "Sometimes I wish I had never seen that arrangement of toys. Maybe it would have been better for everyone if the secret had been kept, "Roberta said, shaking her head in woeful frustration.

She continued, "My little girl started telling me about animals some people killed in front of her, rabbits, and kittens. They warned her that, if she ever told anyone, the same thing would happen to her. When I told my husband, he said he'd help me find out who was tormenting our child. My naivete' prolonged the suffering, because I thought he was on my side. Not until my little girl told me she had to kiss her daddy's . . ." Roberta choked and then began to weep softly. Isabel moved her chair closer to Roberta and put her arm around Roberta's shoulders until she stopped crying.

"Nobody believed me, not even my parents. My husband gave me a divorce, but by the time the custody case got to court, I was a nervous wreck. The judge ruled that I was an unfit mother. Dan, my husband, had all kinds of important people testifying on his behalf. He was awarded custody of my daughter. All I got were weekend visitation rights. But after what I'd been through, I determined that the first weekend I saw her would be the last he ever had her." Traces of anger crept into Roberta's voice as she fought to maintain control.

"You can stop if you'd like, Roberta," Darcy interrupted. "I know this is difficult for you."

"No, I want to go on. I've never told the whole story, and I need to now," Roberta replied. "There are some things I have to say." Roberta put her hands back on her knees and straightened again, summoning strength to continue. "When I ran off with my daughter, I had no idea where to go. We packed a few belongings in suitcases and paper bags and left in the middle of the night. The divorce hadn't left me with much, but I gave up what I had to protect my child. That was six months ago, and to this day I don't know whether I'm a saint or a sinner for what I did. At times I feel as if my whole life is a lie. Then, I remind myself I'm saving my child."

Roberta was interrupted by the sound of a door swinging open. Michelle Milthorpe walked into the room with a pot of coffee in one hand and several cups in the other, her fingers hooked through the cups' handles. "Thought you'd like something to drink while you're talking," she said. "If you're not coffee drinkers, there are soft drinks in the refrigerator."

Michelle set the pot and cups on a small table at one end of the room. I'll be right back with more coffee cups."

Everyone moved slightly in their chairs and breathed deeply to break the tension in the room.

The Roberta continued. "I had no idea what my daughter had been through, so I didn't know what to expect. She developed a stuttering pattern and started sucking her thumb. At one point, I had to put her back in diapers. Nights are the worst. It's more than her sleeplessness; it's the nightmares. Sometimes, she wakes up screaming. Other times, she talks in her sleep, dreaming about rituals they put her through. When she finally wakes up, it's hours before she'll go to sleep again. During the daytime, I have to worry about the triggers."

Darcy noticed Wes's puzzlement and said, "Let me jump in for a minute and explain a trigger. It's something an abuser plants in a child's mind. Some abusers convince a child he's got a bomb inside him, that it will go off if the child tattles. So when he thinks about telling what he's been through, his heart starts pounding, he begins sweating, and he thinks a bomb is going to explode inside him. There are other triggers. Some groups perform 'magical surgery.'

"They put the child to sleep by drugging him," Darcy explained. "To the child, it's like an anesthetic. They may scratch the child's stomach or cut him a little. When the child awakens, they show him the scar and claim it's from an operation. Cult members often convince a victim that an evil heart has been put into him. That way, the child thinks he'll always be bad, that he doesn't dare do anything about the abuse."

"Are there other kinds of triggers?" Wes asked.

"Yes, several we know about. The child may be told that his stuffed animals will spy on him. Kids can be programmed to believe that someone secretly watches them, like anyone in a blue dress or every green car that drives by. Another trigger tactic is to have the abuser dress in a professional uniform. One victim told me that a man in the group wearing a policeman's uniform killed a baby. She still isn't sure if he really was a policeman, but for years she was terrified of the law. That's why she didn't go for help, even after she got free."

Nurse Milthorpe entered the room and put down several more cups on the table. Darcy poured coffee for Roberta, who encircled the steaming cup in her hands, as though warding off an evil chill. Angelo got cups for Isabel and himself, and Wes did the same for Annette.

Roberta lifted her head and continued talking. "What angers me most is the way they manipulated my daughter's mind. These abusers are experts at mind control. They made her feel so dirty and worthless, she wanted to die. She actually asked me to kill her a couple of time, like they killed the baby rabbits."

Roberta clenched her fists until the muscles and veins of her arms distended. Darcy reached for the coffee cup that Roberta had set down in frustration and anger and offered it to her. Roberta sipped the steaming liquid and said, "We tell our children to obey their parents. I always did, anyway. Didn't you?" she asked.

Marie, Isabel, and Annette nodded.

"And yet, they twist that into brainwashing. My daughter thought she was being a good girl by obeying her daddy, and yet she knew it was evil and horrible. Even today, she seems confused about loving her daddy and doing what he wanted and feeling guilty that she didn't tell me what was going on . . . my daughter, my own flesh and blood! I've spent the last six months trying to rebuild her respect and trust in me."

Wes looked at Annette, and his eyes said, "We've finally found some people who understand, some people we can trust." Annette nodded in agreement.

"People have been very kind," Roberta said. "Some knew I had no job resume. They hired me to do household chores. I think some of them sensed the strangeness of my situation, but they knew I loved my daughter. I guess they felt that whatever was going on was my business. Still, it's tough being a criminal and knowing I can't run forever, that sometime, somewhere, I'm going to get caught. Still, every day in hiding is one more day my ex-husband can't sexually abuse my daughter," she said firmly.

"Why don't you take a break?" Darcy said. "I know you have more to tell us, Roberta. You've been very brave to go this far, very brave. Isabel, do you want to share your story?"

Isabel nodded as Marie and Roberta on either side of her took her hands in a gesture of solidarity. Angelo, still standing behind her with his hands on her shoulders, squeezed her gently in encouragement.

"My perspective is a little different," Isabel said. "I'm a victim. Both my parents were part of an organized, generational cult that abused me as a child. That was more than twenty years ago when no one knew much about this kind of thing. Thank God for people like you, Darcy," she said. "You give people like me the courage to come out of our closets and speak the unspeakable."

Darcy Linmore nodded her head to acknowledge Isabel's compliment. "I only wish I could do more," she muttered.

"I'd like you all to understand," Isabel said, "that a child who has been ritually abused develops a false sense of reality. My parents' group killed babies. I saw some of them skinned alive. Now, I hope that they were just dolls. I thought they were live babies at the time, and the terror was real enough. Most of it was done by candlelight, and I was always given drugs. Those people were good at knowing what kind of drugs to use. I didn't hallucinate. They wanted me to see what was happening, but my senses were so dulled that it was hard to understand what was real and what wasn't.

"At times, the floors or the walls seemed to move. I don't know whether it was the drugs or a way they manipulated what I saw. All I know is that it created confusion. Imagine! I couldn't even trust the floor I was standing on or the walls of the room.

"But the worst distortion was the way they handled spiritual matters. They convinced me that God had abandoned me. After all, my own parents were tormenting me. They said Satan owned me and that, if I gave my soul to him, I would grow up to be a powerful person, like them. I would also have control over other people. It's a crazy way of twisting the mind. You know you're being abused, but they convince you the way out is to get even with other people someday by abusing *them*."

Wes touched Annette's arm and leaned over to whisper, "Are you all right? We can leave any time, you know." Annette squeezed his hand to let him know she wanted to stay.

"You said something about our group being generational. Could you explain?" Wes asked.

"Yes, of course. That's the kind of group that goes back for generations, sometimes centuries," Darcy explained. "Usually, it's within a single family and maybe passed on to a son or daughter. In some cases, the grandparents as well as the parents are involved in the abuse."

Wes thought, *generational! That explains Gregory's parents. They all must have been part of the Order.*

"To this day, not even my therapist knows everything that happened," Isabel explained. "Little by little, more keeps coming out through my multiple personalities. I have a tendency to split emotionally, disassociate into one of my alters—when the most gruesome details about my past surface. You see, that's how I had to cope as a child. I pretended what happened wasn't real. I crawled inside myself and hid. Sometimes, I pretended I belonged to another family and removed myself from whatever situation I was in. My abusers may have forced my body to participate, but my mind wasn't there."

That must be what Jennifer is doing. Wes thought. He remembered the two shifts in her personality at the apartment. One had been submissive and almost adult in desire, and the other a rage against Annette. *Jennifer's mind is fighting to save her sanity. It's hiding the Order's perversion deep in her subconscious.*

"Teachers were amazed at my math skills," Isabel continued. "They didn't know it was a way for me to cope. When I was seven, I knew the multiplication tables, because I would do them over and over again in my mind when they were torturing me. It was a way of disassociating, and it helped me survive."

Isabel closed her eyes and leaned back in her chair. Everyone sensed the conversation was becoming difficult for her so Darcy turned to Marie. "You're new to our group, Marie. Since this is only your second time here, we don't know much about you situation yet. I don't want to push you, but it might be good for you to talk about what happened."

"I'll do my best," Marie said quietly. "I'm not very good at expressing myself." The small young woman took a sip of her coffee and then set the cup on the floor beside her. "My daughter's abuse pretty much runs the gamut. Cannibalism, baby killing, indescribable torture. They ate the flesh of sacrifices. They killed babies. Sometimes, they kept fetuses in bottles to display their grisly preoccupation with slaughtering the innocent. The leader of the group had a strange name. They called him Ravensky."

Annette jolted backward as if an electric shock had struck her. Trembling, she rose slowly to her feet and walked to the other room where she threw herself face down on the couch, muffling sobs of anguish in the cushions. Wes followed her and stood helplessly, wondering what Marie had said to affect her so profoundly. Wes sat down on a corner of the couch and gently touched her back. Slowly, she pulled herself upright. She looked at Wes, tears streaming down her cheeks.

Eighteen

Darcy entered the room and knelt by the couch where Annette was sitting. "If what Marie said was too traumatic, it's all right if you leave now," she said.

Annette shook her head. "No. I need to hear the rest of what Marie has to say. I'll be OK."

Darcy put her hand on Annette's. Then she continued, "The purpose of this evening is to heal. You can't process these things quickly. I know you're anxious to find out everything you can about your daughter, but your emotional health is at stake too," Darcy advised. "These situations are often harder on the parent than the child. Your daughter is used to being abused. You're not. Before she can experience emotional healing, you'll have to work through the pain she suffered. That begins with accepting what happened, not just intellectually, but emotionally as well."

Darcy eased herself up from her knees by the couch and sat down next to Annette. "I know what's going through your mind right now because I've been there. You want to crawl inside yourself and deny it. When I first found out what my husband was doing to my child, I would go into my bedroom and turn up the radio as loud as I could to drown out my sobbing. Sometimes I'd be eating with my daughter and thoughts of the horrible things she went through would flash through my mind, and I'd have to excuse myself and go to the bathroom to throw up. One of the therapists we work with told me that mothers like us go through something similar to the post-traumatic stress syndrome war veterans suffer. In a way, they're right. We've been victimized as much as our children."

Darcy reached into her pocked for a tissue and handed it to Annette to blow her nose and dry her tears. "I keep these handy," She said, smiling. "A lot of crying goes on in our support groups." Darcy stood up to leave. "I'll go back with the others and chat for a few moments until you're ready to come back. One more thing. Don't let your mind get carried away. I know that mental images of what your daughter endured flash through your thoughts. At times, you wonder if you're blowing it out of proportion or if those images can capture the full extent of the horror. That kind of speculation will hurt you. You'll never know everything that happened, so don't try to visualize it. Above all, remember that "Believe the Victims" will always be here when you need us."

Darcy left the room. Annette turned to Wes and said, "I'm glad we came here tonight. This is very painful for me. If you go back to Clarion, I'm going to need these people."

Annette blew her nose again, stood up, and tightly clasped Wes's hand as they walked back to the room where the others were. When they stepped inside, Marie rose and hugged Annette. "I don't know what upset you," she said, "But whatever it was, I'm sorry."

"You have nothing to be sorry about," Annette said. "Right now, we all need to hear your story. Please don't hold anything back because of me."

Annette and Marie smiled at each other. They all resumed their respective places. "When you feel comfortable, Marie, please continue your story," Darcy said.

Marie crossed her legs and tugged her skirt over her knees, fumbling with the slit in the hemline. "My daughter is ten now," she said. "I discovered the abuse two years ago. Ironically, it was a Sunday morning. My husband never went to church and seldom let me take our daughter. He said things were too hectic during the week, and he wanted to spend quality time with her. I insisted it was important for her to get a religious education, but he said no, he'd tell her Bible stories, which would be better coming from her father. Then one Sunday morning, I got sick and had to leave the service early. There was a strange car in our driveway, a cream-colored late model Ford.

"The front door was locked when I got home. We never locked the door to our home. We probably should have, but my husband and I grew up in rural Illinois where you never locked your front door, at least not when somebody was home. I thought it was strange and rang the doorbell several times. Finally, my husband came to the door. He was angry that I was there. Inside, he introduced me to a tall blonde-haired man he called Albert."

Annette gripped Wes's hand so tightly that her fingernails dug into his palm. He could feel the muscles in her arm growing tense.

"I asked where my daughter was—let's just call her Melody. He said Melody was asleep. That was strange, since the whole idea of them being home was to spend time together. I didn't pay much attention to the guy named Albert. I went straight to Melody's bedroom. I tried to awaken her and could barely get her attention. He body was limp, and she didn't get up until the middle of the afternoon. Even then, she was groggy. I suspected she was drugged.

"My husband and I didn't have a good marriage. We didn't communicate well at all. I decided not to talk about what happened, just bide my time and watch. Then one night several months later, while my husband was away on a business trip, the truth started coming out."

Marie took several sips of coffee, savoring each mouthful. Wes knew she wanted to tell the others what Melody had revealed that night her husband was out of town, but on another level, she probably wanted to keep it a secret, as if doing so would lessen its credibility.

Slowly, she continued. "I don't know why Melody started talking that night. Perhaps she was so full of torment that she had to break the silence. She described being burned with candles, having hot and cold water thrown on her alternately, being dragged out of bed in the middle of the night and taken to cemeteries. I wanted to believe she was making it all up. But no child could dream up what she told me, like being locked in closets, hung upside-down, and put in cages with snakes."

Again, Wes saw the innocent long-haired child reaching out to him in the moonlight. The mental picture became clearer until he could vividly see the cage and the snakes writhing in it.

Marie went on. "I know this is hard to believe, but Melody said she saw people killed. Afterward, the bodies disappeared. She said they were put in big tunnel, very hot. It must have been a crematorium or kiln of some sort." Marie paused, then said, "I want to tell about the worst thing Melody went through, but I'm not sure I should."

"You can say as much or as little as you want," Darcy said. "There are no rules here. If you want to hold some thing back, that's OK. Remember, we're listening, not judging."

Marie smiled her thanks to Darcy, but she continued to play with the slit in her skirt, nervously rubbing the edges of the fabric. "I need to talk. I need it as much as Melody did."

"One night, Albert, the man I had seen in the house that Sunday, told Melody that either she or another little girl her age would have to die. Both of them were handed knives, but neither would strike out against the other. So they were punished. She described being thrown into a pit with snakes and the remains of animals they'd killed. Melody even said that down in he pit there were . . ."

Marie quickly covered her mouth with her hand. A spasm gripped her throat. The others edged forward in their chairs with intense concern, wanting to reach out to Marie. She swallowed deeply and said, "It's OK. Sometimes there's a sickness in the bottom of my stomach that I can't squelch. Anyway, as best I can figure out, the pit was filled with the remains of the animals and b-b . . . babies they had killed! Marie blurted.

"May I say something?" Isabel, the Spanish woman, interrupted. Darcy nodded in consent. "What Marie's telling you is true. I've seen this sort of thing too. It may be hard to believe, but you've got to understand the brainwashing methods of these groups. The more they torture their victims, the more their victims shut down their feelings—the more they become robots, zombies."

Isabel paused, looking at Marie to see if she wanted to go ahead. Marie's eyes closed tightly, her body tense, as she sought to regain her composure. Darcy nodded at Isabel and motioned for her to continue.

"Darkness and death, that's what it's about," Isabel said. "They keep you in the dark so you lose all sense of time and reality. There's lots of blood. To them, it's the sacred fluid to worship evil. When you're a child and they pour blood on you, you feel like you're dying. You've seen them kill animals, maybe humans, and you know that following blood is the sign of death.

"These people are insane! There's nothing so evil they won't do it. I saw cult members tied down and their genitals mutilated. Men were castrated. One young girl was forced to perform oral sex on animals to bring out the penises so cult members could cut them off and feed them to their victims. Do you understand what I'm saying?" Isabel screamed, raising her hands over her head in defiance and frustration. Finally, unable to adequately express her outrage, she slapped her hands on her thighs and shook in anger.

Heavy silence settled over the room. Wes glanced toward Annette, who stared straight ahead, entranced by what she had heard.

Isabel eventually resumed her account by exclaiming, Cannibalism! That's what it is, the belief that predators have supremacy. They made me eat human flesh. I knew people would never believe me, but my therapist did. He called in a doctor. I described what it was like to chew certain kinds of internal organs. The doctor stood there and shook his head. The therapist told me later that the doctor admitted I had described in perfect detail the texture of the organs we had to eat. To them, it was an honor to eat the flesh of a dead person! We were consuming the strength of the one we destroyed.

"One more thing. They used me as a breeder. They gave me doses of hormones at an early age so I'd develop faster. I've forgotten how many times I was pregnant or how many of my babies they aborted and killed. But who's going to believe that? What if I testified in a court of law? I would be on trial! People just can't accept what we in this room have been through. We're the victims, but somehow it's all twisted around, and we become the guilty ones, the ones who have to keep quiet, the ones who are called liars. People think we're mentally sick."

With that, Isabel sighed deeply and sagged into her chair. Angelo stroked her shoulders. Everyone was thinking the same thing: Would justice ever be done for any of them? Despite his habitual cynicism, Wes believed that the very fact he was here and these people were openly sharing their grief in a supportive atmosphere was evidence that evil had its limits.

Darcy stood and paced back and forth across the room. Then she turned to the group and said, "All of us in this room share similar experiences. We don't trust easily. We may not want to be around children because of what we've seen done to so many innocent young ones. We're afraid of churches, robes, ceremonies, candles, prayers. It's frightening to us. It shouldn't be, but it is. It reminds us of all the wrong things."

She went to the small table and poured herself a cup of coffee. She started to lift it to her lips, then hesitated. "Fear dominates us. Our self-confidence has been destroyed. We feel guilty that we didn't know what was happening, that we didn't do more. Now, we're faced with giving our children the childhoods they were robbed of, right under our noses. At night, we hear their screams in our minds. Every time we pick up a knife, a needle, or a pair of scissors, we look at it dumbfounded, wondering if one like it was used to torment our child.

"We even wonder if our children imagined all of it. A therapist who works with us once told me, 'Darcy, you can't produce a flashback if an event didn't happen. What you child remembers is real, not a hallucination.' If we don't watch it, we will do what our children tried to do . . . pretend it didn't happen or involve ourselves in endless activities to occupy our minds.

"Sometimes we feel we're incapable of being good parents, but we can't let the past intimidate us. We must trust our instincts. We must listen to our children and be ready for that moment when they let go of the pain and lay it before us."

Darcy continued, "Now, what do we do? Where do we go from here? I don't have all the answers, but my own experience taught me a few things."

She went back to her chair, sat down, and looked at each person in the room, trying to assure them of her concern. "Don't be too philosophical or you'll start believing the whole world is diabolical and that will create more terror. And don't suppress your normal desires. If you're like me, you want to be married, to bring another life into the world, believing that goodness is more common than badness. We're a long way from being there, but if we don't believe we'll be whole again, we'll remain in pieces. And the pieces will fragment further, until there's nothing left of our lives. We can't let those who tormented us and our children win that victory. We owe it to our children and those who love us to fight back and to believe that someday this will be over."

Darcy stretched out her arms and gestured upward with her hands, saying, "Let's stand together. It's been a long, traumatic night for all of us." Looking at Wes and Annette, she said, "Before we leave, we always join hands and share a few moments of silence in honor of our children. It draws us together and reminds us there's strength in our silenced when we call upon a power beyond ourselves."

One by one, they stretched out their hands to the next person. Wes took Annette's hand in his left and Darcy Linmore's in his right. They bowed their heads as stillness settled over the group. Only the sound of breathing could be heard.

When their moment of mediation ended, Darcy Linmore pulled Wes aside. "We have to blindfold you again. I'm sorry, but that's the rule. Until you've attended two meetings and everybody trusts you, we'll transport you back and forth."

"I understand," Wes said. "It's all right. What's being shared here is so important. I wouldn't do anything to endanger it."

Wes took Jennifer's coat from the hall closed. He and Annette stepped to the kitchen door, curious about what Jennifer and her new friend had been doing. Wes quietly opened the door to peer into the room. Jennifer and Nurse Milthorpe were seated at a table with drawings like the ones Jennifer had done earlier scattered in front of them. Jennifer was listening excitedly as the nurse spoke.

"Heidi, the Bible talks about the angels God sends to protect us so we don't have to be afraid when nasty people try to hurt us. Could you draw me a picture of an angel?"

Jennifer nodded and reached for clean paper and some worn crayons. Her simple sketch bore a striking resemblance to "Annette's soft, curved face and patient gaze, but the feathered wings were large and overpowering compared to the body. Nurse Milthorpe watched Jennifer as the unusual angel emerged from her subconscious. Then in an intense final stroke, Jennifer shaded the wings with thick, black crayon.

"Is that OK?" Jennifer asked.

"You did a great job, Heidi. But why are the wings so big and black? Most people think of God's angels with bright golden wings. The wings you drew look dark and evil."

Jennifer scooted her chair closer to the nurse. "But I've never seen God's angels," she said. "All I know is, the nasty people do bad things to me. How can they if beautiful angels with pretty wings are around me?"

Wes wondered if the nurse was prepared for such a serious question, one that, in slightly different words, he had often asked himself.

"The devil tries hard to win against God," the nurse responded. "Sometimes, people who are lonely or very angry let the devil into their hearts, and they become bad . . . like your angel with the black wings. But if bad people open their hearts and let the light of God inside, all the darkness will leave. Sadly, just like you, they're afraid of being hurt again."

"I don't want to be afraid anymore, but sometimes when I sleep I can hear big black wings. I know you asked me to draw a good angel, but sometimes the good and the bad get all mixed up in my head. Do you understand?"

"Yes. But remember, you're safe now." Nurse Milthorpe placed a reassuring arm around Jennifer and hugged her. As Jennifer settled into her arms, the nurse rocked her softly and murmured a quiet prayer: "Littlest sheep, returning to the flock, rest your tired soul, and know that the Lord's angels will be all around you."

Taking advantage of the lull in conversation, Wes and Annette pushed the door open and entered the kitchen.

"Mommy!" Jennifer said, rising from Nurse Milthorpe's embrace. "I have angels, good angels with bright golden wings everywhere, and they're looking out for me."

In spite of the painful things she had heard that evening, Annette beamed in relief at the joy in her child. She smiled and extended a hand toward Nurse Milthorpe. "Thank you again. You've been a bit of an angel yourself."

The nurse smiled politely and turned to Jennifer. "Just remember who's around you all the time."

"Angels!" Jennifer exclaimed, throwing her arms open and gesturing around her. "Everywhere! Lots of them!" She paused, then asked, "Can I take one of my pictures?"

"Sure. Which one?"

Jennifer looked through the pile until she found one colored with tones of dark green and brown depicting exaggerated shapes of people. In the bottom corner stood a tiny blue stick figure with yellow hair. It didn't take long for Wes to realize the little person was Jennifer.

"I like this one best. I'm real small and hiding so they can't find me," Jennifer explained.

Jennifer looked up to see Wes and Annette standing by the kitchen door preparing to leave. Wes gazed back at Jennifer and the picture she prized. The change in circumstances from the terror and shock he had undergone since Jennifer's first call on "Talk about Town" to the serene comfort to Darcy Linmore's support group was like the satisfaction of crossing the final yard-line marker during a practice sprint.

"Let's get ready to go," the nurse said, reaching to take Jennifer's coat from Wes's arm.

As Jennifer and Nurse Milthorpe exchanged final hugs, Annette whispered in Wes's ear, "I want to speak to Marie." She tugged on his arm as they left the kitchen and approached the brave woman who had bared so much of her soul.

"Marie, thank you for your courage tonight. I know it wasn't easy to share your story," Annette said as she took Marie's hand. "I've been through something similar with my daughter. I've known only a few weeks, and I still don't have the whole story. I look forward to joining the group again. Perhaps after a couple more times I'll have as much courage as you had tonight, and I'll tell my story."

Marie reached out to hug Annette, and they clung to each other. Annette started to walk away, then stopped and turned back. "Marie, I have to tell you something else. I can't bear to see your pain without your knowing it."

Annette stared at the floor. Wes saw that she was struggling to get the words out and put a reassuring arm around her shoulders. Annette looked at Marie, tears streaming down her face, her hands trembling, and said, "Marie, the man who abused your daughter was my husband, Gregory Ravensky Simpson."

Nineteen

Horror shrouded the ride back to 2519 Calhoun Street. The brutal realization that Gregory had been involved in such a violent group left Wes and Annette exhausted. Jennifer laid her head in Annette's lap and was sound asleep minutes after the car began moving.

"Ravensky was a family name," Annette said to Wes, "handed down to Gregory from his mother's side of the family. It was his middle name, but he never used it, only the initial *R*. I used it once and he got angry, told me never to speak that name again. Gregory wouldn't even use Ravensky to sign legal documents."

The meaning of the name didn't dawn on Wes at first. Then the recognition of its meaning flashed through his mind: *Raven-sky . . . R-a-v-e-n. That's it! The Dark Raven.*

Wes's mind fled miles away to Clarion, Indiana. Tomorrow, he would say good-bye to Annette and Jennifer and head back to whatever awaited him in Columbus County. It was an unappealing prospect. The gnawing sensation in the pit of his stomach was linked to fear of Hancock and his henchmen: Blackwell. The Simpsons—and Lord knew who else.

"We're here," the driver said. "Calhoun and Ogden."

The abrupt interruption startled Annette. She jerked forward as she realized where she was. Then she nudged Jennifer and began talking to her so she wouldn't be startled. The car pulled to the curb. As Wes took off his blindfold, he noticed the car had deliberately parked on a portion of the street beyond the nearest street lamp. Wes clasped Annette's hand, and she took Jennifer's. They filed out of the car and it sped away. Wes stood on the empty South Chicago intersection, wondering if the saga he'd been through was real.

Then Wes looked at Annette. Standing forlorn in the dark, cold autumn night, she had pulled her borrowed overcoat around Jennifer, who snuggled close, holding tightly to one of Annette's legs. It was real all right, and the two most important people in his life had suffered beyond his comprehension.

The chilly Chicago air pierced their clothes, biting sharply. None of them had brought adequate wardrobes in their haste to leave. Annette only had Hannah's thin cotton coat to ward off the chill, and Wes felt bad to see her huddled uncomfortably against the strong wind coming off Lake Michigan.

I can't do much for her in my financial condition, Wes thought, *but I could drive up to her home in North Chicago, pick up some clothing, and be back before morning.*

As they walked back to the apartment, Wes asked Annette, "Did Jennifer have many friends in your old neighborhood?" he asked.

"Yes. She was a popular kid in Lincoln Heights. But Gregory had to approve the children she associated with," Annette sighed, weary of the memories she'd dealt with the past few hours. Then clenching her fists deeper into her coat pockets, she said sarcastically,

"Yeah. What a great guy he was, caring so much about what friends she played with during the day, then molesting her by night!"

Wes listened as Annette spoke. She obviously felt some responsibility for the past events. Silence settled between them as they continued to walk along the sidewalk. Wes kicked at a stray candy wrapper that had been dropped by a previous pedestrian, and looked across the street, seeing his reflection in the glass store fronts. Wes interpreted Annette's silence as an indication that she was hurting more than she let on. He sensed her deep frustration and anger, and touched her shoulder. *Perhaps I could do more than find her a warmer coat. Maybe I could find some personal things that meant a lot to her and Jennifer—like that cat . . . what's it's name?...Tickles. Maybe I could get a picture of Tickles or a favorite stuffed toy.*

"Annette, I'd like to go by your old home, tonight."

"Why, Wes? What's on your mind?"

"You'll see. I'm not up to anything sneaky, just something I think is important. Nobody will know I'm there. It's not far, is it?

"No, about forty-five minutes. But what if someone from the Order is watching the house, just waiting to see if we'll show up?"

"Well, even if they do see me, they still won't know where you are. I'll be very careful so no one can follow me back here.

"How do I get into the house?" he asked Annette. "Do I have to break in and add to my sins of kidnapping and harboring a fugitive?" he said, smiling at his own effort to lighten their mood.

Annette laughed. "I hid a key in the rose bush on the left side of the front door. It's under a small gray rock, darker than the other rocks there. Gregory didn't want me to leave a key. He thought it was risky, but I hid it for Jennifer. Gregory never knew it was there."

Wes smiled. The Order seemed so diligent and thorough in their ways of evil, but Annette's hidden key indicated that they couldn't control everything.

Although the conversation had momentarily concluded, Annette and Wes continued walking. Wes reached the intersection in front of the apartment building a few steps before Annette and Jennifer and pushed the crosswalk light. The warmth of his hand adhered to the chilled metal pole, and Wes shivered, although he wasn't sure it was from the Chicago chill, Annette's pain, or his plan to return to Annette and Gregory's house.

As they walked slowly back to apartment number three, Wes made some mental plans for that evening—how he would enter the Simpson home, what to look for once inside. He also told Jennifer of his earlier decision. "Tomorrow, I'm going back to Clarion. I'd have waited to tell you in the morning, but I didn't want to upset you at the last minute. It's not something I want to do, you understand, but you need proper medical attention, and we've got to get money somewhere."

"I'm OK, Mr. Wes. I don't *need* to see any doctor! I told you and Mommy, I don't *like* doctors!"

"Jennifer," Wes said, "I understand why you don't want to be near a doctor, but you must. Dr Ben is a good man. Remember, Nurse

Milthorpe will be there to look after you. You like her, don't you?"

"Yes! A lot!" Jennifer responded, the warmth from her voice creating wisps of white smoke that swirled about her head. "Why do you have to leave us and go back to that bad place?"

"I don't want to, Jennifer, but you and your mother need money, and I don't know any other way to get it."

"Mommy can get a job. And I can work. I'll help!"

Wes smiled. "That's very thoughtful, but your mother couldn't make enough money to pay the rent and feed you, plus pay the doctor bills. Don't worry! We'll talk on the phone every day. I can even come up on weekends if you'd like"

"You promise?"

"I promise."

They walked a few more feet in silence, then Jennifer said, "What about the nasty people? I don't want them to do bad things to you."

Wes wasn't sure how to respond. He didn't want to give Jennifer a flippant response. With everything she had been through, she would see through any trite answer. Then he heard himself saying, "Angels will look after me, Jennifer!"

Jennifer looked up at him, her brown eyes opening widely. "You mean, like the ones Nurse Milthorpe told me about, the ones around me?"

"Yeah," Wes answered. "Just like that. Angels everywhere I go."

As they walked on, Wes wondered if his answer was merely acquiescing to a small child's need for assurance or if deep within he believed that angels would look after *him*. The words of his childhood prayer went through his mind: *Now I lay me down to sleep, I pray the Lord my soul to keep.*

He remembered a picture that hung on the wall of his bedroom while he was growing up, a picture he hadn't thought of in more than thirty years. He didn't remember his mother hanging it there. It had always been there, a scene of two small children looking over the edge of a steep cliff. Unseen, a bright, shining being with feathered wings stood in front of them with outstretched arms to prevent them from falling over the edge. No one had talked about religion and angels in his childhood home, but that picture said everything his mother and father failed to say. The last thing he did every night as a child was to look at that picture. First, his "now I lay me down to sleep" prayers, a kiss on the forehead from his mother, and then that picture. Whatever happened before he should awake, that beautiful being with the graceful feathered wings was there in his mind . . . and, he believed, would stay all night by the side of his bed.

The walk up the stairs to apartment number three was emotionally as difficult for Wes as if was physically uncomfortable for Jennifer. Each step took him closer to morning when he'd drive away from these two people who were so precious to him.

Once back at the apartment, Annette immediately put Jennifer to bed. Then it was time for Wes to begin his journey to Lincoln Heights. It was nearly midnight, and with the long drive back to Clarion ahead of him the next day, he wouldn't get much sleep. He scribbled some directions from Annette and headed north to the Simpson home.

Wes had no problem locating Annette's neighborhood, which was exactly as she had described it. In the glow of street lamps, Wes saw the neatly manicured lawns and immaculate homes with porch lights smiling a warm welcome, the ideal place to raise a child and to live out the American dream.

Minutes later, Wes turned off the main street onto Juniper Avenue. Straight ahead stood the white and blue Simpson house. He parked two houses down and quietly shut the car door. No barking dogs announced his arrival. Not even a stray car meandered down the streets to interrupt the silence. As Wes walked toward the house, his footsteps echoed in the night, making him feel as if someone would appear momentarily and alert the local Neighborhood Watch Program.

Wes noticed the newly mowed lawn as he walked up the sidewalk to the front door. *They must have paid someone to take care of the place. I suppose the service continued in their absence,* he mused, vaguely uneasy. Then another thought struck him. Who owned this place now, and who lived here? There was no For Sale sign on the lawn. Wes surmised the whole affair was tied up in estate court.

The rose bush was exactly as Annette described. In the faint light, Wes fumbled around the rocks, avoiding the rose thorns. He picked up one rock and found nothing under it, then another. Finally, he noticed a darker one and lifted it. The key waited there, cold and damp in its earthy hiding place.

Wes eased the key into the lock and turned it. The door opened smoothly. With only moonlight to guide him, he fumbled with a flashlight he'd taken from his car. It hadn't been used in a long time, and he hoped it would work. Instantly, a pale beam of light shone a few paces ahead.

Wes carefully studied the interior furnishings in pale earthen tones that bore Annette's unmistakable touch. He walked through the living room, past the dining area, and into what he thought was the master bedroom. Several pictures stood on a dresser, including one of a young girl and her parents. They were dressed casually in sweaters and slacks, seated in a wooded area near a small stream. Wes shone the flashlight upon the three figures in the photograph— Annette, Jennifer, and Gregory. How beautiful Annette had been before the tragedy, so seemingly carefree. Wes directed the beam into Gregory Simpson's face. He was surprised to see a face that women would look at twice and a smile that would beguile any unsuspecting person. Jennifer had inherited his blonde hair and gentle features. Gregory Simpson looked like the ideal father.

Next to the family portrait was an individual picture of Jennifer. Wes had often wondered what she had looked like before he came to know her as an abused, terrified child. He was struck by the lack of sparkle one would expect in a normal child's eyes. *It's a good thing Gregory is dead,* Wes fumed. *If I could get my hands on him, I think I'd kill him for what he stole from Jennifer.*

Looking around the bedroom, Wes spotted a large walk-in closet.

Inside, he selected several dresses and accessories he thought would be appropriate for Annette this time of year. He tried to pick sensible clothes, but it had been years since he had paid any attention to a woman's wardrobe. Then he returned to the hallway and found Jennifer's bedroom.

Everything in the room was coordinated, and he could imagine Annette carefully selecting each piece. This was a room where a little girl could dream and laugh over secrets. A canopied bed encircled in pink ruffles held dozens of stuffed toys. Wes smiled, remembering how he and Misha had collected colorful pieces of fluff and stuff, bringing joy into her life. Now, they were memories, collecting dust somewhere.

Wes noticed a gray, stuffed bunny and picked it up. *This looks like something Jennifer might have loved once*, he thought. *Perhaps this will make her happy, especially if she once cuddled it as a source of security.*

Wes saw a chest that he presumed held Jennifer's clothes. Small roses and little green turtles sprinkled around a design of pale yellow daisies made a border for the chest. He looked in the drawers and began gathering an assortment of clothes he hoped would match, including Jennifer's shirts, which were printed with characters he faintly remembered from television cartoons he had flipped past one Saturday morning. There were large orange cats and an array of colored bears. *This is what childhood is supposed to be*, Wes thought, as he picked up the clothing. *Nameless stuffed animals, giggles, and colorful clothes that make a statement all their own of happi-*

ness, not pain and abuse.

Time was slipping by, and Wes had to get back before daylight. Reaching down by the frills of Jennifer's bed cover, he found a duffle bag labeled "School Daze" in neon pink and green swirls. It was stuffed with dolls in various stages of undress and hair design. *Sorry, ladies, but I need this more than you do,* Wes muttered as he dumped out the dolls and filled what he could in the bag.

Wes considered how he looked—a gray bunny with floppy ears and a neon duffle bag tucked under his arm, a nearly expired flashlight in his left hand, and his right index finger hooked through a half dozen clothes hangers filled with women's apparel. Suppose someone had seen him enter and the police arrived? How could he explain trying to escape with these "valuables"? *At best, they'd think I'm some kind of nut or pervert,* Wes thought.

Setting his collection down by the front door, Wes checked to see if he had dropped anything in his haste. He became aware that his throat was parched. He headed toward the kitchen to satisfy his thirst, hoping the plumbing hadn't been shut off. Water immediately poured from the tap, and he downed several glasses, feeling the quench only when it hit his stomach. Sated, he set the glass on the counter top and sat at the kitchen table to collect himself.

Crash!

The shrill sound of breaking glass caused Wes to lose both his breath and his balance as he spun around to seek the enemy with the failing beam of his flashlight. The shadowed walls reflected nothing at first, except for the broken water glass that lay in sparkling pieces under his beam of light. Then from the ebony emptiness came a glint of two reflecting slits of light. As Wes edged closer, his quarry unexpectedly leaped into full view. He dropped the flashlight as a frightened cat sprang over his shoulder in a desperate attempt to escape, its claws scratching Wes's cheek. He instinctively drew his hand to his face, which was moist with fresh drops of blood.

You must be Tickles, he thought as he reached for the fallen flashlight to see where the cat had gone. *Odd that you would still be alive after six months.*

As the thought subsided, Wes heard a crunch under his feet. He jumped at the noise, flashed the light, and saw crushed brown flakes that had once been famous high-protein Kitty Stars, the kind of treat all-American cats crave. Wes directed his flashlight to a torn sack of cat food that had obviously been purchased for the little beast by a frugal Annette.

"Twenty-five pounds of Kitty Stars!" Wes laughed out loud at being caught off-guard. Then he spotted the pet door neatly installed in the solid oak back door. Tickles had been enjoying a well-fed bachelor's life.

I wonder if I can get him to go back with me? Wes thought. Searching randomly illuminating the room with his flashlight, Wes concluded that the mysterious cat was hiding. *Poor thing. Probably hasn't seen another person in here for months.*

Returning to the kitchen table, Wes hastily wiped the blood from his cheek. He reached into the glass-paned cabinet over the sink and got another drinking glass. His hand shook nervously as he filled it to the top and drank hastily. A newspaper lay spread out on the table. *This is odd*, he thought. *Annette is so tidy. Why would she leave for a trip without cleaning first?*

"Hey, tickles, you into finance or the comics?" Wes laughingly called to the cat. Amused at the sound of his voice and the conspicuous silence of the cat, Wes wiped the back of his hand across his chapped lips.

He surmised that a realtor or an estate executor might have gone through the house and left the newspaper lying there. He focused the flashlight on the front page. The news was basic—presidential hoopla, football scores, news about the economy. Suddenly, Wes noticed the date on the newspaper: Tuesday, November 3, 1992. It was today's!

At that moment, things fell into place: manicured lawn, the utilities still operative, no realty sign out front, today's paper spread out before him.

Instinctively, Wes jumped to his feet, turned on the light switch above the stove, faintly illuminating the room, and walked to the refrigerator. Inside, he found fresh eggs, milk, juice, and sandwich meats.

Someone has been here today, maybe minutes ago! Wes thought, terror rippling through him.

Wes gathered what he had come for and fled from the house. He found himself speeding back to apartment number three, running from a nightmarish certainty that their lives were still in jeopardy. He wouldn't tell Annette and Jennifer what he'd found in their home. He now understood how Annette's red dress had made its way to Clarion to terrorize her daughter. Someone in the Order must have returned to the house while Annette was in the hospital and taken one of her dresses to add to the collection of horror meant for Jennifer.

The next morning, Wes awoke early. He wanted to sneak out before Annette and Jennifer awakened. It would be easier this way. No emotional good-byes. Wes could still be the hero, go back and get the money, save the day, and maybe he wouldn't have to deal with feelings that seemed more intense than friendship. His thoughts were broken by Annette's voice.

"Good morning," she said, as she walked into the kitchen. "I smelled the coffee. You weren't going to leave without saying good-bye, were you? You haven't even told me about last night."

"I was just having a cup of coffee before waking you," Wes answered. "There's not much to tell. I picked up a few things for you and Jennifer. Hope you like what I selected." He pointed to the clothing on the couch, hoping this sparse wardrobe would get them through the next few weeks.

Annette walked over and put her arms around his chest, hugging him tightly. "Has anyone ever told you what a warm and kind person you are?"

Of course, no one ever said that to me, Wes thought. *Warm and kind don't get you ratings in the media. Abrasive and obnoxious do.*

"Wes, I said you're a very sensitive person."

Wes set his coffee cup on the table and awkwardly responded, "Thank you. No one has ever told me that before."

"Well, maybe they never had an opportunity. Or maybe you never faced anything like this, so the best in you came out."

Wes put his arms around Annette and hugged her. "Let's not wake Jennifer. She needs all the sleep she can get. I'll slip out quietly, and you tell her good-bye for me."

But at that moment, Wes heard the door open and the sound of shuffling feet coming down the short hallway.

It was Jennifer, rubbing her eyes and wobbling from side to side in the stupor of a child's awakening. "Mommy, my tummy hurts! It burned all night. If it will go away, I'll go see Dr. Ben., He'll make it stop."

Annette knelt and took Jennifer in her arms. "That's a brave girl! We'll go see Dr. Ben just as soon as Wes lea . . ." Annette interrupted herself and looked at Wes.

He couldn't avoid the situation, so he knelt between them and said, "Jennifer, remember I told you last night that I'd have to leave for a while."

Jennifer jumped away from him. "You can't! You can't!" she cried, forgetting the previous night's conversation. "You're my best friend." Jennifer poked out her lower lip, pouting and summoning what feminine wiles she had at that tender age. Her shoulders drooped, hands clasped tightly behind her. Balancing partially on one leg, she twisted back and forth, coyly expressing hurt and rejection.

Wes took her hand and said, "Jennifer, if you want you tummy to stop hurting, you have to see the doctor, and right now your mommy and I don't have any money to pay for that. I've got to talk on the radio again, like I did when you first called me. That's how I earn a living."

"But the nasty people will hurt you!" Jennifer protested. "They're mad at you, I know they are! You took me away from my husband."

Jennifer didn't realize she had said husband. Even after she did, the shock on Wes's and Annette's faces didn't register with her. Stunned silent, Wes's mind raced. Husband? He didn't have time nor would it have been appropriate now to ask her about it.

"I'll never be far away from you, Jennifer. If you need me, I'll be here in a matter of hours. Remember, I promised! And don't forget Nurse Milthorpe's angels."

"They're not Nurse Milthorpe's angels! They're my angel's," Jennifer protested loudly. "My very own special angels to keep the nasty people form hurting me again."

Wes opened his arms and reached out to hug both of them. He had never served in the military, but he surmised this was how it must feel for a soldier to go off to battle and leave his family. In a very real way, that's what he was doing. If Annette and Jennifer thought he was brave, Wes didn't. He couldn't imagine the worst coward in the world refusing this mission.

Wes arose, put on his coat, and walked to the door. Annette came to him and reached up to kiss him gently on the cheek, whispering," "I'll find out what she meant by the word *husband*. Don't worry about it. Please be careful, and know I'm praying for you."

Annette and Jennifer will be OK, Wes thought. *She's a resourceful woman, and she can call on Darcy Linmore and Nurse Milthorpe.* Wes smiled and stepped out the door. He didn't want to look back for fear he'd be tempted to stay.

Twenty minutes later, he was heading south on the freeway. The Chicago skyline diminished in the distance, until all he could see in the rearview mirror was the tip of the Sears Tower piercing the low haze of an icy early November morning. Eventually, that too faded from sight.

Before him, the flat farmland of Indiana stretched toward the horizon. In cornfield after cornfield, golden mulched stalks were lying in the fields, awaiting the turn of a plow blade to make fertilizer for the next kernel of corn dropped in the soil. The farmland reminded Wes of his roots, the belief that hard work and respect for the land brought rewards. Calloused hands and strong hearts turned Indiana clay into the bounty that filled feedlot troughs, which in turn supplied Chicago's slaughterhouses. People standing in line at McDonald's didn't care that the cycles of the seasons were necessary ingredients in their cheese burgers. But it mattered to Wes. In his shaky, uncertain life, he recognized the shortened days of winter as precursors to April's warm rains, which would cause these dormant fields to sprout.

While speeding down Interstate 360, Wes realized nothing happened by chance. In spite of harsh winds and cold winter days, the seasons balanced and brought life from death, the assurance these Indiana farmers lived by. No matter how deep the snow or how harsh the December cold, the brick-hard clay of winter would soften in the summer sun and yield bright yellow ears of corn, completing the cycle of life, death, and rebirth.

When at last the outskirts of Clarion came into view, the muscles in Wes's jaw constricted and he clutched the steering wheel with both hands, as if he wanted to assure his control over the car's direction. Wes flipped on the radio and tuned to WTTK in time for the eleven o'clock news.

As the last report of the hourly headlines concluded, an announcer declared, "From now until noon, you favorites of yesterday on the Late Morning Community Calendar . . . songs of the forties and news of the nineties, right here in Clarion. If you have an announcement to make about a community gathering, a job or service that's available, call WTTK! Don't forget, at noon 'Talk about Town" with your host, Chuck Bailey."

"Bailey?" Wes questioned aloud. At least he didn't have to wonder what had happened to his show. Fifteen minutes later, Wes entered his apartment. The sink was full of dirty dishes, magazines and newspapers were strewn throughout the living room, and a cup of once stale coffee sat on the kitchen table, the liquid evaporated and ark sediment ringing the bottom.

Wes grabbed the phone and dialed WTTK. "Can I speak to Chuck Bailey, please?"

"He's unavailable right now, getting ready for 'Talk about Town.' You can leave a message. May I ask who's calling?"

"Wes Bryant."

There was silence at the other end of the line. Brenda, WTTK's receptionist, had been struck mute. She regained her senses and said, "Just a moment. I'll see if he can be interrupted."

Moments later, Wes heard the familiar voice of his faithful producer. "Wes! Where in the world have you been?" Bailey asked.

"It doesn't matter," Wes answered. "Do I still have a job?"

"Sure, sure! I told Warren you had to take care of some important personal business. He didn't like it but went along with it. I've been doing the show, but I gotta tell ya, buddy, I'm no Wes Bryant. I underestimated what it takes to get in front of that microphone every day, no matter how you feel."

"Thanks! Can I do the show today?"

"I suppose. I was going to talk about the city council proposal to develop that park on the east end of town. You wanna do that? Can you get here in time? It's only a half hour 'til the show."

"No sweat, but I don't want to talk about the park. My return appearance has got to be stronger than that."

"What about discussing Sheriff Arnold Hancock's plan to establish sobriety checkpoints during the upcoming Thanksgiving Day weekend? Ever since Reverend Carmichael was killed by that hit-and-run driver, Hancock has been saying he'd still be alive if the Sheriff's Department had had the authority to stop cars when school use is suspected."

Hancock. Wes's blood boiled at the sound of the name. Part of Wes didn't want to touch anything involving Arnold Hancock, but the rebellious side, which made him an outsider in Columbus County, rose to the surface. It didn't matter to Wes if discretion was the better part of valor. He'd take action today.

"That's a great idea! Let's go with the Hancock thing, but under one condition. You get Sheriff Hancock into the studio to face me, eyeball-to-eyeball."

Bailey picked up on the resolution in Wes's voice. "Where's the win?" he asked. "You know the rule on talk radio—always have an antagonist. The whole town is angry of Carmichael's death. Almost, Wes, it sounds like you've got a hidden agenda of some kind, wanting a head-to-head with Hancock."

The relationship between Wes and Bailey was marriage of sorts. Running a talk show together meant thinking alike, acting on the same impulses, sensing the same needs in the audience, knowing when to go for the throat and when to back off. They knew what got people's attention. Beat up on a guest here, empathize with a caller there. Always just enough tension to grab the listener. If things lagged, yell a little. If they got too tense, put on a white hat and play nice guy.

Wes summoned his innate acting abilities. "No agenda, Chuck. I just think the show would have more punch if Hancock were there. After all, it's his idea, so he should defend it."

"OK. But we've got less than half an hour now. You're going to have to do the topic cold."

"I can handle it. 'Spontaneity is the soul of wit,'" Wes said in a deep-throated oration, but he couldn't remember who had said it first.

"Yeah, and spontaneity can be on-air suicide for unprepared talk show hosts," Bailey laughed.

Suddenly, a thought flashed through Wes's mind. In any other context, it would have been simply a mischievous idea. In this case, he had deliberate design. "See if you can get that young lawyer, Manley Harris, on the show with Hancock. Might make some sparks fly. I once remember he accused Hancock of racism, claiming his deputies beat up some black people who wanted to protest the county's refusal to put up a stoplight at the corner of Gaylord and Fifth Avenue. Remember, that intersection where a car hit and killed that kid several years ago?"

"Yeah, I remember. Wes, you're not going to stir up that racial stuff, are you? You need to have a real win on your first day back, not a dogfight about old animosities."

Wes couldn't explain his true intentions, and he had little time to get his point across. "I'm in a hurry, Chuck. Gotta take a shower. I'll walk in at the last minute. If there's new spot copy to read for some advertisers you picked up while I've been gone, put that right on top of the stuff that needs my attention. One more thing, don't tell Hancock I'm going to be there. I'd like this to be a surprise."

"Wes, you are up to something, aren't you? All right, I'll go along with your ornery game. It's just good to have you back."

Wes changed to a fresh, unwrinkled shirt, a rarity in the Bryant wardrobe, quickly brushed his hair, and put on a tie. He usually didn't bother. After all, this wasn't television. It was radio, the theater of the mind. Donahue and Carson had to have carefully coiffured hair and meticulously selected wardrobes. All talk show hosts needed were a loud mouth and quick wit. Wes had those, but the tie and the unwrinkled shirt weren't for the audience. They were for Hancock, a little something to make himself look more serious and professional.

He'd also make sure Hancock was sitting on the north side of the interview table in the studio. That way, he'd look toward the window to see Wes. At that hour, the sun would shine directly into Hancock's eyes if Wes pulled back the curtains covering the window. Every time Hancock looked at him, Mr. Sun would be an accomplice in the intimidation process. And he'd give Harris the best mike, the table top with the mini-boom on it, which would allow him to sit more comfortably in his chair. Hancock would get the short-stemmed mike, the one Wes hated, the one that made guests lean awkwardly over the table. That would keep Hancock uncomfortably on the edge of his seat. Wes would have a big glass of water by his side. So would Manley Harris. But no water for Hancock. The sheriff would get the message. Wes would do whatever he could to irritate Hancock and throw him off-guard. Dry mouth was small punishment compared to what he'd done to Jennifer, but it was all Wes could manage at the moment.

Wes was out the door and on his way to WTTK only ten minutes after his conversation with Bailey. He usually dreaded that drive. "Talk about Town" was his livelihood, a job, nothing more. Today was different. Wes wasn't going to work; he was going to war.

He quietly slipped into the back door of WTTK without anyone's seeing him and went to his office. He buzzed Bailey on the intercom, and moments later the "Talk about Town" producer rushed through the door and uncharacteristically threw his arms around Wes in a bear-hug.

He patted Wes roughly on the back in macho exuberance, declaring, "Boy, am I glad to see you! Hancock and Harris are sitting in that studio, glaring at each other like World War III is about to start. Nobody's saying anything. Let's get down there before something happens."

"No, Chuck. Don't tell them I'm here. Let them think you're doing the show until the last minute, then I'm going to pop in the door."

Chuck's exuberant expression turned somber. He cocked his head and looked at Wes from the corner of his eye. "Tell me what you're up to, old buddy. Remember, I covered for you while you were gone. My job's at stake, too, y'know."

Wes looked back with a seriousness Bailey had never seen before. "Chuck, you have no idea what's at stake in that studio. Your job and mine are the least important things at risk today."

Wes's adamancy precluded further questions. Bailey said, "I trust you, Wes. You may not always use the best judgment about every-day affairs, but when it comes to the really big stuff, I'd trust you with everything I've got."

As Chuck walked out of the room to the studio, Wes realized he'd never heard Bailey say anything like that. He thought Chuck considered him flippant, like everybody else did—Wes Bryant, all talk, no walk; all blow, no show. He remembered what Annette had said about his being warm and sensitive. Maybe he could learn to like and trust the things about himself that Annette and Chuck recognized.

Wes took a deep breath, pulled his shoulders back, and tightened his belt a notch to suck in his stomach and make him feel more vir-ile. He looked at his reflection in the window and straightened his tie. An errant tuft of hair stuck out on the left side of his head so he spit on his palm to slick it back.

Then he walked quickly across the hall to the studio door. He paused before putting his hand on the knob. This was nothing like facing a 250-pound lineman, bent on destroying his body, or a 190-pound safety, determined to tackle him before he got to the goal line. This was no game. No scoreboard at the end of the field would tally the verdict. The stands were empty. No one watched, except perhaps the angels Jennifer and Nurse Milthorpe talked about. It was hard to turn that handle, but he did. The door swung open, and he stepped inside.

Sheriff Hancock's back was to the door. Manley Harris sat on the other side of the table, facing the door. When he saw Wes, his face lit up with a huge grin. "Bryant! Wes Bryant!" Harris rose to his feet, genuinely delighted.

Sheriff Hancock stayed seated. Slowly, he turned in his chair, leaning his elbow on the table and looking back over his shoulder. He stared up at Wes with a dark look in his penetrating blue-black eyes. He, too, grinned but his lips barely parted.

"Mr. Bryant," said Hancock, "I understand you've been out of town on *personal* business. Welcome back to Columbus County."

Twenty

It's two minutes to air time, and Columbus County is waiting," Wes said, directing Harris and Hancock to take the positions he designated at the table.

Wes walked to the studio board and took his familiar place, humming to himself. On the other side of the big glass window in the producer's room, Chuck Bailey grinned broadly, affirming how happy he was to see Wes back behind the microphone. Wes barely glanced at the board, cart machines, and complex configurations of switches and meters. He'd been there so many times that, in spite of his brief absence, he could have closed his eyes and handled the technicalities with precision.

Seven minutes later the opening jingle, initial spot breaks, and introductory patter were out of the way. Wes said nothing about his absence or return. He acted as if he'd never left the show, and this was just another day. He voiced a couple of farm reports and local civic club announcements, which gave him time to plot his strategy.

Then Wes wheeled his chair around and looked squarely at Sheriff Hancock. "Our special guest today, Arnold Hancock, sheriff of Columbus County for thirty-one years, battalion commander of our local National Guard unit, the man who's kept us nearly crime-free and let us all sleep a little easier at night. Welcome, Sheriff Hancock, to 'Talk about Town.'"

Hancock squinted to shield his eyes from the glare of the window behind Wes. He edged forward in his seat to reach the microphone and put his hand around the stem of the mike stand, pulling it as close as he could. The short cord on the mike prevented him from getting it near enough to be comfortable. As he leaned forward, his bulky frame seemed to wrap around the edge of the table.

Then Hancock responded with equal mockery. "Thanks, Mr. Bryant. It's the first opportunity I've had to do your show, and I welcome the chance to publicly set the record straight regarding some issues that concern all the fine citizens of our county."

"And next to Sheriff Hancock, a brilliant young lawyer, known to many of you as a champion of the underdog, who takes on cases that some in the Indiana Bar won't touch—Mr. Manley Harris."

"Thank you, Mr. Bryant," Harris responded. "I've long admired your blunt style of dealing with topics a lot of folks in Clarion ignore. Like today, a serious issue about civil rights and First Amendment liberties."

Wes reacted to Harris's setup by assuming an offensive posture toward him. "Mr. Harris, what's wrong with cracking down on drunk driving to make Columbus County a safer place for all of us? A close friend of yours, the Reverend James Carmichael, apparently was run down by a drunk driver. That should make you a strong proponent of sobriety checkpoints during this upcoming holiday season."

Before Harris could answer, Sheriff Hancock attacked. "The issue is safety, Mr. Bryant. Safety on the highways. Safety for all our citizens. For the life of me, I can't imagine why Mr. Harris would want any drunk behind the wheel of a car, especially at Thanksgiving, when we should be grateful to God for the blessings of life."

Wes gritted his teeth at Hancock's mention of God and the safety of Columbus County citizens. "Sheriff Hancock, are we sure that Harris isn't concerned about public safety?" Wes shot back. "If someone deliberately drives drunk and endangers the lives of others, he should be ordered off the streets. No thinking person would argue with that, and I assume that an attorney has a fair amount of intelligence."

Manley Harris joined the offensive. "Mr. Bryant is right. I'm not opposed to properly conducted sobriety checks, but that's not what you and your deputies have done in the past. And I'm afraid you'll do more than that this Thanksgiving if someone doesn't stand up to you!"

Hancock leaned back, his weight straining against the chair, and folded his arms over his chest. As he started to speak Wes Bryant motioned him forward to the microphone so he could be heard on the air. Hancock seemed irritated to be chained to the mike.

"Nobody complains when they go through a security check to board an airplane. They don't say that's unconstitutional. Besides, no matter how many drunks we catch, it's the deterrent effect we're after," Sheriff Hancock said.

"Do you know what the Indiana Appellate Court ruled last year about sobriety tests?" Harris asked.

Hancock's shoulders rolled slightly, and he arched his eyebrows, as though asking, "Why should I care?"

One for our side, Wes thought, knowing that the radio audience wouldn't see Hancock's gesture. They would interpret his silence as ignorance of the court's ruling.

"Well," Harris went on, "the court ruled that sobriety checks must be at different spots each time, and the traffic officials should be able to explain later why they chose a certain location. They're also obligated to give the community prior notice about the locations and dates."

"We've done that," Hancock interrupted. "It's scheduled for Thursday and Friday Thanksgiving weekend."

"Where?" Harris demanded.

"What difference does that make?" Hancock retorted sharply.

"I just told you what the court said. Answer me! Where? Is it going to be the same place as last year, because if it is, I might take you to court over it. Picking Applegate Lane was deliberately discriminatory. Ninety percent of all black people in Clarion drive that road. Placing a sobriety checkpoint there is a glaring example of discrimination. It says that you're not only looking for drunk drivers, you're looking for black drunk drivers."

"I'm looking for people with more than .10 percent blood alcohol levels, because that's the legal level that allows us to make an arrest. I don't care what color their skin is. If they're drunk, they're going to jail."

"You don't care?" Harris questioned. "I doubt that, Sheriff Hancock. When you tried this same tactic last year, the number of black people stopped at road blocks was twice that of white people. And in Columbus County, less than 20 percent of the people are black. Smell an attempt to intimidate black people. Sheriff? Maybe you don't, but I do." Harris glared at Hancock.

Wes glanced toward Bailey. His producer could hardly contain his excitement. This was talk radio at its best. Two opposing guests going at it fervently and the incoming phone lines lighting up with callers wanting to join the foray. It wasn't the high drama of "Transsexual Prostitutes on Drugs" or some other frivolous subject you might get on "Geraldo" or "Donahue," but for Columbus County, this was as good as it got.

Bailey cupped his fingers in the vague outline of a "C" for commercial. Wes had been so engrossed in the interchange between Harris and Hancock that he had skipped the second spot break of the hour and was already into the second segment of the show. Now, he'd have to double the typical amount of commercial announcements allotted by WTTK policy. He quickly called a halt to the debate. "We've got to break for our sponsors, then I'll be right back. You're listening to "Talk about Town." I'm your host, Wes Bryant."

Wes hit the switch that shut off all three studio mikes and simultaneously activated cart deck number one, starting the first of three one-minute spots about seed fertilizer, grain bins, and farm equipment sales, plus two thirty-second public service announcements from the local blood bank and the Army recruiting office. He stood, took the pitcher of water always sitting at his right, and leaned over the counter between him and the table where Harris and Hancock sat. He conspicuously poured Harris a glass of water and set the pitcher back down, ignoring Hancock.

Before he could gloat, a banging at the studio window got his attention. Bailey appeared to be in a heated conversation with Warren Crews, who normally paid little attention to Wes's show. The station owner checked the rating, kept track of the amount of spot time sold, and made sure "Talk about Town" was turning a profit. Beyond that, he pretty much let Bailey and Bryant have their way. But now, he was obviously upset. Crews motioned for Wes to come into the other room. Wes excused himself, stepped out of the studio, and hurried into Studio C.

"What's going on, Bryant?" Crews wanted to know. "First, you disappear without notice, then you show up at the spur of the moment, and not this. WTTK's got a good reputation in this city. We've always gotten along well with civic officials, including the Sheriff's Department. Then you bring in this smart-aleck lawyer, who's probably a card-carrying member of the ACLU, and embarrass Arnold Hancock, an institution in this town. Hancock's record of law and order is unblemished, and he's never lost an election. Why are you holding him up to this kind of ridicule?"

Wes was taken back. He desperately needed this job now that Jennifer required expensive medical attention. At the same time, he couldn't allow Crew's objections to stop him. Over the loud speaker in the background, he heard the end of the first one-minute spot.

He had less than three minutes to settle Crews down and get back in his studio.

"Look, boss, no matter who Sheriff Hancock is or what the community thinks of him, Harris has raised some valid points. The Federal Communication Commission gives you a responsibility to serve all your listeners, black and white, the poor and the powerful, and if Hancock's sobriety tests are discriminatory, someone needs to say it. If you want to take me behind the woodshed after the show, so be it. But right not, I've got to do my best job to get the truth out."

Crews glanced at the clock on the wall. He fidgeted with some papers in his hands, rubbed his chin, and shook hid head in exasperation as if reconciling an inner debate.

"Thirty seconds," Bailey interrupted.

Wes stood face to face with Crews. It was the first time since Wes had worked there that they had clashed on a matter more serious than deciding the discount rate on multiple-spot buys by advertisers.

Wes saw a frightened look come into Crew's eyes. He shoved the fistful of papers toward Wes. "Don't push it, Bryant Hancock has a lot of friends in this county, and they could lean on me and make my life real uncomfortable."

"I'll buy you thirty seconds," Chuck Bailey said, darting from the room, running into Studio A, and shoving another commercial into the cart machine. Over a background speaker in the hallway, Wes could hear the works, "Read for the fun of it. Read for the facts of it. Read as if your life depended on it. Your friends at the Columbus

County Library want you to know they are there to serve you with all the information you need when you need it . . ."

As the public service announcement droned on, Wes turned to walk away. He opened the door to Bailey's studio and glanced back at Crews, who stood there slapping the tightly rolled papers against his thigh.

What kind of control does Sheriff Hancock have over Warren? Wes wondered. *He's worried about more than a heated afternoon talk show.*

Wes threw open the door to the studio, leaped three big steps to his chair, and switched on his microphone just as the Columbus County Library announcement was ending. "This is Wes Bryant, back with you again on 'Talk about Town.' My guests today—Attorney Manley Harris and Sheriff Arnold Hancock. We'll take calls in a moment. But first, I want my guests to wrap up any final comments. Sheriff Hancock, you first."

Methodically, Hancock reached up to the brim of his gray Stetson and tipped it back. The elbow of his other arm rested on the table. He pointed his index finger at Manley Harris, like a schoolteacher lecturing an obstinate student. "Harris, let's get one thing straight. I run a clean county. It's a dry county, and there aren't many of those left in America. If the citizens of Clarion want to drive up north to Sweetwater County or out west to Cottonwood County and buy some booze, that's their business. It's a free country. But if they're going to drink and drive afterward, they'd better sober up before heading back to Columbus County. That means black and white.

"We want safe streets in our town, safe from drunk drivers, safe from drug-crazed kids. We want Columbus County to be what America once was, a place where decent families raised decent children. *I am* the law in Columbus County. I'll do whatever I have to do to fulfill the sacred trust people gave me with this badge."

Sheriff Hancock patted the shining silver emblem of authority hanging on his white shirt, which was marked by pinholes in the area below his shoulder from the many times the badge had been put there. The speech was a good one, full of pathos and patriotism. No criminal-coddler this sheriff. He was part Matt Dillon, part General Patton.

There was a momentary silence as Harris slowly put on his unassuming wire-rimmed glasses. He reached into his briefcase by the side of the table, pulled out some papers, and laid them in front of his microphone. He shuffled through then, left to right, as if dealing cards, until he found one with several highlighted paragraphs. He took it in both hands, glanced at it, then with all the high drama of a courtroom lawyer orchestrating a jury's response, Manley Harris took off his glasses one wire hook at a time, and calmly looked at Sheriff Hancock.

"The Reverend James Carmichael was my best friend," Harris said quietly and firmly. "He was not only my pastor, a man of God, and a great leader," Harris said, "he was like a father to me. My daddy died when I was a baby, and Mother raised five of us on a motel maid's salary. The reverend took me fishing, took me to ballgames, even drove me to the circus in Indianapolis one year. He was the only father I ever knew.

"If it hadn't been for Reverend Carmichael, I'd have dropped out of school. Long before this business about the mind being a terrible thing to waste, James Carmichael explained that my brain was God's gift, and I'd better use it. One night, when I was a senior in high school, I stopped by his house. I was going to get a job down at the fertilizer plant after graduation, but James convinced me to go on to college. He said that scholarships were available to bright young black people. He talked about Martin Luther King, Jr.'s dream and how I was part of that dream. He told me how proud my daddy would be if he were still alive and could see me get a college education. Sheriff Hancock, the Reverend James Carmichael was the most important person on the face of this earth to me, outside of my mother."

"This," Manley Harris said, holding the highlighted document in his hands, "is a copy of the coroner's report concerning the death of James Carmichael." Harris shook the papers in Sheriff Hancock's Face. "I'm sure you've read it, haven't you?" he asked, cocking his head.

"Sure, I've read it," Hancock shot back. "So what?"

"It's not what the coroner's report says," Harris responded. "It's what it doesn't say." Harris sorted through papers on the table and pulled out another sheet. "This is a police report on the accident, signed by you. 'cause of death—hit and run.' Is this your signature, Sheriff Hancock? Did you file this report?"

Hancock squirmed. He pulled out a large white handkerchief, unfolded it, and using it like a dish rag, wiped the sweat from his face. "Yeah, I filed that report. I did some rounds myself that night, checking on reports about vandalism in that part of town. I found Carmichael. Whoever hit him was driving like a crazy maniac. He was mangled beyond belief."

"Did you call an ambulance to attempt to resuscitate him?"

"No. Why should I? He was dead."

"Is it your prerogative as a police officer to make that determination?"

"He was dead, I tell you! I don't want to describe what he looked like in front of this radio audience!"

"I'm not asking what the body looked like. I just want to know whether you had the authority to pronounce him dead, and why you didn't call an ambulance. You're an officer of the law. You didn't even have to go to a phone. All you had to do was pick up the radio mike in your police vehicle. You could have had an ambulance there in minutes. Why didn't you?"

"I did what anyone would have done. What are you getting at?"

"No, you *didn't* do what anyone would have done! Anyone else would have had to call an ambulance and a doctor or medic would have had to examine him. If there was no doctor on the scene, he would have been taken to a hospital and pronounced dead on arrival. Was he?"

"I don't remember."

Harris leaned back in his seat and loosened his tie. He shook his head. 'You don't remember? And you're the sheriff of this county? You found a body by the roadside, and you don't remember what you did? Well, let me refresh your memory," Harris said as if Sheriff

Hancock were standing trial before the entire county. "According to this report, you had James Carmichael's body taken directly to the coroner's office. Nobody saw the body but you and the coroner. No doctor, no medic, or other police officer. Since when do you have the right to take that kind of unilateral action?"

Sheriff Hancock leaned forward over the table and twisted both his hands back and forth around the mike stand, as if its slender steel cylinder was Harris's throat. "Young man, I've been sheriff of this county nearly as long as you've been alive, and no one has ever questioned my integrity! No one has ever questioned my handling of the law! No one has ever dared make the kind of accusations you're making."

"Accusations? I didn't make any accusations, Sheriff Hancock. I merely asked how you handled a routine police investigation after discovering a body."

"Gentlemen," Wes Bryant said, interrupting the tense proceedings as if he were an impartial moderator. "According to the log in front of me, we're late again for a commercial break. You callers out there, I promised we'd get to you, and we will. Don't go away! We'll be right back. You're listening to 'Talk about Town.'"

Wes hit the button activating the commercial cart, simultaneously reaching to the speaker volume control for the studio monitor. He turned it up as loud as was tolerable, hoping the appeal to buy Columbus County organic tomatoes would irritate Hancock.

After making his prerequisite marks on the station log, indicating the commercial and what time it played,

Wes continued flipping through the programming schedule, an exercise designed to make him look busy and to avoid any interaction if Warren Crews tried to intervene again.

Wes didn't want to break the tension. Beads of sweat had formed on Sheriff Hancock's brow below the brim of his hat. He tapped his fingers on the top of the table and shifted his weight from side to side.

Two minutes later, the last commercial cart triggered the station jingle, bringing the audience back to "Talk about Town."

"Wes Bryant again. My guests are Manley Harris, a local attorney, and Sheriff Arnold Hancock."

Wes looked at his computer screen for a signal regarding which line to take and which caller would be first. Bailey had typed: "#1, Mary, Center Street Bridge," obviously a question about the old decaying viaduct on Center Street that everybody wanted shut down as a safety hazard; "2, Henry, new patrol cars; "3, Phyllis, school crossing patrols."

None of the caller's questions focused on events in the studio. They either were more concerned with things that directly affected them, or they were too afraid and embarrassed to pursue the matter. Rather than let Hancock off the hook by immediately taking a caller, Wes said, "Mary, Phyllis, and Henry, I'll be with you in a moment. Hang on! First, back to Harris and Hancock for a final comment. Sheriff Hancock?"

"I've got nothing to say. I came here to talk about what really matters. Safe streets, good police protection, keeping drugs out of town, and looking after the proud citizens of Columbus County."

"Manley Harris?" Wes said. "Anything else before we go to the calls"

"One more thing, Mr. Bryant," Harris responded. "I have in my hands a petition to the state Attorney General, signed by Hannah Carmichael, the Reverend James Carmichael's widow, asking that James Carmichael's body be exhumed for an official autopsy. When I leave today, this petition will be filed in Columbus County District Court!"

Twenty-one

If Sheriff Hancock was disturbed about exhuming Reverend James Carmichael's body, he concealed it well. Wes was amazed to see the arrogant look in Hancock's eyes and the defiant set to his chin.

Sheriff Hancock picked up the paper lying in front of him and stacked them vertically, methodically squaring the edges. He placed them in a small, black plastic briefcase he had brought to the studio and turned to Wes, "Mr. Bryant, I have some important matters to take care of. You'll excuse me . . ."

Wes interrupted quickly. "I thought you were going to stay for the entire show. That was our agreement."

Sheriff Hancock's eyes narrowed to slits. His bushy eyebrows tipped downward as he coldly looked at Wes and blustered, "Well, things change, don't they? You'll just have to do without me."

Pushing his chair from the table, Hancock arose and stretched out a hand in Manley Harris's direction. "Mr. Harris, I'm sure we'll meet again. You and Mr. Bryant can handle the rest of this show without me."

With that, Sheriff Arnold Hancock left the studio. Wes was pleased that he had turned tail and run, despite his outward composure. Knowing the evil Hancock was capable of, his comment about meeting Harris again was not lost on Wes, as he faced his mike and said, "Don't go away! Stay tuned. We'll have more in a minute."

Wes hit the cart deck, inaugurating another round of commercials, and stood up to ease his tension. He half expected Crews to glare at him from the other side of Bailey's window. But he wasn't there and neither was Bailey.

"Do you want me to stay?" Harris asked. "I'll be glad to talk about my other objections to the sobriety checkpoints."

Wes rubbed his neck as if loosening the tense muscles attached to his cranium would also unleash an idea about what he should do. "Sure. Stay here. Let's continue the show, with or without Hancock."

The rest of the show was anticlimactic, a one-sided debate. After fifteen minutes, even the callers had exhausted all aspects of the sobriety checkpoints. When the show ended, Wes said good-bye to Manley Harris and completed his usual post-show routing of readying the studio for whoever used it next. Mentally, he relived the moments when Hancock sweated out Harris's questions and smiled to himself at the sheriff's discomfort.

As he walked toward the main lobby of the station where Brenda was answering phones, the late-day sun flickered through the dust-coated Venetian blinds. A beam of light made its way through the cracks and glistened on a wall of the hallway and the infamous rogue's gallery of photos. Wes had passed by these pictures often without noticing them, but today he sunlight accented them strangely.

It must be the angle of the sun this time of year, he thought, scanning the pictorial account of WTTK's influence on Columbus County.

Wes glanced at the photograph of Girl Scouts presenting an award to Crews. Next to him was a famous presidential candidate and shots of other county officials who had been involved with WTTK. Another photo depicted a gathering at the large public funeral of the city's recent mayor, Edward Grimsby. Wes had never met the man and dimly remembered hearing about him as a kind but ineffectual person with few civic accomplishments. The black-suited, leading citizens of Clarion were standing at the entrance of the cemetery. Wes noticed that the person next to Hancock was the librarian. Next to her stood Warren Crews; then, by his side, the county coroner. Wes didn't know the other, obviously important, people in the official photo.

Looking at the photograph, Wes sensed something he hadn't noticed before. He stepped closer and, with his fingertips, brushed aside the dust that had collected on the glass. Impossible! He thought. He leaned closer, eyes inches from the photo. Hancock, Crews, the coroner, and several other city officials had something in common— they were all wearing cufflinks with a triangular symbol. Suddenly, the exhilaration Wes had felt moments ago was exhausted.

The Order! Wes thought. *They all belong—every one of them including Crews.*

Now, he knew why Crews had been so disturbed about Hancock's treatment. And if the coroner was an active member of the Order, what about the death of Larry Bender? Had Larry uncovered something the Order didn't want him to know? Like a hangman's noose tightening around his neck, Wes felt his nightmare choking him.

His thoughts were interrupted by WTTK's receptionist, Brenda.

"Wes, got a message for you," she said, handing him a neatly folded piece of paper. "Your daughter, Misha, called. Here's her number.
She'd like to hear from you today, if possible."

Wes looked curiously at the paper. *Why would Misha call me?* he
wondered. *I haven't heard from her in months.*

Wes had had all the suspense and strain he could stand for one
day. He hurried down the hallway toward WTTK's back door and
accidentally bumped his shin against two massive loudspeaker cabinets stacked against the hall.

He reached down to rub his leg, certain he had drawn blood. The
huge, three-feet-high and two-feet-wide speakers were part of a new
outdoor public address system destined for the Clarion High School
football field. George Rainey, WTTK's chief engineer, had been hired to
install them but he had nowhere to store them in the interim because
they were so large. Crews had given permission to leave them in the
hallway, since almost no one on WTTK's staff used the back door.

The promise of being alone for an evening—taking a hot bath,
watching a couple of hours of television—sounded wonderful. He'd
call Misha later. Right now, he needed decompression time after the
show. People who had never been involved in the media often said
to him, "You've sure got an easy job! What's the big deal about sitting in a chair and talking for a few hours? They pay you for that?"
He smiled wryly. He knew what hard work it was.

Wes stuffed the note with Misha's number in his pants so he'd
find it when he emptied his pockets that evening and stepped out-

side to the parking lot. As he put his key into the car door lock, he noticed a piece of paper stuffed in the crack between the door and the frame. *Probably a solicitation to buy something at a local store*, he thought. Yet he'd never seen one stuffed in the crack of the door before. Wes opened the door and unfolded the piece of paper.

A fair exchange.

The Raven's wife returned or

The daughter taken.

Wes recalled the comment Jennifer had made about her husband. But who was the daughter? *Oh, no! They meant Misha!* The thought shot through his mind. *Have they threatened her? Is that why she's trying to call me?*

Wes crumpled the paper, threw it to the car floor, and ran back into the station to his office. Quickly, he dialed Misha. The line was busy. Wes tried to get through several more times with no success.

I'll drive to my apartment and call from there, he thought.

Wes rushed the short distance across town, speeding in 35 mile-per-hour zones. As he drove, he thought about Misha's junior high school years, a time that was supposed to be carefree and explorative. Instead, it had become a battleground as Wes and Polly jockeyed for position during the demise of their relationship. Misha was trapped in the middle, torn between feelings of loyalty and hostility. Wes and Polly's problem became Misha's nightmare.

After the dust settled, Misha's feminine instincts led her toward her mother. She wasn't bitter toward Wes, but she needed an enduring relationship with at least one parent.

Wes remembered her as a freckle-faced child whose curly auburn locks ringed her head. He recalled the day she had skinned her knee as she navigated solo without bicycle training wheels; the time they raked crisp, copper-hued leaves into a big pile in the backyard and recklessly jumped into them, scattering their collection in all directions; and the day he brought home a mongrel terrier from the animal shelter, her first pet in a long series of dogs, kittens, and hamsters.

In the last seven years, they had gone separate ways. Her auburn hair had darkened, and her moods had turned even darker. It wasn't that Misha refused to spend time with her father or to tolerate his presence. It was just that an unacknowledged tension made it uncomfortable for them to be around each other.

Wes reached his apartment and rushed inside. Without removing his overcoat, he grabbed the phone and dialed Misha's number. "It's your dad," he said when she answered. "I got a message you wanted to talk to me."

"Where have you been?" Misha asked. "It's been several days since anyone at the radio station heard from you, and you haven't been on the air."

Wes was surprised. He hadn't known she listened to "Talk about Town." A surge of pride flushed his face.

Misha continued. "Anyway, that's not why I called. I've got to talk to you about something. Can I come over?"

Wes felt overwhelmed by the unexpected request. Misha had never been to his apartment. After the divorce, he had stopped once to see the small two-bedroom apartment she and a girlfriend had rented, but Misha had avoided his place. She had made it plain she didn't want to visit him because it reminded her of the divorce.

"No," Wes said, abruptly remembering the threat on the note. He surmised it would be safer if she stayed put. "I'll come get you."

"Oh, Dad," Misha said softly. "There you go again, being overprotective. I won't hear of your driving over here. I'm coming there."

Wes decided to concede to her concern about his being overbearing, hoping there was no risk in her driving to his apartment. "All right, drive carefully. You know how to find my place?"

"It's on the left side of that yellow and white two-story apartment off Fifth Avenue, isn't it?"

"That's it. Just ring the buzzer."

Wes wondered if Misha's reaching out to him could mean a new beginning in their relationship. What should he do when Misha walked in? Should he hug her or keep his distance? He had to handle things carefully. He was no expert at intimacy.

Wes showered, then checked the refrigerator for drinks and snacks. Nothing but a couple of cans of Pepsi, some cold Italian sausage, a few slices of bread, some cream cheese, and assorted leftovers. Bending over, his head half in the refrigerator, pushing aside bottles of salad dressing, pickles, and half-consumed edibles, he jumped at the sound of the doorbell.

He went to the front door and opened it to see Misha, looking far too tired for nineteen, her eyes hollow with dark shadows under them. Either she was pretty strung-out or she hadn't slept much lately. She wore blue jeans that were shredded at the knees and the upper part of the thighs, though Wes wasn't sure if it was from wear and tear or conformity to fashion. She had slung a well-worn backpack over her left shoulder.

Misha stood silently at first, staring at the ground. Finally, she looked up, her wide brown eyes gazing intently at Wes. For an awkward moment, neither spoke. Then Wes opened his arms and reached out. Misha let her backpack slide off her shoulder and fall to the ground as she stepped into his arms. It was the first time in years they had touched each other.

"Come in, honey," Wes said, putting his arm around her. Misha grabbed her backpack and snuggled close to Wes, her shoulder barely reaching his armpit. She walked to the tattered couch that was covered with a blanket and slumped down in one corner, leaning on her elbow and looking as if she could fall asleep momentarily.

"Why don't you rest while I get some coffee," Wes suggested, walking toward the kitchen.

When he returned, Misha's eyes were closed and he wondered if he should wake her. "Misha?" he said softly.

She jerked upright quickly as if she had been stirred from a brief frightening dream. Wes handed her a cup of coffee.

"You don't look too good," he observed. "have you been getting enough sleep or are you still working the night shift at that garden hose plant?"

"Naw. I quit there months ago. Been doing odd cleaning jobs for people and picking up a few dollars here and there with baby-sitting. Just haven't had much sleep lately."

"Something bothering you?"

"Yeah, sort of. Well, I guess wouldn't be here otherwise. It's not like you and I get together all the time. If I'm bothering you and you're too busy, I can come back some other time," Misha said, as if looking for an excuse to leave.

Wes responded quickly. "No! Right now is fine. I was just going to watch some TV this evening and get to bed early, but I'd much rather talk with you."

Misha took several deep sips of steaming coffee, slurping it slightly to cool it. "I know we never talked much about religion around our house, but do you know anything about the occult, Dad?"

Wes was stirring the instant coffee granules in his cup when Misha asked the question causing him to jerk the cup handle. Some of the hot brew sloshed over the edge. He winced and grabbed a handkerchief from his pocket.

"You OK, Dad?"

"Yeah, honey. I'm fine. Go on."

"I heard you interview that psychic a few weeks back. You know, the one who wrote the book about aura character analysis and how you can find out what people are really like by reading the colors in the atmosphere around their bodies? I just wondered if you've read any books or run into people who know about that stuff."

"I can't say I'm an expert, but I've read a few articles about extrasensory phenomena, witchcraft, voodoo, that sort of thing." If the Order of the Dark Raven qualified for Misha's definition of the occult, he knew more than he wanted to, certainly more than he could tell her.

"You know, this girlfriend I'm living with, Roxanne Thornbury?" Misha said. "She fools around with that stuff."

"What stuff?"

"Ouija boards, tarot cards, books on witchcraft. You know, that kind of stuff."

"So, why should that affect you, as long as she minds her own business and doesn't bother you with it?"

"Well, that's the problem. She isn't minding her own business anymore. It used to be just a fad with her. Now, she goes to meetings all the time, and she wants me to go with her. What bothers me is the look in her eyes. I don't know how to describe it. Sometimes when I look at her, it's not really her. It's weird. You know what I mean, Dad? Have you ever looked at anyone like that? Someone whose soul was so evil you could feel it when you looked in their eyes? Like, all the bad was looking back at you?"

Misha's words arrested his arm in midair as he lifted his coffee cup to his lips. He had seen that look, too frequently, in fact, in the eyes of the Simpsons, Sheriff Hancock, and Dr. Blackwell. Was Misha's roommate possessed by the same kind of evil that controlled the Order?

"Is this the first time you've thought about this?" Wes asked. "Why bring it up now?"

"Until last night, I tried to ignore it," Misha said, holding her cup of coffee with both hands and tilting it in a circular motion, swirling the coffee to distract her foreboding thoughts. "Roxanne came home after midnight and . . ." Misha stopped speaking. She rubbed the top of her forehead with her right hand and combed back the strands of her bangs with her fingers. Wes sat down at the other end of the couch and waited for her to go on.

"I'm not sure I really want to talk about this," Misha said. "Maybe it was a big mistake, coming over here. I can handle this by myself. I'm probably reading too much into it anyway. I always was super-sensitive about what people thought and said, like my moth . . ." Misha caught herself, embarrassed.

Wes was pleased that Misha had thought to approach him for help. "Yes, you're a lot like your mother. Both of you are very sensitive people. That's the first thing that attracted me to her."

Misha stopped playing with her hair, surprised. She had assumed that the bitterness of the divorce was still part of her father's life.

"You were telling me about last night. What happened?" Wes asked.

"Roxanne goes out a lot at night and comes home real late. I'm not exactly a night owl, so I'm usually asleep when she gets back. But last night, I was reading this really good paperback I bought at Millican's Pharmacy. You know, he's got that section at the front of the store with all the murder mysteries. I'd just turned off my bed light when Roxanne came home.

"She must have thought I was asleep. I guess that's why she wasn't more careful. Our beds are in the same room, and I saw her put some things in a box in her side of the closet. I guess she never thought I'd look there. But then, until last night, I'd never thought I'd look there. But then, until last night, I'd never had reason to. I was curious about what she'd been doing." Misha cupped her face in her hands and cried, "Oh, Dad, I wish I hadn't looked. I wish I had just left it alone."

Misha stood up, wiped her eyes with the back of her hand, and picked up her cup of coffee for warmth. She walked toward the kitchen. "Can I heat this up?" she asked.

"Sure!" Wes jumped to his feet and crossed the small living room to the kitchen where he turned up the heat under the tea kettle on the stove.

"So, how long has it been since you've talked to Mom?" Misha asked, continuing to avoid her story.

"I'm not sure. A couple of months. There was a question about health insurance, and she called me at the station. The last time I saw her was four or five months ago. She looked well."

"I talk to her once in a while on the phone, and every couple of weeks we get together for dinner," Misha said. "You never did say why you didn't do your show this week."

"Out of town. I had some business to take care of in Chicago."

"Chicago? I didn't know you did business in Chicago."

"It's some new stuff I'm involved in, pretty complicated. I'll tell you about it sometime."

"Who looks after your place here? You don't clean it yourself, do you, Dad?" she said, grinning.

"No! I don't have time. The lady who cleans the WTTK offices comes in once every two or three weeks and tidies things up a bit. Keeps it from going completely to the dogs."

"Well, I guess I'd better go," Misha said, setting down her cup of cold coffee on the kitchen table.

"I thought you wanted some fresh coffee? The water's ready to boil."

"I changed my mind," Misha answered. "I want to get back to my book. It's a great murder mystery, but it's not very believable. The kind of stuff that scares people, but everybody knows it doesn't happen in real life."

As Misha walked toward the door Wes said, "Misha, you came here on your own, and you can leave on your own. I won't push you. Whatever you wanted to talk about, it's OK if you want to drop it, but I don't think you should. Can you tell me what Roxanne put in that closet?"

Misha whirled back to him and blurted, "Yes!" Misha swallowed hard, trying to force a big lump back down her throat. "There were bones in the box," Misha said, speaking in a hushed voice. "Small bones, but too big for a chicken or rabbit or anything like that. And there was a knife in the box, not a single-edged knife like the Boy Scouts' knife. A double-edged knife with a fancy handle that had a design on it . . . three overlapping triangles. And on the blade of the knife . . ." Misha took a deep breath. "Daddy! It couldn't be!" she cried, throwing her arms around Wes, burying her face into his chest.

"What, Misha?" Wes said, stroking her hair. "What was it?"

"On the blade of the knife, something brownish . . . all dried and caked. Maybe it was nail polish or something like that, but . . . it looked like blood."

Quiet settled over Wes and Misha. It seemed as if they knew something that neither wanted to speak aloud or admit to each other.

Then Misha added a final detail. "The strangest thing about the stuff in the box made no sense at all. If Roxanne is in some crazy group that fools around with blood, killing animals, cutting herself or whatever, then what did she do with the other thing I found in the box—a long, black feather?"

Twenty-two

Neither Wes nor Misha wanted to talk further about the secret life of Misha's roommate, Roxanne Thornbury. Misha felt better after telling her dad, but she quickly slipped into a state of denial after doing so and had nothing more to say. Wes had his own reasons for squelching the conversation. Questions about Roxanne's possible affiliation with the Order could give him away.

As Misha kissed Wes good-bye, he realized the evil of the Order of the Black Raven had penetrated deeper into his own daily existence. Sure, Annette and Jennifer were like family. But Misha was his flesh and blood, and she shared living quarters with a young woman who probably knew about the note left on his car.

"If you're worried about going back to you place, you're welcome to stay here with me," Wes offered.

Misha smiled and touched Wes's arm. "Thanks, but I think I'll go back. If I need you, I'll let you know."

As Misha walked out the door, Wes determined one thing: from now on, he would make more frequent contact with Misha. The potential danger from the Order wasn't his only reason. Wes also yearned to mend he gap between them.

That weekend and all the next week were filled with a tension Wes had never experienced as he worried about Misha and about Annette and Jennifer, who were alone in Chicago.

Every night at 8:00 p.m., Annette walked to a pay phone at the corner on Calhoun Street to call. Wes worried about an attractive woman like Annette phoning in the darkness, where any unscrupulous individual could accost her, just as her namesake, Helen Logan, had been accosted. But it would be worse not to have the daily reports assuring him they were well.

Wes also made daily contact with Misha. They didn't have long conversations, but he reassurance of Misha's safety relieved him. Things at "Talk about Town" changed little, provincial boredom enlivened with occasional controversy. It was revenue-producing, and that's what concerned Wes most as he laid aside every spare dollar for Jennifer's welfare.

Ten days after Wes's return to Clarion, Annette called excitedly with the news she had gotten a job. It sounded strange that an upper-class suburbanite like Annette would be enamored with the idea of tending petunias and fertilizing geraniums, but Wes understood that her employment at the Flowers-R-N-Art Shoppe was important to her damaged self-esteem. Jennifer had enrolled in school, and her precociousness quickly accelerated her in the classroom.

Annette told Wes that life was lonely and fearful for her and Jennifer. She had learned Jennifer was frightened of red cars, a trigger that had been implanted by the Order. Annette mentioned to Wes that she had kept quiet about Jennifer's comment regarding her "husband," waiting for the right moment to discuss it.

"Jennifer started seeing Dr. Olinger to treat her venereal disease,"

Annette said. "Although each visit is quite traumatic, Jennifer has coped well. Even her fear of doctors has begun to fade away. She knows that they are trying to make the pains in her stomach go away."

"Well," Wes interrupted, "that sounds like the best news I've heard in some time. Good for Jennifer!"

"But that's not all, Wes. You haven't heard the best part! On her third visit Dr. Olinger became the proud owner of a 'Jennifer Original.' She had carefully drawn a picture for him of a sunny day with lots of green trees and a blue sky. Wes, can you believe it? A sunny day! I know she's going to be better."

Wes smiled from ear to ear, and even though he couldn't see Annette, he knew she was smiling too.

"Dr. Olinger was so pleased, he reached out to hold Jennifer in a warm hug. She let him, and there wasn't a trace of panic in her eyes. He told her that it was the most wonderful day he had ever seen, and he is keeping the picture right by his desk to remind him of her when his own days aren't so bright."

"I guess I've worried about you for nothing," Wes chuckled.

"Oh, Wes! I just wish you could have been there. Giving that picture to Dr. Olinger was so good for Jennifer, more important than even the treatment and medication. Dr. Olinger is the kindest man I've ever known . . . well, almost the kindest."

The conversation ebbed away. After hanging up, Wes relaxed in the arms of his favorite chair, reflecting on Annette's words. He could begin to see that caring people were gathered around them to

fight back the darkness. But the Order and their threats of retaliation still had to be faced. If they did intend to harm his daughter,
Misha, they were either going about it the long way or simply bid-
ing their time. Perhaps they were concentrating on finding Annette
and Jennifer. At 11:30 Wes fell into a deep sleep, still seated in his
familiar recliner.

Suddenly, from the warm fog of slumber, Wes was jolted awake
by the commanding bell of his wall phone. It was Annette again,
pushing their lives forward dramatically by a single call.

"Wes, I know it's late, almost 2:00 a.m., and we just spoke a few
hours ago, but I had to talk to you again tonight," Annette said. "I
left Jennifer in the apartment and slipped out to call you. We had a
long talk after I hung up with you earlier, and you need to know
what she told me."

Wes muttered a sleepy greeting and a warning about Annette
being out on the street that late at night and leaving Jennifer alone
in the apartment. Annette protested, "This is just too important to
wait for the morning. When I was tucking Jennifer into bed tonight,
I finally asked her what she meant by husband. I was right about
one thing . . . My husband Gregory was her husband."

Wes said nothing. The tone of Annette's voice and the rapid pace
of her speech convinced him that he shouldn't interfere with the
flow of her conversation.

"Jennifer was married to Gregory in a ceremony last winter, just
before the accident," Annette went on. "She described the whole

thing to me." Annette paused, a silence so long that Wes wondered if she was still at the other end of the line.

"Annette? Are you there?"

"Yes. Be patient with me. Wes. This is hard to talk about. I don't know if I can get through it again, but I'll try."

Annette took a deep breath and continued, "It happened while I was gone over a weekend, attending a women's seminar sponsored by a volunteer group I worked with. One night that weekend, Gregory dressed Jennifer in a black gown, like a wedding dress. He scratched a name on her forehead. When I got back, I noticed her forehead was all scratched, but Gregory said she had taken a bad fall while riding her bike. I wish I had asked more questions at the time, but I just never suspected . . . never suspected that . . ."

Annette choked on her words. Wes knew she was stunned to learn that the man she had called her husband had married their daughter in a ceremony so evil only the events of the last month convinced her it was real.

"Gregory drove her to some place in the countryside. Jennifer was blindfolded, so she didn't know where they were going. When she got there, they went into a room filled with people dressed in black. Everyone seemed happy she was there. It was a festive occasion. They kept calling her a queen and said how honored she was to be a bride of the Dark Raven. Wes, they even put her through a kind of ceremony. She remembered part of it, something like, 'Honor and obey, in death we are reborn,' similar to a wedding vow, only backward, reversed. Then after the vows, they bathed her." Annette's voice fell silent. Again, Wes wondered if she had been cut off.

"Annette!" Silence. "Are you still there?" Nothing. The silence was so long Wes almost hung up so Annette could call him again if they'd been cut off. Then Annette's frail voice spoke.

"They took the black wedding dress off her. She was naked. They bathed her . . . in blood, their blood. Each member in the group cut himself, and then . . . the men urinated in a large pail, and they mixed it with the blood. They poured all that over Jennifer."

Wes wondered if he should halt the conversation. Annette enunciated each word haltingly, drawing out multisyllable words as if trying to speak a foreign language.

"When they finished bathing her, they raped her, all the men. Jennifer doesn't remember how many. She just said, 'Lots.' I asked her, 'Five? Six?' All she could say was, 'More, lots more.'

"Wes, I don't understand. Bad people are bad people! Evil is evil. But this, this is . . . unspeakable, unimaginable." Annette paused again. This time, Wes didn't wonder if she would resume the conversation. He knew there was more.

"Wes, I'm not sure if I believe what Jennifer told me happened next. Maybe she made it all up. If the part I just told you was true, perhaps it scarred her mind and emotions so badly, something snapped, and she thought other crazy things happened too. I don't know. I just don't know.

"Anyway, the building where all this took place was on a farm.

They took her outside to the barn. While Jennifer watched, the killed a horse, a large horse, then split open its belly and cleaned out its insides. Jennifer's hands and feet were tied, and she was put . . . Wes, I think I'm going to get sick."

Faintly, in the distance over the phone, Wes could hear the sound of Annette retching. Then she coughed and spit, obviously clearing her mouth of the acrid taste of vomit.

She shouldn't be going through this alone. Wes thought disconsolately. *Why am I here in Clarion while she's alone in Chicago?*

Finally Annette regained her composure and spoke again. "I'm sorry, Wes. I just couldn't handle it."

"That's OK. You don't have to tell me anything you don't want to."

"No, no! I have to! They laid Jennifer inside the gutted belly of that horse, and they somehow . . . Wes, I don't know how they did it. I don't even know if it's possible. I'm not sure it's true. They somehow enlarged the rear end of the horse and pulled Jennifer through it. The way Jennifer explained it, they told her the horse was giving birth to her. Jennifer was now reborn to serve the Dark Raven. Then, Gregory renounced being her father and declared that he was her husband."

"Am I losing my mind, Wes? Has the strain gotten to Jennifer? Is she going crazy too? Do you believe anything I'm telling you?"

Wes thought back to the sight of James Carmichael's bloody body ripped open, and Dr. Blackwell holding the palpitating heart in his hand. Who would believe that?

"I can't take it anymore, Wes. I can't take living alone! I know that

I have Michelle and Dr. Olinger but, Wes, it isn't enough. This is too much for me to handle. And I can't deal with the fact that the Order, whoever these people are, goes on treating others like they treated Jennifer. I can't live in fear the rest of my life, wondering when a police officer might stop me for speeding or some kind of paper trail will reveal my whereabouts.

"I think one of them is in every car that drives by this phone booth. This has to end, Wes, and I've got to end it. I made up my mind tonight to come back to Clarion and go public with my story. I want you to come get me, and we've got to keep Jennifer hidden until I can find someone, some sane, decent person . . . Is there anyone left like that? I don't know . . . someone in the courts, someone in law enforcement who will believe me and stop the Order before anyone else suffers like this."

Wes stood up. He had been waiting for some extraordinary event to compel him into action, but he had never expected this. Trust the courts to reveal the iniquitous deeds of the Order? If Annette went through with it, Wes knew she'd need all the legal help she could get. Wes decided Manley Harris would be the first person he'd call.

"You're serious, Annette?" Wes asked. "Maybe this is just a reaction to what you've heard. Sleep on it. Maybe you'll change your mind in the morning."

"I told you, I'm going public with my story."

It was useless to argue the issue. "I'll take off first thing in the morning to come get you. Any idea who could look after Jennifer?

It would have to be somebody you know and trust, who can empathize with Jennifer's hurt and rejection."

Annette knew someone. "I'll speak with Nurse Milthorpe early tomorrow morning after Jennifer's treatment with Dr. Olinger. Michelle has become a very good friend to Jennifer, and I know she'll help. Wes, Jennifer has moments now that are filled with hope. She even prays with me at night before she goes to bed. I'm sure Michelle has been a major influence in breaking down some walls for Jennifer."

As he listened to Annette, Wes wondered if an idea he had might be beneficial beyond helping Jennifer. "I agree about Nurse Milthorpe, but I'd also like to bring my daughter, Misha. That way, we'll have a backup when Michelle has to be at the hospital. Don't worry. Annette. I'll have it all worked out. Misha and I will see you by noon."

"What will I tell Jennifer?"

"Leave it to me. You get back to the apartment before she wakes up and is frightened because you're not there. I don't fully under-stand your decision, but I'll support you a hundred percent."

Wes threw on a robe and sat down in his lounge chair to contemplate Annette's call. He wondered why he was central to all the hellish events of recent weeks. He'd never seen himself as an extraordinary person. In fact, the last twenty years had been pretty uneventful, except for the divorce from Polly.

Why was he being thrust into the role of protector and prosecutor? Amidst these unanswered questions, he remembered needing to call Manley Harris.

Wes sat back down in his lounge chair to call Manley Harris. He didn't know Harris well enough to realize he was a deep sleeper, the kind who could peacefully ignore a bomb explosion in the next room. He worked long hours, building a law practice against almost insurmountable odds. By the time he got to bed at night, he didn't sleep like a baby; he crashed like a rock into the depths of slumber. The phone rang so many times Wes wondered if Harris had left town. Finally he answered in a surly voice that made Wes wince.

"Manley Harris? It's Wes Bryant. I know it's late, but this is an emergency."

The urgent tone in Wes's voice jolted Harris awake. "Wes, I've been thinking a lot about you. If this concerns that business of exhuming Reverend Carmichael's body, there's nothing to report. The courts are dragging their feet, like I expected them to do."

"No," Wes interrupted, "It has nothing to do with that. Do you know anything about custodial cases . . . you know, where there's a divorce, and a parent is protesting rights to see the child?"

"I've dealt with a few. Most have been pretty straight forward arguments over one of the parents' feeling her or she got a raw deal. Why call me at two-thirty in the morning about that?"

"Suppose one of the parents disagrees with the custodial decree and kidnaps the child, you know, goes into hiding and violates a court order. Would you handle a case like that?"

"That depends on the reason."

"Child abuse."

"I'd take a case like that."

"Manley, I need you to take a case right now—I'm referring to Annette Simpson and her daughter, Jennifer. Remember, the night Reverend Carmichael was murdered, I asked you to talk with Hannah about the situation."

"Yes, she explained it to me as best she could."

"I haven't got time to go into detail now. I'll get in touch with you late tomorrow afternoon. Annette has been in hiding for two weeks. Now, she wants to go public with her story. I'm afraid to turn her over to the Columbus County courts and Hancock's jurisdiction. Manley, Hancock personally killed Carmichael, and he didn't do it with a car."

"Look, Bryant, if there's any chance that we can bring to justice the people who killed Carmichael, Joshua's battle of Jericho will be nothing compared to the walls of evil I'd bring down. I'd stake my life, my law practice, and everything I've got on it. I'll stay at my office tomorrow until you call."

As difficult as Manley Harris's call was, Wes considered picking up the phone to dial Misha, a tougher task. The last week had been remedial, but years of accumulated hurt couldn't be erased by a few phone calls. What if Roxanne answered? He'd have to risk it, tell her there was an emergency.

Wes was relieved to hear Misha answer the phone. "It's Dad," he said, "don't act startled. Try not to wake up Roxanne. I need to ask a favor of you."

A weak all right was all Misha could muster.

"After Roxanne leaves for work tomorrow morning, pack a suit-case. Leave a message for her, say you've just learned a dear friend of the family is seriously ill, and you must go away for a while. Leave a few of your things behind so it doesn't look too suspicious, but take everything that's important to you. You may not be back."

Wes paused, giving Misha a chance to respond, but he quickly real-ized she wouldn't speak for fear of awakening Roxanne. Wes contin-ued, "I'll pick you up about nine o'clock. Don't say anything to any-one about leaving."

Wes put down the phone, scarcely believing what he had done. Tomorrow, he would drive Misha to Chicago and ask her to stay with Jennifer. If anyone could expose and heal the wounds in Misha's life, Nurse Milthorpe could.

Wes stood up from the chair and stretched his arms over his head, pondering his plans. He thought of all the people whose help he'd need to implement a life-saving scenario for Jennifer. If any one of these people let him down, Annette's plan to expose the Order of the Dark Raven would fall.

Twenty-three

As Wes rounded the corner of the street to Misha's apartment he spotted her sitting on the front steps, a beat-up suitcase at her side, elbows on her knees, her chin resting in her hands. Wes thought she looked like a forlorn waif, running away to parts unknown.

Misha looked up, startled from deep thought, as Wes pulled to the curb. She picked up her suitcase and headed for the car. Wes wondered why she wasn't carrying more clothing, then realized her lifestyle didn't demand an exotic wardrobe. He guessed the suit case contained another pair of jeans, maybe an extra set of sneakers, some sweats, and T-shirts.

"Hi, Dad," she said, opening the back door and throwing her suit-case on the seat, then getting in the front passenger side.

Wes reached over and squeezed her hand. "Thanks for trusting me," he said "I know you're in the dark about all this, but in addition to helping me, you're getting out of that apartment. I've been worried ever since you told me about Roxanne."

Misha tossed back her hair and grinned. "It's not like I have a lot of commitments to hold me here or that I've got something better to do with my life right now. Besides, if you really need me, it does-n't matter anyway."

Wes glanced at her, pleasantly surprised. Misha had always seemed independent and rebellious. Even as a child, she wanted to do things her way. He was unprepared for her cooperative attitude.

Wes waited until they got on Interstate 360 North before explaining things to Misha. "Several weeks ago, I had a run-in with a secret occult group in the county. I suspect it's the same group that Roxanne is messed up in. I discovered they were physically and emotionally abusing a child. I rescued her . . . well, sort of . . . I kidnapped her, but they had already taken her illegally. This may not be making a lot of sense, but the bottom line is this: I helped her mother escape too. The two of them are secretly living in Chicago."

Misha didn't say anything, but she raised one eyebrow slightly. That was her querulous look, the one that asked question without saying a word.

"This making any sense?" Wes asked.

Misha cocked her head sideways. "Sort of. What's all this got to do with me?"

"The mother has decided she wants to expose the child's abuse. She's going to the authorities, but her daughter must remain in hiding, and she needs someone to look after her."

"Wait a minute! You mean, you want me to look after this little girl? How old is she?"

"Nine."

"Dad! I can't be an instant mother to a nine year old! How long is this going to take?"

"I don't know. Don't worry. Someone will be there with you."

"Who?"

"A friend of the mother."

"What if this occult group comes looking for this girl and finds me? What then?"

"That's a risk we have to take."

"You mean, I'll have to take!"

"Misha, when we get to Chicago, you can change your mind if you want to, and I'll take you right back to Clarion. But just give it a chance. Meet little Jennifer."

"OK. But remember, you said if I don't like the look of things, I don't have to go through with it. Promise?"

"Promise."

Neither of them said another word about the purpose for their journey. For the next two hours, Wes caught up on Misha's life the past few years. She did most of the talking; he did most of the listening. As they neared the outskirts of Chicago, Misha refocused the conversation on what they were doing.

"Jennifer's mother, what did you say her name was . . .?"

"Annette."

"Annette. She must be a brave lady to risk so much for the life of her child."

"Yes, a very brave lady."

"Suppose she doesn't want me looking after her daughter? What if she doesn't like me?"

"She will, Misha. She will."

Minutes later, Wes was driving down Calhoun Street toward Hattie

MacKenzie's apartment house. He parked a little distance down from the apartment. Together they climbed the steps and Wes knocked. At first, no one answered, so he knocked again. Then the curtain covering the kitchen window pulled back slightly, and Jennifer looked to see who was there. When she saw Wes, she opened the door and threw her arms around his waist as far as they would go, hugging him tightly, and crying out over and over again, "Mr. Wes! Mr. Wes! You came back!" Wes knelt and enfolded her in a smothering hug. For Misha, it was an awkward moment. She had never seen a child respond to Wes like this. In fact, she'd never seen anyone respond so warmly to her father.

Annette appeared behind Jennifer and also threw her arms around Wes and hugged him tightly. Wes pulled Annette and Jennifer close to him and turned to face Misha. Wes could see the emotion on her face, as she watched Jennifer and Annette express their feelings toward him. Even though it had been years since the divorce, Wes assumed Misha felt some jealousy. He reached out to Misha, pulling her to his side, defusing the pain of the moment.

"Misha, these are the people I told you about. Annette and Jennifer," he said, nodding at each of them alternately. "And this is Misha, the daughter I told you about."

Mr. Wes," Jennifer piped up. "She's pretty! Mommy said she's going to stay with me for a little while, while you're gone. Is that right?"

"Yes, if that's OK with you."

"Guess who else is here," Annette said, pointing behind her toward the tiny living room. Wes looked up to see Michelle Milthorpe, watching the whole scene. "I called and asked if she would come over and meet Misha. I also told her what I'm going to do, and she's agreed to help Misha any way she can."

"That's great!" Wes said.

Michelle Milthorpe poured a glass of milk for Jennifer and prepared coffee for the others. Then she took Jennifer by the hand, leading her into the bedroom so Annette, Wes, and Misha could be alone. For the next hours, they talked about Annette's decision and what it would mean to each of them.

Michelle returned to the living room and interrupted their conversation, offering sandwiches made with tuna salad she had mixed up earlier. "It's a long drive back to Clarion. You'd better have something to eat now, so you won't have to stop on the way."

Carefully thinking through her words, Michelle looked at Wes and Annette, then at Misha. "I know you're preparing for a fight against evil, but remember, you're not alone. God is only a prayer away, and despite how things look, don't give up!"

Michelle paused, as a serious look crossed her face. "I don't know if Dr. Ben told you much about me, but since you're leaving Jennifer in my care, you deserve to have more than a nurse's resume."

Wes and Annette looked at each other, wondering what to expect. "When I was sixteen, I entered the Sister of St. Francis Convent," Michelle explained. "I became a nun serving the spiritual needs of those in a hospital. One day, a young woman with a small infant came to the emergency room in the dead of night. She had been badly beaten, and her child was scarred from repeated abuse. The woman said her husband drank and was very violent. She couldn't take anymore, and she had no one to turn to. The sisters and I took them in and treated their wounds. Unfortunately, the baby was too severely injured and died the next morning.

"I decided that night that God had called me to treat wounds of the flesh as well as of the soul. So I began my nursing studies. When I finished and was accepted at St. Joseph's, I remained a part of the order under a special dispensation. That turned out to be a blessing because, while treating another abuse victim, I met Darcy Linmore. The sisters appointed me to help 'Believe the Victims.'"

Michelle paused and watched Annette's and Wes's reactions. They stood motionless, stunned by the revelation. "I'm sure you must find all this very surprising, but I believe our paths crossed for a divine purpose. Jennifer is safe with me. If she needs to hide somewhere, I won't hesitate to take her into seclusion at the convent."

Wes's eyes were transfixed on the face of this middle-aged nurse. "A nun?" he asked. "You're a nurse and a nun too?"

Michelle laughed, her face glowing from the warmth of her spirit. "I always wonder why that's so frustrating to people," she said. "What's so strange about being a nun?" She patted Wes's hand. "It's OK. I know how to burn toast and spill coffee too."

Annette laughed at Michelle's remark. "I knew you were special the first time we saw you with Jennifer," she said, "but I had no idea now very special you are. Thank God for you, Nurse Milthorpe.

And thank God for you, Sister Michelle."

Michelle went to Annette and hugged her tightly. "I love you, Annette," Michelle said, "and I want you to know that God is ready to go with you into battle."

"I love you too," Annette answered. "With God's strength, we'll make sure no other child ever suffers at the hands of the Order."

The two women shared a final assuring glance. Then Annette went to Jennifer and kissed her good-bye one last time. "I won't be away long, baby. Listen to Nurse Milthorpe and Misha."

"I will, Mommy."

Wes smiled at them and opened the front door. A tear slipped down Annette's cheek as she put on her coat and followed Wes out of the apartment.

Minutes later they were driving through the outskirts of Chicago, headed toward the Indiana state line. Wes and Annette talked about the aching hurt they felt leaving their daughters behind. Annette feared that, once out of her sight, Jennifer would exhibit some bizarre behavior induced by the Order's past abuse.

Wes realized how little he knew about Misha and how much he was counting on her to assume the responsibility of caring for a child. Knowing Michelle was there gave them both comfort. Her parting words touched both of them: "Remember, there's more than Misha and me looking after Jennifer," she had said, as Jennifer chimed in, "We've got angles on our side!"

Annette leaned over and tenderly kissed Wes on the cheek. As she slumped down in her seat and leaned her head back against the head-rest, she said, "You're a very special man, Wes Bryant. What went wrong between you and Polly is really none of my business. Maybe you were both at fault. I don't know. But I have the feeling you've grown a lot since then, and you're not the man she knew. I can tell you this much. I like the man I know. I like him a lot." As she said those words, a beautiful smile crossed her lips.

Wes looked at her out of the corner of his eye and realized she had just said the most affirming thing he'd heard from any woman since his first romance with Polly. It was good to feel needed. Wes had wondered if he'd ever feel like that again and had almost convinced himself it didn't matter. But now, sensing a warm surge of self-accept-ance, he realized he had been kidding himself.

As the suburbs of Chicago gave way to the farmlands of rural Indiana, Wes quietly passed the time watching the scenery slip by. He thought of the dramatic events that had passed through his life recently and realized how valuable time and life were. His thoughts scattered like so many dried cornstalks.

We are doing the right thing, Wes thought to himself. *Jennifer deserves the normal life of any other nine year old, and I'm going to see that she gets it!* He paused in thought as his car hurried past a small weathered church. Although Wes was not one to attribute much sig-nificance to symbolism, the appearance of the church at that moment brought a deep warmth to this heart.

As the outskirts of Clarion slowly came into view, Wes nudge

Annette's arm. At first, her limp body moved without any sign of waking. Wes gently touched her again. "Next stop, Clarion, Indiana," he said in his best imitation of a train conductor. Something about the finality of that statement abruptly awakened Annette.

"Wes," Annette said, "I'm not sure what to do next. I've made this decision to come back, but where to I start?'"

"First, we're going to call Manley Harris. He's waiting to hear from us," Wes said as he eased his car down the off ramp of the freeway at the Clarion exit. "There's a pay phone at the gas station over there." He pointed to the busy gas station fifty yards beyond the exit.

A dozen eighteen-wheelers sat behind the truck stop. In front, ten pumps stood ready to dispense diesel fuel to an ongoing stream of shiny semis. Clarion was a good place for them to stop. It was far enough from Chicago that they needed to refuel and handier than pulling off at a busy Indianapolis exit. The station also provided a wide array of services: a restaurant with homecooked hash truckers called "real" food, a mini-mart where you could rent videos or buy a loaf of bread, and a large restroom with shower stalls.

Wes pulled alongside the west end of the station near the restroom entrance, where a pay phone hung from the wall. He searched through his pockets for a quarter and dialed Manley Harris.

"Manley? It's Bryant," Wes said.

"Wes!" Harris exclaimed. "Boy, am I glad to hear from you! I never got back to sleep last night, trying to figure out this situation. It's not going to be as easy as I thought, Wes. Is Annette with you?"

"Yeah," Wes said. "We just pulled into town. Where can we meet?"

"Not at my office," Harris said. "How about Hannah Carmichael's? We'll be safe there. Besides, you're going to need a place for Annette to stay, and I assumed that's where you planned to take her."

"Hadn't really thought about it," Wes said.

"See you there in ten minutes?"

"Sure. Ten minutes."

Wes got back in the car and explained where they were headed. He didn't mention Harris's comment concerning problems. He wanted to wait until he heard more about what Harris meant.

Ten minutes later, Wes arrived at the Carmichael house, familiar surroundings that held for him a mixture of hope, fond memories, and deep pain. Buried somewhere behind that house was a dead cat, a bloody symbol of the Order's hatred for religion and civility.

Wes drove his car around the east side of the house where a grove of trees and some leafless lilac bushes provided obscurity.

As Wes and Annette walked to the front door Wes's mind went back to that night nearly three weeks ago when he first brought Annette to James and Hannah Carmichael. How things had changed since then.

It only took one firm knock on the door for Hannah Carmichael to answer. She flung open the screen door and engulfed Wes and Annette in her big, strong arms. As she did she broke into convulsive sobs. Several times, she tried to collect herself and say something, but she couldn't. She stood at the threshold of her doorway, leaning her head between Wes and Annette, weeping in sorrow for the loss of her husband and the return of her dear friends.

Hannah lifted her apron to her face and wiped the huge drops from her eyes until her apron was visibly wet. "Come in," she said. "Forgive me for acting like this. I just seem to feel things so strongly these days."

Hannah reached out both of her hands, took one of Wes's and Annette's hands and, stepping backward, led them through the door. Wes saw the old piano in the living room and remembered Hannah singing "Rock of Ages." Wes felt as if he were walking into a peaceful harbor, where love and faith somehow survived destruction. Manley Harris rose from the couch to greet them, shaking Wes's hand vigorously.

As Hannah and Annette began chatting, Harris motioned for Wes to follow him through the living room into the kitchen. It was unusually warm for mid-November and comfortable enough to sit outside in the sunshine. Harris pointed to a couple of aluminum folding chairs, the kind with brightly colored plastic webbing that dotted the backyards of Columbus County homes. Tucking the chairs under their arms, they slipped quietly out the back door and unfolded the chairs under a huge cotton wood tree that had shed its leaves and now lifted stark limbs against the deep blue sky.

Harris looked at Wes soberly. "I wish I had good news for you, but I don't."

"Aren't you going to take the case?"

"It's not that. This isn't a simple issue. A custodial hearing wouldn't help you."

Wes leaned forward, curious to hear what Harris was talking about.

"I sat down this morning and thought this whole thing through from every angle," Manley said. "If Annette wants to go before a judge and get a reversal of the custodial decree, that wouldn't be a criminal proceeding so it wouldn't be public. It's a closed hearing. She'd have no chance to tell her story beyond the courtroom. You couldn't be there. Annette would be all by herself with Jennifer and the grandparents. I don't think you want to subject her to that.

"I thought about the Grand Jury route, but I don't know how we'd pull that off, either. You'd have to go through a prosecutor's office, like he district attorney, so you'd have to convince the D.A. of your story, and that proceeding would be private too. Again, it would be Annette's word versus the Simpson grandparents in a closed setting.

"There is one other angle," Manley went on. "If Annette pleaded guilty to kidnapping her daughter, she might be indicted. But that would only be for contempt of court, not a criminal violation, since there's no missing person report. The Simpson grandparents never filed one because they didn't want the whole state knowing Jennifer was missing. Without filing some type of a charge, you can't get this thing before a judge."

"You mean, Annette can't just walk into a police station or into a judge's office and say she's kidnapped her daughter and violated a custody decree?"

"That's not the way the legal system works. Anyway, if she went to the police and said she kidnapped her own child, they'd immediately want to know where she found Jennifer. You can be sure that if the police checked with the Simpsons, they wouldn't want the authorities nosing around. And what would you tell the police in another county about not going to Hancock in Columbus County?"

Wes hung his head and shook it from side to side, stretched out his hands on the sides of his chair, gripping the armrests tightly in frustration.

Harris continued, "Wes, I know this isn't what you wanted to hear, but I'm a lawyer. I've got to tell you what the law says. Your best hope would be the district attorney, but even confession that a crime was committed isn't enough. He's got to have some evidence. Jennifer's not here, and if she were, that's still not evidence."

"But we kidnapped her!" Wes blurted. "I kidnapped her! Won't someone indict me? I'm willing to go to jail, if it'll give Annette a chance to stand up in court and tell her story."

"Where's the ransom note?" Manley Harris asked. "There's no evidence that you tried to take Jennifer in exchange for money or made any kind of threat. The worst thing we have is the violation of a custody decree, and that's a civil breach of the law, at worst punishable by contempt, and even that, in a closed hearing."

Harris stood to his feet, walked about ten feet away, and leaned his right shoulder against the deep ridges of the bark on the cottonwood tree. He stared silently into the distance for a moment, the turned to Wes, bent his right leg, and propped the sole of his foot against the tree.

"I want to bring the Order of the Dark Raven to justice as much as you do," said Harris. "I want to get them for killing Reverend Carmichael. I want those people put behind bars so they don't keep tormenting children like Jennifer, but I've exhausted every legal angle I know."

Harris pushed himself away from the tree and paced back and forth, as if hoping for a miracle solution to pop into his mind. Wes sat in silence, his body, mind, and emotions exhausted. He had hardly slept in the last twelve hours. He had hoped Annette's courageous act would bring an end to the Order's evil. Now, he realized that her willingness to be publicly ridiculed and to place her life on the line wasn't enough.

"Wes," Harris said, "what I've told you is the hardest thing I've ever said to any client. I'm sorry. If you're looking for the law to end the Order's reign of terror, forget it. If you think justice can be served by forthrightness, that's not the case. This thing is beyond the law. It will take a power a lot higher than you and me. If James Carmichael were here, he might know how to pray and get an answer, but I don't know how."

Harris walked to where Wes sat dejectedly and put a hand on his shoulder. "I'm sorry," he said. "Hannah told me Annette is welcome to stay here as long as she wishes. If you want to think this over a few days and get back to me, I'll be happy to talk with you."

Harris started to walk away, then turned to face Wes. "I remember what Reverend Carmichael told me once. He said, 'Manley, I'd rather face the devil himself than a man gone mad.' You know what he meant by that, Wes? He believed God had power over the devil, and he could call on God to defeat the devil. But a man gone mad, that's another matter. As Reverend Carmichael put it, 'You can tell the devil to get behind you, but you can't stop a crazy man from pulling the trigger of his gun.'"

Wes said good-bye to Manley Harris and listened to the lawyer's footsteps crunching the crisp, dead grass as he walked around the side of the house back to his car.

What could Wes do now? He knew nothing about theology, and he wasn't sure about this business of fighting either the devil or the devil's henchman. The Order held a loaded gun to his head. How could he keep them from pulling that trigger?

Twenty-four

After Manley Harris disappeared from sight, Wes sat motionless, waiting for something to nudge him toward incomprehensible action. He knew it would take something crazy to end all of this, something as crazy in the name of right as the raping and killing of children was in the name of wrong. He was obsessed with a driving desire to force the Order into open atonement for its sins.

A sudden cool wind whistled through the bare limbs of the tall cottonwood tree and scattered leaves across the Carmichael backyard. The chill reminded Wes of his surroundings and forced him to realize he couldn't sit there forever.

Wes rose from his chair, folded it and the one Harris had left behind, tucked them under his arms, and headed back into the Carmichael house. He found Annette sitting in the living room, drinking a cup of Hannah Carmichael's freshly brewed coffee.

As Wes entered the room, Annette patted the couch and motioned for him to sit beside her. Hannah Carmichael excused herself, saying she had some ironing to do in a small room off the back porch.

"You look upset, Wes," Annette said. "Manley Harris didn't have good news about our situation, did he?"

Wes nodded despondently and explained all the reasons why she would accomplish nothing by coming forward to the police or a judge or a jury.

"But there must be a way!" Annette insisted. "Manley Harris is a good lawyer, but he can't think of everything. Surely there's something he hasn't considered. I won't give up that easily. I *can't*."

Wes smiled to encourage Annette, but inside he floundered. "I'm so tired," he said. "I can't think straight right now. I'll go back to my place and sleep on it. I'll come back for you later."

Driving back to town, Wes's thoughts careened through the options that ranged from murderous revenge to Annette's returning to Chicago. He pulled up in front of the apartment and trudged inside. Fatigued, he dropped his clothing to the floor in a heap. He set his faithless alarm clock for 6:45 a.m., crawled into bed, and pulled the covers over his head, like a child trying to shut out the world.

Something jolted him from deep sleep. Wes bolted upright, thinking it was early morning and he could sleep another couple of hours. Then he noticed the sunlight and realized he had overslept. Bleary-eyed, he peered at the alarm clock. Seven-thirty, nearly an hour beyond the time he'd set the alarm. Wes grabbed the clock and shook it, punishing the old timepiece for its errant ways. He glanced at a corner of the room where he had tossed soiled shirt for the laundry and angrily threw the clock into the pile. *I could have slept through an atomic bomb for all the good that stupid thing does! I'll take it into the shop on my way home tonight. I should have had it fixed a long time ago.*

Quickly, Wes showered, dressed, and headed for the station. After the run-in with Warren Crews over the Hancock-Harris confrontation, he didn't need more strikes against him. When he got to the WTTK studios, Wes slipped through the back door. Briefcase and laundry bag in hand, he carefully edged his way down the hallway past the speaker cabinets. He hurried into his office, hoping no one had noticed his late arrival. But someone had: the past person he needed to deal with—Warren Crews.

Wes had barely stepped inside his office and hung his suit jacket on a hook when Crews pushed open the door, stuck in his head, and said, "Been waiting for you to get in. You and I have to talk about some things. How about right now?"

The tension in Crew's voice indicated it wouldn't be a casual conversation about program topics and advertising quotas. Wes knew he had no choice. "No problem. Come on in, have a seat. What's on your mind?"

Wes walked behind his desk and sat down in his chair. Crews took one of the two molded plastic chairs sitting in a corner and placed it near the desk. He leaned forward, drawing himself close to Wes. "I'm not happy with the job you've been doing lately."

Before he could continue, Wes interrupted. "What's the problem? Our spot sales are up, double from this time last year. I've done every advertiser endorsement you've requested. I know there's not much competition in the county, but we've still got the most listened-to-station during my show. If that's not good enough, what is?"

Crews dropped his eyes and rolled the fingers of his right hand rhythmically across the desk—little finger, then the third, middle, and index finger, and back again. "Why were you absent from the micro-phone? Chuck covered for you, but that's not good enough."

"Hey! I haven't had a serious vacation in three years, so what's the big deal?"

"That Hancock and Harris interview didn't help matters any."

"What's wrong with that?" he said. "Hancock deserved to be nailed."

"That's your opinion, Wes, but not the opinion of most people in this town. I'm still getting complaints about how you embarrassed Sheriff Hancock." Crew's eyes narrowed and flashed with anger. "Don't ever do that again, Next time, you're through with 'Talk about Town.'"

Wes had to make a split-second decision. He could either back off and wait for a better opportunity to deal with this issue, or take it head on. A poor night's sleep, a stubborn alarm clock, and yesterday's conversation with Manley Harris had pushed him to the brink. He was in no mood for compromise. "What's the problem, Warren? Are they leaning on you? Are they making life difficult?"

Crews cocked his head and looked at Wes out of the corner of his eye. "I don't know what you mean."

"I think you do, Warren. Do they have something on you? You're one of them aren't you?"

The question hung in the air unanswered. Finally, Crews responded. "I don't know what you're talking about." His voice rose to such a level that Wes wondered if those outside the office could hear.

"The Order, Warren, the Order of the Dark Raven."

Crews pushed his chair back, scraping the metal caps on the legs against the bare wood floor. He looked at Wes, his face white. "You're pushing too hard," he said, "You know what happened to Bender and Carmichael. You know, Wes, I don't want that to happen to you . . . or me."

Crews slowly undid his tie, took his jacket off, and draped it over the back of his chair. He unbuttoned his shirt, pulled back the left panel, and exposed his breast. Tattooed just above Crews's left nipple were three interlocking triangles.

"There's only one reason I showed you this, Wes, and it's for your own good. Five years ago, I was destitute and needed money. Someone told me where I could get it. I didn't know what I was getting into. It was just a loan on the side. Then I missed a couple of payments. They roughed me up a little. Finally, I signed over the station to some guy named Ravensky. Don't mess with these people! I learned the hard way." His voice trailed off, and his lips tightened in anger.

"I know all about Jennifer and Annette," Crews said. "It happened to my stepdaughter, Roxanne, too."

"Roxanne!" Wes felt the skin on his neck bristle. Misha's roommate was Warren's stepdaughter. He realized why the Order's threat had not been carried out in the week since he received the note about Misha's life. "She had been theirs for the taking when they wanted. Roxanne was her guardian angel from hell.

Wes looked at Crews and tried to gather his hate together, but all he could feel was disgust and pity.

BOB LARSON

Crews dropped his arm to his side and slumped his shoulders in hopelessness. He leaned forward on the desk, bracing himself on his balled-up fists. "Annette and Jennifer are alive only because the Order fears this thing could get out of hand. They have every reason to keep it quite, and, if you stay quiet, they'll back off."

Crews leaned away from the desk, and said, "At first, I didn't want to be involved, but now I'm a willing participant. I was even there that night at the Mounds of the Elders when Jennifer was coronated. Hancock told me you were there too."

Wes clenched his fists and jumped to his feet. He wanted to lunge at Crews, and the effort to restrain himself caused his body to tremble.

"What the Order does isn't always pretty, but they rule this county. Nothing of any significance happens without their approval. You could join us, you know. Then everyone would be safe."

"I don't believe you!" Wes shouted. "Do you think I'm crazy?" he pounded his fist on his desk, wishing it were Arnold Hancock's face. "What you're involved in, Warren is evil! You're insane to think I'd go along with this! Insane! What do you take me for, anyway?"

"The way of the Raven isn't evil," Crews said in a guttural whisper. "It's the way to power, to control, to all the things we truly seek in life. The Raven rules with strength. There's so much I could explain to you, Wes. You'd understand if you knew the rest. You're prejudiced by a lot of myths, like the meek inheriting the earth. That's a lie. God is jealous—jealous of the Dark Raven's ability to bring meaning and order to our lives. Wes! That's what it's all about.

→ saw vision of S.R. when
reading this.

Justice in the name of the Dark Raven!"

A cloud of hot fury settled over Wes. What perverted madness allowed Warren Crews to feel justified in his evil?

"It's two hours to show time," Crews said, looking at his watch. "I want to know by then if you're going to join us. It's the safest thing you can do for everyone. We're reasonable people, Wes."

"Reasonable!" Wes snorted. "You kidnap a child, torment her with despicable ceremonies, sexually abuse her, and brainwash her! Are you calling that reasonable?"

"It was for her own good, Wes. She is a Chosen One, a queen! She had to be prepared. She had to serve the Dark Raven."

Crews grabbed his coat from the back of the chair, flipped it over his shoulder, and stepped toward the door. "I know what you're going through," he said, glancing back at Wes. "I had to make the same choice five years ago. The Order of the Dark Raven is the true way. You'll see. You don't understand it now, but you will."

Warren Crews left, the regular cadence of his footsteps fading down the hall toward his office. Wes was incensed by the insanity of what he'd heard and enraged that Warren actually believed what he said. He pounded his fist against the wall.

If Wes had slept through an atomic bomb and awakened to a devastated world, it couldn't have wreaked as much havoc in his life as all this had done. He was more certain than ever that he alone was obligated to bring the secrets of the Dark Raven into the light of public scrutiny.

Standing in the dead silence of his office, Wes again felt the faint brush of something against the hair on his arm. The peculiar sensation manifested itself every time he thought about Jennifer at the Mounds of the Elders. It wasn't a muscular twitch. It felt like the edge of a soft breeze barely reaching his skin.

And then, as he was experiencing the feeling, Wes remembered a similar touch of a feather stroking his arm . . . long ago, on a hot summer day in Clarion. Wes squeezed his eyes shut and dived far back into his childhood to reach a painful, suppressed memory.

He had met his friends on the street near his house.

One of them brandished a BB gun with all the macho confidence a twelve year old can muster. The boys were laughing, kicking something on the ground. Drawing closer, Wes saw a small bird, felled with a single BB pellet, severely wounded and dying. Its beak gaped for air, and one wing flapped desperately toward impossible flight.

The boys laughed at the helpless creature, kicked it around with their feet and tumbled it from side to side. When they tired of that sport, they knelt next to it. One pointed the BB gun at the little bird. "Naw," said the other, "don't shoot it. I never saw a bird like this one. Let's have some fun with it. I'll show you what to do."

The bird was different. Wes had never seen one like it before. The vision from the past was so strong, Wes felt as if he were there.

"Let's see what happens if we yank out a feather! Come on, don't be scared!" one of the boys said.

The helpless bird struggled less energetically now, most of its life force spent. Its little legs twitched, the wing flapped spasmodically. Then one boy pushed the bun's barrel against the bird's head and held its legs taut with his free hand. The bigger of the two boys plucked a long tail feather from the bird, laughing at his own cruelty. The nearly lifeless bird jerked violently, as if extruding that feather were a pain beyond any it had yet suffered.

"Stop it!" he yelled, filled with revulsion. "Don't do that! Leave him alone!" But the more he protested, the more the boys laughed at him. Wes wanted to run, and he wanted to fight. It was useless to intervene because both boys were bigger. He could run, but what would that prove? Then the biggest boy pointed the tail feather at Wes and slowly walked toward him.

"Get away from me! Don't touch me with that thing!" Wes cried.

"What'sa matter, scaredy cat? 'Fraid of a bird feather, huh?"

"It's not fair! That little bird can't fight back!"

"Scaredy cat, scaredy cat!" the boy insisted, grabbing Wes's arm and running the feather up and down the flesh on his arm. "Tickle, tickle!" the boy giggled.

Wes looked away and covered his face with his other arm. He began crying, then tore himself away and ran home as fast as he could. Although he had never told anyone about the mangled little bird, he had never forgotten it. He also never forgot that, while the innocent creature was being senselessly tormented, he had run away. Even now, he felt that feather lightly touching the hairs of his arm, the soft sensation striking him like a knife.

Wes released the rightness of his eyelids, opened his eyes, and looked around him. His heart pounded as it had the day he ran away.

Wes knew his days of running were over. He breathed deeply and started cleaning out the drawers of his desk, putting things in his briefcase. While doing so, he picked up the phone and called Manley Harris.

"Manley," he said, "I need you to be here at the WTTK studios, twelve o'clock sharp."

"Why, Wes? What's up?"

"I can't tell you. Just be here! If the receptionist tries to stop you, ignore her. Walk on past her. If my ON THE AIR light is glowing, ignore it. Come on into the studio."

"Wes, what are you up to? Nothing crazy, I hope."

"No, nothing crazy. I'm saner than I've ever been in my life."

After Wes hung up the phone, he thumbed through his address book for Hattie MacKenzie's number and called her. He asked her to bring Misha to the phone. Several minutes later, Misha was on the line. "Misha, I don't have much time to talk. Do what I say, and don't ask questions. You and Jennifer and Michelle get on the first bus back to Clarion. One leaves around eleven o'clock. I checked in case I ever had to get Annette here in a hurry."

"Daddy, what's wrong? I just got here! Now, you want me to turn around and come back!"

"I know, I know. But you *have* to. Do *it!*"

One more call to make—Hannah Carmichael. Wes told her, "Bring Annette with you to the radio station at twelve o'clock. Don't ask why. Just be here!"

Stunned, Hannah blurted, "But you wanted to keep Annette in hiding! Someone at the station might recognize her!"

"Hannah, I realize it's confusing, but I know what I'm doing. Trust me, please."

"I do trust you, Wes" Hannah said. "We'll be there. So will our prayers."

It was done. In little more than an hour, Manley Harris, Hannah Carmichael, and Annette Simpson would be at WTTK. About two hours later, Misha, Michelle, and Jennifer would arrive. It was all coming together. It was Wes's turn to drop his own atomic bomb. He picked up his briefcase and the laundry bag of dirty shirts with the hitchhiking alarm clock inside, and set them by the door. He also took a cassette labeled "Jennifer's Call" out of his desk and put it into his briefcase, and no matter which way it went, a few dirty shirts might be all he had left.

Wes sat down and rehearsed what he would do, changing this, omitting that. His strategy had come together in quick detail, so extraordinary he could only hope he had what it would take to pull it off.

Twenty-five

Wes wouldn't give Warren Crews an answer before the show. He would act, not talk. At ten minutes to twelve, he gathered up his briefcase and laundry bag and headed for Studio A. Once inside, Warren couldn't corner him undetected. Wes put his brief case and laundry bag on a shelf of the studio console to this right. It was silent in the studio, so quiet that the ticking of the alarm clock sounded loud enough that listeners cold hear it when Wes turned on the microphone, a crucial part of his plan.

Two minutes to show time, Warren Crews stepped into Studio A. "Wes, we were supposed to talk. I need your answer."

"I have one."

"Well, what is it?"

"I've decide to join forces with you," Wes said.

Crews grinned widely. "I knew you'd see it our way! You've made the right choice," he said, walking over to put his hand on Wes's shoulder. "Annette and Jennifer will be fine now. A whole new life is beginning, a life you never dreamed possible."

Smiling in return, Wes said, "You don't know how right you are, Warren, a whole new life."

"We'll talk more right after the show," Crews said enthusiastically. "I can tell you so much now. Meet me in my office."

"Thirty seconds to air time!" Chuck Bailey said over the intercom.

Crews looked at Wes approvingly, like a slick TV preacher exult-
ing over a new convert, then strode confidently from the studio.
Wes put on his earphones and slipped into his seat, watching the
wall clock countdown: 5 . . . 4 . . . 3 . . . 2 . . . 1.

Fifteen seconds after the opening "Talk about Town" jingle, Wes
Bryant faced his moment of truth. "Good afternoon, Columbus
County. I'm Wes Bryant. This is 'Talk about Town.' Today's show is
going to be unusual. I have several in-studio guests, including Warren
Crews, owner and general manager of WTTK, and Sheriff Arnold
Hancock. We'll also have several unannounced, surprised guests."

Wes looked through the window of Studio C, where he saw Bailey
looking at him questioningly. "I'd like my producer, Chuck Bailey, to
ask Mr. Crews to come in here and also to call Sheriff Hancock's office
and ask him to get over here as quickly as possible. While we're waiting, here's a commercial announcement from our friends at DeGroff's,
where you'll always find the lowest prices and the freshest food."

Wes hit the cart activating the spot, leaned back in his chair, and
took a deep breath. He glanced at the bag of laundry with his alarm
clock. Tick tock. Tick tock.

DeGroff's commercial was in its last twenty seconds when Crews
burst through the door. "What's going on here? Why do you want
me in the studio? I thought you were one of us now!"

"I'm a man of my word," Wes responded. "That's why I want you
in here. Sit down in front of the mike, Warren."

For a moment, Crews didn't move, stunned by Wes's abrupt

actions and the stern tone in his voice.

"*Sit down*, I said!" Wes commanded.

As the closing strains of the commercial faded into the "Talk about Town" jingle, Crews slumped into the guest chair that Chuck Bailey affectionately referred to as the "hot spot."

Wes started things rolling. "With me in the studio is Warren Crews, my boss for the last five years. Recently, I've gained a new understanding of Warren's role in making WTTK the most listened-to station in Columbus County. Perhaps it's time for you to meet the man behind the man at the mike. Warren Crews, welcome to 'Talk about Town.'"

Crews loosened his tie and rubbed his index finger on the inside of his collar to give himself breathing room. He leaned toward the mike and responded, "Thank you, Wes. Happy to be here," though his extended neck veins showed that he wasn't happy at all.

"Tell us about yourself, Warren. You know, all that biographical stuff. Let the folks get to know you better."

Beads of perspiration formed on Crews's brow. He wiped them with the back of his hand and leaned toward the mike. "Well, I'm forty-seven years old. I've been running this station for twelve years. I'm married, have three stepchildren, and consider Columbus County the greatest place in the world to live. I'm proud of how WTTK serves our community."

Wes leaned on one elbow, smirked slightly, and gestured toward Crews with a pen he held. "Things are going pretty well here at WTTK. Has it always been that way? Ever fallen on rough times, Warren?"

"You know how things are in business, Wes?" Crews responded with a sheepish smile. "There are good times and bad times."

Wes shot back a stern stare. "Tell us about the tough times."

Crews squirmed in his chair as sweat trickled from his temples to his cheeks. "Like I said, there have been good times and bad times."

"Warren, take a good look at the bag on the shelf next to me. What's it look like?"

Crews shrugged his shoulders, gesturing toward the shelf. "It's a bag . . . just a bag."

"My laundry's in there, Warren. Dirty laundry. You ever have any dirty laundry?"

Crews's eyes narrowed. "Sure. Every week. My wife does it on Saturday."

"Some dirty laundry doesn't wash easily, does it, Warren? In fact, it can explode right in your face when you least expect it."

Crews didn't respond. He leaned back in his chair with his hands on the armrests, straightening his body in an attempt to intimidate Wes.

"There's something else in that bag, Warren. You can't see the dirty clothes, but you can hear what else is in there. Listen! What do you hear?"

Wes glanced at Chuck Bailey, who leaned close to the window separating Studio A from Studio C as if hoping he could hear too. Crews cocked his head so his left ear pointed directly toward the bag.

"Hear anything, Warren, like something that would catch the attention of Peter Pan?" Wes said, chuckling. "It's not a crocodile,

Warren. It's a clock. You hear it, don't you?"

"Yeah. A clock," Crews said. "Sounds like you've got a clock in your laundry bag."

"Something else is in that bag. The clock is attached to a motion-sensitive bomb. Any abrupt action, like dropping it, would detonate it."

Bailey shot erect, a look of horror on his face. Crews stiffened in his seat. "You're kidding," he dared.

"Would I kid about something like that?" Wes asked. "Why do you think I want Sheriff Hancock over here? We're going to talk about dirty laundry. Mine, yours, Sheriff Hancock's, and some other people you know real well."

Studio B had filled with WTTK staff members, who peered through the pane to see what was happening. Wes leaned toward his microphone. "We won't take commercial breaks the rest of the show." He looked at Bailey. "As soon as Sheriff Hancock gets here, usher him into the studio. I want everyone out of the building, except Crews, Hancock, and Bailey.

"One more thing. Don't anybody try to cut off the electricity or take me off the air. I've got a monitor feed directly from the transmitter. It was installed so the person in the studio would be the first to know if technical difficulties interrupted our broadcast signal. I'd know in a split second if anyone tried anything funny. If they do, I'll throw this laundry bag on the floor, and everything in here goes BOOM!"

Wes turned off the radio mike and switched on the office intercom. "Get out!" he yelled into it, causing Crews to jerk back violently, nearly

BOB LARSON

tipping over his chair. Wes could see WTTK staff members running out of Studio B toward the front door. Then Wes reached over to the board and turned the studio mike on again. "Remember several weeks back, the phone call from a young girl named Jennifer?" he asked his radio audience. "She talked about the 'Dark Raven,' said she was being hurt. In case you don't remember that call, listen carefully."

Wes leaned down and reached into his briefcase for the cassette of Jennifer's call. His hands were damp with perspiration. As he heard the distant piercing wall of a police siren rapidly approaching, his grip tightened around the soft cloth of the laundry bag.

His mind raced. Did Hancock and the Order have a plan of their own? What about the National Guard? Would Hancock order them to intervene? More importantly, could he really pull this off now that the main players were coming onto the field?

Wes's senses were overloaded and he went blank. He forgot he was holding Jennifer's cassette in his sweaty palms. Crash! The sound of the cassette falling to the floor forced him back to reality. He quickly retrieved the tape.

Suddenly, it dawned on him. Dead air . . . ! The mike was on, waiting for the tape. He had panicked hearing the siren and, in the confusion, left it open. *Radio silence . . . dead air . . .* the cardinal sin of a broadcaster. The lull could have given Hancock and Crews a chance to intervene.

Wes hurriedly put the cassette in the deck and hit the play button for the cassette deck audio. Jennifer's taped voice broke the deathly silence in the air and declared, "I'm afraid of them . . . They hurt me . . . The Dark Rave . . ."

When Jennifer's tape finished, Wes reached for an auto switch that would send continuous music over the air. He couldn't afford another moment of dead air, giving the impression he wasn't in complete control.

Wes sighed deeply and glanced around the studio. Bailey looked inquisitively at Wes, knowing moments before the mike had been open, leaving Columbus County and the listening world cloaked in unknowing silence. He had remained calm, a beacon for Wes. They shared a brief, reassuring glance, which was shattered by the arrival of the menacing police siren of Sheriff Hancock.

Without warning. Hancock burst into the studio, his gun drawn. Two deputies stood behind him. Wes reached for the laundry bag and edged it toward the corner of the shelf.

Crews leaped to his feet with outstretched arms and backed away, restraining the sheriff from coming further. He screamed out, "Don't do anything, Arnold! He's got a bomb in that bag! The crazy fool is ready to blow us all up!"

Hancock slowly lowered his pistol and put it in his holster. Wes faded out the music that had been playing, opened the microphone, and said, "Our other guest has arrived, Sheriff Arnold Hancock. Hand your gun to the men with you; then tell them to get out of here."

Hancock hesitated momentarily, then handed his gun to the nearest deputy, and said, "Go on, guys. Get outta here. I'll take care of Bryant."

"Chuck, get a chair for Mr. Hancock," Wes ordered Bailey. "The sheriff has a lot to say."

As Wes waited for Bailey to get a chair from an adjoining room, he went on. "Mr. Crews and Mr. Hancock know each other well. You might assume that, since they are community leaders, but these men are acquainted in other ways, aren't you, gentlemen?"

Bailey rushed through the door with a molded plastic chair from Wes's office and shoved it behind Hancock. Reluctantly, the sheriff sat down and Wes placed an open microphone in front of Hancock.

"Scoot up closer to the microphone, Sheriff," Wes said. "Columbus County is waiting to hear from you."

"I don't know what you're up to, Bryant, but you won't get away with it. My men, along with some state troopers, are surrounding this entire building. They're all listening to the radio. They know what you're doing."

Wes grinned broadly. "Perfect! Just what I want. Hello, everyone out there," he said. "In case you've missed anything, I've got a tape recorder running. Everything that's said this afternoon will be recorded for posterity—and the courts."

"You're crazy, Bryant!" Hancock screamed. "Nobody's going to believe anything you tell them. You're committing a criminal act—taking hostages, threatening lives, commandeering a radio station. Before this day is over, you'll be behind bars!"

Wes didn't lift his hand off the laundry bag. He scooted it as close to the edge of the shelf as he could without pushing it off. "We're waiting for some other people you both know," he said to Hancock and Crews.

Wes turned up the continuous music tape again and switched off his mike momentarily so he could speak to Bailey on the intercom. "Inform the wire services and CNN about what's going on. See how quickly they can get a satellite uplink here. They like this sort of stuff—live, on-the-spot coverage. Make sure UPI and AP know about it. Call the network television stations in Indianapolis. They might want to send camera crews up here. I want the whole country to hear what's going to happen. As a backup, start the auxiliary recording deck in Studio C."

Without hesitation, Bailey set off to fulfill the requests. Wes felt that his producer acted as much out of loyalty as out of the threat of the bomb in his laundry bag. He threw back his shoulders and voiced his best imitation of a disc jockey's voice. "And now, for your listening enjoyment, the easy sounds of light rock. No elevator music. No talk. Just good music."

Wes reached for another pre-recorded tape of music from the shelf and put it into a second tape deck that would activate when the cassette in the first deck ended. The station always kept a tape like this handy in case anything went wrong with one of the studios and they couldn't air live programming. But for Wes Bryant, it was a way of further intimidating Crews and Hancock. They'd have to sit here—who knew how long?—until Misha, Jennifer, Annette, Hannah, and Manley arrived.

Wes kept his hand on the laundry bag. Tick tock. Tick tock. The sound seemed to grow louder as emotions heightened and sensory responses became more acute. With his microphone shut off to the outside world, Wes motioned Bailey to come into Studio A.

"Grab yourself a chair and sit down, Chuck. We're going to have a little chat about the weather, hog prices, the fall harvest, all those things that should interest these sterling citizens of Columbus County," Wes said mockingly, gesturing toward Hancock and Crews.

"That's not a bomb," Hancock said. "You're bluffing. What do you know about bombs?"

It was an obvious question. Wes paused, then said, "There's a lot you don't know about me, Hancock. Like what I learned in Chicago. But you knew where I was, didn't you, Sheriff?' There are some interesting people in Chicago, and not all of them are on the right side of the law. I'm not going to tell you how I hooked up with those types. Lets' just say they showed me a thing or two and gave me a little present to bring back to Columbus County." Wes patted the laundry bag gently.

"You can't get by with this," Crews said, asserting himself.

"Oh, I don't know," Wes answered. "Look at what you and Hancock have gotten by with for years. You've hidden your dirty laundry a long time. What makes you thing I can't come out of this squeaky clean?" Wes added, enjoying the play on words. "Anyway, I'm not interested in talking to you guys until everyone else is here. By the way, would you like to know who's coming?"

Hancock shrugged his shoulders. "It doesn't matter."

"It might matter, Sheriff. Manley Harris is one of them."

"So what? I've dealt with him before."

"Then there's Hannah Carmichael, the Reverend Carmichael's widow."

"So? Should that bother me?" Hancock shot back.

"Perhaps you'd be more interested in knowing that two other ladies are going to join us—Annette and Jennifer Simpson. Jennifer's got quite a story to share, and the whole country's finally going to hear it."

Twenty-six

During the next two hours, Wes and Crews and Hancock sat in Studio A, listening to the canned music, pop hits of the last two decades reduced to bland orchestral arrangements Each time Wes changed a tape he alerted he listening audience to the situation inside Studio A. Crews shifted nervously in his chair, one leg over the other, swinging back and forth. He acted as if he was on the verge of speaking, but didn't.

Sheriff Hancock never flinched. Occasionally, he adjusted his position in the chair, but he never diverted his attention from Wes and the laundry bag.

Wes carefully monitored the audio feed from the transmitter to make certain there was no dead air, and he changed music tapes whenever necessary. At the end of two hours, Wes realized that if Manley, Hannah, Annette, and Jennifer were to get into the studio, they'd have to pass by a police cordon. For all he knew, they might be out there now, waiting behind the blockade.

Wes turned down the volume on the cassette channel playing music and spoke over the air. "This is a message to the police surrounding the building. Let the following people come into the building— Manley Harris, Hannah Carmichael, Michelle Milthorpe, my daughter, Misha, and Annette and Jennifer Simpson. They should be out there by now, so if you don't let them come in, I'll blow up the place."

Wes repeated the names of the people, along with descriptions, and then resumed the music. Moments later, he heard footsteps coming down the hallway toward the studio. Everyone turned to see who it was.

Harris, Hannah, Michelle, and Annette cautiously stepped into Studio A, closing the door behind them. Wes told Chuck Bailey to get chairs for the four of them from a nearby office.

Manley Harris spoke first. "What are you doing, Wes? Man, I'm a lawyer. I've got to advise you, you're in dangerous territory. I hope you've got a good reason for doing this."

"I do, Manley. You'll see."

"Wes," Annette said, "I trust you. Just tell me how I can help."

Hannah Carmichael stood silently. Her large, dark eyes darted about the room. Wes knew her husband's death had left unhealed emotional scars, and these present circumstances obviously terrified her.

"Don't worry, Hannah," Wes said. "James death will be avenged."

Hannah stepped from her place and leaned over the broadcast console, kissing Wes on the cheek. "I never had any children of my own, but I couldn't be prouder this moment of you and my Manley than if I had birthed you both." Despite her grief, she glowed with strength.

Wes turned to Bailey. "Go outside, and let me know who's here from the media." He paused, then spoke to Annette. "Sit down at the end of the table, near the microphone. As soon as Bailey gets back, I'm going to interview you. You don't have to say anything you don't want to, but now's the time to tell as much of your story as you can handle."

DEAD AIR

Wes waited impatiently for at least ten minutes. He wondered if the police had kept Bailey from returning when he heard footsteps down the hallway. Bailey opened the door to Studio A.

"You're not going to believe what's going on out there. It's a three-ring circus," he said. "I've never seen anything like it. CNN has moved in a satellite uplink dish. So have two network stations from Indianapolis. This is a major media event. When I got outside the building, they stuck microphones in my face wanting to know what's going on. Wes, I didn't tell them anything. How could I? I don't know any more than anyone else here."

"You mean they're broadcasting live to the whole country?" Wes asked.

"Yeah. Seems there was a tanker truck accident and fire on the freeway, so CNN had come in for coverage, as well as the Indianapolis stations. That's why they got over here so quickly. They've got radios on in the parking lot and microphones next to the speakers so they can get live sound from in here. Wes, they want to know all about you. They think you're some deranged terrorist or something. Man, if you wanted publicity you sure picked the right day, because they're all out there just for you!"

Sheriff Hancock jumped to his feet. "I'm calling your bluff, Bryant. There's no bomb in that bag. Even if there is, I think you're scared to use it."

Wes picked up the bag and dangled it by his index finger, swinging it back and forth gently. "Remember, Hancock, it's motion-sensitive, and dropping it on this floor would be a real abrupt motion. There's enough explosives in here to blow this whole station sky-high."

"You wouldn't kill everyone here! They're your friends! You wouldn't sacrifice their lives too."

"Maybe I'm crafty, Hancock, and maybe I'm crazy. If I'm just crafty, you may be right. If I'm crazy, nothing will stop me. You don't know if I'd kill them to kill you. Sit down before I decide this whole thing isn't going to work, and I might as well drop the big one."

Hancock's fists doubled, and the veins in his neck stood out. He seemed to be calculating his options. They all looked risky. Finally, he sat back down. Wes made sure he expressed no sense of relief at Hancock's acquiescence, though inside he sighed deeply.

He turned to Annette. "I'm going to shut off the music now. Are you ready to talk?"

Annette nodded as Wes slowly faded the volume on the cassette deck. He activated his microphone and said, "A woman named Annette Simpson is in the studio with me. She's thirty-four years old and is the mother of nine-year-old Jennifer Simpson. She's going to tell a story you'll find hard to believe, but it's true."

Wes smiled and winked at Annette. "Mrs. Simpson, start at the beginning," he said. "The whole country is listening. Say what you've always wanted to say, but thought no one would believe."

Annette leaned toward the microphone and began. "It all started when Wes Bryant visited me in the hospital." Annette went on to tell the story of her escape, her reunion with Jennifer, and the truth she discovered about the Order of the Dark Raven. Once the basic facts were out of the way, Wes pressed her further.

"If you can handle it, tell them about the ceremony where your daughter was married to your husband"

Annette carefully constructed each detail with amazing accuracy and calmness. She spoke of the terror her daughter had experienced, of bloodletting ceremonies, and sexually perverted rituals. Wes wondered how seasoned network reporters were handling the story. It wasn't the kind of fare network television usually aired. Fiction was one thing. This was fact.

Wes carefully studied Crews and Hancock. Even though they were obviously nervous to hear their evil behavior exposed, they displayed no regret. The more of Annette's story they heard, the more detached they became. Emotionally, they refused to admit their involvement. Somehow they must have been brainwashed to believe right was wrong.

Even as Annette told her story, Wes faced the truth that he was still the guilty party in the eyes of the law. There was no tangible evidence to convict the Order of any crime. He was a crazy man threatening lives, and Annette was a disgruntled widow soiling the reputation of her dead husband. Jennifer? Who would take the word of a child against the reputation of a respected public official like Arnold Hancock?

Wes reached down with his left hand to rub his shin. It was still sore from his banging it against those huge speaker cabinets sitting in the hallway outside the door of Studio A.

Wes muttered to himself, *All I need is a pain in my shin to distract me from what's going on here.* A thought flashed through his mind: *those speakers might be useful for something there than announcing a football score.*

As Annette approached the end of her story, Wes motioned for Bailey to come near him. Hesitantly, Bailey got out of his chair and leaned over the studio console as Wes whispered in his ear. Bailey left the studio immediately. A few minutes later there was noise in the hallway. Through the window leading to Studio C, Bailey could be seen pushing and shoving the large speakers from the hallway into the room and stringing strands of wire in different directions.

For the first time, Hancock took his attention off Wes Bryant's laundry bag. His eyes darted back and forth, looking at Wes and then at Bailey to see what he was doing in Studio C. Bailey returned to Studio A as Misha and Jennifer walked in.

"Mr. Wes!" Jennifer cried out, letting go of Misha's hand and running toward Wes.

Wes started to lift his hand from the laundry bag to embrace her, then reached out with only his left arm to hug her tightly.

"I've missed you so much," Jennifer said. Then out of the corner of her eye she saw her mother. "Mommy!" she shouted. "You're here too!"

Jennifer turned to run around the corner of Wes's studio console, then stopped. Her body froze instantly as she looked directly at Crews and Hancock. Wes switched off Annette's microphone, turned on his own, and said to the listening audience, "Jennifer, Annette Simpson's daughter, has just walked into the studio. You just heard her. My daughter, Misha, brought her here. Right now, Jennifer's looking at Warren Crews and Arnold Hancock. Jennifer, come here a moment. I want you to say something about those men."

Wes reached out his hand to Jennifer, and she haltingly stepped toward him, never taking her eyes off Crews and Hancock as if they were deadly snakes poised to strike. Wes put his arm around Jennifer, pulled her close to him, and directed her face toward the microphone.

"I want to ask you some questions. Talk right into this thing. It's called a microphone. People who listen to me on the radio can hear you. Tell them who those men are."

Jennifer lowered her head and snuggled more tightly into the crook of Wes's arm. Then she threw her arms around his neck, looking away from the microphone. "They're the nasty people," she said. "They hurt me. They hurt me bad. It was cold. Dark. I was afraid. Nobody would help me. I wanted them to stop. They poked me. They put me in that cage."

The safety of Wes's arms enabled Jennifer to release the emotions she had held captive for so long. For the first time since Wes had known her, Jennifer broke down sobbing.

Gradually, Jennifer release her tight grip on his neck and turned her head around to face the microphone. "Those two me. They hurt me."

"How did they hurt you?" Wes asked.

"Bad. I don't want to talk about it."

"Please try! It's important for everyone to know."

"That man," she said, pointing at Warren Crews. "He killed a baby rabbit."

"How?"

"In his hands. He squeezed it tight 'til there was blood everywhere. Then he put his bloody hands all over me. I . . . I . . . I didn't have any clothes on," Jennifer said, as she buried her face in Wes's shoulder.

Annette whimpered slightly, and Wes could feel his shoulder growing moist from Jennifer's tears. "And the other man?" he said. "The big guy sitting there with the badge on?"

"He hurt me too."

"Can you tell us how?"

"He poked me. Put things inside me. He said something about making me belong to the Dark Raven. If I hurt, it would make me belong. But I don't belong to them! I belong to you and Mommy, don't I?" Jennifer burst into tears again and clutched her arms around Wes's neck.

"Yes," Wes said. "You belong to us, not them. Not anymore."

"No one will believe this stuff," Sheriff Hancock blurted out. "What kind of a kangaroo court is this anyway?" he yelled.

"If you've got something to say, say it into that microphone," Wes shot back.

"All right, I will," Hancock, said, grabbing the microphone in front of Annette and jerking it closer. "I've been sheriff of this county almost as long as you've been living, Bryant. How dare you allow an emotionally disturbed child to accuse me of molesting her! And so for this . . . this woman sitting here, I don't know who she is. Maybe she isn't the mother. How do I know? You expect your audience to believe this crazy story when a maniac like you is threatening to blow us up?"

Wes looked toward the window of Studio C. Bailey gave him a thumbs-up sign, indicating his mission was complete. The speakers were ready for action, and the auxiliary deck was still recording. "Maybe you'd like to hear Annette's and Jennifer's story again, Hancock, in a way that would emphasize it to you? I want you to get out of that seat, open the door to the studio, step around the corner to Studio C, and walk in there. Don't try anything funny. If you try to run down the hallway and escape, you won't get very far. All I have to do is knock this laundry bag on the floor, and it's all over for everybody."

"What do you want me in there for?" Hancock retorted. "If you've got something to say, let's say if face-to-face, man-to-man."

"I've got a lot to say, but I'll say it when you get in Studio C. Now, get moving! You're testing my patience." Wes barked, lifting the laundry bag again by its drawstrings.

"OK. OK. Just don't drop that bag."

Slowly, Hancock edged his way out the door, around the corner, and stepped into Studio C.

Wes let go of Jennifer and reached to his board. He turned on a switch that activated the audio feed from Studio A to Studio C. "Can you hear me, Hancock?"

Hancock nodded.

"If you've got something to say, there's a microphone in there, and we can hear you in here. The whole country can hear. All I have to do is hit the right switch. Got that?"

"Yeah, I got it," Hancock answered sullenly.

"Now," Wes said to Hancock, "let me tell you something about those huge speakers Chuck Bailey just installed in you studio. Normally, a studio of that size would have tiny speakers, maybe three or four inches in diameter, not huge fifteen-inch speakers like those. Know anything abut sound electronics, Hancock?"

"Why should I?" Hancock responded. "I'm a sheriff, not an electrician."

"Well, those speakers were designed for a football stadium. They're powerful, and I can control the volume from in here. For example, let me give you an audio tone. It's a high, shrill sound that we use to test the sound level of our equipment. Normally, it sounds like this," Wes said as he hit a button, sending the shrill shriek over the air. Then he turned it off.

"If I want to, I can make that just a little louder," Wes said, grinning, "like this."

Wes gradually turned up the volume on the test tone to an ear-splitting level. The sound from the speakers rattled Studio C's window, and Hancock clasped his hands over his ears, screaming in pain. Then Wes turned the sound back down.

"Get the idea. Hancock? You've got a football stadium full of sound in a six-by-eight room. It could get uncomfortable in there if I think you're not paying close attention to what's being said. I can see every move you make through that window. If you try to go out that door; you'll have to deal with my dirty laundry," Wes said, picking up his laundry bag again and swinging it menacingly. "One more time. Can you hear me?"

"Turn that thing down! I can't stand it! You've got it too loud," Hancock said.

"Good," Wes said. He nudged Jennifer slightly toward the microphone. "Is that the man who hurt you?"

"Yes!" Jennifer yelled, as she pointed toward the window. "He's one of the nasty people! He's a friend of the Raven."

Hancock clasped his hands to his ears again and shook his head violently. He pounded on the walls of Studio C in frustration and pain.

"I think maybe you heard that, Hancock. Right?"

"What are you trying to do, Bryant?" Hancock pleaded. "I can't take this! I'll get you. Bryant! If I can find a law about attacking somebody with sound, I'll nail you on it!"

"Pardon, Sheriff Hancock? I'm not sure we got that. Would you mind repeating it?" Wes said, turning up the volume on his voice.

Hancock screamed at the top of his lungs. "Stop! I can't stand it!"

"Jennifer, did you ever beg that man to stop hurting you? Did you ever cry out in pain?"

"Yes," Jennifer said. "All the time! I begged him not to put those things inside me. I begged him not to put blood on me. I begged him to let me go. He wouldn't. He just laughed and did it more. I hate him! I hate him!"

As Jennifer spoke Wes turned up the volume to the speakers, sending Hancock berserk. He pounded the palm of his hands against the side of his head.

Wes turned the volume as loud as possible, shattering both Hancock's eardrums and the plate glass window separating Studio A from Studio C. The sound of glass splintering and crashing to the floor mingled with the sheriff's howl of agony.

"Yes, I did it!" Hancock screamed. "I'm the one! It's all true. Just turn those speakers down!" He put his hands to the sides of his cheeks and then held his crimson palms in front of his face. "Blood on my hands! There's always been blood on my hands. Someone's blood. Any one's blood. But I did it for the Raven. I had no choice. The Raven wanted it that way."

"Because that's the way of justice!" a strange voice said.

Everyone turned to see who had spoken. A tall, blond-haired man stood motionless in the doorway.

"It's Daddy!" Jennifer exclaimed.

Silence saturated the atmosphere like a thick fog. Sheriff Hancock could be heard from on the floor, where he had collapsed in pain, muttering, "Blood on my hands! Blood on my hands!"

Warren Crews cringed fearfully before Gregory Simpson's presence. Wes Bryant grinned with the satisfaction of a private investigator closing a case.

Before them stood a man devoid of emotion and love, who had stolen the bloom of innocence from his own child. The immaculately combed blond hair, piercing blue eyes, and muscular physique Wes had seen in the photograph now came to life with a hideous severity. His self-confident stance projected a magnetic presence. Like a

powerful beast poised to intimidate his prey, Gregory smugly folded his arms across his chest. The impeccable tailoring of his dark
pin-striped suit gave him the appearance of a corporate captain
assuming control over his surroundings.

"Gregory!" Annette gasped and went limp. "You're alive!" She
reached protectively toward Jennifer, and the two of them edged
closer to Wes's side. Gradually, Annette changed her composure and
looked defiantly at the man to whom she had once pledged her trust
and eternal devotion. "My only peace of mind was thinking you had
burned in that accident straight back into the hell you came from!"

Gregory watched her revulsion, amused that this woman dared
offer her mindless opinion, considering he was the Dark Raven. Wes
remembered Annette's saying her only purpose had been to bear
Gregory a child and wondered if she had only been a vessel to per-
petuate the Raven's dynasty. Her weakness had been a source of his
power, but now she was an obstacle. Jennifer was the Order's future.
Her very conception had been detailed by the hands of hell.

"Did you really think *you* could stand between me and my daughter?" Gregory challenged Annette as he walked toward her. Wes
reached out to put his free arm around Annette, his other hand still
firmly gripping the laundry bag.

"Jennifer is *mine!*" Gregory insisted. "She was planned by the Order—a
symbol of the Dark Raven's power bred by your innocent soul. Do you
think I met you by accident? You, the humbly born daughter of a minister? You were ideal for the part with your little cross of gold and well-

read Bible pages! Your selection was carefully arranged by the Order. Jennifer had to be born of a woman pure of heart so that by corrupting your goodness the Raven's power would be strengthened.

"It was easy for me to make you think you were wanted and needed. I offered a life beyond your stupidity and pious upbringing, and you swallowed it without hesitation. My only obstacle was getting rid of you when the time was right. The car accident was planned in detail for weeks, and it was just a matter of time for the weather to help. You were meant to die, Annette! You were supposed to be in the front seat and thrown from the car and mangled beyond recognition! Instead, you panicked when the car spun out over the ice, and you dove into the back seat to shield Jennifer. *You, Annette! You should be dead?*"

"No!" Annette screamed. "God was there with me, Gregory. *We* saved Jennifer's life, and he chose to let me live too. *I* am Jennifer's hope for the future, not you!"

"Get out of my way! Give me my daughter!"

Annette stood firmly, her grasp around Jennifer growing tighter.

"Jennifer," Gregory whispered to his scared daughter. "Come with me, my queen. You belong to me. We must go now." His voice was etched with determination as he extended his hand to the sobbing child.

Jennifer clung to Wes, Annette's arm securely encircling her soft young shoulders. Tears streamed down Jennifer's cheeks. "No Daddy," she said. "I belong with Mr. Wes and Mommy. Go away!" Then she buried her head in her mother's chest.

Wes took the laundry bag in his hand and boldly stepped toward

Gregory. The broken glass from the studio window cracked under his feet, its crisp sound invading the atmosphere of Studio A.

"You've lost, Simpson!" Wes shouted. "The Order is as worthless as the mindless souls who believed your lies!"

An angry blush of color crept up from the collar of Gregory's shirt and continued into his cheeks. His eyes flashed hot with intensity. Shifting his weight, he turned his head toward the moaning sheriff, who had slumped to one side of the studio. Hancock was framed within the borders of the broken pane, its webs of fractured glass suspended along the edges like farmhouse spider webs refusing to fall.

To Gregory Simpson, his former compatriot in evil was now a useless, despicable pile of human refuse. It was plain—if justice were to reign supreme—he, the Dark Raven, would have to enforce it, and the moment was now. He grabbed Annette's arm, forcing himself between he and Wes. Gregory shoved his face toward hers. She gasped with pain and her eyes grew wider with fear. She tried desperately to run.

"You should already be dead! I'm only finishing what the Order couldn't do," Gregory yelled, sweat beading on his brow.

Annette shrieked and pulled away, unable to release his grip. "Gregory! Look at what you're doing! Look at the evil inside you! Think of Jennifer . . ." Her voice trailed off.

"I *am* thinking about Jennifer! She's all I ever think about!"

Then without warning, Jennifer's grief-stricken, pleading voice cried out: "They hurt me bad! It was cold, dark. I was afraid. Nobody would help me. I wanted them to stop."

Wes turned toward Studio C's shattered wall of glass. He saw Bailey hovering over the auxiliary tape deck, which had been running while Jennifer told her story.

Bailey had slipped back unnoticed into Studio C, re-wound the tape to Jennifer's plea, and replayed it in an attempt to defuse the confrontation.

Jennifer's taped voice startled the Raven. He whirled to see where the sound was coming from, losing his grip on Annette, who ran to stand behind Wes.

Wes glared intently at the stunned Gregory, whose jacket had been flung open when Annette escaped. Wes saw the gleam of a cold steel knife blade tucked neatly into Gregory's belt. He knew there would be three triangles on the handle—it was the same knife he had seen gleaming in the moonlight, the knife used to slit the goat's throat at the Mounds of the Elders. The sparkle of the studio lights reflected off the blade, and Wes envisioned goal posts from his distant past. This time, no injury would bar him from scoring the most important play of his life. This win wasn't for his glory. It was for the glory of good and the end of evil.

Forgetting the ruse of his fake bomb, Wes dropped his laundry bag and lunged toward Gregory Simpson with a tackle more vicious than any in his football days. Gregory was surprised to see Wes leap from behind the radio console. He fought off Wes's blow, stumbling backward, struggling to steady himself.

Gregory reached for the concealed knife, and, in his haste, reached past the handle, firmly gripping the blade in his bare hand. The pain of the blade slicing his flesh further enraged him. He quickly repositioned his hand and held the handle tightly. Gregory ignored the blood running down his wrist, creating a crimson pattern on the cuff of his shirt.

Wes grabbed Gregory's bloody wounded hand and fought for control of the knife. They struggled and fell to the floor, glass confetti scattering across the room and matting into their hair. As Gregory wildly slashed the air with the knife, Wes shoved him backward, causing the Raven to hit the console with an outstretched leg. The telephone and intercom on the console tumbled to the floor on top of Gregory, entangling him in a slithering mass of cable vipers.

Strength he hadn't felt in years surged through Wes as he shoved Gregory aside with a swift kick. As Gregory rolled to disengage himself from the wires, Wes tottered to his feet and leaned against the console, one hand holding tightly for balance, the other wiping away the salty taste of blood from his split lip.

Gregory also staggered to his feet, the knife still in his hand, and charged Wes again. Wes returned the assault with a brutal block. Everyone in the studio winced. Gregory's eyes, once filled with hot rage, now watered in response to the impact. His muscles jerked, and he took a deep painful breath, grasping his stomach.

Ignoring his own pain, Wes lunged back at Gregory. As the two collided, Wes felt his shoulder thrust against something solid. A sharp, unrelenting pain shot down his arm, competing with the familiar agony of his injured knee giving way. Wes fell to the floor. Sidelined again, white stars flashed before Wes, as he clutched his knee and pulled it to his chest. A damp shiver rippled across his hand. Wes looked down and saw blood dripping form his finger. Red droplets splattered onto the floor, changing the shattered glass jewels beside his feet from sparkling diamonds to deep red rubies. His shoulder had obviously rammed into Gregory's knife, slicing deeply into his own flesh. Seeing the flashes of pain on Wes's face, Annette rushed to his side.

Reeling from Wes's attack, Gregory stumbled backward toward the pitiful sheriff. His hand withdrew from where Wes's shoulder had delivered the final blow. Blood poured between Gregory's fingers. The blade of the Order's dagger protruded from the Raven's chest. Wes's attack and the force of his shoulder against the knife handle had turned the deadly weapon against its owner.

Hancock staggered to his feet. Fresh blood trickled down his face, collecting in a clotted mass. Pain sapped his once-arrogant strength, as Hancock reached through the shattered window frame and offered his trembling hand to catch Gregory, who was now dying by his own sword.

In slow motion, Gregory agonizingly fell backward toward Hancock in the direction of the one remaining shard of glass protruding from the frame of Studio C. It ripped through his flesh, as his full weight came to rest in the arms of the one man he had trusted—Sheriff Arnold Hancock.

"No!" Hancock screamed, as Gregory's blood mixed with his own. "You are the Raven, the keeper of Justice!" Hancock desperately clutched the dying body, trying to remove the knife with its polished triangles looking as if they were grinning at him in a sneer from hell.

Gregory's chest gushed warm puddles of blood to the studio floor, a few feet from where Hannah and Michelle stood in horror. His eyes fixed upon Jennifer, and his lips curled upward in a sadistic salute to Wes. The Raven was dead.

Wes held Annette's hand tightly, his own pain only a faint whisper compared to the gore and death that surrounded them.

"It's over," Wes declared. "It's finally over." His childhood image of the picture on his bedroom wall flashed before Wes. Once again, he was the protective angel whose safety and security he had trusted. In a half-whisper, half-prayer, Wes spoke the words: "I pray the Lord my soul to keep."

Fiction

OTHER ELM HILL FICTION TITLES
Now Available

ANGELWALK and STEDFAST

BEN HUR

ESCAPE

NOW I LAY ME DOWN TO SLEEP

SERENITY BAY

THE THOR CONSPIRACY

THE HOUSE ON HONEYSUCKLE LANE